WHO KILLED NICOLAI

A NOVEL

WHO KILLED NICOLAI

A NOVEL

BASTIAN R. CARDEN

Cover Design by Chris Babental, www.babental.com.

Silhouette of angel girl fleuron © Irina Solop.
Silhouette of girl on flower © Irina Solop.
Bound by Fate fleuron © Irina Solop.
Fluerons used under license from DepositPhotos.com. All rights reserved.

Interior layout and design by www.writingnights.org.
Book preparation by Chad Robertson.
For information about permission to reproduce selections from this book, email bastian.carden@gmail.com.

Or write:

Shwio, LLC
200 W. Portland St. #620
Phoenix, AZ 85044

ISBN: 9781730715396

bastianrcarden.com

Printed on acid free paper in the United States of America.

24   23   22   21   20   19   18   178   7   6   5   4   3   2   1

Dedication

For JMC, who loved me obviously.

And for Dad, who taught me how to write right.

You owe me a beer. Probably both of you.

Contents

WHO KILLED NICOLAI

A NOVEL

BASTIAN R. CARDEN

PROLOGUE:

Right Angel, Wrong Ring

osmic heartbreak, astronomical pain, but as I wither, I hear the whispered warning of a familiar voice. She is full of foreboding.

Nicolai. It's finally here, the last night of your life. And remember, all you have to do is not *die, and remember, all you have to do is* not *die, and remember.*

Last time, I was falling from a balcony. Now, she's back for my execution. How wonderful, how absolutely convenient! Maybe it really is all like they say.

Who knows?

Maybe it's just a feeling, a bastard idea born of Father Earth or Mother Nature, but not both. I'm zooming in from outer space, reduced to volcanic heartbreak and earthquakes in my legs. Tastes like ash. I was whole a second ago, but that's when I saw the ring, and I can hardly see anything anymore. I'm surreal in the window, staring through what remains, like that's not me standing there, like that's not my own self. My eyes hate ghosts, so they roll away, circling back to the matter at hand, back through the window and the sand, back to the traitor standing inside. She's an angel, so she'd probably prefer biblical tsunami, apocalyptic flooding, and the foam of acid rain burning my lips.

"Pick a poison," I say to no one. "Get out."

But I already picked. I picked *her.*

Either that or she chose the wrong victim.

Who knows?

Like everything else in the shop, the window is pristine, but I'm not quite sure she can see me—with the lights and all, I mean. It's bright inside and dark out here, so I probably look like a ghost. Maybe that's just a feeling too.

What it really feels like is fire—*I* feel like fire. My angel is wearing a diamond ring the size of a Mini Cooper on the fourth finger of her left hand—but it *damn sure* isn't the one I gave her! It's bigger and better and far more brilliant, no doubt a reflection of the man who bequeathed it.

Bequeathed?

Fuck!

Retreat beckons me, flames my cowardice, begs my legs to flee, to abandon the sight of this angel and the atrocity she wears on her ring finger. It probably came from Mordor.

She accepted me, you see. She accepted me once and then she murdered me and now I'm standing here like a dope, too scared to run, too terrified to stay, hanging again in the in-between.

I shouldn't be standing here. My eight-year-old Honda Civic, faded blue like my life, waits impatiently behind me. I should've left already. My Civic knows this. When left between rocks and hard places, I tend to avoid both, and she is my escape. I can trust my Civic, because my Civic has carried me to paradise and back on several occasions.

Hell, maybe we can stay this time…

I turn away and by sheer happenstance I see lightning terrifically far away. It flashes enormously, then its bolt spiderwebs the sky, tearing at the darkness like a white-fingernailed goddess.

They're not fingernails. They're tiger claws.

It is very dark, but not very late. I'm guessing it's about twenty to nine, but I can't make out the time, and I keep my eyes on the night, awaiting the thunder. This storm was unpredicted. It rolled into our little neck of Georgia uninvited and unwanted, a late season hurricane's death throe. A damning boom rocks me, and I notice many of the patrons in the store looking with big eyes at one another, wondering comically if the thunder is an omen.

It's not, I think.

It's revelations.

So for the first time, I say my truth aloud.

"Fuck forgiveness."

And with that I forgive myself my love for this girl.

It raves, my heart, and I hate it. I let a scar settle in as breathless seconds pass. I let her burrow deep in a way I've never allowed, and that's right when she sees me. My angel lifts her gaze from whatever it is she was doing by the snack counter, and as she does, she sees me, just as I hoped she would—dead.

I watch her—no, I perceive and peacefully observe—her, and I see in her every mannerism, from every direction and in each squint, until it hits her who I am.

Joy drains from her face like rainfall to a sewer.

If I deserve it, she deserves it. It is nectar, watching that glee melt into worry. It is ambrosia to my soul, seeing her see me so broken. I feel the storm's first drop land on my ear, and I am overwhelmed with fearlessness: this, despite the pain. You might think falling five stories onto some bleachers would hurt more, but I know from first-hand experience that this isn't true. An angel pushed me off a four-story balcony once, like five years ago maybe. Like I said, I've lost the time.

Is she the One there, wearing the ring on the other side of the window?

Who knows?

As I watch the joy drain from her face, I decide it's finished. I know where I am and it's not where I belong. I get in my Civic, close the door, and retreat into its chamber, my sanctuary, a place of known error and regret: the past. It's where I go to get back out. It always starts the same way, here, and I have to start somewhere. I screech out of the parking lot, happily ignoring the rain, and as I turn onto the freeway, I begin to think of him.

This, *I know*, is just a feeling.

Dad.

Maybe *he* wasn't real either.

Maybe I made him up.

Mom told me once that it is the earliest raindrops which make the road slick, but her teachings are a part of my hell too, so I let them go. My feet become tires and I race away, escaping into the safety of a thunderstorm, ignoring the dangers that I now realize were never real. Between the towns of the Georgia and East Alabama, it's all orchards and beauty, backwoods and oaks. I can't see them now in the dark—maybe it's twenty past nine.

I'm thirty or forty miles into my great escape when I hit something in the road, probably the corpse of a critter. I'm not even close to campus when it happens, and I immediately sense the imbalance.

Shit. I'm hydroplaning. My face is pressed to the door.

I look up—rage is pouring from the sky, and I know something's terribly wrong: I can make out every raindrop, they splash in slow motion on the driver side window.

Fire flows from my heart. I was doing ninety, maybe eighty-five, now I'm doing sixty but I'm going backwards—

—and I've completely lost grip of reality.

Next, I lose grip of the wheel.

My hands float before me, hovering like helium balloons. One by one, I feel the rumble of individual striations on the highway shoulder. My Civic whips forward, my headlights shine onto something long and gray—a wall—and I see the six-foot tall concrete barrier dividing the freeway.

I'm on two wheels, about to flip. I feel it.

"Wait!"

I close my eyes, one by one, rumbling on the road—

—*Oh! Wait?*

Wait! It's too simple. The joy drained from her face.

I realize.

Then, *NO!* I saw it—I see it. Paradise, dividers, women, hell, and it's still too late. Steel meet concrete meet Earth meet water. Fire or flood. I dive in.

Finally.

Who knows.

Did I not mention yet that my Dad's dead.

No?

How interesting…

Nicolai

"Love means never having to say you're sorry."
— FROM THE BEGINNING OF *LOVE STORY*,
BY ERICH SEGAL

y father died of cancer when I was four, so there's that. Whenever I think about him all dead and everything, I call him that—father—but usually he's Dad, a best friend who was there for me until one day he wasn't.

I don't remember anything about that night—the evening my father got stolen—except that it was the worst, most awful night of my life. For three days he laid and wasted away, and then, like yesterday's sunrise, he was gone forever.

My mom—through forgetfulness or poor parenting, take your pick—failed to tell me until recently that Dad and I shared last words. Or, better put, that Dad shared last words with me. It was *Dad* who diverted my attention away from sports and superheroes. It's his fault I fell in love with women to begin with—the idea of women, I mean, the joy of their companionship, the earning of an angel's heart, chivalry, all that old romance jazz that died out decades ago. And so it's always been women for me—always—girls then ladies then women going back as far as I can remember.

In Kindergarten, for example, my teacher sent me to the Principal's office because I said to some kid, "You're the dumbest-ugliest-stupidest idiot on Earth." An unjust punishment, I say, because I was refuting his absurd argument that, "Girls are totally gross and disgusting!" (To be honest, I don't remember Chester-field's words. I am, however, 100% sure of mine: Ms. Bridges wrote them verbatim on an incident sheet for Mom, and Mom still has the carbon copy in her house.)

Two years later, in second grade, our teacher organized a millennial version of "What Do You Want to Be When You Grow Up." Instead of choosing an oc-cupation, we chose a purpose. Even though the game had been rigged, nothing changed: everyone but me stuck with the classics; protect people (cops), explore the universe (astronauts), move to L.A. (join the dark side), and so on.

I presented last. I straightened my navy clip-on tie—the one Dad gave me—and stood tall at the box podium Mrs. Pride had set atop a crafts table. Then, ignoring the faces of my twenty-three bored-to-tears classmates, I announced proudly and perfectly in a practiced voice, "When I grow up, I want to become the very best at loving women." (Another trip to the principal's office. Another piece of carbon copy blackmail.)

The words aren't right. With imaginations, they never are. I guess maybe I meant, "to care for women," or, "become the best at making women smile," or chivalry and romance. Whatever the case, that was it. That was always it. In my dreams and nightmares and drifting thoughts, that was always it.

"What do you want to become?" they asked me, and I shared with them my noblest intention. The response always came back the same too: "Kill your fantasies or keep them yourself, and if you must dream, dream silently."

I've obeyed both for as long as I can. Somewhere in between, I lost Dad, and now that I've found him, now that Mom showed me who he truly was, I'm appar-ently supposed to die.

I close my eyes.

I accept.

I believe right now, as I always have, that if you've earned the love of a good woman, there is no place so warm. There are no arms so soft. There are no mo-ments more present. No home run or promotion or one-night stand compares; not if it wins game seven, not if you become CEO of Google, not if you ménage with supermodels. There isn't an experience greater than love. That's my truth. I'm happy to die with it.

"Is there more?" my heart monster asks a third time.

More? There have already been six angels who, for better or worse, shared with me their hearts, mentoring me in the philosophies of romance as I failed them one after another, all done in the hope that I might one day fulfill my greatest and grandest, most fortuitous and foolhardy ambition: *to become the very best at loving women.*

"Yes. But is there more?"

JESSICA COMES

"All the reasonings of men are not worth one sentiment of women."
—VOLTAIRE

1.

essica.

My genesis.

I remember her like yesterday's sunset.

One magic afternoon in May, Jessica floated onto the stage of my life. I was expecting a Jehovah's witness when I answered the door, or at worst some salesperson, but I opened it to find the mythical creature who'd haunted all my childhood nightmares to date.

A girl.

"Hi, I'm Jessica," the girl said. "I'm here to see Mona."

The sun was right behind her head, casting shadows through the willow tree that adorned our little front yard. I stood uncontrollably speechless in her shade. She carried by her right side a reusable cloth bag of books and in her right hand a pair of ballet slippers. I beheld her—or bewitched I was—for she was closer to me now than any girl before.

"Uh, hello. I asked if your sister's here."

I remember her perfect blue dress with its perfect yellow sunflowers, and I remember the dress matching perfectly to her blue earrings. Even the sun cooperated with her whims, shining perfectly off her black ponytails and unblemished skin as she looked past me into our less-than-perfect bi-level.

Jessica squinted at my silence a moment. "Look, we have recital practice, see." She lifted her slippers, shaking them daintily like two pink bells. "This *is* Mona's house, right?"

Then, I heard the beast roar behind me. "Nicolai, move!" it screamed.

My sister, Mona.

Mona quickly rescued Jessica from my awkwardness, chided me for being a "weirdo," then the two of them vanished up the stairs. I remember little else from that day, spare a pinch of spying and the avid vow I proclaimed to the world and to myself that I'd win Jessica's heart.

Three weeks later, Mona's ballet class threw a Spice Girls themed party at Cooper Creek Park. Mona told Mom over breakfast who was coming, and Jessica's name was included, so I told Mom I wanted to go. Mona, in predictable big sister fashion, objected viciously. I persevered by skillfully walking Mom through the cost-benefit of tagalong versus babysitting fees.

Survey says: Nicolai wins!

The glee I felt at defeating Mona meant zilch next to the glee I felt upon seeing Jessica at the park. Right as we arrived, right after passing a tiny, unmanned inspection shack, we came around the first bend and there I spotted Jessica walking along a path beside the reservoir lake. Hundreds of white, pink, and lavender lilies blossomed around its marshy bank. Jessica turned away and crouched beside a colorful batch, then our car turned down a side road. Mom parked in a rubble lot and we arrived at the festivities a minute later.

At my earliest convenience—Mom opens beer, Mom tastes beer, Mom converses with other moms—I began my investigation. I found the flowerbeds Jessica had been examining. There were signs every twenty yards or so, little yellow ones that warned passers-by about the laws of the park. I read and reread the four-word warning a hundred times—DO NOT REMOVE FLOWERS.

Eureka!

My plan came together like a puzzle.

I used an overgrown batch of wild reeds to hide my work, and sacrificed my first Jordans to the slimy green muck of the reservoir bed—sacrilege, I know! I returned to the party every ten minutes or so, that way Mom wouldn't grow suspicious.

I cut a dozen of the prettiest, fullest lilies with a plastic knife. It was rough going at first, and I accidentally frayed the first several into ugly fibers, but once I'd collected eight good ones, I bundled them into a purple rubber band, and took my first steps towards the tree under which Jessica had been reading. Altogether, I spent an hour on her bouquet. It was the hottest weekend of summer too, and that's saying something in Georgia humidity. I sweat bullets the whole time.

Satisfied at last, I hid the flowers behind my back, closed my eyes, and whispered, "Jessica."

Nervous as a chihuahua, I began my journey.

I was eight years old, going on nine.

2.

Most of the dads were playing a needlessly serious game of volleyball in a hard, hot sand pit with a net that sagged like old boobs. Most of the moms were gossiping about local riff-raff, paying scant attention to the blue, above-ground swimming pool adjacent to the gazebo. In the big blue pool, twelve overenthusiastic girls— plus my sister; she went thirteenth—shrieked like sirens.

Jessica didn't enter the big blue pool, and not because she was afraid of the glut of girls. Where I, Nicolai, began life as a romantic, Jessica, it seems, began life as a queen. She just had this *way* about her, a standoffishness, something beyond introversion. I imagine, like me, she was mostly looked at as an oddity.

In any case, Jess spent most of the party reading in the shade of our town's oldest and most famous tree, *Ol' Sam*. Framed on a boulder beside the tree, a decorative gate and bronze plaque celebrated its history. Apparently, some naturalist in the late-sixties claimed he was the oldest tree in the South, and though this was later deemed fraudulent, the plaque remains. And the tree remains a marvelous, spidery thing, with arms thirty yards end-to-end, and bullish roots like steps all along its trunk.

I was pretending to examine said plaque and its decorative iron gate when I slipped on a fallen branch. For balance, I palmed the knob of the gate and by good luck alone it didn't creak. It opened as if it'd been waiting on me, and I passed through. When I heard the crunch of leaf litter under my wet sneakers, I froze.

It was a rebellion.

I tried to supply my feet with courage, but my mind reeled with forecasts of the rejection most likely to befall me should I continue. Somehow—through Dad's grace probably—I steeled my nerves with a few seconds of shut-eyed, self-composition. I managed a step, then another, and before I knew it, I'd journeyed all the way around Ol' Sam. I knew I'd arrived too, because I heard the alarm of a familiar voice.

"Hi, Nicolai," she said.

It was *her*. It was *her* voice.

Jessica, my genesis.

She was sitting on a big root, her back to me but her head turned like an owl's. Her eyes were on mine, and automatically, my hands and the flowers I carried behind my back revealed themselves. She smiled at the bouquet, then studied me a moment. A soft breeze fluttered the ends of her white dress as she stood.

"Nicolai," she said. "Are those for me?"

At last, I knew what to do. "I think you're awesome and super pretty." That's what I needed to say. I'd practiced it a thousand times.

Unfortunately, a series of evil happenings conspired to kill my day. An invisible frog jumped into my throat, blocking my words. Then, a sunbeam flared directly into my eyes (what else could explain them tearing up?) In harmony with those, a mini-earthquake shook me from head to foot: I was the only one who could detect it, obviously.

"Nicolai?" she asked.

How many agonizing seconds I stood there—a silent, shaky, teary-eyed fool—I could not tell you. I dropped the bouquet at Jessica's feet and fled for the safety of the party.

For shame, I didn't look back.

I ninja-climbed the pool's ladder in two big leaps, barreled into the water, and suffered the piercing screams and bruising chaos of Mona and the Sirens. Still, I hid my head beneath the horizon of the pool. I foresaw Jessica reducing my bouquet to a pile of petals, stems, and shattered dreams.

Yes, in terrible shame, I didn't—couldn't, wouldn't—look back.

3.

Worn out after fifteen minutes of shrieks and thuds and howls and elbows, I poked my head above the horizon of the pool. What I found was the most thrilling surprise of my young life.

There she was, Jessica, dancing in plain view beside Ol' Sam. She was dancing with the flowers—my flowers!

She lifted the bouquet over her head, brought it to her waist, bowed, twirled twice more, and, grinning like an aristocrat, she ended her imaginary waltz with her imaginary friends: a slow and lovely curtsy.

Brava!

Had my lips had been flexible enough, a smile would've consumed my face. I dropped to the bottom of the pool, clasped my knees to my chest, and shouted happy bubbles as I spun about. When I came up seconds later, Jessica was grinning in my direction. She waved, then she giggled, then she sidestepped to hide behind Ol' Sam.

An invitation, I thought.

I sprang up the ladder and out of the pool and slid into my coolest Teenage Mutant Ninja Turtles t-shirt. Never before had I felt so fulfilled, so happy. My life made sense suddenly. I needed to be indisputably excellent in matters of the heart. Beyond all my senses, beyond sight and touch and sound, beyond sports and video games and chocolate—even chocolate!—I wanted to make my life sentence, "to be the very best at loving women." I didn't have the words. All I had was a feeling; the *idea of it*. Consider a boy who commits himself to baseball after his first home-run, or the pop star who inspires a million girls to sing. A love of baseball *becomes* a Major League dream; a love of music *becomes* the ambition of a musician; and although my dream offered no specific career path—outside of Nevada, anyway—I felt for the first time in my little life a sense of place and of purpose and of excellence.

As for what happened behind Ol' Sam, that's between Jessica and me. It's not a story I can share because Jessica made me promise never to tell anyone, ever, under any circumstances.

And Ben Franklin made it clear: honesty is the best policy.

And all the stories always say don't lie and keep your promises and the like.

So I, thinking the task an easy one, did just that. I made that promise. I said I'd never tell anyone.

Then I told almost everyone I knew immediately.

4.

Jessica kissed me behind Ol' Sam—for, like, a whole minute!

Sure. I told Jessica I wouldn't tell anyone—that's true—but it was the first time I ever told someone that I wouldn't tell other people something they asked me not to tell. It's not like I'd taken an ethics class yet, I was eight! I had literally no romantic equipment. And besides, I *meant* what I said *when* I said it.

C'est la vie.

Okay. Here's how this disaster played out. We were hidden from the party behind Ol' Sam's enormous trunk. I was caught off guard, you see, and—well—let me back up.

Jessica was standing on a great big root when I rounded Ol' Sam, holding the lilies with both hands near her belt buckle.

"Did you make these for me?" she asked.

She wasn't smiling or frowning, it was like an almanac question. I felt anxious and foolish all at once, and in the brief wait of words, Jessica grew impatient.

"Well?" she pestered.

"I rubber-banded them for you," I blurted out.

"You rubber-banded them?" Jessica said. "You rubber-banded them? You know what I mean, Nicolai, now stop being a little boy and tell me. Did you make this bouquet especially for me? I want to know."

"I looked for a while, for the prettiest ones," I said.

Jessica hopped down from the root. Her sundress flew up like a little parachute and she floated to the ground.

"Why would you, a little boy, give flowers to me, a young lady?"

A rebellion of moths fluttered in my belly.

"Nicolai?" she insisted.

"I just, well earlier, I saw you and—well, there you were, just—"

"Just tell me the truth," she snapped. "You know you're not supposed to pick flowers, right? There were a million signs. Don't you pay attention to the signs?"

I glanced at the flowers, steadied safely in their natural resting place by her belt buckle. As sunbursts popped through Ol' Sam's head of green leaves, I remembered something. Dad once told Mom who once told me that when poetry occurs to you, you must share it. To not do so is a sin.

So I said to Jessica: "I picked them because I thought they were pretty and I wanted them to be with you. A girl like you deserves pretty flowers."

Jessica gasped a little gasp.

"Also," I said, looking now at my feet in the dust, "I think you're awesome and super pretty."

Her eyes went wide with surprise, and then, without warning, she stepped forward and buried her lips into mine. Her tongue touched my lips, you see, and I wasn't a fan of that. I just had this thing about spit and it all came together lousy. Long story short: the first kiss *totally* freaked me out!

Jessica must've seen a PG-13 movie or read a book recommended for teenagers; either that or she was awfully curious about tasting my face. I wanted the girl to notice my existence, not moisturize me.

It was the flowers, I hear, and I'm swung away from my flashback and into the reality of my whispering heart monster. *It's always the flowers,* she says.

And suddenly it's dark again, and it's raining, and I'm speeding into a wall and towards my death. The past recoils with new freshness. I remember I'm on the highway, and I remember Jessica. She wore flower-patterned clothes every day, drew flowers in her notebooks and on chalkboards. She stopped and smelled the roses everywhere she went.

Then I gave *her* a bouquet—I was first—and as a result of my blunder, Jessica made a terrible mistake that day.

She fell in love with me.

On Love

"You know you're in love when you don't want to fall asleep
because reality is finally better than your dreams."
—THEODOR SEUSS GEISEL

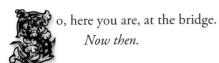 o, here you are, at the bridge.
Now then.

And there you were, with Jessica, all the love of childhood in your heart. You'd won her attention with a gift well-given.

Now what?

Look, I had this thing about spit (not your fault) and it came together lousy (also not your fault). Should I have been honest? Been mean? Ended it? Shouted out, "Ha! Joke's on you, Spit Monster! Give me back my bouquet!" I didn't try to stop liking her. It just happened, like a switch, and that's not a switch that flips back, and that's because it's not a switch at all, really: it's a big red button with a sign saying, "DANGEROUS EQUIPMENT! STAY OUT!"

But you don't read signs. Signs are for sheep.

Maybe I'm looking for the red. Maybe I'm looking for wolf-love.

You're looking for the girl with the joy-drained face.

No, I'm looking for *my* princess.

A princess?

No. Mine. The One wearing the Ring. The girl with the joy-drained face.

Jessica's surprise kiss wore on, but for chivalry's sake, I bit my lip (literally). When Jessica finally freed my face from her smothering—it must've taken five whole seconds!—I resisted the urge to wipe my mouth.

A lesser romantic might've. A lesser romantic might've tipped an imaginary cap to Jess and walked away. But I was not a lesser romantic, so I stayed, awaiting Jessica's next move.

Based on many hours of sneaking romantic comedies into my television diet, I knew I couldn't express any dislike. It was a first kiss, and the rules are pretty clear about those. I'd stopped liking Jessica, true, but that doesn't mean I stopped caring about her. She was pretty and super awesome after all, and she was the girl who invited first romance into my heart, short-lived as it was.

So, here I am, and there I was. I'd won Jessica's attention. I'd approached, but then I immediately stopped liking her.

"Now what?" was the question, and like I said, I stayed.

I've shared this story many times since, and most disagree with my opinion here—that a good lover, man or woman, should take care to reduce their partner's pain following romantic failure. The common advice seems to be something like, "deliver romantic hurt quickly." "Rip off the band-aid!" many of these butchers say. But this crime—a swift slice through the heart—serves only to buy the perpetrator time, to earn her a freedom from a failed promise, or worse, to inflict pain willfully due to some gross sense of superiority, fairness, or time. "Oh, I don't know, I just sort of realized this was all wrong," he'll say, or, "I was talking to my mother and realized you're not the right one for me," she'll say, or any of the other billion versions of the same, all including some synonym of "I just realized," and often done so unlovingly that it handicaps the ability of the hurt one, the victim, to recover. And that's exactly what you are if someone stops loving you suddenly: a victim. I refused to turn Jessica into one of those.

I did not and do not regret the bouquet and the kiss.

What I did not then but do now regret is everything that came after.

Jessica Goes

"First love is only a little foolishness and a lot of curiosity."
—GEORGE BERNARD SHAW

5.

Mercifully, there was no encore.

Jessica pecked me on the cheek—I almost flinched but managed to just grimace. She picked up her bouquet, inhaled the flowers like crack, looked on me quizzically as though I was a Picasso, then ran off giggling the way a drunk cherub does in renaissance painting, *sans* wings. I realize now she wanted me to chase her.

Minutes later, the party moved to cake and ended. Mom, Mona and I returned home. No one at the party saw Jessica kiss me behind Ol' Sam.

For a month and a half, I didn't see Jessica at all, but then Mom agreed to let Mona throw a random back-to-school slumber party. Jessica's name was written fourth on the guest list. On the day of the party, Jessica arrived thirty minutes early. She was the first to show up. I heard her voice and retreated into our tiny den to enjoy my Game Boy in privacy. Ten minutes later, I heard the world's most famous three-word phrase come from under the den's entryway.

"I love you," this voice said quietly.

I looked up. It was Jessica.

I squinted at her and said, "I love you too," as though it were nothing. And to me it was nothing; that's what the people on TV always said, so I said it.

Jessica retorted, sharply and unpleased, "You can't just say I love you if you don't mean it, Nicky. You're such a little boy."

"Don't call me Nicky!" I said, forced to pause my game.

She began shouting, "Nicky, Nicky, Nicky!"

"Stop calling me that!" I yelled back. "Go away!"

"I will," she said, "I don't like you and I'll go away forever and you'll see how you feel." She sneered, stuck her tongue out at me, slapped the doorframe in frustration, and rushed out. She returned to the slumber party where the girls were probably flipping through *Seventeen* or *Us Weekly*, their heads filled with fantasies of becoming celebrities someday so that they too could be examined and/or mocked by the public.

Relieved of Jessica's presence, I proceeded on my Game Boy journey of *Skate or Die!* I was just about to beat the third level when my sister Mona barged in. I had only one life left. (This is a critical fact in the upcoming dispute.)

"What did you say?" Mona asked, hollering with authority the way big sisters do.

"What did I say to who?" I asked, keeping my eye on my game. (If I was going to finally break through to level four, it would require focus, tenacity, and treating my sister like she didn't exist.)

"What did you say to Jessica?"

"Nothing," I muttered. "What did she say I said?"

"She won't tell me but she's crying and then not crying and saying everything's okay, but Mal said she heard you and her talking and then she was like…" and all I heard for another thirty seconds was blah-blah-blah-blah.

When Mona finally stopped her rant, I said very calmly, "I didn't tell Jessica anything. She was calling me Nicky."

"So what?" my sister asked.

I ignored this. I wanted her to leave me alone, and she knew that I wanted her to leave me alone, so naturally she didn't leave me alone. Naturally, she stepped closer.

"So what, she called you Nicky," Mona asked again, hovering over me now like a helicopter.

"So I told her she had to stop. What's it to you?"

Right at that moment, I lost again on the third level. Now I had to start all over. (Never mind I'd lost a hundred times before: I was never much of a gamer.)

"Look what you did!" I shouted at Mona. "I lost."

"That's because you're a loser, Nicky, and you suck at life."

Mona had just finished taking a shower; her skin still wet, her black hair wiry and unkempt. Her face had an awful, sour look to it, enhanced by the lemon shape of her head. She was an odd look altogether, trapped in the purgatory of pre-teen feminine growth spurts, that tennis-ball-boobs-no-butt-squeezy-torso weirdness.

"Now tell me," she said, "what did you say to Jessica?"

"Leave me alone. I told you I didn't say anything, you freak!"

"That doesn't make sense," Mona shouted. "And what's your problem with the name Nicky anyway? You don't get to pick your name."

"Will you please leave me alone so I can play my game? I didn't say anything to your friend."

"Her name…is Jessica," my sister said. Then she slapped the Game Boy out of my hand like a dictator-in-training. "I don't care about your stupid game, or your nickname, Sticky Nicky."

Between Jessica's awkward presence in my house, Mona's bad attitude, and my repeated game failures, I had no choice but to retaliate. "OK, Bony-Moany," I said, extending the vowels for effect.

My sister hated that name, and she'd long ago convinced Mom to criminalize its use in our house—censorship, I say!

Mona threatened to tell Mom.

I dared her to do so.

She started calling me Nicky again, so I escalated the war. "Boo-hoo Bony-Moany," I said, and later, "who's your friend now, Bony-Moany?"

Our volume escalated, alerting Mom that sibling trouble had risen to code red. As usual, I caught the whole blame—sexism, I say!—and Mom commanded me to keep away from the girls for the rest of the night.

I obeyed gladly, but due to the interruption, I did not overcome level three of my game. Ever.

Mona and I squabbled often as children, but really this conflict was heaven-sent. Boys with older sisters have a considerable romantic advantage over boys without. One needs experience to anticipate a woman's breaking point, and boys with older sisters learn this much more quickly—an unintentional side-effect of coping with tyrants.

6.

By the following morning, Jessica had returned to her affection for me. This was made obvious by the footsies she played with me underneath the breakfast table. (I neither reciprocated nor understood what was happening at the time.) Then Jessica and Mona's other three friends left, and for the last two weeks of summer, I was spared Jessica's company. I remembered the romance of the kiss, but I also remembered the slime. It was mission critical to avoid her lips touching mine ever again.

Our elementary school was called Kaplan. Students in different grades typically didn't see much of each other because we were separated into different halls and took lunch at different times. Yet, somehow, almost every day, and often more than once, even though she was on the opposite side of our building, Jessica found me. She'd loiter near our entrance before and after school, walk in late from recess as my class went outside. She was always smiling, so I always smiled back, but I got lost in the triangle of shame, guilt, and irritation.

Then irritation took over.

Jessica forged a BFF-grade friendship with Mona to be near me. I know this because I asked her once, "Are you being friends with Mona because you like me?" to which she answered, "Duuuuuh!"

Now she was at my house twice a week, winking, leaving little notes in my backpack, interrupting my TV shows with her valley-girl accented girly stuff stories. Even if I still liked her—which I didn't!—I didn't trouble her with my unsuccessful *Skate or Die!* missions. Romance requires empathy, and it was becoming apparent that this invader had none.

As Christmas approached, irritation vanquished shame and guilt entirely. I'd had it! I needed to end this once and for all. My plan was the obvious one: make Jessica not like me.

Seems easy enough, right?

Round 1 – The Dinner Burp

In her own mind, Jessica was a princess, but to everyone else she was just prissy. Things needed to be neat and clean and classy; everything from her spotless, shining shoes to her pressed dresses spoke of early-stage O.C.D.

So, one day in early November, many months into this first romantic trial of mine, I chugged a can of Coca-Cola as fast as I could just before dinner. As I muscled the building gas in my belly, we sat for dinner, filled our plates, and right as Jessica was about to take her first bite of Mom's lasagna, I let out a terrific three-second burp, and let me tell you: it was quite a thing. A professional trumpeter couldn't have done much better.

Mom was abhorred. Mona was embarrassed. Jessica was…grinning?

…Then smiling?

…Then giggling?

Then defending me with, "I don't mind. I think it's funny."

Through the blinding magic of that bouquet, my revolting burp became a rebellion cry.

I guess love does that.

Round 2 – Camp Nicolai

Of the few memories I have of Dad, none are clearer than our spontaneous backyard camping adventures. I was only four-going-on-five when he died, but his spirit and his smile and the feelings on those nights remain alive and vivid in the most sacred vaults of my memory.

After two days of begging and guilting, Mom agreed to let me camp in the backyard for two straight weeks as a birthday gift so long as I showered first thing every morning. I forewent a Sega Genesis 96xx game console in the effort; a mighty sacrifice for me, another money saving negotiation for Mom.

Though my primary aim was to send a clear "Let It Be" signal to Jessica, I loved the backyard: the crickets, the whispering pines, the distant smell of Lake Mathis wafting over our neighborhood on lucky occasions. If the ghost of my father lives anywhere, it is there in the grass and the soil.

When Jessica arrived (her cadence now upped to three times weekly), I made for the tent. Even when it rained on night six, I told Mom I was staying outside.

That was the deal, and Mom was a stickler for deals. Two slumber parties, three random visits, zero trouble for me. My plan was working. Surely Jessica's heart was turning away from me. Surely her mind had processed my behavior as unacceptable ignorance. Surely it was dangerous apathy at the very least.

Surely wishful thinking, indeed.

On day eleven, no kidding, I come home from soccer practice and find a pink tent pitched beside mine. When I peeked inside, I found Mona and Jessica laying on a plush pallet of blankets. They didn't even have the decency to use sleeping bags!

"You have to banish them," I demanded of Mom as she scrubbed a soup pot in the kitchen.

"Banish?" she said. "You're not a prince, Nicolai, and I'm not a queen. We're not in the banning business."

"This was *my* gift. My camp." I repeated it several times. "Camp Nicolai! Camp Nicolai! No girls allowed."

I pressed my point, but she said, "It'd be rude." She wanted me to practice being nicer.

I said I didn't care and that I didn't want to camp anymore.

She laughed at me—a hearty laugh this time. She put a loving hand on my shoulder, crouched beside me, painted a maternal grin on her face, and reminded me that I had two nights to go. (Like I said, Mom was a stickler for deals.)

I deflected Jessica's approaches that night, but after Mona fell asleep on the last night, the fortnight, Jessica snuck into my tent.

"Can I kiss you on the cheek," she asked.

I told her, "No."

She did it anyway.

It wasn't so terrible, I guess.

Round 3 – Kick Her in the Shin

Two nights after Camp Nicolai ended, Jessica was rummaging through our refrigerator for an evening snack. She turned around and found me standing innocently behind her.

"Oh. Hi, Nicolai," she said. "You've got a little something in your hair." As she repaired said imperfection, I kicked her in the shin as hard as I could. It was an impulse, like swatting a gnat or jumping at a crack of thunder.

Jessica cried out. Mom rushed in from the living room and asked what happened. Jessica said a jelly jar had fallen on her toe but that she was fine. She even told Mom I'd come running to her rescue—that liar!

Mom told Jessica to be careful next time, and, without even inquiring about which jelly jar had fallen or why it hadn't broken, she left the two of us alone. I stood sheepish before Jessica's admiring eyes.

"You really owe me now," she said before marching off.

It was clear to me that Jessica would continue pressing her crush onto my life. People say it all the time, "All's fair in war and love," and all those people are full of shit. It's not fair, it's never fair. Jessica and I learned far too young that love and war are the same goddamned thing.

7.

Maybe if I'd had the vocabulary, things would've turned out differently.

But I didn't.

So, it couldn't.

We had a timing problem. Neither of us yet knew anything about what to do between rocks and hard places. We didn't know there were other options, like waiting. Romance—like English, like Latin, like anything—must be learned and experienced and suffered through. Jessica seemed to me unflappable, and I, having already exhausted more diplomatic options—burping, relocation, and kicking—was at a loss about what to do.

Then—lucky timing for once—*Eureka!*

An idea occurred to me while mopping our muggy garage one Saturday morning, a punishment handed down following a loud disagreement with my sister—injustice, I say! I knew Jessica wanted to kiss me, but I also knew she wanted to keep it a secret. She was not above the social stigma that might befall her should her feelings become public knowledge.

The last Monday before winter break, four months after our kiss behind Ol'

Sam, I slipped a note into Jessica's backpack. On a piece of pearl stationary, I wrote in my most patient penmanship:

"Hi Jessica. It's me. Meet me tomorrow at 11:50. Supply room with the blue door. You know which one. Just sneak away. Then come in. You'll find me waiting. Like how I found you, remember?
For you I mean.
It's safe.
I promise.
Love.
Nicky."

It was 11:57. I'd been waiting nearly half an hour. Time was already thin for this sabotage and here she was ruining it! I'd had to wait fifteen minutes. Now it was twenty-two minutes approaching twenty-three. Fear crept into my belly.

What if it doesn't work? Did I even considered that?

Finally, Jessica opened the door.

My belly growled like a baby Chewbacca. (I knew I'd miss lunch, but I'd never missed a meal before that day with Jessica. I was thinking about my hunger. I remember that.)

Then, Jessica slipped in.

The closet had two doors, one on each end. The red door opened to the sixth grade halls; the other, the blue one, opened to the cafeteria. The blue door had a recently broken lock, a fact known to everyone—wisdom passed down from the detention boys—and a sign reading, "Authorized Personnel Only." Inside, the closet was lit by a feint, orange-red bulb that buzzed above the blue door. It looked like the kind of light you see in pools, a thick protecting plastic over its top; smash-proof technology, armor. Upon entering, I'd flicked the two switches beside the door. Neither of the switches appeared to do anything. They certainly didn't affect the armored light, and I nearly got trapped there, looking at it, wondering how long it had gone on shining. The closet was lined with plaster shelves, wooden shelves, locked closets, and hutches, and I'd been hiding in the tallest hutch.

"Nicky?" she said. Then again, she called to me, "Nicolai?"

When she'd entered, she did it like a bandit, opening the door only slightly and slipping in sideways. She shut it fast, and silently.

I thought to myself, *Who could be chasing her?*

She walked across the closet to the other door, looking around all the while, and upon reaching the other side, she huffed, flopping her arms at her sides.

"Hi," I answered as I emerged from hiding.

"What is all this?" she asked, hands on her hips. "We can get in big-time trouble, you know?"

"I think it'll be okay though."

"So what? You've been so mean to me," Jessica said, "and I've been so nice to you. You're just—" she got flustered searching for the right words "—you're just such a little boy."

I was beginning to doubt this plan, but she licked her lips like three times while she whisper-shouted at me, and my resolve about this sabotage doubled. The sword was ready. Or maybe it was a grenade? In either case, I readied my heart to jump atop it.

"I'm sorry," I said again.

To my dismay, Jessica stepped closer. She didn't run away. Instinctively, like a tasty mouse cornered by the housecat, I stepped back. I was stalling, killing time. I thought I'd have to stall longer, but then I saw shadows under the red door; those were the feet of Mr. Jansen, our resident curmudgeon janitor, here to replenish his mopping bucket like he did every day at noon. The time was presently 11:59.

Yup, time's a bitch.

Along with being maniacally scheduled, Mr. Jansen loved getting kids into trouble. He'd yelled at me before, more times than I could count. This was the plan too: he'd catch us in here playing hooky, we'd get in a little trouble, and be on our merry ways.

When the clock struck twelve, he was supposed to enter.

The clock struck twelve. The shadows didn't move.

"So," Jessica said, stepping ever closer.

My back pushed up against the blue door. Mr. Jansen seemed a mile away. "So," I said, reeling back.

"Why are we here? What is this? Where is this even?"

"We're in between the school and the cafeteria."

"You know what I mean, Nicky."

Then, like it was happening in super slow motion, she took my hands in hers and said, "Please. Just once. Tell me the truth."

"What truth?" I said back.

"What do you mean, *what truth*. The truth. Your truth. Whatever."

And for whatever reason, I put my arm around her back, said sincerely, "I love you," and pressed her lips into mine. I felt her smile against my mouth. She wrapped her arms around me, and in my desperation to keep her saliva at bay, I lost my balance and pulled at her sleeve for support. This was an ENORMOUS mistake. Mr. Jansen might walk in at any minute—

Then, we fell.

We slipped against my weight, pulling us both down. We rolled onto a pile of cardboard boxes, our faces still smashed together, my courageous lips resisting her assault. I wanted it to end so badly, but Mr. Jansen hadn't made a move— maybe he was fumbling with his keys or chatting up a teacher. My lips weakened and gave way to Jessica's tongue—a second defeat—a flood compared to the last one.

The red door opened. Hallway light from the school flooded the closet. We were exposed; our childhood crimes of onsite truancy and illicit affection displayed for The Cleaning Man's judgment.

Jessica saw Mr. Jansen and screamed.

I saw Mr. Jansen and exhaled.

"Holy moly! What've we got here?" he said, wearing a big, ugly smile. I couldn't make out his face—in fact, the whole of him was somehow silhouetted against that armored light—but still, I could tell him by his wrinkles. "Two troublemakers alone, ay? We'll see about that!"

8.

Mr. Jansen rushed us to the principal's office. He held Jessica and me by a bicep as he sped to administration. Neither of us could look up at him, we were so scared.

In less than three minutes, Jessica and I were seated on opposite ends of a wooden bench outside the big principal's office. We could hear the muffled exaggerations of Mr. Jansen coming from inside as he regaled Mrs. Bryant with vigilante joy. He didn't even look at me as he passed us on the way back to battle, but I sure as fuck stared at the back of his head when he left. I never quite forgot that, hard as I tried.

Principal Bryant called us in with one shrill word, "Now!"

I chose to close the door behind us.

"Did I tell you to do that?" Mrs. Bryant asked.

When I reached to open the door, she shouted again, "Now!"

In two grown-up office chairs, Jessica and I sat silently as Mrs. Bryant, the old, blonde, blue business suit wearing leader of our school, called the parents. She turned away from us. Spoke quietly. I could tell she left a message with the receptionist at my mom's office before speaking directly with Jessica's father. Mrs. Bryant hung up the phone, turned in her big leather chair, and stared into us; into our souls. Her silence demanded confession. The wood walls of her office felt like a courtroom closing in on me. Her wrinkly fingers steepled into a bent triangle, and she looked at me through the triangle with one eye, then at Jessica. Her big brown eye moved like a metronome between us; unblinking, stern, and invitingly ready.

The tactic worked: in less than thirty seconds, I volunteered my truth.

I blamed Jessica, obviously. Or at least it was obvious in the moment. I swear I only did it because I figured Jessica would do the same, but she didn't. She deflated and somehow fell into herself. She didn't blame me or disclose the note. She said almost nothing. She answered Principal Bryant's questions with yes or no or the shortest answer necessary, and throughout, she sat quietly and pained, her eyes down, her powerless hands cupped in her powerless lap.

Jessica received only a slap on the wrist. A simple written warning with a carbon copy for home. I, however, was sentenced to a three-day suspension, a punishment that would carry me into winter break. It was my third strike, see; the Chesterfield fiasco and my telling a whole class I wanted to be *the very best at loving women* finally caught up to me. Sitting there, awaiting our parents after Principal Bryant returned her attention to the box monitor atop her desk, Jessica glanced at me every minute or so, her eyes were veined with red, and an expression captured in one word: regret.

I couldn't hold her eye—shame wouldn't allow it—but when I did peek, I saw in my periphery the cold drip-drop of tears falling onto her lap and collar. As they fell—ringing it seemed, like bells—my heart recorded her pain.

I started crying too, silently like her, with tears just as big and drops just as steady to match the girl sitting to my left, the girl with the broken heart. And somehow, somehow, I knew even then that this little bit of reciprocity eased her pain, even if barely.

Still, I felt disgraced, like my goal *to be the very best* personified into Dad, then turned its back to me, spitting at my feet on his way back to battle.

It is the earliest memory I have of hating myself.

Maybe if I'd had the vocabulary, I would've apologized.

But I did not, so I could not.

Jessica's father arrived, and Jessica left. We were never left alone again.

My mom showed up ten minutes after that and scolded me all the way home. I didn't hear a single word. I felt dreadful.

When we got home, I was sent to my room and told to remain there until morning. Mom brought my dinner to me, a plain plate of pasta, no parmesan. She caught me crying, so she showed pity when she returned to collect the half eaten plate: a bowl of Neapolitan ice cream. She even took out the strawberry part.

Somehow, pity made it worse. It made no sense to me.

I put on the same t-shirt I'd worn to the party at Cooper Creek, *TMNT*, and I laid in bed, and I stared at the ceiling, and I saw through it and up to Dad. He was the hope of oxygen in an airless room, a foolish hope, an air that would never come. I fell asleep right after the ice cream and a short prayer.

I saw Jessica in passing a few more times before school ended. The following summer, her family left town. Mona said Jessica's dad landed a big job in Philly, but their friendship had already ended, killed by my sabotage. They too were gaining a vocabulary of friendship (and as I've been made to understand, this is a much more perilous curriculum for girls than for boys.)

Through Christmas and into the Spring, two images would settle into my thoughts at bedtime. Right as I laid down, they popped up like little fireworks, and they were my first thoughts too, every morning when I awoke: Jessica's smiling face when I gave her the bouquet and her bloodshot eyes with the principal. Two moments, diametrically opposed, living on two ends of the same path. On April 1st of that year, I swore on whatever it is nine-year-old boys swear on that I would never hurt a girl, not ever again, no matter what—

No, no, Nicolai. You're supposed to not *die, remember? The wall's right there. No need for B.S.—her and that white car of hers.*

It wasn't a white car, it was a black truck.

The order's all wrong anyway. Serena came first, not Becca. So it's not B.S. Honestly, it's not.

Serena came first, you say. Did she now? Who knows?

Someone does. Someone must. With Jessica, I held onto at least that much.

SERENA

"*Even the handsomest men do not have the same
momentary effect on the world as a truly beautiful woman.*"
—JONATHAN CARROLL

1.

My late elementary and middle school days were barren ones, entirely lacking in romantic success. This limbo, a wait of six years, threatened my whole quest. I gracefully lost the memory of those times—the desert of it, I mean, its cacti and trappings and snakes—but I sure as shit remember the heat.

Who knows?

Maybe it's all waiting there. Maybe without the strength of that skin, I never would've stood a chance. I never really stood a chance anyway.

I somehow managed to keep hold of my great aspiration to be *the very best*, and into high school I brought with me great hopes for my future. I was only fourteen, but my skin was much darker by then.

No one noticed though.

Not even Mom.

2.

Holding on wasn't always easy. I stopped often to recuperate.

One night during the winter semester of sixth grade I journaled for over two hours because I gave a girl named Molly a love note. Molly took said love note, origami-ed it into a swan, then smashed said swan beneath her Timberland boot.

Another time, around Spring Break in seventh grade, when I was eleven, I played hooky for three days because of a girl named Cecilia. I asked to sit next to her at lunch, but she said sharply the seat was for one of her girlfriends. Following a gamely inspirational talk I addressed to myself, I bravely returned halfway through lunch to find said seat occupied by an asshole kid named Dirk, who earlier that day had gotten a "D" on his geography test...a "D," in geography, about America.

Adding to the wasteland of my early pubescence, the few friends I had simplified into savants of Pokémon, sports, and first-person shooters. They deflected all my affectations for women, all my suggestions that they were not Sirens, but Divine Ones. As we aged, my casting out worsened. I learned through demoted draft slots at playground pickup games that romance is not cool for boys.

Lacking superior options, I volunteered as the wallflower and fell into myself. I stayed on the wall for as long as I could, which turned out to be for as long as I wanted. Mercifully, middle school ended, and my anticipation for high school swelled. My soul begged summer to end.

My enthusiasm for school arose because I had it on very good authority that high school boys have girlfriends, and I very badly wanted one of my own. The last one lasted only the duration of a kiss. I'd certainly earned more than that!

I did pushups and sit-ups every day, practiced my coolest pick-up lines, and shopped carefully for clothes that made me look like I didn't shop carefully. I fantasized constantly about my first day of school, then one day I woke up, and like Christmas to a kid, it was upon me.

High school!

And on that glorious first day…

…absolutely nothing happened.

I can't remember a single girl even glancing at me. But on the second day, right at sunrise, I stepped on the bus and saw Serena.

3.

I climbed the stairs, nodded to the driver, told him my name, and he marked me off on a checklist. I lost balance as the bus lurched forward. I grabbed the back of the first seat. It was just enough to keep me standing. When I looked up, that's when I saw her: Serena. She was the only one there, and she was smiling at me for avoiding the fall.

Serena resumed her meditations out the window. I watched as the morning sun painted her, its shadow falling softly across her jaw, reflecting little white dots on her light pink lip gloss. Her curled black hair fell as naturally as a waterfall, and I felt immediately her manner and her way: she was the opposite of cheerleader flamboyance, earning attention through subtlety and polish, but earning it nonetheless.

I took my seat a row behind her on the opposite side. We were the only two on the bus until it picked up five kids in the next neighborhood.

For many days, this was our way; riding together in silence.

Serena made friendly with a girl named Eleanor. Serena talked to Eleanor. On occasion, I overheard them. (Only a heart-monster would call this spying.)

I bought a pair of green Adidas with white stripes because green was Serena's dominant dress color and she loved the number three. I bought a hemp wristband patterned with musical notes because she carried a violin case. I hummed the melody to "This Is How We Do It" in earshot because it was her favorite song.

Then, in early October, she finally talked to me.

"Cool," she said as we stood to get off the bus.

"Huh?" I asked.

"Your wristband. I think it's cool. I like forest."

"Gump?"

"Green," she giggled. "Forest green. That's the color."

I lifted the wristband to inspect it, knowing well its shade.

"Thanks. Cool," I said, but before I could build on the moment we were off the bus and she was vanished.

The next morning, I wore the wristband again—*duh*. Serena smiled upon seeing me through her window at my bus stop.

"Hi," I said, getting on.

"Hey," she said, sitting up a bit.

I sat down across from her. "I'm Nicolai," I said. "You might already know that from us being on here every day."

She laughed politely. "I'm Serena. I like your neighborhood. It's so pretty."

"Well I hate to inform you, but I live two blocks up that way. This part here's way, way better."

"I'm sure that's not true," she said.

"No. Really, it is. Where I live we've got quicksand and giant dragonflies, but in good news the lava and the Great Floods are over so you wouldn't have to worry."

"Sounds lovely. I like dragonflies," she said.

"What about quicksand?"

"I've never seen quicksand. In fact, I think it's not real, right? Somebody told me that once."

"Who?"

"Who what?"

"Who told you quicksand's not real?"

"I think it's something everyone just kind of knows."

I looked away and said, "I guess we should shake hands now."

It was awkward, but she accepted, taking my hand lightly. Acknowledgment had become talk. Talk had become touch. Her hand was silk, but I didn't dare linger in the grasp.

"So where do you live Miss First-on-the-Bus."

"Lark Pond," she said.

"That's way off Macon, right?"

She nodded.

"You're so far away."

"Yeah. My father thinks it's worth it for the music. But you're right though, I'm on here for like twenty whole minutes before you get on and I can't sleep or anything."

"Why?" I asked

"Oh, I don't know," she said. "I can't sleep when I'm moving. Cars. Busses. I can on, like, planes though. Which is weird, right?"

"Maybe you belong in the sky."

She smiled at that.

"See me. I can sleep anywhere," I said. "Watch." I let my head drop and pretended to snore. She laughed louder than my silliness deserved.

The bus came to a stop to pick up Serena's friend Eleanor and the other invaders. I knew Serena enjoyed Eleanor's company, and I didn't want to give her pause about making a choice between her or me.

"Cool talking," I said. "I'm gonna get on some homework."

Maybe I feared rejection.

Who knows?

Maybe I was pushing up against time.

Is she the One?

"Yeah." She said. "Cool talking."

Is she the One who kills me?

4.

I came to know Eleanor—we were mutual Serena enthusiasts—and I could tell in the subtext of Eleanor's comments and in the undertones of Serena's looks that a problem was brewing. Serena *wanted* me to ask her out and my waiting threatened to cross that bridge from chivalrous patience to unreasonable hesitation.

But I stood still. I waited...

It felt purposeful, inclinations born of my lifelong quest *to become the very best at loving women.* Waiting challenged me on days when Serena was particularly pretty, or moments when we connected on shared interests like Legos. I succeeded every day in resisting the urge to formalize our mutual attraction.

I stood strong, and I waited.

On Halloween morning of that year, it finally happened. I finally won a moment.

"Oh hey," Serena said, interrupting our conversation about the school's new principal. "Do you have a date for the dance?"

"For Homecoming?" I asked.

She nodded.

"I don't," I said. "Do you?"

"No, I was seeing if you maybe wanted to go together?"

"What? Yeah! Yes—" quieter now, getting a grip "—absolutely." I sat up straight and turned to face her. "I was gonna ask you but I thought you had a boyfriend." (This sentiment was true enough.)

"What? No! Why? I mean why would you think I had a boyfriend?"

"How do I put this? Well," I said, counting on my fingers, "you're pretty, and you're fun, and I see you around with some of the music guys laughing all the time, and music guys get all the girls, as everyone knows."

"Like quicksand," she said, throwing me a bone.

"Yeah. Quicksand. I guessed—well, I mean—you're cool and smart too and…never mind—" I was smiling now, big and toothy "—I'm rambling but yes—yes. What I mean to say is, I'd love to go." We locked eyes and I told her with the sincerity of a Priest, measuring the level of my chin and settling my hands beside me. "More than anything. More than anything I'd love to bring you home."

She squinted at me. I'd spoken in disbelief. It had finally happened.

"Homecoming, I mean. I'd love that."

Serena blushed pink and turned away and smiled at Eleanor. Eleanor smiled back at her, but when Eleanor's smile reached me, it vanished like mist. I didn't interpret Eleanor's change of heart. Maybe I should've.

From the outside, it looked like nothing had happened, but it'd been a lightning bolt, the biggest I'd ever felt. The world had changed. Serena had me in her heart now. It had taken us two months.

5.

It had been ten years since Dad died.

The night before Homecoming, Mom, Mona and I celebrated overcoming the decade with a picnic near the graveyard where Dad lay. We ate in silence, thinking and sharing looks, and in the silence I could feel them crying. I hoped they couldn't feel me. I was smiling inside, excited for the sun to set and rise again so I could take my girl to the ball.

So, the sun sets and rises, and it's the last night of November.

Mom and I arrive to Serena's dad's house. The complex was a boxy two-level stucco type, and the inside matched. The furniture was all gray and plastic and functional, but none of it was uncomfortable. He'd cooked some stew earlier. The place smelled grand. (Serena's parents divorced when she was two.)

I was wearing beige slacks, a blue button-down, and, on Serena's request, a pink tie. I sat on a white couch with porcelain side tables. It was big and fluffy and deep, and my feet dangled from its edge. I sank in, toes tapping, thumbs twiddling, as Mom and Serena's dad shared parent-talk across the breakfast bar.

Without forewarning or announcement, we three went mute.

Serena began her descent of the staircase. How the world seemed to fold under each *tap-tap* of her heels on the birchwood steps. In order through my eyes; her glittering, silver two-inch heels; the slit that ran foot-to-knee up her pink dress; streaks of darker pink silk decorating the dress's belly and back; red-pink streaks covering her chest and neck, three spaghetti straps over each shoulder, multiplying and crossing into a spiderweb across her bare back; her face, turning to me and smiling as I stood, holding an inadequate corsage in my inadequate hands.

Mom left.

I sat in the back of her Dad's extended cab F-250. Serena sat up front and we three departed.

Her father dressed in a white T-shirt and blue jeans, and wore a well-mani-cured blond mustache. I caught him glancing at me in the rearview, so I looked out the window. It was as simple as that.

"Nine-thirty," he said as we pulled into the short line of vehicles idling along the curb. "I'll be right here to pick you up."

"Dad. Ten," Serena pled.

Her Dad looked at me and said, "Okay, but not a minute later."

Serena waved to her father as he drove off, then she turned to me and said, "Come quick!"

She took my hand and walked us briskly through the fountain courtyard and into the school's central stairwell. The dance was about to start in the cafeteria, but we were heading in the opposite direction: up.

"Where are we going?" I asked in a whisper.

No answer.

We climbed a flight in the stairwell, then flew through the dimly lit halls until we stopped. We were standing in the school's heart, before the doors of our brand new 1,500-seat auditorium.

The metal doors banged and reverberated in the emptiness as they closed behind us.

Then, Serena released me.

She descended the aisle towards the stage, where dark purple curtains climbed four stories to hide the settings behind it. She ascended onto stage, where her heels echoed *tap-tap.* There she stood, center stage, and she looked at me, and signaled with a wave of her hands for me to come nearer.

Looking up at her, I said, "We shouldn't be here. Not yet. The dance is just starting."

"Nonsense, Nicolai," she replied. "This is exactly where we should be."

An outreached hand, a nodding gesture: all the persuasion necessary for me to join her rebellion.

On stage, I took her hands in mine. They were as cool as the moonlight now pouring in through the west-facing windows. She rose as high as her tip-toes would take her.

Then, finally, she kissed me.

It was soft and slow, and the feeling silenced all my thoughts and fears, my phobia about kissing—along with spiders and spinach and boogie-monsters—a thing of the past. I soaked up the moment. I felt her vibrations in each movement of touch from her fingertips to her hips to her cheeks to the tip of her tongue. We stayed on stage for many minutes, exposed to our invisible audience.

When it ended, she lowered herself onto her heels. A sculptor of moments, she'd just completed a masterpiece. "Come on," she said. "The dance, remember?"

Like a cat thief admiring his perfectly-cut six-carat diamond, I looked in her eyes and answered, "I do, but who knows? Like you said, it's where were supposed to be."

Then I kissed her, and I realized.

It had finally happened.

A girl finally liked me.

6.

As Serena and I danced, turning with each other to the music, my fingers laced behind her back, her fingers laced around the back of my neck, a pair of eyes shattered my euphoria like the boom of a gunshot.

A pair of eyes, a pair of blazing green and unmistakable eyes, the eyes of Becca Odalis, a sophomore.

It had been a perfect night to that point. Serena and I snuck in kisses during slow songs. She rested her head on my shoulder. I kissed the top of her hand, tasted her neck, ran my fingers through her hair. We even escaped the cafeteria twice more to explore the wonders of making out.

This new pair of eyes threatened all that.

Becca was only a sophomore, but she had four years of sultry in her blood. Five-foot-two, blonde hair dyed with blonder tips, hairspray-stiffed bangs on a shoulder-length haircut, Coca-Cola bottle body, eyes like a Caribbean shore framed in the gray-blue clouds of heavy mascara and artificial lashes, all done precisely to compliment the green dress that flowered above her knee. Her shoulders were always bare, and though she was barely a B-cup, she looked voluptuous. Presently, Becca's forearms were hanging off the broad shoulders of a blue-eyed, blonde-haired senior linebacker whose name I would later learn was Jake.

But presently, her eyes were on me.

I quickly looked away, but just as quickly looked back. It was very dark, and she was ten yards away maybe, but those eyes shined like a lioness's, beaming at me.

Serena's head was resting in the nook of my neck when it happened. Knowing no better, I smiled to one side and winked at Becca.

Then, in an attempt to curse me, Becca Odalis—not the most popular girl at school but maybe our school's biggest pop star—blew a kiss back at me so loud I heard it. It whacked right into my forehead. I couldn't get out of the way in time. My stomach dropped. I felt a pang, a rush of wind from the space between Becca and me. This space filled quickly with pedestrians, and the song came to an end.

Following a smile for Serena, I stole another look in Becca's direction. She was already walking towards the exit, arms wrapped around her boyfriend and vice versa.

Then, she left.

Serena kissed me on the cheek and tugged at my tie and suggested I come nearer for some treasure.

"I love you," Serena whispered to me. It was the first time she'd ever said it. "I do. I love you, Nicolai."

I said the words back, and we kissed, and any concerns I'd had about Becca Odalis thinned and vanished like every storm that's ever threatened land.

It was nothing to her. Just like that, Serena had returned me to good.

7.

Three weeks had passed between Serena asking me out and homecoming itself, and during that time we spent many hours together on the bus and on the phone. I replaced Eleanor as Serena's company.

We ended every morning the same. "You'll call me tonight?" Serena would ask. "Of course," I'd say, and I always did. Always right at seven thirty, and the next day repeated anew, just like that, like clockwork.

My feelings for Serena grew, but they lacked overwhelming force, and overwhelming force seemed like a requirement in how I'd read it in books and seen it in movies and heard in it songs. I battled the asymmetry, tried to force my feelings into a speedier maturation. I felt like it was *me,* like some*thing* was wrong with *me.* I journaled often about love after homecoming. It seemed different. Homecoming had changed it. Hoping the confession might unlock some safeguarded passion I hadn't discovered, I wrote of betrayal, and how my lack of reciprocity made *me* feel to *myself* a traitor. I would say the words, "I love you." I'd volunteer them and offer them in reply, the way good men do. What other option did I have anyway? Tell her, "No! I don't love you." She was my girlfriend, which means she was the most important thing I had going. Love sounded a close enough word to me.

Who knows?

Serena and I couldn't properly date. Neither of us could drive. Our relationship was restricted to evening talks of about an hour, and our conversations ended always the same.

"Father said I need to get off the phone now," she would say. "Alright. I'll see you in the morning," I'd answer, and she would express her great regret in not being able to spend more time talking with me, and I always reciprocated the words, and I always meant them, and the next night repeated anew.

We held hands, kissed often, and found windows between classes to meet in the halls or at each other's lockers.

Christmas came and went.

Serena's Dad allowed her more time on the phone in the evenings, and she became bolder in her proclamations of love. I took those proclamations into my heart like a sponge. All was well in my world; I'd arrived at my destination, having earned the love of a prized girl in our freshman class.

Then, one winter afternoon, Becca Odalis made her encore on the stage of my life.

Really, I never stood a chance.

BECCA

"In love, women are professionals, men are amateurs."
—FRANCOIS TRUFFAUT

1.

Becca found me because of Mom, while I was sitting on the stone steps of my school one afternoon. She was late, and I'd been waiting.

Naked spruce trees lining the driveway rustled in a gust. The sudden noise chilled my bones, like skeletons shaking. Down the hill, I caught a crew of groundskeepers stuffing their fresh fallen leaves into big black bags. Two math team kids were waiting for their own chaperones a few steps above me, geeking out over a graphic novel with anime babes on the cover. These two pock-marked juniors, Walter Wicker and Ben-Hoo Young, were the top students at my school. They ultimately went on to become co-valedictorians and very successful Internet entrepreneurs.

I was reading *Catch-22* for English when the gust interrupted me. As the wind slowed, a small white truck came to a stop in front of us. I peeked over the spine of my book.

It was Becca. She was looking at me, an eager smile spelling "U" on her lips.

Memory returned like a flash. I hadn't remembered Becca once since the kiss she blew me, hadn't thought about her at all: her green jewelry, her green dress, the way she left so suddenly, her soft shoulders, her neck, how she puckered before she blew that kiss.

"Your name's Nicolai?" Becca asked, leaning over the console. I nodded like a dumbass.

"I'm Becca. I saw you at homecoming?"

"Yeah, I remember. Sure, I'm Nicolai," I said out of turn.

I adjusted clunkily and got my left wrist trapped in the straps of my bookbag. *Catch-22* fell away from me in the jumble, and I reached for it desperately, grabbing the novel just before it rolled off the stairs.

"What's your number?" Becca asked me.

"Twenty-two," I said.

She looked at me quizzically.

"Wait, what?" I asked. "What number?"

"Your phone number," she said. "I need help, and it looks like you're the one to help me."

"The one to help you with what exactly?"

Becca smiled and tilted her head. "You gonna give me your number or not? I can't be idling like this for you."

For the sake of traffic, I obliged Becca and gave her my number. She removed the cap of a red pen with her teeth and scribbled me onto her forearm. (Man, did I think she was cool.)

After confirming she had my number correct, she asked, "Now. When are you 'round?"

"What? Is that like a riddle?"

"A riddle? No. I mean when do you get home?"

"Oh, umm, I'm not going home," I said.

"What do you mean you're not going home."

"I mean, not right away. My Mom's picking me up."

"It's late," Becca said. "Sure you don't need a ride?"

"I'm covered. Thanks."

"Have it your way then."

Had I made a mistake?

I reached out for a second ending, hollering to her, "And anyway—" Becca looked at me "—I was taught not to get in cars with strangers."

"Well," she said, shifting into drive. "It's a truck. And we aren't strangers anymore, now are we?"

Then, she drove away.

Right away, I got that feeling you get when someone's spying on you. I turned around slowly and discovered Ben-Hoo Young and Walter Wicker, the soon-to-be millionaires, staring down at me. They said nothing, but their confounded looks asked a crystal-clear question: "How did you get a girl like *that* to talk to *you*?"

I had no formula or blueprints to offer. Walter and Ben-Hoo were architects, not painters, and my world was all about color. It must be how they feel when a fool begs to understand Calculus: they can't offer words, only numbers and variables that you already don't understand.

I returned to *Catch-22* and the story of Yossarian's jaundice—

The wall, remember?
Do you remember the question?

No, but the philosophy abounds: angels don't date nerds in high school, but they sure as shit do later. Apparently, it's just a matter of waiting to see which of the Walters and Ben-Hoos pan out in the end.

It's clear Becca mistook me for one of them.

Or maybe she got it just right.

2.

Becca didn't call that night.
She didn't call the next night either.
On the third night, our house phone rang.

Mom answered and shouted, "Nicolai, for you."

I hurried downstairs and found Mom in the kitchen.

"It's a girl," she whispered.

"That's alright," I said.

"It's doesn't sound like Serena."

"I'm pretty sure that's alright too."

Mom handed me the cordless, eyes squinting with suspicion.

"Hello," I said.

"It's Becca," the voice on the other side said back.

I was looking straight at Mom as confusion stretched my smile.

"Hi there. You...you—"

"Can I see you tonight? I need help, remember?"

"Tonight?" I replied.

I smiled at Mom. Mom didn't smile back.

"Hold on a second, would you?"

I turned my eyes away from Mom, then my head, then the rest of me. I trotted upstairs, closed my door, and sat on the bed thinking: *calm down. Be cool.*

"What am I doing tonight?" I said. I had tons of homework, a European history exam to study for, and a weight training session early the next morning. "Nothing," I answered. "Nothing really."

"I need your help," she repeated.

"Tonight?" I asked.

"It's all catching up with me. Can you? Can we meet?"

"What's catching up? What is it you need help with exactly?"

"I'll tell you when I see you."

"I don't know—about tonight I mean. And I don't have a car yet. I'm only—"

"A freshman. Figures," she said. "I just got mine. I'll come to you. Where do you live?"

Meet Nicolai: Deer-In-Headlights. I had no clue what Becca could possibly need, but I *definitely* didn't want her coming to my home.

"Does it have to be tonight?" I asked.

"Nicolaaaaaaiiii," she said.

I'd never heard my name said like that. It was a pleading, the way she let the last syllable hang on so long and so desperately. "Stop being such a freshman. I promise it's safe."

A brutal silence followed, but nothing concrete occurred, so I said, "Yes. OK."

She exhaled satisfaction in having persuaded me, and I still knew near nothing about her.

Only one thing stuck out, and of only one thing was I sure.

Becca never belonged. She was stuck there, just like me. It turns out that's exactly what she needed help with.

I told Becca to pick me up from a shopping center near my house. She summarized the details, "Milton and Mill. Six-thirty. There's a blue bench next to the pay-phones. We'll meet there."

We said goodbye, and then for a minute I sat on the edge of my bed thinking: *I should call Serena.* I picked up the cordless and began dialing, but my pointer finger stopped itself and floated over the final digit, an ominous 7.

What would you say?
Do you think it's trouble?
Would she want to know?
Would I want to know?

I was sure Becca had made a mistake, either that or she really did need my help. I decided it'd be better to tell Serena afterwards, so I set down the phone, slid into my leather jacket, and walked downstairs.

I told Mom I was going to a friend's house.

"Be careful," Mom said to me, and I thought nothing of her choice of words.

I'd been waiting only a few minutes when Becca's white truck pulled into the parking lot, blew by the Dollar General, and screeched to a stop in front me, on the blue bench where I sat.

Stay cool, I thought to myself as she leaned over the center console. *Just stay cool.*

"Hi," I said.

"Hi you," she replied. I barely heard her over a pop song blaring on the radio.

"Hi," I said again.

"Well? Are you gonna get in or do I have to pull you in?"

"No. No, I'll just get in," I said, then I sat down, closed the door, and buckled up.

Becca's left foot was perched on her seat. Her short hair was in a high ponytail that stretched and beautified her neck. She wore jean shorts, half-calf cowboy boots, and a white sweater with lavender stripes that rendered bare her toned shoulders. She was art: intentional and unique. I remember thinking how comfortable she looked. I remember wanting that, and I remember feeling immature and lost in the rules of my life.

I noticed she wasn't wearing her seatbelt.

"Where we goin'?" I asked.

"There's a bowling alley on Buena Vista called Stripes. There's pool inside too. You know it?"

"Yeah, I know it."

I didn't know it.

"Do you like bowling?" she asked.

"I guess. I've only done it a few times."

"That's alright," Becca said, shifting into drive. "You just grab a ball and throw it at some sticks. We'll put the guard rails up if you suck."

On that note, we sped away, and Becca hummed the songs on the radio.

I very much wanted to ask how I could help, but I was worried I'd make an ass of myself by asking. It was loud because of the radio and the wind that blasted through the cab since both windows were halfway down. My lips took to shivering, it got so cold, but Becca appeared immune.

As we ascended the Interstate on-ramp, my nerves mellowed, my comfort grew. But then, as one might a lapdog, and without a word of warning, Becca laid her right hand on my left thigh. She didn't grab me or rub me; her fingers tapped my leg lightly to the rhythm of the radio. When I looked down, her hand appeared to me a strange little animal, unknown and unwelcome. I considered swatting it away.

But I didn't.

If I knew what I know now, I would've done it. Or I would've said politely, "You've misunderstood me. I'm not for the having."

But I didn't.

Maybe I worried it'd be rude.

Becca kept her eyes on the road, kept humming those pop songs, kept being awesome and cool and comfortable and sexy. *Stay calm*, I thought. *Stay calm, Nico.* Maybe I liked her touch so much it sealed my lips.

Do you think it's trouble?
Would she want to know?

We pulled off the highway a few blocks from the alley, and Becca lifted her hand from my thigh, and I exhaled, and she heard it over the wind, and she looked at me, smiling in "U" again.

I couldn't help it. I smiled back.

Then, we got to where we were going.

4.

A vertical billboard flashed its white boxes along the entrance to the dilapidated yellow building. Each white box carried a letter, and they spelled B-O-W-L-N-G. The "I" had gone out of the sign. At Stripes, I imagine this happened often. A marquis beside the white "N" box was advertising "2-for-1" night, whatever that meant.

Becca rode by several empty spaces along the back row of the lot until we reached its most remote corner. She parked, killed the engine, and lowered the radio volume to ambient. Light streaked in from lamps overhead. Nevertheless, it was very dark.

"That girl you were dancing with," Becca asked. "Who is she?"

"What?"

"The girl at homecoming, duh. You two were dancing all night. Is she your girlfriend?"

"Serena?" I asked. "Is that what you need help with?"

"No," Becca said. "I just wanted to know her name and now I know. Can't a girl ask a question?"

"Was the guy you were hanging from all night your boyfriend? The big jock-looking guy."

"I knew it. You were looking at me all night."

"No—"

"He's not a jock first, but *nyet*," she answered, and her smile vanished, and she started scraping a smudge on the windshield with her fingernail. "Not since homecoming," she said sadly.

"Did something happen at homecoming with you and this giant non-jock-looking jock?"

She muffled a laugh. "I imagine you already know, but thanks for playing."

"Know what?" I said. "I don't know anything about you."

In (very) slow succession, Becca told me the jock's name was Jake, that he was a senior, and that they'd dated for two months. "He broke up with me when he dropped me off after homecoming. Like, who does that?" I didn't have gossipy friends—still don't—but apparently, everyone at school thought Becca stole Jake from Tatiana, his girlfriend of six months. Becca said girls at school were calling her terrible names, and that she didn't have many friends left.

It seemed like a terrible state of affairs, 'man-thief' or not.

"We never fucked though," she said. "At least there's that. I think it's probably the real why, if I'm being honest."

The casual way she referred to sex made me feel childish. "Why not?" I asked, adjusting the seatbelt I was still wearing. "I mean, why didn't you and Jake, you know…"

"Jeez, Nicolai," she said. "You can say 'have sex' at least. Nobody's gonna arrest you."

"I'm not so sure."

"Try it. Say it."

"I'm alright."

"And you can take off your seatbelt."

"I'm definitely not so sure about that."

She leaned back as if to examine me under new light. "You really are a fresh-man, huh?"

"I am actually. I'm a freshman."

"Well, nobody's gonna arrest you." She lifted her left hand and said, "I hereby guarantee your safety."

I exhaled. "That makes me feel much safer," I told her.

Is this the first time I'm seeing it? I thought, then the empty feeling of not knowing where the question had come from. It shocked me how suddenly her feeling followed mine.

There's no way to know who follows who.
And I've maybe forgotten the question.

Becca laughed and looked away. When she turned back to me, she'd changed. She was charged.

She was gazing at me, peering into my soul in that way women do when they first consider the promise of a man, that first gaze of intentional consideration. She must've talked for over an hour and a half with nothing more than my questions of clarification to interrupt. I lost not an ounce of patience. I can't be sure as to the Freud of it—maybe Becca had never been listened to before, maybe the rumors at school were hurting her—but at some point, due to some wisp of word or switch of insinuation, in the backdrop of my listening, and accompanied by the radio which had tempered its melody to the slow songs of evening, Becca began hearing a telepathic voice in my silence.

It said:

I hear you. I understand you. I have no judgments to pass.

Her gaze then transformed into that of the hypnotists. I forgot where we were, and why, and that she needed help. Worst of all, I forgot about the girl awaiting my call—I'd forgotten about Serena—and in losing myself to my affectations generally, I let feeling take full control of my life for the first time ever.

Accordingly, I sinned.

5.

It was almost nine. Becca's hypnosis had almost worn off. I almost got home free.

I stopped her mid-sentence. "Becca," I said.

I was going to ask her to take me home, but she defended the night, and reached out and touched my cheek. I looked into her eyes, then closed my own as

I pressed my cheek wantonly into her palm.

"Slide your chair back," she said.

I did without a word.

"Not like that. Go all the way down. Lean all the way back."

I did.

"Just relax, OK?"

I did that too. I relaxed.

I heard Becca's body shift over the center console before she perched atop me. I tried to avoid touching her thighs, but her first move was to move my hands so that my fingertips teased the cusp of her jean shorts. Her skin was so soft, so warm. Each time she kissed me with her strawberry lip-glossed lips, I licked my own lips to prolong the taste of her. She moved to my neck and tickled me into a fever by teasing my ears.

Again, she said my name. "Nicolaaaaaiiii."

I adjusted and slid my hands up and around her back—an attempt to take control—but she guided my hands away.

"You're one of the ones Mom told me about, aren't you?"

"Huh?"

"You're one of the ones who knows."

"Possibly."

Lost in her completely, lost there in the dark corner of that bowling alley parking lot, my hands found the sides of her legs as her hips pressed into me. The anticipation was maddening. She lowered herself, sliding into the space between me and the floorboard, lifting my shirt as she went, kissing my chest. Her kisses reached my belly button before the occurrence occurred to me. Even as Becca was unbuttoning me and reaching into my underwear, I didn't *actually* think it was going to happen: the blowjob lives mythologically in the male mind until the moment it begins.

But begin it did.

I suffered many side effects from Becca's excellent treatment: vertigo, a shaking leg, goosebumps, sweat condensing on my forehead. I became quickly aware of the impending climax but was gentlemanly enough to warn Becca ahead of time. She was a lady in reply, seeing me through to the finish.

It was the most exhilarating forty-five seconds of my life.

Then, accordingly, we went back home.

On Lying

The wall, Nico. Remember?
Do you remember the question?

There's nothing to remember. It's done. The tires rumble over the striations of the highway shoulder. I find my hands, and they float back to find the wheel. Too late.

Flames melt metal melt flesh. There is a smoldering. Dark streaks on the concrete to mark the occasion.

The car and I smash into the median at forty-five miles per hour. The Civic's old. The airbags probably don't work. I lose the wheel for the last time.

I remember the question, but it's not a question, it's a quest, for the girl with the joy drained face.

No, Nico. For the One who killed you.

I only remember the fall. Nothing more.

Oh, Nico. How you lie! And here we are, smoldering.

There was little ceremony after Becca finished. I zipped up and said, "Thanks." Becca said, "You're welcome," and we sped to my neighborhood. It was a quiet drive, and the sky was gray, and I got the sense that Becca was in a greater hurry to get back than me.

When I walked in, Mom was watching a hospital drama called *E.R.* She'd forgotten her worries about the earlier phone call, and anyway, nothing could pry Mom away from George Clooney, who happened to be smiling at the mother of a comatose kid when I passed by the living room like a ghost.

I snatched the phone, walked to my bedroom, and flopped on my bed face first. Immediately guilt cascaded over me, drowning out my awareness and draining away every other emotion I'd felt that evening—gratitude, confusion, fear. Guilt tightened my gut. Guilt squeezed my fists. Guilt crystalized the choice before me: *to tell Serena or not?*

My ears rang. My eyes burned. I felt afloat. I rewound and repeated the progression of my choices: giving Becca my number, getting in Becca's car, allowing Becca to touch me, sharing a conversation, surrendering to intimacy. My head rose from the pillow as if lifted by a magnet, and it occurred to me that *none of it* was my fault.

Alleluia! Guilt had done its work quickly!

It was hardly a choice. I felt free from my sin, so I picked up the phone and began dialing Serena with a moral-minded smile on my face.

It came down to two pieces of advice, advice I'd heard countless times before; Ben Franklin's famous phrase, "Honesty is the best policy," and the other one, like Mom said, "Everyone makes mistakes. All you can do is learn from them and grow."

Sound direction from great minds, right?

Let's slow down.

What I hadn't yet learned is that mistakes in romance often lead to permanent endings. I also failed to consider how Serena might react. I hadn't learned the difference between fibs and lies, how fibs annoy but lies annihilate. I did not yet know that a lie is a sin that has gone untold.

So, to recap, my equipment going into this massacre; honesty and the promise of growth. It seemed like a mighty arsenal at the time. All I had to do while smothering my face in the pillow was summon the many stories of my youth; the fairy tales and cartoons, the grown-up movies dealing in dishonesty. The hero was always vindicated by the truth, and usually he earned a prize, and always the relationship moves forward, bettered by the turmoil the lovers overcame.

Only later do you read the love stories where everybody dies.

I *wanted* to right it. I didn't want to lose Serena: she was the centerpiece of my life. My guilt melted into redemption as I found refuge in the bunkers of truths. I sat up in bed and dialed Serena's number, prepared like a good boy to share with her my story.

With that, I'd like to say thank you to all the story-tellers out there who built these myths: you really fucked me good on this one.

Serena

8.

It was nine-thirty, two hours later than usual for our evening talk. Serena picked up before the second ring.

"Hello? Nicolai?"

Only then did it occurr to me that this might not be such a good idea.

The sound of her voice mixed terribly with my blood. It bubbled and swirled about in my veins, locking my lips and freezing my lungs. Breathless, I became light-headed with terror: I felt like a medieval warrior charging across a plain into rows of armored opposition, but I'd vowed to charge until it was over. Victory was the aim, and the aim here was honesty.

"Hey, it's me," I said.

"Of course it's you. Is everything OK? It's late."

"Sure. Of course. Everything's fine. Just got tied up." *At least it's not that*, I thought. "What'd you do tonight?"

"Well, I was telling you about Mrs. Cairo, right? She got in one of her moods again and got mad because Aaron won't stop bugging this new girl Harper. Aaron keeps passing her notes, like she likes him. She doesn't though, so now we all have this pop quiz tomorrow, like a graded actual test. So I was studying for that. I can't stand Aaron."

I wanted to say something, but I couldn't find the words.

"I watched *Friends* earlier with Dad," Serena said. "We laughed for like thirty minutes straight. Did you watch? You promised you would."

"No," I said. "But I've seen it. I just don't get *Friends*. It's not really my thing."

"Stop it," she said. "I like to think I have an idea about what you'd like?"

She laughed.

I noticeably did not.

I had begun pacing my room like a patrolman—desk to closet to bed to desk to closet to bed—a trap, my own little prison of integrity. I caught myself red-handed in the mirror.

"Is everything OK?" she said.

Not victory, but honesty, my reflection corrected.

"Do you know a sophomore girl named—" but the name hid itself somewhere in my throat. For many seconds it lingered there.

"Who?"

"—Becca?"

"Becca? Like…Becca Odalis, Becca?"

"That's her, yeah. Becca Odalis. The sophomore."

"OK."

"You know her?"

"No. I just know *of* her," Serena said. "Everyone knows *of* her. What *about* her?"

"Interesting thing," I said. "The other day she asked for my phone number."

Serena said one word, samurai sharp: "What?"

One question, and time stopped.

I continued meekly. "I was waiting for Mom in front of the school and Becca rode up and sort of asked for my number. It was weird. I'd never talked to her before that."

One question became two. "What? Why?"

"I have no idea," I said. "I didn't really think about it. I just sort of gave it to her."

"Did you just say you gave Becca Odalis your phone number? Is that what you just said?"

"I just said that."

"What? Why?"

"You just said that."

"I know, but why did you give her your number?"

"What do you mean why?"

"You know what I mean!"

"Because she asked. I'm not sure how to answer that."

"Because she asked? I asked *why*. *Why* in God's name would you give, of all people, Becca Odalis, your phone number?"

"Like I said, it was weird and she said she needed help with something and I just did."

"You're lying."

"No I'm not! What do you mean I'm lying?"

"You know *exactly* what I mean."

"I'm not lying. I was sitting in front of the school. She asked. I gave. Seriously. Which part do you think is the lie."

"What could she have possibly needed your help with, huh?"

"I didn't know at the time."

"Well what then?"

Mine, here, was honesty.

"Actually," I said, dumbfounded, lost in the question. "She never got around to it. Hmm."

The sentence had spilled out. I knew it didn't look good.

"Nicolai, are you joking? Is this a joke? If it is, it's awful and I want you to stop right now."

"No," I said. "This all happened."

"What all happened? Get to it already."

"I am," I said. "I'm literally in the process of telling you the truth. It's not like you're figuring it out."

"You're freaking me out, Nicolai. What happened?"

"Well…she didn't call at first."

"What?"

"She didn't call for, like, three days."

"I don't care! I don't need a damn backstory, just tell me what happened!"

"I will when you calm down and stop yelling at me."

"That's not fair!" She screamed. Then she whimpered, "What happened?"

Before I could answer, Serena began to cry. It sounded like a suffocating inhale, then it faded into vibrations, leaving only an echo. Like a symphony's movements, the volume rushed back and away and back again, until finally, when she began to speak, her words came out muffled. I couldn't understand her at all.

"You have to stop crying," I said. "I can't make out what you're saying."

"Tell me what happened."

"You have to calm down."

"This is as calm as I can be right now, just get to it."

"Alright," I said. "Alright…."

I almost rewrote this tragedy mid-act. I strongly considered a late retreat. "Becca called," I said, "and she said she needed help with something, so I agreed to meet her and she picked me up."

"When?"

"This happened tonight?"

"Tonight? She picked you up tonight?" Serena asked.

"Yeah," I said. "In her truck."

"I don't care about her truck," Serena snapped.

"I didn't say you cared about her truck," I shot back.

"Stop talking about her truck."

"OK, fine" I said. "So, anyway, she picked me up and asked if I wanted to go bowling and—Serena, you have to stop crying."

"I'm not crying," she said, but crying overtook her as she spoke. Another minute passed.

"Are you alright?" I asked.

"Goddammit, Nicolai. Please," she begged, "for the love of God, tell me what happened! Just tell me the truth."

"Look. We got to the bowling alley. Instead of going in, she parked the car and we talked."

"You talked? Talked about what?"

"About her boyfriend, mostly."

"Becca Odalis doesn't have a boyfriend, Nicolai. Now I know you're lying."

"Her ex-boyfriend. You get what I mean."

"Did you tell her about me?" Serena asked. "Huh? Did you? Did you tell her there's a girl who loves you that you talk to every night waiting for you to call? Did you?"

"She did ask about you."

"Oh! She did? What a shock! Becca Odalis asked about me. Becca the man-thief asks my boyfriend *about me!* How classic. Well, Nicolai, what did you tell her, huh? That I was a friend. Or you know what, I bet you pretended like I didn't exist. Didn't you? Didn't you! Tell me right now, and if you hesitate, you lie."

"I didn't tell her anything about you, but it wasn't on purpose, okay!"

Alas, mine was honesty.

"Oh shit!" Serena exclaimed. "Not on purpose? How convenient! Wouldn't want Becca Odalis to know there's a girl who loves you out there, now would you? Wouldn't want that to get in your fucking way!"

"I've never heard you say fuck before," I said.

"Get used to it."

"Look," I answered, angry now because she hadn't applied any credit to my telling of the truth. "You gotta believe me. I didn't plan any of this."

"Sweet Jesus, convenience again. Mister Nicolai, mister very convenient, do you think that if I tell Mrs. Cairo tomorrow—" a pedantic voice now "—*'I didn't plan to not study*,' that she'll give me a goddamned A-plus. Teach me your ways."

"Come on, Serena—"

"Nicolai, goddammit. What, happened!"

"I didn't have sex with her or anything."

"What then?" she shouted. "What did you do? Why are you telling me this?!"

"I—"

"Tell me!"

"Serena, honestly I—"

"Tell me," she cried, desperate for the end.

I hadn't considered her heart, hadn't considered what a shock it would be. I did, however, fulfill my duty to honesty, and in doing so, I introduced Serena to victimhood.

"OK..." I said again, and hesitated for a metaphysical hour before my closing statement. "Becca went down on me in her car."

Serena shrieked as though she'd seen a ghost.

Then, nothing.

Then, silence.

(Then I remembered it was a truck. Classic. I'd ended on a lie.)

How convenient. Then, silence. Then, nothing.

9.

The dial tone told me she'd hung up. She'd actually done it.

I tried calling back. She didn't answer. I called again ten minutes later. After one ring: pick up, *click*. I didn't call again.

She wasn't on the bus in the morning, and she wasn't at school either. That was a Friday.

The weekend that followed was the loneliest I'd ever known. I kept to myself, hiding in my room with my video games and self-pity. Mom could tell it was bad, but I managed a good enough smile and did well in convincing her not to worry. I couldn't convince myself of the same. I couldn't *not* worry. A great fear that I'd lose her kept me awake hours past midnight. I called her twice each day, but all weekend long, she refused my calls.

On Sunday night, I dialed her number and waited.

I couldn't believe it when she picked up. She'd answered my call.

10.

"Nicolai?" Serena said.

"Hey!" I replied, sitting up at my desk and smiling at the sound of her voice. "Yeah, it's me."

"I want you to listen to me." she said. "Don't talk."

"I want you to know how sorry I am. I'm going nuts—"

"If you say anything else I'll hang up and never talk to you again. Can you do that? Can you actually have a heart?"

"Yes," I answered. "I'm listening."

Several times she attempted to begin, but each time, crying stole her voice. I waited silently, as instructed, and I looked to my left at the full-body mirror hanging from my closet, and there I saw a hideous troll wearing my clothes, staring back at me where I should've been standing.

"I love you," she finally said. "I have since you did that sleeping joke on the bus that one day when you finally talked to me. I didn't think you'd *ever* talk to me. I had such a crush. It was so stupid."

"Serena," I said.

"You agreed not to talk," she interrupted. "Or was that a lie too?"

"I didn't lie to you. I told you the truth."

She shouted at me. "Shut up and let me speak!"

No woman had ever yelled at me like that before; not a teacher, not even Mom. If I'd been magic, I would've shrunken myself into a ball and disappeared in the nothingness. But I wasn't magic, so I stayed there with the mirror-troll, warts and moles and all of him. I was trapped.

"You know," Serena said with a sad laugh, "I just knew we'd get married and have beautiful children and live happily ever after. But Dad always says, 'Remember, it's high school,' and I'm just another girl to you—" I stopped myself from talking, but she was *not* just another girl: she was precious. "I honestly believed that if I could convince you to feel towards me what I felt about you, that…"

"That what?" I asked.

She began sobbing. It wasn't like before; this was like what Adele sings about, gut-wrenching stuff.

"Serena," I said.

"Never again," she said back. "Never again, Nicolai. Do you understand me?"

"Of course, never again!" I exclaimed, joy ringing in my heart. Forgiveness had come! "Honestly," I said, "it just happened. And then George Clooney was on the T.V. when I got back so I figured—"

"No!" she shouted. "No—No, you—you're not understanding me. You aren't listening." Her sobbing stopped cold. Samurai sharp, she said, "You will never be able to hurt me again. When I said never, I meant never talk to me again, never call me again—"

"Serena—"

"And if you ever say my name again, I'll tell my father what you did, and he'll tell your Mom. I doubt you're *actually* brave. I doubt you're one of the ones who know. You don't have it in you."

"Brave?" I said desperately. "Please. Sere…. Serena, you can't do this."

"Nicolai. Don't. Fucking. Tempt me."

Then, she hung up.

And we never talked again. Not ever.

11.

The rest of that school year, Serena and I didn't exchange a single "hello." Not a word passed between us.

And for the next three years, when I'd see her in the halls or cafeteria, or walking through our courtyards, or at football games and assemblies in the auditorium where we shared our first kiss, those rare times our eyes met, hers eyes would turn away instantly. It left me feeling cold, and I always felt I deserved it. I felt like she deserved her vengeance.

When she hung up on me, I fell into myself. I remember the minutes right afterwards, the deep darkness of it. I nearly fell over while pacing my room. I sought refuge in the only emotion bunker I knew: Mom's arms. I raced downstairs. "Serena broke up with me!" I cried like a beaten-up kid. Even Mona came down to say, "It'll be okay," before promptly returning upstairs.

Mom's bunker wasn't as cozy as I'd remembered. She used phrases like "it's all normal" and "just a part of growing up," words I'd heard a hundred times applied to a thousand situations, like making a mistake in soccer or getting a bad grade. Something was very suddenly and very clearly different now, and I knew Mom knew I could tell. The feeling ravaged my heart. It exploded into existence, a monster of terrible misfortune.

I longed for my Dad: my father.

A feeling of isolation sucked me in, its gravity enormous. The loss of my father rang like new, like the news, like it happened yesterday—a headline shouting: *DAD'S DEAD;* subtitle adding: *And he ain't coming back.* So powerfully did this swell come on that I felt awoken from a coma, the obviousness of Dad's deletion now rupturing my sense of place, the way a streak of lightning ruptures the dark, and I squeezed into Mom's shoulders, and I was thinking of him, thinking of how I wanted *his* arms to wrap me up, a king to his prince or a master to his apprentice, a man who could say with stern jaw and honest eyes, crouching with honest eyes to meet mine, the wither of experience and empathy in his tone: "It's normal," he would say, "just a normal part of growing up, son," but father didn't say it because he couldn't say it because he was dead, and it materialized to me only then, in that bottomless moment, when all I had left was Mom, that I could see him, but only a face from pictures, and I couldn't feel anything but *her*, and no one would ever call me son, not in the way I needed, no matter how long I breathed air or how long I loved women.

"It's alright, Nico—" *Nico?* She'd never called me that before "—you'll be alright. Rest your thoughts."

I pressed away and looked at her. "Nico?"

"That's what Dad called you. To him it meant the sun. Don't overthink it."

We were the same height now. I hadn't noticed before.

Mom got me to bed with food in my belly. She stayed up with me until one o'clock. I felt guilty knowing that no matter how well mothered I was—and I was, as well as any boy—I'd be forever doomed to Dadlessness. The emptiness had never before appeared so vast, so impossibly dense and impenetrable.

I always wondered what it was like for Serena. Her pain was the pain of victimization: *I* had hurt her. I think maybe I was supposed to reach back out. Or maybe that would've made it worse. Maybe it went just the way it was written. Maybe shunning me was all the healing she needed.

Who knows?

I can feel my hands on the wheel again. I can feel heat all around me.

"Who cares" might be better than "who knows," you know. You're running out of time.

We're running out of time, and nobody knows what time will do. Maybe Serena will talk to me again someday, maybe at a high school reunion. As I'd done once before, I resolved thereafter that I would never hurt a girl, not ever again, for as long as I lived.

As with all my other promises, I meant it when I said it.

Becca

6.

Just as it requires freakish athletic talent to become a sports star as a teenager, so too would it require a freakish romantic talent to succeed at navigating a first relationship. It should be apparent by now that I was not born with such talents. A man can avoid dangerous paths with a good romantic map, but it is experience that does the mapmaking. If someone does ever find a girl-obsessed, fifteen-year-old boy who turns down blowjobs, someone will find him playing poker with Santa Claus, the tooth-fairy of Atlantis, and a humble Donald Trump. A teenager turning down *that!?* Truly, it is a mythical concept.

In the days following my banishment from Serena's life, I thought myself a scoundrel. I'd been great with Serena. I'd had it all under control—the house built well on a calm beach, its walls sturdy, its windows backed and boarded—but then hurricane Becca came through and that was that.

I kept to myself for weeks, believing I could hide from my remorse by hiding in my room. Mom checked on me often, but she never pried, never pressed for details on how or why it ended.

School, however, had no such reservations.

Chance crossings with Serena happened all the time, so most days I left the school feeling cold. My few friends would ask what happened, and I always deflected the question, pleading the fifth or playing the privacy card. I only had one conversation about it, with three down-the-street friends of mine named Sean, Ryan, and Steve. Their questions regarded the chronology and details of Becca's blowjob. It was a very short conversation.

My world had ended, and I was alone. The nights were sleepless, the days were worse, until one day in late February, when Becca returned.

7.

She called me on a Monday.

Mom answered the phone and handed it to me as I passed in the hall. It was Becca.

After brief salutations, Becca made her case. I was standing out back in the wind. It was a moonless night, and I realized I'd been fighting a smile.

"You owe me," Becca said. "You know that?"

"I owe you what exactly?" I asked.

"You owe—come on Nicky."

"Don't call me Nicky. I hate that name."

"How about Nico then? Nico sounds nice."

"How about Rebecca instead of Becca."

"How about no, that's not my name," she answered. "That's not on my birth certificate."

"Nicky and Nico aren't on my birth certificate either."

"Yeah, but there's a difference between adding parts and taking parts away. It's name rules or something. Can we move past the name thing, seriously."

"We can't, but please continue."

Becca resumed her pitch. "Like I said, you owe me, and don't get all shy pretending like you don't know what I mean either. You haven't so much as called or left me a note, and it's been like a month."

I bumbled over a few words before getting it.

"Ooooooh…"

"Good. You get it. And it's only fair. Reciprocation, like we learned in Algebra the other day. Reciprocals are what make things whole."

Becca then shared a meandering anthology of the various mistreatments she suffered at the hands of various teachers. She called me every two or three days. We talked maybe twenty times, our conversations always short and coy, snarky and charming.

There was more to why Becca and I were required to share a second date at the bowling alley. There was research and the recovery of a lost gem, but mostly it was her plea for reciprocity. That word weighed mightily in my world: my sister and Mom's too. Reciprocity was the first, last, and only mandate we ever got from Dad. Many years after he died, he made it my law. I never really had a choice, you see, so I never stood a chance.

8.

"Reciprocity is the currency of relationships," Mom would tell Mona and me. Then she'd remind us, "Those were *his* words."

When I turned ten, Mom showed me the truth.

It was a winter weekend, and I'd gotten angry at Mona for not bringing our Nintendo upstairs. She was sprawled across the couch like a spoiled brat, like a princess-not-yet-saved, and as credits for a reality show called *The Real Housewives of Who Gives a Shit* flashed on the screen, I demanded she do what she said she'd do. She said she wanted me to leave her alone, so naturally I didn't leave her alone. Naturally, I leaned in.

"You're so fucking lazy!" I shouted, but when I turned to perform my dramatic exit, I bumped into Mom. She'd been standing there like a sentinel. She'd been standing there all along.

Who knew?

My look was of horror: I wondered if she had it in her to murder me.

Instead, she smiled, and calmly said, "Upstairs, Nicolai."

I went up.

Mom followed.

Mom pointed at her bedroom door.

I entered.

Then, she pointed to Dad's side of the bed.

Reluctantly, I sat, my feet dangling over the edge.

"I'm sorry," I said when Mom sat down beside me. The queen-sized bed she and Dad shared, the one from their first apartment together, creaked under her weight. "I mean, like, really, really, really sorry."

"For what, Nick?" Mom said. "Do you know why you're sorry?"

"I said the, uh…. The F-word."

"The word's alright. You might need some age and context, but you'll get it. I don't mind so much that you said a word, it's why. You used a word like a gavel today. Your father would be very disappointed."

My dangling feet froze.

Mom had never invoked his name like that, she'd never said anything like that at all. My jaw shook. All around us were memories of Dad, his side of the bed having gone mostly untouched since he died of cancer; an analog alarm clock, two encased watches, a white mug filled with Bic pens and highlighters, a stack of his favorite books and a bunch of Hemingway beside them. Over his nightstand hung and still hang three pictures framed quietly in wood. The first: Dad, alone, smiling in cap and gown on graduation day at Western. The second: Dad with Mom on their Honeymoon in Michigan. The third, the one hanging highest: Dad with Mom, Mona, and me. We're roasting marshmallows at a camp on the Chattahoochee. It was our last family vacation. Father had been told about his terminal condition a few days before we went down there, but he hadn't even told Mom yet.

"On the last day—" Mom said, then she interrupted herself, "—do you remember?"

I shook my head and said, "I don't think so." That's why Mom continued.

She wiped a building tear from my eye. "It's okay, Nick. Having a man like your Dad as your father…you were always bound to disappoint him. He was a great man."

"Really?" I asked.

"Yeah, babe. Really. We're lucky to have him in our blood."

Mom told me two stories Dad shared that night on the Chattahoochee. I don't remember either, but I'm sure Mona does. She remembers everything.

"Alright Nicolai, listen to me," Mom said. "You forget things, I forget things, but that doesn't make us lazy. Mona's watching trash right now. She forgot about the game system. Trash will do that."

"I know, Mom. That's why I was yelling."

Mom chuckled. "You've always made me laugh? Like three days after your father died too. I can't remember what it was you said."

She stood, took down the picture of us camping, sat back down, and set the frame on her lap.

"I don't talk about your father a lot. I know. I know that and I'm." Mom smiled and shook with feeling. It was a smile to hold back a reservoir of tears. The reservoir was fast failing. "I'm sorry for it. He asked me to share something with you at 'an opportune moment,' and there aren't many opportunities with you. You're really a good guy. Right on your way to great."

"Really?" I asked.

"Yeah babe. Really."

She rubbed my hair, and lost a teardrop.

"Your father asked me to deliver this. It's the only one. There's nothing else after. He also asked me to read it to you. Then you can have it forever, ok?"

I nodded, and from the nightstand's only drawer, Mom withdrew a security envelope. Inside was a single page of twice-folded paper. On the paper was Dad's handwriting.

Mom read, and the room glowed:

"Keep your heart aware. Remember that love and judgement are opposites. They cannot swim together, and they cannot know each other. They do not eat the same food, they do not drink the same water, they do not breath the same air.

"Judgment lives in our instincts, son, but love lives in the soul. Souls who share substance are soulmates, and that's what we are. You, Mona, Mom, me, all of us. That's what we will always be, because our souls belong to the same tribe.

"In all matters, reciprocate, and strive to over-reciprocate where possible, especially for important friends (but girlfriends too!) Give more than you take, whatever the cost, and this action will fill your life

*with goodness. This is the only promise I'm prepared to make you, my
son."*
*"Oh, and take care of your Mom, otherwise I'll come down and haunt
you. Capiche?*
"Love from out there,
"Dad."

Then Mom cried and cried and cried. I'd seen her crying before, but never
like this. I embraced her as much as my little frame would allow. She returned my
embrace and kissed me on the forehead. That afternoon, I began to understand the
tragedy of love, but I was still far from understanding the depth of Mom's loss.

I am far away still.

"Your Dad put it plain as a paper," she said. "Do not be quick to judgment."

(Though I've never reread it, I keep the letter in the glove compartment of
my Civic.)

"I'm sorry I called Mona lazy," I said. "I shouldn't have. She just has really
bad taste in television."

Mom laughed.

"Is that judgment?" I asked.

"No, Nicolai. That's a fact."

We hugged again. It was warm, and I wanted to stay, until she stretched her
neck, and whispered into my ear something I *definitely* never forgot. "And Nicolai—" her mouth was right next to my ear "—if you ever swear like that in my
house again, I'll punch you in the nose. *Capiche?*"

9.

With reciprocity in mind, I decided to oblige Becca. She had skillfully guided me
to third base, and I planned to reciprocate in full. (It took her less than a minute.
How hard could it be?)

How can you be sure that's what she meant? "You owe me."

Who knows?

Back then, I knew nothing about anything sexual. The Internet barely existed, and the connections we did have were way too slow and way too scary for that kind of research. No sir. Back then, when one needed to study, one went to the library.

Mom dropped me off. I told her I had to work on a chemistry project, which, metaphorically, was true. I climbed the stairs and bravely entered the four-storied gothic building. Once inside, an obvious dilemma stopped me cold.

How to ask the question?

"Ummm, Hi, Mister Librarian. Yes, my name is Nicolai, I'm about to be sixteen and I'm looking for your best textbooks about sex. More specifically how to be good it. Even more specifically, oral."

So no, I didn't talk to any librarians.

Luckily, finding relevant titles on my own was easy. I began with one called *A History of Sexual Liberation: From Taboo to Titillating.* I read the word "cunnilingus," and my face soured: not at the thought, but at the disharmonious sound of the word (especially next to *fellatio*, which sounds like a string instrument: the violin, the cello, the fellatio—see!)

I hid my books behind the walls of a writing desk cramped against the end of a shoddy metal bookshelf in the library stacks on the third floor. I learned body parts and theory, but four hours of research in, it felt like I was getting nowhere. All I had were facts. I could find no authoritative protocol or process regarding pleasure of the P-word. I considered calling off the whole affair.

It was during hour five that I opened an Eastern philosophy text thinking it might contain a section on Kama Sutra. It didn't, but while flipping through, I stumbled across a page with a picture of a fit brunette sitting cross-legged in yoga pants in a park, a pond lined with lilies behind her, her fingers pinched, her eyes shut, her smile serene. The subchapter was titled: *"The Science of Meditation."* It explained how turning off the senses could turn on solutions: apparently, if I shut my eyes and breathed—*poof!*—I'd be good.

Though I'd hardly seen anyone all day, I peeked around in search of spies.

Privacy confirmed, I closed my eyes, set my hands in the shape of a cup on my lap, and took five deep breaths.

Holy Fuckin' Buddha! It was an absolute miracle.

I'd been knee deep in anatomy all day, and then, in less than a minute, the complexities of my task simplified into sexual ones and zeroes. I hollared, *"Allel-iau!"* accidentally, my brain felt flared and blue, and I foresaw all the glory of my impending success.

I called Mom to pick me up.

Once home, I called Becca.

We agreed on the same terms: same time; 6:45, same day; Monday, rendez-vous at same strip mall, head to same bowling alley. I was sure I'd lose my virginity in less than forty hours. It was planned. It was meticulous. It was researched.

And it all backfired gorgeously.

10.

Seven o'clock rolled around and I was still waiting for Becca under the canopy of walkways lining the strip mall. We were supposed to meet at 6:30, and I was about to call her from the payphone when a sedan screech to a stop in front of me, a Lexus, a newish one I figured, sleek and black and maybe three years old.

The window rolled down. "Nicky," an energetic voice said from inside the car.

I bent down, and looked in. It was Becca, sexy as ever.

"I'm not Nicky," I said.

"Nicolai, Nicky, whatever."

I squinted at her, at the leather seats, at the futuristic interior.

"My Dad's," she offered. "Get in."

I stepped in and buckled up. It was the nicest car I'd ever sat in.

"Ready?" she asked.

"Yeah. I'm ready," I answered, and we made haste.

A few minutes into our journey, Becca set her hand on my thigh. Unlike the first time when I froze, I placed my hand atop hers. I faced her to appreciate some details, her sharp chin, her glowing green eyes, her pink lipstick. I'd never been with anyone who wore pink lipstick before, and Becca blushed upon noticing my admiration.

We made small talk for ten minutes under the lamplight in the parking lot. We occupied the same space. Like a starting gun, the streetlamp above us timed off, which meant it was now dark again. We stretched over the center console, and our lips quickly found each other's.

"Back seat," Becca said when we paused a second time. (The first time, she stared into my eyes. It felt like she was scanning me for evidence.)

I slinked and squirmed between the two seats and nearly dislodged the shifter before landing clumsily in the back seat. Becca exited then entered through the back door like an adult. She chuckled, and as I helped her remove her skirt, I noticed how the bowling alley was crowded with pedestrians. Maybe it was league night, the alley abuzz with competition.

"Ready?" I asked

"Ready for what?" she answered

I grinned at her, and descended, and I must say my over-reciprocation was a tremendous success. Becca banged and slid her palms against the windows. She grabbed the clothes hanger for leverage before falling again as she moaned with pleasure. It was an exaggerated, strange noise—haunting in a way. She repeated in no particular order, "Oh God," "Don't stop," "Right there," "Amen," and various simple profanities. Most notably, she shouted many times, "I love you, Nicolai! I love you!"

I was very much enjoying the experience, and very literally becoming the very best at loving women, when fatigue due to breathlessness set in. She disregarded the signs, though. She kept me playing. Through tugging and pivoting, she kept me in the game. Put another way: Becca wouldn't let me stop.

My mission to over-reciprocate was satisfied, yet every time I came up for air, she begged me to continue. This lasted for nearly half an hour, and I learned a key gender difference that night: when he's done, he's done; when she's done, she forgets.

This was not the gorgeous backfire. I don't might putting in overtime. No, hindsight makes our *real* oversight dumbly apparent: you simply cannot scream like a Banshee in the backseat of a luxury car idled at the edge of a dirty bowling alley parking lot for very long before someone takes notices, especially when you look like me, especially in The South.

Our 'date' was abruptly interrupted when blinding white light flooded the darkness. I looked up, shielding my eyes with one hand while wiping away a silky film from my mouth with the other. There was a *tap-tap-tap,* stone against glass. Standing on the other side of the window, a young, light-skinned, black lady cop with a buzz cut, rapping at our chamber with the wedding rings she wore. She looked a bit like Mom actually, only with darker skin and no hair. Hell, she looked a bit like me, I guess.

The cop signaled.

I rolled down the window.

We were fucked.

(Figuratively, of course. Losing my virginity would have to wait.)

11.

I felt confusion mostly as the officer instructed me to wait on the curb while Becca got dressed and stepped out. Becca hardly looked terrified.

"Name, young lady?" I overheard the officer asking.

"Rebecca Odalis."

"Becca Odalis? Like Mark Odalis's little girl Becca Odalis?"

"Rebecca, ma'am. My name's Rebecca. Has someone contacted my father?"

The lady officer turned to me. "I reckon so," she said.

Rebecca stepped into a police cruiser across the street. It had just arrived, trailed by a black Suburban.

They didn't handcuff Rebecca before she got in the cruiser. She just stepped into it.

They sure as shit handcuffed me, though. I was lifted and handled by an un-necessarily physical, fat officer who shoved me into the back of a third SUV which had just arrived, its red and blue lights serving no purpose other than providing a beacon for the growing crowd of diverse bowlers who seemingly had nothing better to do than stare at and speculate about the Lexus, the two teenagers, and the now eight cops loitering around their five tax-funded vehicles in the parking lot.

A very young-looking officer, but with an old-man sneer on his goateed face, read my rights and told me I was under arrest for public indecency.

"How old are you?" he half-shouted through the cracked window.

"Fifteen, sir," I said, smiling at him.

My joy offended.

"You're lucky, you know? One more year and we'd 'a had you done up for."

He wanted to scare me, the dork, but it didn't work. I was grinning like a kid at a circus. I couldn't help myself. The lady cop who'd first found us, the one who looked like Mom, stepped into the SUV's passenger seat and looked back at me through the cab divider.

"Why in heaven are you smilin'?" she asked. "You're in a whole heap of trouble, son. That's Mark Odalis's daughter."

I didn't know who Mark Odalis was. My blank look confirmed this for the officer.

"Mark Odalis is an assistant to the D.A., just a notch below people like the Mayor, the Police Commissioner, the Controller or Comptroller now or whatever."

"What's a Comptroller? That's not real."

"Nevermind that. In city work, these are the kings and queens, and Mark's a prince. Careful what you say. He's protective of his little girl. That's his only child. You hear me?"

My grin had morphed into a full-blown smile.

"You crazy?" she asked of me.

"No," I said. "It's just—"

"Just what?!" she interrupted, irritated.

"It's nothing. It's stupid. Thank you for the advice."

Then, she left me again.

As I saw it, trouble could only amplify the romance. I looked out the window and watched the cruiser ride away with Becca. I had not a care in the world.

Not long after that, reality set in, and I came down with it.

Such is the nature of highs.

12

I'd been alone just three minutes, and already the stupid smile I was wearing had vanished, replaced with a brink-of-tears-holy-shit-I'm-in-deep-trouble look of dread.

Dread escalated to terror when Becca's father, assistant district attorney and aspiring small town Mayor, Mister Mark Odalis, sat beside me. He wore a black suit with a stop-red tie. He had a big voice, but I was about as big as him at five-foot-six. He had three kernel-sized moles under his right ear—hair poked out from two—and he hid his freckled bald head under a starving bald combover. I still don't get how he produced something as exquisite as Rebecca. (My honest guess is he didn't.)

"You want to explain yourself?" he asked, impersonating a mobster, I guess.

I was a kid from the South. Mom taught me at the very least when *not* to say shit.

He held out for nearly a minute, but I wasn't budging. Mark Odalis then commanded me to stay away from his daughter. Throughout his rant, he reminded me several times of his holy stature in the city. His threats made me nervous, sure, but really he couldn't do squat. I was giving his daughter head: even if it is a crime—and I'm not so sure that it is—anything I got in trouble for, his precious little girl would too.

But, Mom…. Mom on the other hand could do shit.

And she did. Mom shit all over me.

We arrived home following a wordless drive of contemptuous glances. Once home, Mom paraded through my room and found the only dirty magazine I had, a *Penthouse* that had recently become my best friend. "Is this where you learned about cunnilingus?" she snarled.

"Ewww, Mom! Gross. Never say that again."

She'd been furious for more than an hour, but that got a giggle out of her. "I'll never say it again," she told me. "Scouts honor." Then she put a hand on my right shoulder, sort of like how they knight you in England. "Two months," she proclaimed.

"Two months what?" I asked.

"You're grounded. For two months. Sports and school. That's all you get. Two."

"That's cruel and unusual punishment."

"That's two too."

"You can't."

"Do I look like George Washington to you?"

"What?"

"Not George Washington. Not a democracy."

"Oh…" I said, "I see what you did there. Clever."

Mom smirked. I had her hooked. Charm was my only way out, my only chance to avoid this. Charm was my secret weapon. Charm and I were like two old maids sitting on rocking chairs gossiping about—

"Charm's not gonna work, Nicolai. Two months."

"Come on," I begged. "Becca said I wouldn't go to jail."

"I work for the city," Mom said. "This *will* get around."

"I can appreciate that. And I'm sorry. But how 'bout we say one month? Meet in the middle."

In her work for the city, Mom had to do a lot of buying. She always encouraged us to be vocal and to ask for what we wanted. I reminded her of these teachings during my plea bargain negotiation.

She said to me: "Two months. There's another lesson here Nick." Mom lyricized that lesson. "You can't, always, get, what you want."

Story of my life, I thought. *If only I could be George Clooney.*

13.

Becca was a comet: luminous and mysterious both. Cavemen didn't understand comets because they knew nothing of orbits, and that's what Becca was to me, a comet to a caveman. She dazzled me.

As predicted, we weren't charged for a crime, but that didn't stop our parents from handing down punishments. Theirs were different, handed down with gavels from different podiums.

I received a two-month grounding, and was released early on good behavior. Becca received two-and-a-half years of social purgatory for a crime unfathomable to her father. It is actually true that rules of boys and girls are tragically unjust, especially in high school.

Becca's clothes changed. Her hair changed. She became notably regular. The gossip factory output was awful, so she moderated entirely, and all the school forgot. By the next year, she'd become a brunette. By graduation, her pop stardom was mythology.

Between the guilt I felt about hurting Serena—a guilt that raced back in the absence of Becca—and the borderline statutory rape incident at the bowling alley, I seriously reconsidered my priorities. I thought: *maybe this whole "being the very best at loving women" lifestyle isn't such a good choice.* I was only fifteen and already I was miserable.

I promised myself I would change, and that I'd stay away from girls for good. Through the end of freshman year and into the summer, my anti-girl declaration survived. I talked to nary a one. I ranked twenty-third in my class and made the bench for varsity soccer. I grew another few inches, my thin arms and legs took on some muscle, and I felt my choice to forego *the quest* AND *the question* altogether had been well made.

Oh, how often this sentiment rises from the ashes of failed romance.

We fail, or we've been failed, and we say things like "I'm not trying to date right now," or, "I like being single," or, "I love the freedom of having no one tell me what to do. A significant other just wouldn't fit." But this is what happens, see: she walks through the door, he buys you a drink, your friend brings her to the table, the cute guy at work invites you to breakfast. Soon you'll add your entire history, regaling your friends about your destined loved. No one speaks of romantic purgatory once relieved of service. Seriously, it's like saying, "I'm not trying to be rich right now." "I like being broke." "I love the freedom of having no wealth to worry about. A huge bonus just wouldn't fit my present lifestyle."

In my case, in mid-September, two weeks into sophomore year, *she*, quite literally, walked through the door.

When Winter ended, she was Spring, but in one word, hers was the Autumn. Everything about her rested between amber and green, and gray sometimes too, but no contrasts. From the crown of her brown-black hair to the bottom of her black-soled sandals, she was always Summer to me.

AUTUMN HILLS

1.

nother year of high school began. I didn't see how I'd survive four. I shared one class with Serena, who still wouldn't look at me, which meant American History with Mr. Lapadula was a daily headache, and Becca was a junior now. She'd adopted a low profile, wearing less makeup and more conservative attire.

Our day consisted of four ninety-minute blocks, but because my high school had 2,000 students, only two kids shared my schedule; a Goth kid who presided over our school's chess club, and a quiet, religious girl named Cynthia.

Mrs. Havelik was just about to begin home room announcements when a new student entered, escorted by our new vice principal, Mr. Caldwell. Mr. Caldwell introduced her, and among other details we learned that her family had just moved from Colorado, that they grew potatoes, and that she was a talented skier.

"So please be kind to your newest Warrior Eagle. I'm pleased to introduce Autumn Hills."

"Summer," the new student corrected sharply. "It's Summer."

Mr. Caldwell checked his sheet. "I could've sworn...," and he scratched his head saying, "my mistake. Summer Hills ladies and gentlemen. Greener than the Fall kind." He tried to laugh off his mistake and awful poetry, then he looked up and saw that no one was listening. He was clearly trapped between relief and embarrassment. He rolled his eyes at the absurdity of his name mistake.

"May I sit?" Summer asked.

"Yes, of course," Mr. Caldwell said.

Then, Mr. Caldwell left. I can't remember ever seeing him again. He was fired for some undisclosed violation later that semester. I'm sure it had nothing to do with the seasons.

I thought nothing of the new student: she seemed plain. There was a bit of blonde in her wavy brown hair, and a dimple on her left cheek. I saw no other nuance.

But, Summer was in my biology class next period.

Then, I saw her across the room in economics. I still didn't think a thing of it—a coincidence no more or less special than Christ Cynthia or the Goth Guru of Chess.

But then, she was there after lunch, in Latin I.

And trigonometry too, my final class: she was sitting two seats behind me. I felt eerily aware of her eyes.

Summer's schedule matched mine exactly.

2.

Later that day, two of my friends peer-pressured me into attending the lady's basketball game. They both had girlfriends on the team, and ultimately I joined them in the gymnasium just before tipoff.

The three of us sat on creaky plastic bleachers ten rows up. There were maybe seventy people total in attendance, which made for decent energy, but as the game approached the end of the first quarter, boredom set in. I had plenty of homework to do, so I began plotting my exit. Midway through the second, as I stood to make my escape, Summer stood from the bench, turned, and our eyes connected.

It's her first day at school. How can she already be in the game? I thought.

I sat back down.

Summer checked in and readied herself on defense. She blocked a pass, darted towards her basket, and scored an uncontested layup with her first touch. It didn't let up either. Into the second half and right through the game's end, I watched Summer, hardly speaking to my friends. When she was on the bench, I stared achingly at the back of her head.

Summer scored fourteen points. They'd won against a superior opponent, and it was her effort that carried the upset. She was a fine leader and natural athlete, but she had something else too, something everyone could smell. Something everyone wanted.

Grace.

Summer moved evenly like a figure skater; powerful and smooth, physical but delicate. Her smile was regal, her manner precise. I remember wanting it too; her grace. I remember wanting it very badly for myself.

My two friends and I waited in the parking lot for their girlfriends. It was 9:00, unseasonably cold, and very dark because the parking lot lights were off for some reason. I was loitering now: a curious scavenger waiting for one last scent, one last clue about the girl who shared my schedule.

The girls' team emerged from metal doors behind the gymnasium. They were walking up a paved hill in our direction when I spotted Summer among them. Chance, however, deprived me of an introduction. Summer rounded the building the other way and disappeared into a station wagon, kissing her mother on the cheek before they rode off into the night. All I could do was watch as the Colorado license plate vanished around a turn. My buddies' girlfriends arrived to meet us. Their hugs and little affections stabbed me with jealousy.

I got home at nine thirty. Everything was going fine. I ate dinner, knocked out some homework, watched some baseball, then I settled into bed and closed my eyes. And I started smiling. I lay there in bed, just smiling like a circus clown. I couldn't sleep. I caught myself hugging one of my pillows. I got up and did fifty push-ups to try and woo my body into rest. It didn't work. I was up past two in the morning: I couldn't get Summer off my mind.

It was terrible: I knew what was happening and it was terrible, like the captain of the *Titanic* must've felt. I'd liked Serena plenty, and Becca—well, Becca was a comet. This was different. I'd fallen into a romantic abyss, a curse reserved for the lonely hunter that lives inside the heart. It is a worst-case scenario for high school boys, and even worse for the monsters living inside them.

Goddamn it… I had a crush.

On Crushes

Every morning, I readied to approach Summer. I would practice varying salutations while trying to charm my reflection in the mirror. Every morning, my reflection replied the same.

It's not you.

I'm telling you; a crush on a girl is an utterly terrible thing.

So you thought you might go right through the wall, dear Nicolai?
It's not a gate, and you don't have keys. Walls are for crushing, so even if you did have keys, which you don't, it wouldn't be you. There are no keys for walls, only catapults and battering rams. There is ear-cracking noise and pain in the soul and the streak

of fire and metal against flesh.

It's not that simple. The angel and I shared a schedule. Loving this girl almost killed me.

Almost?
We're back in the thunderstorm, back to the road, and I can see it again, as if from across the highway, as though from atop the pines, as you crash into the concrete barrier. There was a mighty explosion, but not a passer-by or deer or living creature to see, not one beyond me.

Many cars on their many journeys pass you by, going north or south, but none go both so none stop as the rain slows to a drizzle. It is almost enough to douse the fire.
Almost.

Crushes are the worst.
Until you fall.

In what I've gleaned from social media and pop music, a crush on a boy is quite different. Hope and imagination intersect into a love story shared freely at slumber parties or via text messages.

"OMG, he's so cute!"

"I think he likes you, like, seriously."

"I think he likes Caroline."

"OMG, you're way prettier than Caroline. Like, by a lot."

"Oh, you think? Please tell me more!"

When a boy has a crush on a girl, however, it is a private, lonely business, espionage and counter-espionage warring in the soul. There's no opening up about it because there's no one to open up about it to. There's no health kit. Maybe there's something in sex ed, but there aren't grades or tests or anyone to open up to. Teachers don't teach us about our new sex obsession. Counselors don't counsel us about all the hair growing in strange, new places, and still, there is no one to talk to, forgiving the most modern, most forward-thinking men. Standard fathers are predictably underequipped, most having foraged through puberty alone, many convinced that emotionalism was, is, and will always be an exclusively female privilege.

So, who do boys turn to for advice about women? The answer is all too often the same: no one, or television, and television won't let you open up to it either.

I am on the road once more. Full speed this time, I strike something in the road, and it occurs to me my heart-monster was right.

This really is it.

It's over.

I just witnessed the most tremendous flash of lightning too.

What else is there to remember?

Who knows.

Summer Nights

3.

Summer turned my world to darkness. All I could do was wait, and watch. I couldn't even muster friendship. I was reminded daily of my shortcomings.

She sat two rows ahead of me in Mrs. Gottlieb's biology class. From this vantage, I watched her like the hopeless admirer I was. I began to seriously question my philosophy about approaches, about waiting, about my own aptitude. Summer and I shared a whole day of classes, and the fact that she hadn't talked to me began its work. As weeks became months, as they exhausted my semester's worth of chances, at my lowest point, sometime around Thanksgiving, the fact that Summer hadn't talked to me took on a life of its own, warping my nerves into a poisonous idea that played on a loop in my head, singing in Elvis Presley's voice: *you ain't good enough for that girl. You ain't now. And you ain't never gonna be. Son... oh son, Just let 'er go.* (It's not a real Elvis song or anything, it was just in his voice.)

I remained spellbound into December, and I hadn't even said hello, but a week before winter vacation, a fortunate twist provided a first hope. I overheard Summer telling Mrs. Portwood about a manger scene at her church. (Call it spying if you'd like.)

"What church do you go to?" Mrs. Portwood asked.

"Star of the Sea," Summer answered (short for "Basilica of Saint Mary Star of the Sea Holy Catholic Church.")

What luck! What tremendous luck!

My eyes bugged. My soul sang. Fate, the cruel devil, had offered me an olive branch. It just so happened that I knew someone who'd started going to Basilica of Saint Mary Star of the Sea Holy Catholic Church, just last summer in fact: my sister, Mona.

Turns out she had a purpose after all!

4.

Mona was old enough to remember Dad. She was eight when it ended. She saw it all, and understood the ramifications: Dad was dying. Through my much younger eyes, Mona carried grief like a feather, like it was nothing at all, but when she left home for college to attend Western, Dad's alma mater, all that changed. Her soul collapsed under the feather's weight. It was the first time she'd been so far and so long away from Mom.

Mona took leave after one semester.

She was diagnosed with and suffered from a sudden and tremendous depression. Mom did much to assuage the crying that sometimes overtook her, bouts that could last hours. We weren't a religious family, which meant recovery after Dad's death had been a secular affair. Mona, however, was always the spiritual one. She was born that way. Most of us boys have to become it.

Against her former judgments, Mom compelled Mona to join a Catholic support group, and there, Mona met a 23-year-old soccer coach named Sean, to whom she's presently engaged. Sean was a transfer student from England and happened to be running a Catholic food-packing charity in my town. He was charming and kind and handsome too: I couldn't understand what he saw in my sister!

Mona began attending church with Sean every Sunday, and that church was, of course: *Basilica of St. Mary Star of the Sea Holy Catholic Church.*

Alleluia!

Sean came over for dinner to meet Mom in mid-December. I ambushed him at the table, asking if I could join them for Christmas Mass. Sean said, "Sure, mate? Why not." I'd moved too quickly for Mona to intercept.

On Christmas Eve, a Thursday, we met Mona's boyfriend and two other Brits for lunch at a diner. After eating, we headed to Star of the Sea. As we approached the church in Mona's new Civic, the one she'd soon pass down to me, me scrunched between her boyfriend's two friends in the back seat, I read an announcement on the main lawn's scheduling placard: The Basilica of St. Mary Star of the Sea Holy Catholic Church would host four—I repeat, four!—services that day. We'd arrived for its midday service, the third, and it was only Christmas Eve! There'd be even more tomorrow.

Oh No!

Hundreds of people entered and exited and socialized and worked, dusting poinsettias and handing out brochures and selling donuts and hot coffee beneath pop-up tents unnecessary for so cloudy a day. Mass was far more pleasant than I expected; a children's choir was singing, everyone was smiling, doormen greeted visitors and members with warm hellos and cordial nods. I'd been to church services twice before, but never Catholic Mass. There must've been at least five-hundred people crowded into the sanctuary, many forced to stand along the back walls of the main floor and balcony.

As the priest evangelized, my thoughts returned to Summer, and I didn't hear a word of the Gospel because I was scanning the faces of the congregation trying to find her. Under the guise of a bathroom break, I left my sister and the Brits at one point so I could walk out of and back into the church by a side entrance. I couldn't see into the easternmost part of the sanctuary.

My happiness hinged on the Church, and on fate, and on my own focus, none of which I controlled. Still, I just had to find her—she had to be here!

The voices came back to me at my weakest. First, the singing one:

You aren't good enough Nicolai, and you never will be.

Then, a voice conjured up from the dead.

If you must dream, dream silently.

(Welcome, everyone, to the mind of a boy with a crush.)

When Mass began, stage ministers built a manger scene on the steps before the alter. The priest's introduction described, "A foundation of Fear in God," hence their setting up the show's "foundation" during the sermon.

Get it?

Maybe there's no sarcasm in heaven, because after just thirty minutes of Catholicism, God rewarded me with a miracle.

Summer came!

Dressed as the Virgin Mary, she slowly ascended the shallow stairs. She held in her arms an African-American infant who, I quickly deduced, was little Baby Jesus: a controversial Mass, indeed! Summer sat on a low stool flanked by a rail-thin, middle-aged man playing Joseph, the Priest, a Deacon recounting the birth, dogs dressed as donkeys, three wise men wearing ties, and an outrageously talented six-year-old kid *Pa-Rum-Pa-Pum-Pum*-ming to the audience's delight. (He was black too…obviously.)

Summer's face was awash in the joy of the assured believer. Grace hovered about her person like a halo, and I ached to be inside. Butterflies fluttered in my stomach, my throat kept drying up, and as it usually went in her presence, I felt breathless. I suffered another fifteen minutes there, alone in my agony as the service dragged on with stages and announcements and sacraments and whatever else it is that happens during Mass.

The song changed—*finally*—and the congregation began lining up to receive communion.

"Just cross like this," Mona said, instructing me to fold my arms across my chest.

I squinted my eyes to near-shut. I hoped this would convey my absolute confusion.

"It's important. It tells them that you're not Catholic," she said, "but you should come up, since you're here and everything. They'll bless you—yeah, Nicky, even you—but you can't take communion. It's important."

"You said that twice."

"There's a reason, Nicolai."

We moved slowly towards the stage, me trailing my sister, my sister trailing the Brits. I watched Summer as we neared. Her eyes bounced around the church, but they missed me with each pass. Before I knew it, it was Mona's turn for communion, and as she crossed her arms to alert the minister she wasn't Catholic, Summer finally looked over Mona and down at me.

Finally.

Summer's graceful grin grew into a surprised smile upon seeing me.

I smiled back, big teeth and all.

"Son," I heard from a barreling voice.

Right in front of me, there stood a tall man. He was dressed in black slacks, a white shirt, and a black tie, and he bore a startling resemblance to Mr. Jansen, the janitor who'd arrested Jessica and me. This man was not a janitor, however, he was a communion minister.

The man gestured at me with a little Communion cracker, so I took it, ate it, and did a little cross over my chest because that's what everyone else was doing. I looked up again at Summer and she waved to me, fluttering a few fingers near her side. I played cool, nodding slightly (a noteworthy accomplishment when you consider the jungle thumping of my heart in my chest.) It wasn't until days later that I recognized my potential predicament in having taken communion. Summer might think I was Catholic—especially considering I also accepted the wine and performed a second cross with the next minister.

The priest ended Mass, saying, "The foundation you set in Jesus Christ must be thoughtfully laid. Once arranged, you may only build your faith in certain ways, or risk having to start all over again. You must be sincere. You must be in earnest."

The old lady next to me yawned. He should've stuck with the classics. Certainly we would have all been better served with a reminder of the rules.

Exodus 20:13 The 6th Commandment: Thou shalt not kill.

(Not sure if he was reading out of the King James Bible…so just in case, from the New International Version…)

Exodus 20:13, The 6th commandment: You shall not murder.

You get the point, right?

Who knows?

6.

Holidays ended, and classes started up again the first Tuesday in January. I was switching out books before first block on the first day back when she said my name. It'd been so long since I heard her voice. It sounded like middle C, she was so familiar.

"Nicolai."

I turned around and found my crush, Summer Hills, standing a few feet away. She was hugging a text book and a Five Star binder, and carried over one shoulder her pink backpack adorned with yellow bells.

"Hi, Mary," I said.

"It's so embarrassing," she replied.

I couldn't believe it. We were having a *real* conversation. It was as though we'd talked a hundred times before: I couldn't believe how natural it felt.

"Not at all," I told her. "You were very Mary up there." (That line I'd practiced.)

"Sure, sure," she said, unable to subdue her smile. "Who was that you were with?"

"Who?"

"At Mass. Is that your family?"

I told Summer about Mona and the exchange students. She followed up by sharing some background on the manger scene and her fear that she'd drop the baby.

"Well," Summer said. "It was good to see you. I mean, funny, you know. Like fun. It was a good surprise."

"Me too, yeah. So random." I said, even though it wasn't random at all. "What do you have for first period?" (Our schedules had changed: I'd be lucky to have even one class with her.)

Summer withdrew an index card from her back pocket. "Trig two. Room 204," she said.

"No shit?" I exclaimed. "Me too!"

A stroke of good fortune, yes, but I could tell I'd erred. Her furrowed brow expressed dissatisfaction with the phrase, "No shit," and I remembered immediately how Mom said Dad swore rarely. I made a mental note to keep all bad words—even 'heck' and 'dang'—out of my vocabulary.

"I'll walk with you to class if that's cool," I said, and she accepted my offer with a nod, and we made small talk as we went, and I never loved the halls more, not even when Serena snuck us into the auditorium at homecoming.

I didn't sit beside Summer in class, but afterwards, I walked her to second block. She was worried I'd be late, and I was, and I was scolded for my tardiness. It wouldn't be the last time. I met her the next morning, and then every morning for the rest of sophomore year. We didn't go on any dates in January, but we talked throughout the day and most evenings too. Ultimately, Mr. Lee separated our seats in trigonometry, the only class we shared. He said our romance was distracting and apparent. The following week, he had a stern talk with us about passing notes.

Then, Summer kissed me on the cheek one morning in early February and asked, "Are we together?"

"Of course, we're together," I answered.

And really, that's all there was to it. Finally, I stood a chance!

The question of my faith never really came up. Summer was a fervent believer, but not filled with religiosity. She lived for harmony. She lived intentionally to balance. I didn't recognize these qualities as they happened, but I certainly felt them. I felt lucky to be her boyfriend, and I later learned that Christmas and Easter Catholics were common, and that she assumed I fell into that bucket.

In late February, it finally happened. The moment was doubtless as the storyteller foretold.

I can't recall the exact day, but I remember that the day was sunny, and that the time was between second period and third, and that we were walking the central corridor of the school. Summer was wearing a new blouse, gray under white polka dots, and new, pinker blush. An announcement reminded the student body about a track-and-field match later that day—our star sprinter, Xavior Zax, was competing for a city championship in the 10K, and many people thought he had a legitimate chance. Summer took my hand in hers, and we proudly walked as one, our first ever signal to the world that we were each other's. I swear I could pinpoint the very spot of my footfalls. We were passing by the auditorium when it actually happened, the very heart of the school where a decades-long history of awards and pictures and past principals lined the atrium, where ten-foot tall, twenty-foot wide trophy cases housed sixty years of sports victories. We stopped; or rather I stopped with a jerk.

"What?" she asked.

I couldn't tell her. Somehow I knew to not even try. She wouldn't understand yet.

The doors to my right led to the stage where Serena had kissed me, and the doors to my left led outside to the steps where Becca Odalis asked for my phone number. I'd felt it, right there and without a doubt, and for the first time, I could remember the moment exactly. I remember the feeling perfectly, because it's the exact, perfect moment that I fell in love forever with Summer Hills.

Love had finally found me, and it was the finest feeling of my life, the only thing worth dying for that ever stumbled my way.

Then, gravity.

Then, I forgot.

7.

Summer and I volunteered together on a soup line for Saint Patrick's Day. I was doing it for my college resume. Summer was doing it because she volunteered often. It was her grace.

During a break, Summer told me she'd never seen a church so big, and that she was awed by its arena-sized sanctuary, comparing it to the humbler worship-centers in Colorado.

"Where are you from in Colorado?" I asked.

"I tell people Denver, but I'm not actually from Colorado," she answered.

I missed what she said at first. We were outside between buildings, and it was cold, and I stopped with a jerk, recognizing the riddle.

"Wait," I said. "You've told me you're from Colorado? More than once, haven't you?"

Summer looked around to see if anyone was spying. "Can you keep a secret?" she asked.

"Yeah, sure," I said.

"You can't tell anyone. Not even your mother. I'm being serious."

"I can keep a secret. I'm an epic secret-keeper."

"It's about Mom," she said. She paused to clear her throat. "Mom made up the Colorado stuff. Most schools don't verify out of state records, and definitely not overseas stuff. This town's perfect because if things turn weird, we can just jump the river to Alabama."

"Trust me, you don't want to do that," I said, taking the opportunity to crap on a rival. "Alabama? Wait? What are you talking about?"

Summer and I had been official for more than a month, but we'd never discussed our families. We talked about sports or school or nothing at all. For me, talking about family meant talking about Dad, and talking about Dad was something my mind avoided without effort.

"I've been meaning to tell you this," she said, "and I'm sorry I kept it a secret."

A long, nerve-rattling sigh. "We're here illegally—me and Mom, that is."

"Come again?"

"I'm Irish. We're Irish. I grew up there my whole life."

"I'm sorry, what?!"

And in a perfect Irish accent, she says, "I was barn 'n raised in Dooblin. Pa stays back in Ireland, and we've been jumpin' 'round schools a few years now. We've had no choice but to make our way here any way we can. Circumstances, Mum says."

"Whoa whoa whoa whoa whoa, wait wait wait," I said like a spaz. "No way. No way. Stop. How does that work?"

She reverted to American. "I go to school and Mom stays home for now. She's looking for work but it's hard without good papers."

"So it's like. You and your mom. And you're here illegally. From Ireland. Is that what you're saying?"

"Ay, we left when I was eleven—Sorry."

"Sorry for what?" I asked.

"My accent, the classes."

"Which accent?"

"Just," she said, "Just forget I said anything."

I stepped nearer. Took her hands in mine. "Go back," I said.

"To Ireland?" she asked, shocked.

"No. In the story. I mean to the story. I mean, just tell me whatever you need to tell me."

Summer leaned in, and whispered in Irish for effect. "This here's the secret part. We left 'cause the cops told Mum Dad was I.R.A."

"Like with taxes and stuff?" I whispered

"How is that like taxes?" she asked loudly.

I opened my eyes as wide as they would go. I hoped this would convey my absolute confusion.

"Oh…" Summer said forgivingly, "That's I.R.S., Nicolai. Not I.R.S. I.R.A. The 'S' is an 'A.'"

My silent idiot expression held steady.

"I.R.A., as in Irish Republican Army."

I didn't know what an I.R.A. was at the time, and also, this seemed suddenly far-fetched. "This is a joke, right?" I asked. "You're not a domestic refuge. I could never believe that."

"Domestic refugee?—" then, in stunning, sexy Irish, "Look at you and your big American words."

She shook her head and turned to walk back towards the serving hall. I ran after her.

"Sorry," I said. "Keep going. I'm sorry. An I.R.A., you were saying?"

"The I.R.A. They're like rebels. Stands for Irish Republican Army. They're kind of like rebels or terrorists, depending on how you look at it, I guess."

"Terrorists?" I asked, almost laughing, "In fucking Ireland?!" We'd had a nice long conversation about swearing just yesterday. The F-word was strictly out-of-bounds. "Sorry," I said again. "I'll get better. It's just a lot to take in."

"I guess so."

"So wait, you're like, what—a nomad? Like my girlfriend is a real life drifter?" Then I asked, "What's it like?"

She answered right away. "Lonely."

I kissed her on the forehead, and I embraced her.

She began to shake; not with tears, but with laughter. A chuckle broke through in a splutter, she pulled back, shook her head, and grinned at me. "I like you Nico. More than ever," she said.

"What do you mean?"

"And to think, all I needed was a silly Irish accent."

She rubbed my cheek with her thumb. She really did try to be a sport about her victory, tried to temper her laughter at having tricked me with such a preposterous story, but it spilled out in snorts then grew to a barrel.

"You shoulda seen it," she finally said, bent over to catch her breath, like it was really that good.

"Seen what?"

"Your face! Oh, did I have you. That makes me the new champion right?"

"For what it's worth, I thought it was a good accent."

"How many Irish do you know?" she asked mid-laugh.

"Apparently zero. So let me get it straight. What you're saying is that you are not, in fact, an illegal Irish immigrant on the lamb with your mom."

"Well, I am on the lamb with mom. We lived in a suburb of Denver called Lakewood to answer your original question, and Dad stayed back. They got a divorce."

"Sorry," I said.

"When I was little," Summer corrected. "I mean, like, we stayed there in Colorado. I think my mom thought he might change and want to be involved with me again."

"He didn't?" I asked.

"Worse," Summer said. "He got remarried for a second time. I've maybe seen my father ten times in the last two years. And the part about my mom not having a job is true. The one she was supposed to have was at a bank, but the bank shut down a month after we got here."

Everything Summer said during the epic *gotcha!* was a lie; everything but that one word: *lonely*. She said she felt lonely, and that part was true. I knew more than her what the chasm of Dadlessness felt like, how the echoes don't dampen. Knowing she was without a father made me love her even more.

"How about you?" she asked. "What're your parents like?"

"I live with my mom. My sister just started college, so it's only me and mom at the house."

"Are your mom and dad married?"

"Yeah. I mean they were."

I looked down.

"Oh," Summer sighed. "How old were you when they divorced?"

"They didn't," I answered.

Putting it into words was an automatic emotional hazard. I could feel the fight in my brain as it coursed across my temples. That's why I never did. I never talked about Dad; I never had to. Nobody ever asked because everyone just sort of knew that I was the kid without a father. A wash of sadness powered through me, but in seconds it vanished; gone like a ghost.

"My dad's dead," I continued. "He died when I was a four."

"When you were a four?"

"No, duh. Me a 4? No, when I was four years old."

"Caught ya!" Summer tilted her head at me. "Nicolai. I'll give it to you—that was good. Pretty convincing. You should be on stage."

"What?" I asked.

"That's an awful joke," she scolded lightly, stepping back and putting a hand on her hip. "I know you're sore that I got you being all Irish, but you should never act like your parents are dead. And anyway, I'm not as gullible as you."

She trotted off ahead of me, proud and haughty.

"Alrighty, then," I said under my breath. (*Ace Ventura* was a recent thing.)

Summer didn't know that vengeance was already mine; I let my victory brew for several glorious days. She finally learned the truth through a friend, and she apologized to me every day for weeks. I made a regular habit of bringing up her awful insensitivity. We laughed every time.

This was the central feature of our relationship: laughter. It was the cornerstone of our mutual affection. Now I just needed Summer to fall in love with me.

Then, everything will be perfect.

8.

Summer's birthday fell on April the thirteenth, a Friday. I took her to a horror movie to celebrate.

During a lull between cinematic murders, it finally happened. Summer kissed me. I mean, really kissed me. I reached my hand around her hip, but she slid it gently away—a reminder about her position on sex. She told we wouldn't "do it" anytime soon, and I always respected that. I never tried to change her mind.

Because it was Summer's birthday, her mom said she could stay out until midnight. I drove us to a clearing behind Flat Rock Park in the Blue Honda Civic I'd just inherited from Mona. I planned well; sparkling grape juice, soft blankets, a little boom box playing classical music. We lay down alone, surrounded by darkness, our fellow stars and a fingernail Moon playing audience company.

Maybe if you don't move, you can stay.

That's maybe the first time I heard it. Her head was resting in the nook of my shoulder. She angled at me and announced in a practiced voice, "Nicolai Recker. I love you."

I lay silent; eyes on the stars.

She shifted her body, propped on an elbow, looked down at me a breath away, and repeated with playful irritation, "I said I love you, Nicolai."

Almost interrupting, "I love you too," I said. "I really do, Summer. I love the way I feel when I'm with you. I've been in love with you for months."

"Months? Why didn't you tell me?"

I shrugged. That was enough for her.

"My real name's Autumn, you know?"

I shrugged, and ditto.

She returned her head to my shoulder, and for the next hour we shared the chirps and crackling of the forest and the twinkling of the stars. We didn't say a word. We hardly moved, sharing The Young Lovers' Hope.

Maybe if we don't move we can stay.

There we were, in love, hardly moving.

If we don't move, we can feel this way forever. Maybe we can keep it just for us. We can keep it for us, just us, until the sun comes up again.

We stood, and we kissed, and we held hands in the car on the way to her house, and everything was finally perfect. When I dropped her off an hour later, after she'd closed the car door, after she'd come back for a final kiss, after she vanished into her house, I remember thinking to myself, *what happens now?*

On Margin

hen, there will be a mighty explosion, but not a passer-by or deer or living creature to see, not one beyond me.

Last time it *was* a mighty explosion.

Last time? There are no last times, Nico. It's time, as real as margin itself. Not a passer-by or living creature, but there will be a mighty explosion.

For six months, Summer will smell fresh as flowers.

Through the end of sophomore year, into and out of that evening when we shared our first words of love, and well into summer break, our love grew richer with discovery and experience. We went running together twice a week, always on different trails or tracks around town. We read two books together in May and June; *Harry Potter* for us, *East of Eden* for summer reading. We even shared a Moleskin notebook that we exchanged every few days, and in it we'd doodle and sketch and write love notes and poetry. She bought the expensive notebook specifically for the cause, and we filled half its hundred pages with the most romantic words and ideas we could formulate, and I never resented any of it; not a drop. Our journey from January to June was sweet as sugar.

Then, margin.

I don't mean to single out my disagreements with Mr. Franklin—the old Quaker is certainly my favorite Founding Father—but what Ben should've said here was, "death, taxes, and the law of diminishing returns." Not as poetic, but if mankind does achieve an immortal, tax-free utopia, the law of diminishing returns and its evil twin, margin, would continue like time itself; unrelenting, unmerciful, unapologetic.

One of the rare times Mona came down from on high to help me was when she was a senior in high school. I was still a freshman. It was shortly after Serena broke up with me.

"Alright, Nicky," she said.

"Stop it."

"If I'm helping you, I get to call you what I want."

It was for economics, and Mona was good with social studies. We were on the second chapter, the one that comes after opportunity cost.

"Fine."

"Fine," she replied. "So, listen. Imagine yourself at the beach on a very hot day. You've got no water, and you walk by a little lemonade stand selling twelve-ounce cups for three bucks each."

"What kind of lemonade?"

"Shut up, Nicky."

"I guess I deserve that," I said.

"You buy the first without hesitation," Mona continued, "and after drinking it, because you have no self-control, you quickly buy another. But here's where it gets tricky. You want a third cup. You consider the time of day, the weather, the money in your pocket, even the impact of sugar on your health."

"Well, I wouldn't."

"That's because you have no self-control, Nicky, but in the example—" she poked the page, keeping her eyes on me "—you're supposed to *not* take the third cup. The law of diminishing returns makes this clear. If you want to stay in the margin, that is."

"Well...what if I didn't?"

"You don't have a choice. There's either margin or there isn't."

"But...what if I really want a third cup."

"Halfway through, you'd realize you're completely over lemonade."

"At that point, there's nothing to do; there's no transaction, no sharing. It's not worth the money in your pocket, and there's nothing you can do to advance the utility of the seller and buyer.

"That means there's nothing."

"Except for stealing," I corrected her.

"Yeah, Nicky," she said, impressed with my banter. She smiled and rubbed my head. It's the fondest memory I have of my sister before she left for Western, that time she actually shared a battle wisdom. "There's always stealing," she agreed, "but they've got laws for that too."

And fabulous as love is, she is not above the law.

What now? I had asked myself. *What's happens next?*

By mid-summer, there were no new paths to find. I often wanted to run alone so I could push my pace. I had no interest in sharing a third book to read (though I agreed to two more all the same) and when I held my pencil over our notebook, I'd flip back through the pages, recycling ideas, wondering where my inspiration had gone. For my last entry, I wrote, "GOT NOTHING," across two pages. To avoid discord, I illustrated it with rainbow colors and stamped a dozen happy faces in the paper's margin. (See what I did there?)

I had no equipment to identify the tidal wave nearing our shores. As it neared, the intensity of my affections slipped from uncontrollable to passionate to calm, until, on one very hot morning in August, without warning, the wave blocked the sun and came crashing down atop me, salty like the sea, salty like sweat.

The Morning of the Fall

"I keep on falling,"
"in and out,"
"of love,"
"with you."
—FROM *FALLIN',* BY ALICIA KEYS

9.

I woke up to a voicemail from Summer.

"Hey, Nico. It's early, I know, but I thought you might be up and just wanted to start my day off by telling you I love you. I was thinking last night—it kind of made me worried...and sad and—well not sad really, just, like...it's weird, right, knowing if me and Mom didn't move here I probably never would've known you and...anyway, well, I love you, and I just really wanted you to know that."

It was August seventh at seven in the morning; I remember that. School had ended months ago, so Summer and I were seeing less of each other, but we still talked on the phone every night. We'd talked just ten hours before this.

"Call me about the schedule stuff too," the voicemail continued, "right when you wake up, or right when you get this. That'd be after, before, well anyway, we've only got like a day and a half 'til registration and I know you don't believe me but I hear from everybody that the lottery works better if you enter it at the same time. OK... Okay, Love you. Bye."

As juniors, we could select our classes for the upcoming year; although the process was somewhat randomized, most kids got the classes they wanted. For weeks, Summer had been pitching me on her favorites. She assumed I wanted to align our whole day.

I sat up in bed, slid into running shorts and my new trainers, tossed on a tank-top, and was out the door in less than five minutes. I didn't grab water or a snack for fuel; I fled with the urgency of a burglar. I thought of the voicemail as I ran; its overreaching, its eerie pointlessness. Around mile two, I became suddenly aware of my behavior changes as a result of summer leave. I considered the excuses I used to win space and time, nights of missed calls that I blamed on whatever white lie came to me. It wasn't that I didn't like Summer; it's that I wanted it in less regular chunks. What could be wrong with that? Around mile seven, I became angry with Summer for how she always lingered about the end of our conversations, how she always prodded me about my emotions. I became angrier as my mileage climbed. I was about to lay blame at her feet for my withering promise, but before I crossed *that* horizon, I somehow circled back home.

It was humid from the week's rain. My training runs usually lasted twenty to forty minutes and four to seven miles, but that morning, for the first and only time in my life, I'd run more than ten. Eleven and a half, I figured. I bent over panting, hands on knees. My breath was impossible to catch. I felt flushed as I climbed the driveway to our split-level, and twice I almost slipped on the walking stones. When I entered the house, a blast of air conditioning rattled me. My skin froze. Goose-bumps charged up and down my arms.

Mom happened into the entryway, keys in hand. She was about to leave on some errand. "Nicolai," she said, eyes-wide.

I looked at my reflection in the mirror, the one that hung over our front door's console table, the one decorated with pictures of Mom and Dad's small lake side wedding in Ewing. My skin looked pale brown, and my brown eyes were bottomed with dark, sucked-in bags. It looked like they were suffocating, and I looked like a malnourished Moroccan kid fighting the plague. Before Mom could reach my side to prevent it, my vision went blank, my knees buckled, and I collapsed.

Then, darkness.

10.

I came to a few seconds later with a bruised elbow and a dizzying headache. Mom said that I should relax for the rest of the day as she pried into the cause of my exertion. I didn't lie to her, I said nothing; the reason for my needing to run was beyond me. Summer was asking for all my time; every minute of every weekday of the upcoming school year. I was too afraid to commit so great a fee to the cause of our love—I mean, what if my resentment grew? What if I fell out of love with her entirely? What then, if we were imprisoned *together*?

Lacking options and equipment, I did what most teenage boys do when confronted with first doubt: I hid. I avoided Summer like the plague I'd become.

I hardly knew my own feelings, certainly I didn't know my feelings well enough to craft words about them. Emotional honesty requires emotional intelligence, and just in case you haven't looked around lately, a high school boy has about as much emotional intelligence as a tractor.

So, I hid.

The afternoon of my first faint, I left a message with Summer's Mom while Summer was at youth service. I told her mom that I wouldn't be able to take her to the movies that night, but that I'd call about it the following day. When Summer called later seeking a full explanation, I was gone, playing laser tag with some friends.

I stayed out most nights, many spent with new classmates who'd moved into our neighborhood earlier that year, and every night I found a new reason to be away from the house, and after about a week, Summer's calls stopped. I worried that she might come to my home, but she never did. She knew that'd be against the rules.

Then, one day, as if from the nothingness itself, like the calendar itself had lied, school started. I was flung suddenly back into the dark center of my wilted, romantic promise.

The morning of the fall had begun.

11.

I found myself in the school's center, the hallway where I fell in love with Summer. My eyes bounced about like prey terrified of tigers. I felt like a surrendered spy in enemy territory.

What would happen when she saw me? What would I say? How would I react?

Making matters worse, I didn't know her schedule, didn't know where she'd be. I needed to survive four classes. It was a big school, so probability was on my side at least, and I'd avoided Summer's favorites when I registered.

I arrived to each class just before the bell. I peeked in and surveyed the rooms. (It's not like I had a plan of escape if Summer had been in attendance, but still...that's what spies do.) I'd gotten through three classes and approached the fourth; room 322, physics, with Mrs. Hudson. I peeked in.

Summer was nowhere in sight.

I took my seat in a corner near the teacher's desk. I'd made it through the entire day without an encounter. Luck was on my side!

And of course, as I exhaled, Summer entered.

Our eyes connected. My nerves freed themselves instantly, released into my gut like a bull seeing red. To my surprise, however, Summer turned away from me and chose the open lab desk on the other side of the room. I didn't know what this meant, but we got through the eighty minutes fine. Every time I looked over, Summer was totally occupied with Mrs. Hudson's orientation.

It was a ruse; an act. After class, she followed me to my locker.

"Nicolai."

I turned around and found my former crush, Summer Hills, standing a few feet away. Her arms were crossed, and though she looked angry, her beauty stunned me.

Somehow, I'd forgotten.

"Hi. Summer," I said.

"Don't you fucking 'Hi Summer' me." My eyes bugged. I couldn't believe she'd sworn! "First question. Are we still together?"

I squinted at her. "Apologize first."

"What?"

"Apologize first. That's a rule—*your* rule."

"Apologize for what?!" she shouted. A few students near us pretended their ears hadn't perked up to our little drama; we had a *real* audience now.

"You swore at me," I whispered as I neared her.

She stepped back. "You swear all the time, don't flip—"

"Apologize and I'll answer your question."

She crossed her arms and stomped a foot on the ground. To me, the whole world shook.

"Yes," I said, caving. "Obviously we're still together."

"Do you still love me?" she followed up.

"Of course."

"Then talk to me," she begged. "I figured you needed some space, and I get that you didn't want to take all our classes together, but now I'm in physics and you know how I *hate* physics."

"Then why'd you sign up for it?"

Through gritted teeth, she said, "It was the only class I knew you would take."

"Summer. I didn't need you—"

"I can't talk. Not now, and not like this," she interrupted. "I have to go. Mom's waiting for me. I don't know what's happening or why you thought it was cool to shut me out but it's making me—" Right then, God as my witness, Serena walked by; a living, breathing reminder of how dangerous the truth is "—Well?" Summer asked suddenly. In seeing the apparition, I'd missed Summer's words.

"I'm not shutting you out. Honestly. It's just…" I trailed off, seeking words but finding none.

"What, Nicolai? What's going on? Just tell me the truth."

How? I wondered.

How can I tell you a truth I myself don't understand?

"OK," I said. "I'll call you at seven tonight. I promise."

Summer calmed. The word "promise" still carried weight in our relationship. She looked on me with a sad smile; an analog for her bittersweet victory. She'd won my agreement for a call, but she still didn't know what was wrong. Maybe she felt I was slipping away but lacked the equipment to find the words. Maybe if she'd had more vocabulary, she could've helped me.

She palmed my cheek, kissed me on the other, then clutched her hands behind my neck and embraced me. Her touch was pure, loving warmth. I wrapped my arms around her. I wanted to stay. I could've stayed forever. But she let me go.

She pecked me on the lips, smiled sad again, said she looked forward to hearing from me, then she disappeared down the hall and around a corner.

I was left thinking again, *what happens now?*

The answer is in the question, Nicky. It's all right there, right in the third margin.

12.

I called as I said I would: 7:00 PM on the dot. Summer's voice shook during our introductory hellos. As for me, I panicked at the start, and without any cause or planning, took the route of the bald-faced lie.

"So, look," I said, "I've been sick for the last three weeks." (Terrible, I know.)

"What do you mean, sick?" she asked.

"I'm not sure exactly. I collapsed after a run. That's when it started."

"What?" she said unconvinced. "You collapsed?"

"Yeah. I just fell over."

"You fainted?"

"I guess so, yeah. Mom freaked out and everything, and now I'm exhausted all the time and I have stomach pain and bad headaches. Like migraines. You know what migraines are?"

"Everyone knows what migraines are, Nico. What did the doctors say?"

"Huh?"

"You didn't go to a doctor?"

"No," I answered. "I just take Motrin or Tylenol. Pepto every now and then. I started drinking coffee too—that helps for some reason. Do you ever drink coffee?"

"You know that I don't drink coffee, and I don't want to change the subject so stop trying."

"I'm not trying anything," I said. "I'm just talking."

"You're saying you didn't call me because you didn't feel good."

"I didn't want you to worry."

"Really? So sick you couldn't pick up the phone? Was your hand sick too?"

Feeling suddenly dumb, I stopped myself from saying another word. I wanted to surrender physically, so I sat on the floor, my back against the closet door.

"Just tell me the truth, Nicolai. What's going on?"

I was new to this brand of lying—I'd never done it before—so I pivoted, thinking again that the truth could set me free. "It's not just that I wasn't well," I confessed, "it's that I didn't know how to put it exactly. I just didn't have the energy. But I am sorry, that's true. I really am. I wasn't thinking. Seeing you today made me see that. I don't know what else to say."

"Nicolai," she said, choking up. "That's horseshit. Stop lying to me. You don't have to be afraid. Just trust me."

"This has nothing to do with trust."

"It has everything to do with trust. Just tell me."

"Tell you what?"

"The truth, Nico. Just tell me the truth."

I hated myself in hearing her heartache, for the uncertainty I'd fostered in her heart. All I wanted was to soothe her, to return her to the same page, even if that page held consequence for me. So my third strategy, one I picked up in childhood, was linguistic sleight-of-hand: I'd admit a small sin to distract from the truth, which was that I couldn't handle the truth, that Our Young Lovers' Hope had faded into mist, and ascended back to the clouds.

"OK," I said, standing up, and too excitedly I said, "It's about Jesus."

"Jesus?"

"Well, kind of. Not really Jesus so much as the church."

"What does this have to do with church?" Summer said, surprised. (The building panic from earlier: gone. Or vanquished, I should say.)

"The day we met at church."

"Well what about it?" I could hear she was shifting positions.

I continued, dropping an octave. "I'm worried you'll take it the wrong way, but remember at the Christmas service? When you played Mary? I know it's way too late and it's a terrible thing, but, I'm not really religious that much. I knew you were gonna be there and that's why I went."

"What are you saying?" Summer asked.

"My family's not Catholic. I went there because I wanted to meet you. I had a crush on you for forever."

"So what? Your family's like what? Like…Baptists?" (I wonder if that would've made it worse.)

"No. We don't practice. I mean I don't practice. Like…never ever."

"You're not even Christian?"

"Well I didn't say *that* necessarily."

It isn't that I expected her to jump up and down with joy. That's not what I'm saying.

"Summer… Summer, are you there?" But I got nothingness from it: thirty seconds of cold nothing. "Summer? Summer?" I kept saying her name. "Are you there?"

She didn't answer, so I switched.

"Autumn?"

"Oh, I'm here," she said, fire in her voice.

Then she kicked my ass for what I did to her, for messing about in the margins of the third story like I had some say in the rules. I got punished, basically, for making shit up, and this was a bad one, and yeah, she definitely kicked my ass. She won the battle overwhelmingly. (Or vanquished me, I should say.)

If you seek truth here, Nicolai, beware.

It came to pass twice.

This was the first.

What follows is my first ever experience with, "The Filter."

13.

It's called an *EDF*: stands for *Emotional Distress Filter*.

Okay. Here's what we know so far.

People can only take so much. We all need help, and sometimes we get it. If a woman's emotional intensity reaches unsustainable levels, an invisible contraption known as an EDF will often appear, as if from nothing, which makes sense, since its invisible. It wraps itself around her ears, and plays coach. Once attached, The Filter inputs a man's communication—his answers, his explanations, his expressions, his posture—and outputs the most cynical, fear-ridden interpretation available in popular culture. Though science has yet to validate this hypothesis with "evidence," I believe in The Filter like I believe the sky is blue on a clear, sunny day in the middle of Montana.

"Nicolai," she said. "I told my Mom you were a Christian."

"It got out of hand," I said. "I get that now. But you gotta understand—" I paused here, hoping to emphasize this loving counterpoint "—I went to Mass because I liked you."

-- Input: "I went to Mass because I liked you."

-- *EDF processing...processing...processing...*

-- Output: "Our love is based on a lie."

"You lied to me," she said, almost asking.

"What? No, I didn't lie to you," I said, shell-shocked. "I liked you. I overheard you talking to Mrs. Portwood—wait, how's that a lie?"

"You took communion," she said. "You lied to God."

"Whoa."

"That's right. You took communion because you wanted me to think you were Catholic?" It was an accusation intonated as a question, but it wasn't a question at all.

"No," I answered sharply. "No, not at all. That's not what happened. You're missing the—"

"I remember," she interrupted. "Like it was yesterday, yes. You're not allowed to take communion if you're not Catholic. I *remember* you," she bellowed.

"But I'm *not* Catholic," I said, "so how was I supposed to know that?"

"Oh, come on! Everybody knows that! Just tell me the—"

"Everyone doesn't know anything, not even that the sky is blue in Montana, but look!" and I shouted that to my own surprise. I literally covered my own mouth to calm myself, and then there were a few seconds of silence, and then I said, "I don't know. I don't remember exactly, OK? But neither do you."

I wanted to calm her—that's it!—and return her to the softness she expressed in the hallway at our school. *How though?* I felt like an amateur chess-player staring across the board at a Grandmaster; any move I chose was sure to be bested on my way to checkmate.

"I really do love you," I said, opting for the safest play. "I love you more than anything."

-- Input: "I really do love you…more than anything."
-- *EDF processing…processing…*
-- Output: "I don't want to talk about this. It's stupid."

"Do you think you can just say you love me and that makes everything better?"

"Umm, do you think I had some evil plan that started *last year* and it's now coming into effect. Like you're an angel and I'm a demon bent on fucking you over."

"So now you're swearing?"

"No, I'm not. We call that a slip, but that's not what I said, and that's not why I said it!" I shouted while jumping up from my bed, and that's probably the shout that got Mom's attention.

"Stop shouting," she said.

"I'm trying, but you're blowing this all out of proportion. I don't want to fight with you, and I'm sorry that I didn't tell you sooner that I'm not Catholic or religious or whatever, but it wasn't a lie no matter what you call it. If I hadn't gone to that service, we never would've gone out. It's because I wanted to know you, and now I know you, and it's as simple as that."

A half-minute silence followed.

"So look," I continued, calming in the confidence that my words had worked. "I honestly don't know why I ignored you over the last few weeks, alright. It wasn't cool and I'm done with it. A short phase. And I really do love you. I don't think it makes everything better, and I'm not changing subjects and I just want you to know that I love you, and that I'm sorry, and I won't do it anymore.

"Is that fine?"

-- Input: [blah, blah, unimportant commentary, blah, blah.] "You're blowing this all out of proportion." [blah…additional unimportant commentary…blah, blah.] "Is that fine?"]

-- *Filter processing…Filter processing…no, it's not fine.*

-- And Nicolai says, "Summer. This is your fault."

"So now you're blaming me?" she said.

It was the most irrational response I'd ever heard to anything ever. I was un-equipped and unprepared, and my love deflated and farted and swirled chaotically about like a recently released birthday balloon.

"What?!" I screamed. (I did. I actually screamed at her.)

-- Input: "What?!"

-- *Filter noting heightened volume! Confirmation! Confirmation!*

-- Output: "Yes, I really *do* think this is all your fault!"

"If you're gonna act like a baby," she said, calm as a therapist, "I'm gonna hang up."

"What?!" I screamed again. Then, calming, I called her bet. "Go ahead," I said, thinking it a bluff. "I dare you. I dare you to hang up. Do it! Go ahead. See what happens."

To varying degrees, as a man ages, he gets better at recognizing the point of no return in an argument. In these situations, he learns to calm, assuage, and, by any means necessary, avoid further escalation. I hadn't aged yet, however, so all I felt when I heard the dial tone was shock, and I thought to myself, and wrote it in a passionate plea to myself later. It *was* her fault.

She'd hung up on me; she actually had!

As I set down the phone to begin coping about the madness, my eyes connected with Mom's under my bedroom doorway. She'd clearly heard the end of our fight, and returned my juvenile, give-me-some-space smirk with a maternal, I'm-here-for-you-always grin. Just before she closed the door, Mom told me this: "It's all very normal, honey. Just a part of growing up. You'll figure it out."

It's all very normal…

I'll figure it out?

No. It's not, I thought. *It's not normal at all. It's madness.*

I dialed Summer's number right away. She didn't answer. I dialed again: same result. I set down the phone and lay in bed. As I stared at the ceiling, Mom's words returned to me.

"It's all very normal," she'd said.

How could it be normal that my anger and love grew in unison? How could it be normal that I wanted Summer more than I ever had before, right after she plowed through my words like a harvest. I felt consumed with the idea that I'd been consumed. A panic rose slowly like bubbles in my gut. The bubbles invaded my chest. I began pacing in circles around my room; I was so tense I thought I would hyperventilate and suffocate at the same time, another paradox that made it all the more worse.

How can it be, I thought, *that I need her more the faster she's running away?*

It wasn't long before I caved to exhaustion and fell into a deep sleep.

14.

A rejuvenating clarity woke me well before dusk. I'm not sure if it was some unremembered dream that unlocked it, but when my eyes opened in the dark, I felt that I'd arrived to a full and beautiful understanding of my predicament. I suddenly recognized the tantalizing magnetism between fury and love.

I sat at the edge of my bed, covered myself in a blanket, withdrew my journal, and wrote these in the dozen or so pages I filled, back and front: *"I might feel love* *quickly or slowly, I'm okay to wane and wax...it could take a day...a year maybe, that's all I need...You cannot <u>know</u> love until you've left the battlefield longing to return...and I long to return...Maybe it's in my nature to see it and maybe she can't. Or maybe it's her nature and I can't, which would be the same. Maybe that's the fight."*

I ate breakfast and got to school and realized only then that I didn't know her schedule. I didn't know the location of her locker. I didn't anything about her now that summer break was over. I scanned the halls for any sign of Summer or her friends. I happened upon a tall senior named Monique who played basketball. She pointed me in the right direction, and I arrived at Summer's locker just before the first bell rang. We had precisely three minutes to get to class.

"Summer!" I shouted.

She turned, disapproval in her look.

"What's the matter with you," I said, stepping near.

"What's the matter with me?" she said. "What's wrong with you, yelling at me like that in the halls?"

"Listen," I said, "do you want to be with me? You asked me yesterday if I still loved you. I said yes, but you never said it back."

"Don't twist this," she said. "You didn't call me for weeks. That's the issue here. And—"

"—and I already apologized for that," I interrupted. "I tried to open up to you and you hung up on me like a middle schooler?"

"That's not what happened," she snapped. "You were rude and mean and let's not forget," she lowered her voice to a whisper, "you lied about your religion and being sick and who knows what else!"

"Answer the question," I repeated. "Do you want to be with me or not?"

"I do," she said, "but we have class to get to now, don't we?"

"I'll walk you. You can tell me all about it," I said.

"You'll be late. You know the rules. We can talk after fourth."

"I don't care if I'm late. I want you to say you love me and that you still want us to be together."

She shouldered her backpack as she began walking. "I love you, Nico. You know that. And you know I want to be together, otherwise all this nonsense would be moot."

"Moot? My, my. You're vocabulary has improved in my absence. Maybe you should be thanking me?"

She smiled at that, hard as she tried not to. I'd fought for her, and in doing so, she felt a spark of romance.

That night on the phone, we forgave each other our trespasses.

The next night, over a fancy steakhouse dinner I arranged with the help of Mom's "work-friend"—Tony, a man whose name always seemed to bring a grin to Mom's face—Summer hardly mentioned my weeks of neglecting her. That didn't stop me from apologizing a hundred times.

It was from this foundation that our mad love began.

It was a spectacular affair.

Our madness wasn't captured in events themselves or specific moments. It was simply the new way of us; the new way of things. Though toxicity had entered our love story, and though we shifted regularly from callus to warm and moody to accepting, we persevered for the rest of that semester without significant trial: neither she nor I ever suggested breaking up. We seemed crazy to our friends, but we also seemed crazy about each other. It's fairy dust for romance—magic, see—because when love is war, peace is sublime. A thing is much more sacred if you know it's going to end.

I learned how to apologize. I learned when to give a gift. I learned about the perfect love note snuck into a locker the morning after a phone fight. I learned how to palm a cheek when her tears finally came. We were no longer boyfriend-girlfriend; we'd ascended. We'd become lovers. We weren't sleeping together, but that is not at the core of the word. If it were, they'd call it fuckers.

With an earned power of will and a mutual faith in each other's intentions, our destinies merged, surrendering themselves to the ulterior wisdoms of choice, an imbalanced proving ground for aspiring lovers. We knew the stakes. We were choosing for ourselves.

It wasn't until nine months later, when, on April Fools' Day, balance finally returned.

15.

Fall semester flew by. The holidays came and went. Spring semester began.

Summer and I decided to celebrate our one-year anniversary with dinner at a new Applebee's. We were two weeks into the year.

In honor of this, our first of many planned years together, we agreed not to argue. We succeeded with gritted teeth—whenever touchy subjects flared about the edges of our evening, we bit our lips in turn.

Summer and I had aligned three of our four classes, so were seeing plenty of each other. Summer was my escape from the *real* stresses of high school, and regardless of our fluctuating states of war and peace, I looked forward to our time every day. Our skirmishes seem silly in retrospect, but at the time they consumed us. In February, for example, I told Summer I didn't believe in Valentine's day. "What do you mean you don't believe in Valentine's Day?" she said. "It exists. It's February fourteenth." I told her it was contrived and that I wouldn't buy her anything, so she didn't talk to me on February fourteenth because, well, it didn't exist. This cost us five days of fighting, and shortly thereafter—a passive aggressive overreaction to the Valentine's Day controversy—I returned the favor when, without telling her ahead of time, I didn't speak to her on St. Patrick's Day. I even pretended to be sick so I could miss school. The next day, I pointed to her I.R.A. father as my motive. This cost us a week and a half.

I was reactive and thoughtful and angry and warm; all the time reflecting on my actions, all the time considering our madness as the normal madness of love. I was learning, and I was happy, and I thought she felt the same.

She didn't. I'd probably been dead wrong from the start.

In all the warring, I lost the core of it. I never assured her that my heart was hers to have. This isn't to say I was derelict; I told her I loved her often, wrote her poetry, took her on dates. I didn't notice Summer's changing mood because it shifted like a cloudscape, too slowly to see. I'd been staring right at her, but I'd missed her in the reflection behind me.

April Fools' Day changed all that. I planned a prank to convince Summer that I'd been hit by a car.

It was a dumb idea, but I'd put several safeguards in place. My friends Andrew and Dennis would tell Summer about my hospitalization right after fourth period, the last class of the day, then Summer would sprint to her car, open the door, and find me in the backseat with a big fat *gotcha!* If something went wrong, she had a cell phone.

Best-laid plans, right?

Well...

First off, her car was locked, so I decided to surprise her in the building. Hindsight tells me that I should've just waited by the car, but hindsight's a prick. We unfortunately took different paths and I passed her by, and by the time I returned she was gone. In the same instant I got there, Andrew and Dennis arrived and confirmed that they'd started the prank. Now the joke was on me. Dennis lent me his cell and I called Summer. Voicemail answered straight away.

"Jesus. I've told her a million times. How hard is it to plug in your phone?" I complained to Andrew and Dennis. Although I was in the middle of an epic mistake, I was berating her. I felt like a schmuck, then I realized I was wasting precious time, so I darted to my Civic and sped to the hospital like Steve McQueen. I probably averaged ninety on the freeway. If they weren't building a new median and expanding the road, I think I could've gotten there faster.

I arrived to the hospital in thirteen minutes. My speed didn't help. The situation worsened.

Each reception nurse prolonged my frantic search. Summer had gone from E.R. to general admittance to an outpatient clinic four blocks away. That's where I lost her scent. Forty-five minutes passed as I searched up and down halls and sped between buildings; forty-five excruciating minutes before I finally found her.

"Summer," I shouted.

She was in the E.R., crying in one of the plastic chairs, her powerless phone resting in her powerless hands.

"You piece of shit," she said. There was no semblance of relief in her eyes at seeing me in good health.

I told her it was all just a big misunderstanding, but she wouldn't calm down. "You're acting totally crazy right now, can't you hear yourself," I said.

Of course she couldn't, so she did what many high school girls do when confronted with an assumed and assured asshole.

She ran.

She scoffed at me, did an about-face, and left the hospital after saying she didn't want to talk to me ever again. She called me cruel and she called me stupid and I called her a fool for saying she thought I could be both. I followed her out, screaming at her about how silly *she* was being and how *she* was overreacting. We argued near the entrance, right in front of automatic doors that kept opening and closing, my jeering and volume enough to stop her retreat. Two smiling paramedics watched us from the seat of their idling ambulance, either spellbound by our energy or entertained by our immaturity. When she turned to walk away again, I reached out and grabbed her wrist.

What happened next was pure reaction: Summer turned on a dime, slipped out of my grasp, and slugged me light lightning on the side of the head. That's right; she punched me—punched me right in the face! Right beside my right ear.

It felt like a cathedral bell ringing in the middle of my face. She'd gotten me, but she moved too fast, and her balance was lost. She fell gracelessly to a knee. She popped right up though, gasping at what she'd done. I could feel the shame washing over her.

She apologized profusely, leaning down to check the spot on my face where I'd soon have a fresh bruise. Thank God it was a Friday; by the time Monday came back around, it was mostly gone. I could walk into school with my head lifted high.

I was seriously hurt, but I was more relieved that her mistake would overshadow mine. Like magic, we were returned to center for a opportunity to connect, to restore our Young Lovers Hope. The cathedral bell calmed, and again it sounded like middle C. We were laughing; at the foolishness, at the moment, at our love. I caught a glance at the paramedics exchanging a high five, and I realized laughter had become rare in our relationship; it was her bellowing and bizarre chuckle, a sound unique to her, that revealed to me my cold objectivity, how I'd transformed our passion from a blooming rose into some petri dish experiment. This was *real* life and *real* love happening to us, and it was about time I returned to the truer version of myself, the one who very desperately wanted to be the very best at loving Summer. The punch unlocked that. Maybe it knocked something straight.

Still, I should've remembered her temper.

16.

The two months that followed were our smoothest since the early days. When we talked, we lingered on the phone. We arrived earlier and earlier to school to spend more time together. We didn't go on many dates—school, swimming, and soccer interfered—but when we were together and alone we laughed frequently and kissed often.

Then, junior year ended. It was time for another summer, and this time we faced the challenge of geographical separation. It was our first vacation from each other since my three weeks in hiding, and this would be three times longer than that, but none of this had anything to do with *our* choices.

Shortly after they fled Colorado, Summer's father returned to the long-dormant affections he held for Summer's mother, Ruth. His third marriage had been a disaster, annulled after just four months, and he'd visited Ruth and Summer twice, visits that Summer enjoyed even though she still called him deadbeat more than dad. To accelerate their reconciliation, Ruth brought Summer to Colorado for most of June, all of July, and half of August. The night before Summer left, my mom cooked pulled pork, and afterwards, Summer and I walked around my neighborhood for an hour or so while the moms discussed strategies for keeping Ruth's heart safe. On our walk, Summer cried and cried, predicting how much she would miss me and worrying that her mom was putting their stability at risk. I told her everything would be fine, and I believed that—I really did.

We kissed, she left, and the summer's Summer vacation commenced.

Within days, I felt a shift in my mood. Resentment rolled into my life like a steady San Francisco fog. I'd discovered romantic warfare the last time this happened, and we found peace in the months following April Fool's Day.

So why did this second change of heart have to overcome me? Our peers and even some teachers said they envied what we had.

Who knows?

The answer defies me. It'd be nice, yes, if I could recall a movie-moment, a whispering pine, a flying crow, or a celebration with friends that crystalized the caused, but I can think of none. If I had to judge it in its simplest, cruelest form, I'd say that change changed us. Two fourteen-year-olds may have much in common, may have compatibility in abundance, but by the time eighteen rolls around, mighty changes will have swept both bodies away, leaving two new people ready to tackle the world. Only fortune can gift such lives, and it was becoming apparent that fortune was not about to shine on the beaches of Nicolai.

I came to dread Summer's return. I didn't know why. The shore was so sweet, yet the waters were drawing me, and drawing me in. I knew the loose days would end; no more lounging about the house on my PlayStation, no more training whenever and wherever I wanted. I assumed Summer felt *at least some* of the same changes I did. I believed she found our bi-weekly conversations boring, and that deep down she recognized the withering state of my promise. Certainly her mind and heart were preparing against the growing winds.

I was dead wrong.

I had misinterpreted her heart a third time. Summer's wave blocked the sun and came crashing down atop me, fresh like a waterfall, drowning nonetheless.

17.

Summer returned in mid-August, two weeks before school started. She arranged a surprise for her first night back, taking me to Flat Rock Park for a revival of the moment when she first told me she loved me.

I felt cold the whole night, a liar, a sheep in wolf's clothing, afraid and undeserving. I didn't have what it took; the difference now was that I *knew* it. I tried to show good face. I planned to persevere the whole year, awaiting a more mutual discontent. At worse, we would agree that a college relationship would limit our growth, stymie our progress, etcetera. That, as I saw it, was the best case scenario. All I had to do was enjoy her presence under the guise.

My charade didn't last nearly that long.

During the first few weeks of school, we only went out twice. On our second date, I was chummy at best, emotionally absent at worst. It was a beautiful evening ended on the high-note of a stunning orange sunset. We'd gone to a movie, then stopped at a diner for some pie on the way home, at a place called Tod Durch's, where a pretty barista with purple bangs served us two slices of pie. As we exited, Summer cracked. She palmed my arm, and then she asked me very softly, "Do you love me anymore?"

"Yes, of course," I said, because that's what they say in the movies.

"I don't feel anything from you," she said. "Just tell me."

"Tell you what?"

"Whatever it is. Whatever's the secret, Nico, you can trust me."

"Summer," I said. A blankness inscribed itself on my forehead.

I felt one thing: I didn't want to hurt her. That was it. It was my all-consuming motivation. I wondered sometimes if I lacked bravery—maybe I was and still am a coward. But even if that's true, it wouldn't be my fault. I didn't *choose* to be a coward; I chose Summer. And anyway, there was no secret to tell. I was working, she just didn't know it.

"Summer, it's nothing. It's just that I've got a lot going. My mind's not here."

The next day, I reverted to loveless affectations. This pattern of hot-cold-hot-cold continued for just under six weeks, and just as it would to a slab of granite, so too did this pattern begin to crack my Summer's heart.

18.

Hunt County High School was in a town far more southern and rural than mine. Their pride was football, and every few years our team had to play theirs, and on every occasion, we got crushed. They were known as the Hunt High Saints, and when they marched in, you paid a price for even thinking you could beat them.

Hunt County sits three counties east of mine, and its football stadium was built at the very edge of our region. Looking over the river, you could see to the other side, to region eleven. Although we were destined to lose, thousands of students and alums attended this particular game because the county didn't care much if students snuck liquor into their enormous stadium; revenue, I guess. They'd just built a second level of seats above the home side stands; it was the only two-tiered high school stadium in Georgia. It held something like twelve-thousand fans. The draw from nearby towns was such that the county had begun building a second tier on the away side as well, where we were sitting, but the stairs leading up to the balcony seats were closed with caution tape, and bordered with steel warning signs announcing danger in huge black and red letters.

We were sitting twenty rows up at the seventy yard line. I was sitting next to Summer among our group of friends.

Summer and I hadn't exchanged a word in the car on the way to the stadium. We hadn't uttered a word on our way to the ticket kiosk. Not a one.

Maybe it was just the right time.

I don't know for sure, and I don't care who does.

It doesn't matter anyway: what happened happened for hundreds of different reasons.

"What's wrong?" I finally asked, nudging.

She didn't answer—couldn't answer. It was halftime, right at kickoff, the middle of the game, and the middle of the story. My friends and I had just returned from the parking lot where we shared shots from a leather flask.

When I reach for her hands, she pulled away and covered her face.

"Summer. Love," I said, "What's wrong? What's happening?"

She stood up and pressed by the fans and parents in our row. I trailed right behind her. She caught me following and yelled, "Stay away from me! You're so…mean or cruel or stupid…just…stay away."

She ran up the stairs to the concessions concourse, and was out of sight before I knew what to do. Dozens of people witnessed her outburst, including our friends, and I stood there, paralyzed with embarrassment.

Do I leave her alone or follow her up?

I decided to go up; to right the wrong, to patch the hurt, to reassure. When I reached the concourse, she was gone. There were no nearby exits or bathrooms, but there were tunneled stairs to the unfinished balcony. I saw Summer just before she escaped my view. She went up to get away from me, I realized, but I'd seen her leg stepping away around the dark turn just before she disappeared.

I pressed on. Followed her up like I told myself I would. I passed beneath many warning signs as I did, their bold red and black letters exclaiming:

DANGEROUS EQUIPMENT! STAY OUT!

19.

Ninety-two percent of the kids at my school graduated. At Hunt High, the number was right at fifty. Like I said, they killed kids.

I emerged from the stairs. I overlooked two dozen rows of bleachers. Found Summer sitting in the front row overlooking the field.

I walked slowly down the steps and sat a seat away from her. We were hidden away, contrasted in dimness against the Friday Night Lights, but still she looked forlorn; red eyes, snotty nose, face damp with tears. She looked straight ahead. We didn't share a word for two minutes.

I stood, then took the seat beside her. To my surprise she wrapped her arms around me and buried her head in my shoulder. Calming, she looked at me and said, "We're not gonna make it, are we?"

"Not make it—what do you mean?" I asked.

"We're not gonna make it and I don't know what to do, Nicolai. I don't sleep. I don't eat, I don't cry really, I don't run. I'm just—" she flopped her hands onto her lap and looked to the stars "—I'm just this all the time, but without the snot. Look at me."

I already was.

"No," she said. "Really look. This is how you make me feel. I'm like this all the time on the inside."

"I'm sure it's not all the time," I said.

-- EMOTIONAL DISTRESS FILTER ACTIVATED:
-- Input: "I'm sure it's not all the time."
-- Output: "You're exaggerating. It's not that bad."

Summer got mad quick. "You have no idea what it's like, do you?" she said. "You just go through your days and play your soccer and wait for your scholarship, and you've got girls salivating over you and then there's me, plain old me, alone, and snotty, and ugly, waiting by until you—"

"Slow down," I said. "I'm not making you wait—"

"For what! Why do it. And yes. You do," she shouted, posturing away from me. The crowd shouted for a complete pass. Hunt was about to score again, even though they were already way up. "You have me waiting. You *know* you do. But you don't tell me you love me anymore. You don't call me. I always call you. Do you realize that?"

"I call you plenty," I said.

-- Input: "I call you plenty"
-- Output: "Be happy with what you get."

Arrrghhhhh! was the first thing she said, then she said, "It's not just the calls. This game is the first thing you've asked me to do since I got back from Colorado. That was two months ago."

I had no words. She was right.

-- Input: *{...silence...more silence...}*
-- Output: Attack!

"I know what you're doing," she said. "I'm not stupid, you know. I know you're doing it on purpose too. It's like you want to see me suffer. It's like you get off on my pain. Is that what it is?"

"That's crazy," I said, defending myself.

-- Input: "That's crazy."
-- Output: "You're crazy!"

Summer stood, pressed by me, then turned up the stairs to abandon me again. I stood and shouted after she climbed a few steps, terrified this was the moment of truth. "Summer, stop now!"

She did. She looked down at me.

"Come here."

I had warmth in my eyes and love in my heart, and set about fixing us again. "This is the first time you're telling me this. I'm not a mind reader, and I can't know what you're thinking, but you must know that I'd never want to hurt you. You've gotta give me at least that much, right?"

I began, in the silence that followed, to strategize an amends; maybe I'd go get some liquor from a friend and mix drinks and we could have a little romantic adventure here on this abandoned upper deck, alone, just the two of us. But as she descended the stairs nearing me, she looked different. She looked worn. I now understood what uncertainty had done to her, how it had stripped layers from her grace. I felt villainous. An irresistible urge to vindicate myself with a more truthful action overtook me. Viscerally, and without much thought, I abandoned the romantics. I really thought she was ready to hear it. I really thought it was the right time. Summer was standing two steps above me on the aisle. I was standing two steps above the balcony railing. (That'll be important here in just a minute.)

"Summer," I said once more, "I don't want to hurt you. I never did. But maybe we should take a break, huh? Maybe this isn't right anymore. I mean, if you're really like this all the time."

-- Input: "We should take a break...this isn't right..."
-- Output: "You're not good enough for me. I'm done with you. My promise is dead and you killed it. Oh, and generally speaking, go fuck yourself!"

What happened next was pure reaction—her eyes flared with fire and she pushed me with all her strength. I fell back a step, losing my balance, then my right foot slipped on some kind of goo—maybe plaster, maybe a spilled liquid from construction earlier in the day—and the back of my thighs hit the three-foot railing and I tumbled off and over the edge of the balcony!

Summer shrieked.

As I fell, I reached up in desperation.

My heart thumped.

Blood raced into my arms.

Time slowed to a near stop.

In the luckiest microsecond of my life, I reached up and out with both hands. My left hand missed, but my right hand landed squarely on the lowest rail. I grabbed hold, but I was now hanging with one arm three stories above the Earth. I immediately lunged up, grabbing the rail with my other hand.

Below me, commotion built to a roar in seconds. I heard people shouting and screaming, but I didn't dare look. I knew it was death, waiting.

Summer reached through the rails and grabbed my wrists, but she couldn't pull me up. She was barely an anchor. Tears welled in my eyes. I had nothing on my mind but survival. I didn't want to die: not here, not like this, not some boy that fell from the unfinished balcony at Hunt High, his life nothing more than a newspaper headline and a week of local TV stories about stadium safety, his ultimate legacy relegated to the statistic of 'accidental deaths.'

I looked up at Summer, and another panic overcame me. I had to live. I had to live for her! Her life would already pivot on this awful, confusing, terrible moment, but it might be ruined if I fell. There'd be no one to defend her. There'd be no coming back to reality with that grace that distinguished her most. They might arrest her. They might put her in jail!

The world went mute. Terror blinded me with tears. All I could sense was sweat loosening my grip on the rail and Summer's firm hold on my wrists. She was screaming, crying out to me, "Hold on Nicolai! People are coming! Pull yourself up!"

I could barely hear, barely think.

My legs swayed hopelessly; if there was some miraculous nook or latch beneath the balcony, I had neither the knowledge to find it nor the skill to maneuver myself up. My strength was failing, and a deep pain began to sear in my hands against the sharp-cornered rail. I felt like I'd been hanging there my whole life.

You have to live, I thought. *For Summer. You can save her by saving yourself.*

Sound returned to me. I could hear people yelling from below. I *knew* they were coming; I finally had hope for rescue.

It was a teasing hope. Right then, my left pinky finger slipped.

Summer cried out. "Help! Help! Help me! Help me!"

One-by-one, the other fingers of my left hand surrendered, and I swung off center, the torque ripping at my palm. I held on with one hand, but I had little strength left. My shoulder ached and the muscles in my forearm burned for release.

You have to live, Nicolai.

Pain begged me to let go.

Not for Summer, but because that's the point, don't you see?

Summer screamed frantically, but she had no way or time to help me.

I looked down and saw the height; it was a dizzying distance. I moaned in agony, and very much in sadness. *This is it,* I thought. *This is to be my story. This is what becomes of boys like me; boys who aspire to become the very best at loving women.* I hung there, death waiting below, and was tempted with a calming proposition. *Maybe mercy has given me a gift! I can finally put away this worry about women and romance and just say fuck it once and for all and forever. I can be free!*

This temptation was but a breath; an exhale to expunge the terror and return to my center, to bring me back to my real self.

A barreling strength rose within me. Not one of muscle, but one of soul, *for the boy born to love a girl.* My resolution came on forceful and brave, and it swept away any inclination I had about retreat. The pain in my arms and hands disappeared, and I aspired.

Now, Nicolai!

I'd come too far. I refused to fail. So powerful was this sentiment, it replaced all my doubts and anguish; my fear fluttered away like wind-swept dandelions. I could feel Summer's grip, could hear her voice begging me to climb. I thought only of her—*only her!*—and I thought, *maybe, just maybe I can do it, maybe I can be it for just one moment.*

Even though I'd hurt her and lost my heart, even though I'd piled up a list of mistakes, *maybe in this moment I can be the very best.*

It is the way you aspire that distinguishes you, I remembered. *Not simply that you do or do not.*

I'd received love because Summer allowed it, because she believed in me, and in us, and in my promise. And I felt a glow and a fearlessness that shouted:

Now, Nico. Aspire.

And in that very last moment, my very last thought—swear to God—was: *I forgive you, Summer. Completely and forever.*

And I smiled at Summer—*my Summer!*—with love booming in my heart. I smiled as I looked her straight in the eyes through those rails and with a forward hope that she'd know I didn't blame her. I smiled in forgiveness and in love and with a pride that sang this sentiment without words, *Not even death waiting below is powerful enough to overcome us. You'll know this forever.*

It was my greatest moment. It was beyond trophies. I'd succeeded—albeit for just an instant—at becoming *the very best*: if I was going to die tonight, I was going to die a lover.

The skin on my right palm tore open against the corner of the rail, I lost my grip, and slipped through Summer's fingertips.

Then, gravity.

Then, I fell.

On Forgiveness

"To forgive is the highest, most beautiful form of love."
—Dr. Robert Muller

Hanging there,

I finally remember,

who killed me.

It was you,

which begs the statement:

who brought us back.

I can't remember the pain, just my revelations. I saw forgiveness and judgment linked like two ends of a magnet, impossible to isolate, impossible to bring together, cursed in limbo. I saw in colors clear as Crayola why my journey headed north *or* south but up *and* down, and then I was back to the magnet, back to the moment of my death. And I remember. I was looking up at Summer. She was shrinking into the sky. At this rate, she'd soon be reduced to a star. I prayed that she knew my truth in her heart; that mine was an honest forgiveness, and that it was hers forever, to treasure as she liked.

That's what it felt like to fall.

My body spun, and I lost sight of Summer. She was the last thing I saw, and I was happy in that.

Then, I crashed into the bleachers and people below me.

Then, darkness.

Summer Ends

"And so with the sunshine and the great bursts of leaves growing on the trees, just as things grow in fast movies, I had that familiar conviction that life was beginning over again with the summer."

—F. SCOTT FITZGERALD, FROM *THE GREAT GATSBY*

20

I didn't die, obviously.

Several parents had gathered underneath me—the enormous parent-of-football-player types. They saved my life, they stood beneath me, eager and ready to help a falling boy, and none more than a man named Mr. Lawrence. Mr. Lawrence suffered fractures in both his hands as he reached up to buffer my fall. He cracked several ribs on his right side, right around his liver. Mom offered Mr. Lawrence money as thanks and recompense, but he turned it down gladly. His honor and a life-long story about a boy whose life he saved provided reward enough. Still, I called him Saint Lawrence in my head. In a way, I consider him the most important person I ever met. To say he touched me is to understate.

Fifty-five feet; four stories in one fall. The full page article on the fourth page of the town paper said I hit the ground at forty miles-per-hour. I broke four bones: my left forearm, my left wrist, and two ribs on my left side, and I also bruised my pelvis, an injury which outlasted the bones. Fortunately, my legs suffered only a few deep welts and a hairline fracture on my lower left shinbone—the result of falling head first. I was able to resume soccer training four months later.

In the calamity of the crash, my head whiplashed into the corner of a bleacher, knocking me out cold. When I awoke six hours later at Hunt County General, the doctor told me my skull opened like a melon, but luckily it didn't chip or crack. I saw pictures of the blood soon thereafter—very melon-like indeed. The doctors repaired me with two dozen stiches and a handful of staples that ran from behind my left ear towards the crown of my skull. Most of the scars are still visible today. Many of them will be with me until I die. The thick one on my head makes it look like they planted something inside of me.

A police detective showed up the following morning, but I was barely cognizant due to the (awesome, amazing, unbelievably fun!) painkillers streaming into my blood. The cops returned thrice more over the next four days, each time asking for clarity about what happened.

"So explain again how you fell, just one more time," the old black detective asked me for a millionth time. He reminded me of Mr. Jansen.

"Backwards," I responded sarcastically. (Because the police had been so persistent, I worried that Summer may have let slip a suggestion of malice. Maybe they had video evidence or an eye-witness.)

"No, young man," the cop said to me, sternly this time. "Where were you? Where was Summer? Just tell us the truth."

I winced and closed my eyes and made like I was having a recurrence of migraine. They'd been pestering me for nearly half an hour, but that finally did the trick. The cops left and never troubled me again. Like Becca, Summer was never charged with a crime. (Yes, the rules for high school boys and girls are tragically unfair.)

Then, six days after they completed their repairs, the doctors released me, and I began to rest for the first time. I took leave from my life.

My head really was a mess; migraines erupted that debilitated me for minutes at a time. The hours that followed these migraines ranged from uncomfortable to unbearable. I cried often from the pain. To reduce my stress, the doctors basically prescribed laziness, and I happily filled that prescription with video games, reading, and daytime television. (It made me sad—and angry sometimes too—that nobody ever told me *The Days of Our Lives* could be so good.)

21.

There are no ground rules for broaching a conversation about near-death; especially since my near-death experience happened right after I tried to end things with Summer.

She never called me. I never called her. It's as simple as that.

I mean really, what would I have said. "Um, Hi Summer. I'm glad you didn't kill me." "Ha-ha," she'd say. "Me too. You said you wanted a break!" And, "Ha-ha," I'd say back. "I guess I should've clarified I wanted to break up, not break my bones!" And then what? We'd laugh some more and go about our day? In this ironically peaceful way, my ending with Summer was the most mutual, most comfortable breakup of my life, if you subtract the whole attempted murder bit.

I returned to school in January, ten weeks after the fall. Whenever Summer and I passed each other in the halls, I saw regret in her eyes. I'm sure she regretted pushing me; maybe she also regretted not visiting me at the hospital. And I came to regret many of my choices too; the fighting, the wasted hours, the not telling her how deeply I cared. The universe remedied this for us, and gifted us a final moment, and it was sweet and it was short and it closed our story with poetry.

Two weeks before graduation, I happened upon Summer at the concession stand during a playoff game for our high school baseball team. She'd been dating one of the outfielders for about a month. When I saw her standing at the counter, I considered returning to my seat, but she saw me before I had the chance. Our eyes connected and she froze, feigning a grin.

"Hi," I said.

"Nicolai," she answered. "Hi. How are you?"

The greeting was awkward, but she had nowhere to go while she waited for whatever she'd ordered.

"I'm good," I said. "Much better, and you?"

"I'm good, you know. I'm—" she glanced in the direction of her boyfriend sitting in the dugout "—I'm good. Really. Hey, I heard about your soccer scholarship to State. That's really great. You must be excited."

"I am," I answered, "but I'm not sure they'll play me much. I'm mostly excited to get on with it." (Her friendly eyes invited me to continue. I happily accommodated.) "I don't understand why they told me so soon," I said. "I haven't done any work all semester. It really does feel like nothing matters anymore."

"Yeah? You like it?"

"What?"

"The feeling? That nothing matters anymore?"

"I guess I never thought of it that way."

"Nicolai not thinking about how he feels? I doubt it," Summer said as she picked up the little pizza and soda she'd ordered. Then she asked a most interesting question. "What happened with you and Gabby? You two looked happy together."

Gabrielle had been my rebound, the girl to whom I lost my virginity in the months after falling.

"Do you know Gabby?" I asked.

"Not really," Summer said.

"Well, I should inform you that she doesn't like to be called Gabby."

"Oh yes, I've heard," she said. "Gabrielle. My apologies."

"Gabrielle indeed," I said in a smarmy British accent.

Summer snorted a bit of soda. She always did that when my jokes caught her off guard.

"Did you hear what went down? Between me and Gabby, I mean?"

Summer shook her head.

"It was almost as disastrous as what happened to us," I told her.

"Again, I doubt that," Summer replied.

I scratched my head, drawing attention to my still apparent skull scar.

"OK, almost as disastrous."

Then, Summer lingered.

I knew what she wanted to say: she wanted to run me through what the days and weeks after my fall had been like for her, and she wanted to explain why she didn't come to the hospital, and she wanted me to know that her heart was good, and that we had deserved each other, and that she missed me often but couldn't overcome the fear of seeing what she'd done, and she wanted to tell me that she was sorry for having pushed me so carelessly. And me, I wanted her to know that only fond memories remained in my heart. It was part of my gift and good fortune that we'd shared a love so rich so young. I knew others our age had loved too—countless others—but their love wasn't ours, and ours wasn't theirs, and when it's yours, it's just that; it's *your* treasure chest filled with *your* gold and *your* silver and *your* moments and no one else can comprehend it.

No one. Ever. That's how it works. It's like a rule or something.

This was my final test with Summer; to leave her with a full knowing.

"I love you," I said. "And I always will and I'll never forget what you did for me. I forgave you before I fell. I know you'd never hurt me. Not if it's avoidable."

Summer relaxed her shoulders. Now was her chance to cash in, a lifetime of closure her reward. "I know," she said. "I saw it your smile. Before you fell. I love you too. I'm sorry."

"Yeah, me too."

And but for another hello or two passed here and there during the last weeks of school, we never talked again. I learned with Summer that romance is an inherently perilous pursuit. It is a dangerous business; that's all there is to it. I lacked the equipment necessary to soften my landing with Summer (and by that, I don't mean a helmet). I also lacked the equipment necessary to slow myself from rebounding the wrong way following our literal falling out.

It was Gabby who taught me this. I'm sure she'd prefer if we used her self-chosen name—

GABRIELLE, NOT GABBY

"Until you get comfortable with being alone, you'll never know if you're choosing someone out of love or loneliness."
—MANDY HALE

1.

Although my fall caused many negative side-effects—a fear of heights, residual pains in my wrists, a limp caused by my cracked ankle, and a lost girlfriend—it came with silver linings. Some were even gold. When I returned to school in January, everyone was interested in me: not just girls, but teachers and jocks and janitors too. Kids I barely knew lingered near my locker. Cute girls I'd never talked to wanted to sign my cast. Punks thought my skull scar was killer, and even the principals asked if there was anything they could do to help. I'd never been popular, and I never wanted to be really, but I was suddenly visible everywhere. It was this visibility that attracted the princess.

Gabrielle Zacapa dressed fashionably, smiled big, walked with purpose, and always wore her blonde tipped, red-highlighted black hair up in a high pony-tail. She was plenty pretty, wildly popular, a fixture on event planning committees, four-time member of homecoming court, and senior class President. Simply put; Gabrielle Zacapa was an achievement junkie.

She approached me in the halls the week after my return. I'd had minor surgery to remove a bone chip from my lower left leg and was subjected to a soft cast and single crutch. I hated those weeks: I felt like a pirate.

"Hi," Gabrielle said, walking briskly to catch me.

"Hello," I said back, continuing onward.

"I don't think we've ever had a class, have we?" she asked.

"One or two. You're Gabby. I know."

"Ewwwww," she said.

"Eww, what?" I asked.

"I'm don't do 'Gabby' anymore," she answered, flashing air quotes. She extended a hand. "Gabrielle Zacapa these days. Nice to meet you."

We shook hands, and I said, "Very nice to meet you, Gabrielle. No hard feelings, I hope. I get misnamed all the time. Now it's apparently 'the guy who falls from balconies,' but usually it's Nicolai."

She laughed politely. "That's actually what I wanted to talk to you about. Would you be willing to do a photo for the annual? You know, like, about your fall? We think it'll make for a great spread, *maybe even get in the first ten pages*," she sang. "We'd get it at an up-angle, green screen the stadium."

"I see," I replied.

"I know it's fresh, but there's this awful deadline. We don't have much time."

I knew Gabrielle's stature, and I had a friend on Yearbook, the goth kid from earlier. There weren't any deadlines until around Easter, and anyway, Gabrielle's body language betrayed her; the head tilt, the giving grin, the little exhale after each sentence. I didn't understand why yet, but Gabrielle Zacapa was into me.

"Sure," I answered.

"Yeah? OK, great! Let's go."

"You mean right now?"

"Yeah, now. We're doing shots in the courtyard and we wanna get you at an up-angle with the third story so it's like…" she trailed off when she caught me holding my breath. Her description brought details back to me. Realizing suddenly that her ambition wasn't respectful to the fact that I almost died, she said, "Sorry." She scrunched her face. "I can be insensitive when I get excited, but I promise I'm not normally this way. I just believe in documentation, if you must know the truth."

For some reason, I believed her word.

"No worries," I said. "It's just that I've got class."

"Which class?" she asked.

"Statistics. Mrs. Floyd."

"Ah, me and Flo are like sisters," she said. Then, without asking, Gabrielle shouldered my backpack. (I welcomed the relief; the thing was a pain to lug on one crutch.) "We'll only be about ten minutes. You'll be fine, I promise."

I nodded to her suggestion and we were off.

As we walked, Gabrielle exhibited her royal quality; quick hellos, cheek kisses with members of her court. She even signed a release from an underling on the prom committee. She had a sense of the air around her, a constant awareness of her effect on people. Where Summer had grace, Gabrielle had fame, and she augmented it constantly, lifting her chin when she turned so her hair would bounce, keeping her expression between generous smile and casual grin; never more or less than those, and rarely laughing. Her teal and white fingernails, freshly painted the night before, matched her skirt, earrings, and low heels, and although I'd seen her a hundred different times, heading events, passing in the halls, or on stage at school assemblies, I noticed her lips for the very first time. They looked soft as room temperature butter.

2.

My opinion on popularity before I met Gabrielle was simple; popular kids are phony, their clothes and behaviors are forced, and their ranks are filled with the spoiled sons of assholes and the pampered daughters of bitches. This opinion collided suddenly into my new courtship with Gabrielle. She was a marquis student-celebrity, princess to many, royalty to all.

After they shot me, Gabrielle asked if I wanted to see proofs the next day. I said yes, and we met alone in the photography lab, and I saw the proofs, and just as I was leaving she asked if I wanted to meet again about print copy. She always secured a next-day follow up, working me more like a client than a potential suitor.

Suddenly, there were whispers about us. I noticed strangers looking at me, glancing my way for a moment or more as I passed in the halls. The rumors themselves were true; only a few days after the photo shoot Gabrielle and I had kissed. (It was in secret between classes, and little more than a peck…well, a peck and a smile, and a lingering clench of fingertips before she pulled away.)

She'd gone cold after that, though. She'd ignore or dismiss me, not return my calls, forget to call when she said she would, sit with me at lunch one day and then not show up the next. This caused me more confusion than hurt, but in either case, concentrating on Gabrielle made me happy. The thought of earning her affection brought me so much peace, in fact, that I surrendered my disdain for popularity. It became an education, a way to rebrand my promise specifically for Gabrielle. Put simply, I transformed myself temporarily into a Gabrielle Zacapa junkie. I invested in a few men's fashion magazines, shaved my facial hair, cleaned my nails, and bought clothes more aligned to her style. I became entrenched with Gabrielle's posse; this brave world of cocky and beautiful teens, and before I knew it, my social life merged with theirs. I hadn't resisted really; I was still the same inside, sure—it was still the same thing driving me, this need to become *the very best at loving women*—but my pursuit had manifested anew.

I knew in real time what this was: a pursuit to take my mind off of Summer, the one who killed me. I couldn't distinguish the joy of new affection from the medicinal way that affection cured my pain. In this way, Gabrielle began as an anesthesia for remembrance, a shortcut out of the woods, and as it goes with shortcuts, one cannot know its perils before travelling the path.

My changes worked. Six weeks after the shoot, we were officially a couple. We became the most apparent duo at school. Thus, was my aspiration returned to me. Gabrielle was my girl, which meant she was the most important thing I had going, and I began in earnest the growing and perfecting of our young relationship.

3.

To her credit, Gabrielle maintained popularity in a way that didn't put-off, success in a way that didn't offend. Her politic was always on, and broadly speaking she was admired by everyone. Underneath this shine, however, Gabrielle owned a complimentary darkness. It spewed out ugly during the short-lived romance we shared, and all of this because I wasn't accustomed to the manner and expectations of her lifestyle.

Simply put, Gabrielle Zacapa was loaded.

She was fourth generation American. One day after she turned ten, her family migrated from California to Georgia, and while their wealth was noteworthy in the posh San Diego suburb of La Jolla, they became local royalty in the rural south; hers was one of the wealthiest families in town.

"What do you think it was," I asked Gabrielle on our fourth date. "What do you think makes your dad so successful?"

"Hard work," she said. "If you work hard, success will come as naturally as a magnet to a refrigerator." She believed this like a zealot. She bellowed it like smoke.

"Magnets don't come to refrigerators naturally. We put them there."

In Gabrielle's eyes, the world began and ended with her father, the patriarch Francisco Zacapa, inheritor of their grandfather's fortune and dictator of family affairs. Gabrielle said he'd earned everything he had, but it struck me as a peculiar brand of hard work considering he'd just completed an eight-week pleasure romp all around Eurasia with Estelle, his third wife, Gabrielle's second stepmother in six years.

"So when you say hard work, how do you mean that?" I pressed.

"What do you mean how do I mean? The magnet thing? Just drop it."

"Hard work," I said. "When your Dad says he works hard, what do you think he means? Hours? Labor? Something else?"

"What are you trying to say?" she asked.

"I'm not trying to say anything. I just want to know."

It devolved from there. In another few sentences, Gabrielle grew so frustrated she stood up and left the restaurant before our cheesecake arrived.

I came to a better understanding of what underlay Gabrielle's resistance to my questions. While it was most certainly an epic tale of hard work for her great grandparents, Francisco Zacapa's "hard work" wasn't the get-up-early-stay-up-late kind; his was the 9-to-3 type of hard work, when you have to talk with lawyers and financial advisors hard work, the hiring and firing of your franchise fast food restaurant shift managers hard work, the tolerating solicitations of charities and 'dinner with my employees at a fancy steakhouse is hard work' type of hard work. After the little restaurant meltdown, I avoided the topic of her family altogether.

Gabrielle carried her reputation for excellence like a toddler carries a blanket; desperately, fearfully, as though letting go for even a moment would invite disaster. This reputation extended to family pride, but honestly, I don't think she ever considered her life in its own context before meeting me. When I'd ask her about the pressure she felt, she'd defer to privilege. "I couldn't be luckier," she'd recite like a newscaster. "It's the least us fortunate folk can do."

4.

One late afternoon in mid-March, Gabrielle and I were finishing an afterschool snack-date at that Tod Durch's place. We'd been together for about two months.

"Do you think I'm making a mistake?" she asked out of the blue.

"Mistake?"

"About Emory instead of the urban project?"

"Oh. That's a big question."

She'd brought this idea to her father; to spend a year working with a non-profit construction firm that built functional homes in Atlanta's poorest and most dangerous neighborhoods. Papa Zacapa preferred she stick to the traditional university route.

"I can't go," she said. "Not don't want to. Can't. You know that, right?"

"Hey, I wouldn't do it," I said. "I'm not judging you. No one is. Whether you're studying or doing the project, it'll be great. Everything you touch turns gold, Gabrielle. Just do what's in your heart."

We ate for a while in silence, finishing the outrageously rich slices of vanilla cake she'd bought us.

"It's just," Gabrielle began before pausing to consider more exact words. "It's just that I always thought I knew what I was doing," she said.

"You do," I interrupted. "You're a G."

"No. I'm not. I'm not anymore. Or I don't anymore. And I think it's you, honestly. I think you're why I'm always confused all the time."

"What?" I was taken aback. She hadn't said it nicely.

"Like how you're constantly asking me about all this stuff; my future, my father, my name."

"When did I say anything about your name?"

"You called me Gabby."

"When you first met me?"

"You don't remember. You met me. Whatever. It just makes me feel weird and anxious, and stupid sometimes too if I'm being honest. Like you've got some answer underneath it all and you're just waiting for me to get around to it."

"Hold on. Are you talking about pressure?"

"Why do you still call it that?" she said. "We've talked about this. Nobody's *pressuring* me. It's not *pressure*. I just…It's just me. You make me out to be a Storm Trooper just because I'm motivated."

"Storm Trooper?" I joked. "I didn't know you liked Star Wars."

"Nicolai!" she shouted, her volume drawing the attention of the coffee shop.

"I'm sorry," I said quickly, and when I took her hand, I felt it trembling. She didn't pull away, but she didn't grip back. Her eyes were moist, her head was down: she was emotionally naked, maybe for the first time in her whole life.

"Hey," I said softly. "Look at me."

She did.

"I think it's just that *I'd* feel pressure," I said. "I don't know or understand how you keep going all the time. But you're right, pressure isn't the right word." (Pressure was *absolutely* the right word, but it wasn't *her* word. She saw *pressure* as a word for people who couldn't handle responsibility.) "We don't have to talk about it anymore," I continued. "Let's get outta here, go watch a movie or something. Or call it a night. Or talk about something else—whatever you want."

This moment, I believe, was the very height of our short relationship. Romance begs its participants to remain in the present, and the consequence for Gabrielle was to put away her drive when she was with me. In my own way, I'd given her an opportunity to slow down and soak up the world, and this culminated in a most important happening: the defining event of most boy's transition into manhood.

"What movie?" Gabrielle asked me. "I like comedy mysteries."

"Is that a thing?"

"It's the only thing."

That's when I told Gabrielle that Mom was out of town for a city manager's conference; she'd been gone all week and wasn't coming back for another two days. Gabrielle said she wanted to come over instead of going to the theater. She wasn't shy about it. Not one bit.

5.

Shortly after Gabrielle overcame the tragedy of my home's not having San Pelle-grino, I prepared a tray with some chips and dips and cheeses, poured box-wine into two plastic cups, and sat with her on the couch. We ate and drank and talked for a few minutes, then I retrieved the throw blanket from Mom's Lay-Z-Boy, covered us, started the VHS, and opened my arms. She curled into the nook of my shoulder like a lazy puppy. She was soft and warm, and the moment was lovely.

About thirty minutes into *So I Married an Axe Murderer,* the two of us having hardly moved, Gabrielle interrupted our calm by sitting up.

"Will you pause it a second?" she asked.

I reached for the remote and did.

She looked at me with a measured grin, then away. From this gesture I as-sumed something heavy was coming: I didn't know she'd be dropping an anvil on my skull.

"Were you in love with Summer?" Gabrielle asked me.

My stomach tightened like a bar mop being wrung at the end of a long Sat-urday night. I hadn't thought of Summer for days, and Gabrielle's question filled me instantly with guilt. *Had it really happened so quickly?* I thought. *Could new affection have pressed Summer out of my mind so soon?* Summer had been so very important to me; for almost two years my life revolved around her.

"Why?" I asked her. "I mean, why does that matter?"

"You ask me all sorts of questions," she said. "I just want to know if you were in love."

Her question was certainly in order. She hadn't once brought Summer into a conversation, and anyway, I had no reason to lie. "Yes," I said. "I did love her."

"Really?" she asked, doubt in her voice.

"Yes," I said doubtlessly. "Yes. Very much."

"Do you ever miss her?"

"No," I said, finding my next words easier to share. "Not anymore. Not since us."

"What were you and her doing up there at Hunt? When you fell, I mean; she was up there with you, right?"

Where Summer had vanished, my fall haunted me every day. Like visions after a horror movie, they flashed in and out of my mind without warning or pattern. Gabrielle's interrogation discomforted me, the gossipy nature of it and the terrible nostalgia both, and I looked away from her with a sneer.

"I didn't mean anything by it," she said. "I only—"

"Do we have to talk about this?" I asked.

"Nico. You ask me about serious stuff all the time," she said. "So yeah, I think we do have to talk about this. I mean if you—"

"We were just talking," I said.

"Talking about what?"

"Nothing. Nothing at all. We were talking about…We were just talking and…"

The words froze in my throat. I paused, staring at the carpet.

Gabby prompted me. "And you just fell?" she asked. "Just like that, outta nowhere?"

"It was a mistake. I slipped. I tipped over the edge, I hung on but couldn't get any footing and then…yeah. Yeah. I fell."

She shook her head in sympathy and asked, "Were you scared?"

"Shitless," I replied.

What I failed to realize quickly enough is that Gabrielle wasn't actually interested in my fall. She'd come for a different reason, and different answers too.

"Did you tell her you loved her?"

"What do you mean?"

"Did you and her say, like, 'I love you' to each other?"

"Sure," I said, not following her angle. "Of course."

Gabrielle huffed. "OK," she said, "so like on Melrose Place—do you watch Melrose Place?"

I wanted to throw a chair and scream, *Hell no, I don't watch Melrose Place! Are you shitting me?!* But I chose, instead, to simply shake my head.

"Well, anyway," Gabrielle said excitedly, "Billy told Amanda the other night—they're boyfriend-girlfriend, well sort of anyway—and they were by the pool in the apartment—that's why it's called Melrose place, because it's an apartment—and Samantha was home early from work because there was this problem with her boss, who, actually…"

As Gabrielle plowed through a four-minute background of Melrose Place, I practically hibernated. Only standby systems held steady: just enough attention to recognize questions.

My I.Q. one point lower, Gabrielle finally arrived to her point. "So anyway," she said, "Billy told Amanda that he just doesn't like to say it. That, like, it's weird for guys to say I love you."

Then, she suddenly stopped talking, and I heard a voice ask:

Was there even a question?

It was all very queer, but my subconscious raced for a response that could fill this gap. "Sure," I answered, "I can see that." (A classic in a pinch!)

"But you haven't said it to me."

Having lost myself in the whole *Melrose Place* rant, and forgetting our lead-in conversation, I blurted out thoughtlessly, "Are you asking me why I haven't told you I love you yet?"

It was a little slip, but it was plenty.

Gabrielle interpreted my answer as: *I do love you. I just don't like to say it.* I was certain of her interpretation because of how she smiled—

Oh, and because of this. "I think I love you," she said.

"It's not really a thinking thing," I replied.

"I don't think it," she said. "I know it. I wrote it down last night, and it felt true. I even wrote my first name with your last name a few times and it felt…Well, it felt…I'm not saying I want to marry you or anything like that, it's just…I love you. I know I do. And I don't care what Papa says about it."

"What?" I asked.

"I love you, Nicolai."

"No. Your Dad?"

"Don't worry about that."

"Like he disapproves of me? Is that what you're saying? Is it because of my skin?"

"Nicolai," Gabrielle interrupted warmly—so warmly, in fact, I forgot about her father. "Just listen to my words. I love you," she said. She wore the relieved smile of a stage performer who's just completed a nerve-wracking solo. She took in an animated breath, wiggled her fingers to expel the anxiety just released, and exhaled the weight of her emotions. Now, everything was right.

Well…almost everything.

Her eyes searched mine. Her ears were waiting. If I was to be *the very best* right now, there was only one response appropriate for the moment. My response practically autopopulated.

"I love you, too," I told her.

Before we even had time to smile, Gabrielle jumped on top of me and unbuttoned my jeans. My thoughts sprinted away from the head atop my shoulders to the head between my legs. My beautiful, popular, ambitious, Latina girlfriend was eager to strip me of my virginity, and I was eager to oblige.

We kissed as we undressed to our underwear. She asked if I had a condom, but I didn't: I'd always considered them presumptuous and unromantic. I felt silly about this opinion when she produced a red-wrapped Trojan from her handbag.

Then, a few minutes later, I lost my virginity on the living room floor, on a carpet that Dad bought for Mom when they were dating.

I remember few details; the location, the pillow I placed behind her head, the shimmery maroon hue of her satin bra. I remember the sex feeling clunky and awkward, and I remember the one thought repeating in my head like wavy vinyl as we repositioned and grunted and attempted to extract pleasure from the process; *this is NOTHING like sex in the movies.*

Frankly, the experience disappointed, and thus I reflected very little on losing my virginity to Gabrielle. When I did, I thought it the most anticlimactic moment of my life. I felt odd about it, and I felt regret that I hadn't shared it with Summer.

6.

Gabrielle and I had sex only thrice more, once in my car, once in my bed, once in the closet of an unfinished, four-unit office building her father owned. This infrequency had nothing to do with morality or a lack of want; she was just truly, awfully, terribly busy. Between family events and school activities and personal hygiene—the waxing and haircuts and facials and mani-pedis and *shoot me*—Gabrielle and I shared only a few minutes between classes here and there and maybe an hour of nighttime phone conversation during the week. As with Summer, the lack of sex didn't bother me.

What *did* bother me—and this came about suddenly after we slept together—was Gabrielle's bickering about virtually everything I did; manners, clothing, the way I ate, my unwashed car, my fingernails not being clipped, my clothes not being ironed, video games, fast food. She even questioned my playing soccer because it offered no career path. Keep in mind, I'd already changed for her—aggressively and on purpose. I'd even befriended her cliques. Still, complaints piled up.

I believed I could make us work, that I could find a balance between self-preservation and change-for-love. I believed I could look beyond her preoccupation with success and the way she generally perceived and treated people like props. Regardless of her politic, and regardless of her father's seeming disapproval, a subject she confessed but wouldn't detail, I never doubted Gabrielle's sincerity. She did *love* me, and told me so, publicly and privately, every time we were together. She smiled at my jokes, left sweet notes in my locker, and always kissed me when we parted, long and sweet, her way of saying, "Looking forward to the next." Not ample, but it sufficed.

I could've, maybe, possibly fallen in love with Gabrielle given more time, but alas, she introduced me to her brother: Adam.

Simply put, Adam had us doomed.

7.

I met Adam at a family event honoring Gabrielle's graduation. I told Gabrielle that meeting her family for the first time at a formal event was a bad idea (especially since there was still the unanswered question of her father's approval) but Gabrielle insisted. She said she loved me. When I tried to say no, she kissed me, then she said please and pretty please, then she touched me, so I agreed to go to the goddamn lunch.

On the last day of March, I received an invitation by courier: "Gabrielle's Graduation Luncheon," it read. Scheduled for 11:30 AM, formal attire was encouraged. Two weeks later, on the morning of the event, Gabrielle arrived to my home at nine on the dot. She shared a bit of coffee and conversation with Mom while I shelved three baskets of laundry upstairs (an unfinished chore from last evening.)

Then, Gabrielle and I left. Mom waved us off from the front porch, and we vanished around a corner.

"I could've driven," I said to Gabrielle.

"Your Civic is what? Ten years old?" she said, hands clutching the wheel.

I tried to laugh her joke away. "Not quite," I said.

"What are you wearing?" she asked.

I didn't quite catch the disdain because I was admiring the lights and features of her Beemer. I'd never sat in one before. "Clothes? A tie?" I joked again. "Is this a trick question?"

She clenched her jaw.

"What?" I snapped? Sure, they weren't the *best* clothes—graduation apparel; khaki's, a blue tie I got from Dad, white button up with thin red vertical stripes— but they were certainly serviceable. "Is this not alright for lunch? Do I need a tuxedo?"

"It's a luncheon," she fired back, "and there's no need to cop an attitude. You're putting me in a position. You know that. You know what my family's like."

"Actually, I don't. I have no clue what your family's like. I've never met them. And if you didn't like what I was wearing, why didn't you tell me that before we left the house?"

"Because I didn't want your mother to think I was superficial, obviously."

"Well," I said, implying Mom wasn't too far off.

Gabrielle didn't appreciate that, so she turned up the radio, and we drove without a word for ten minutes. She made a surprising turn west instead of east on the freeway, but I was too annoyed to ask why we were going the wrong way. The answer rang clear when we turned into the parking lot of a Macy's.

"You're kidding," I said after she parked and turned off the car.

"Please," she said. "I'll pay. Think of it as a gift."

"What? Have you lost your mind? Never in hell would I let you dress me."

"That's not what I'm doing. Don't do that."

"Do what? Tell you your fucking place isn't above me?"

"That's not right, Nicolai. Slow down. You're misreading this. Please, just trust me."

"Trust what?" I asked.

"Trust that you won't like it. You won't like sticking out here. Please. Just—
"

"You're actually serious, aren't you?"

"I am," she said, but with a dramatically downshifted tone. "Don't think the worst of me," she pled. "Just be helpful, will you? I'm begging you. Please."

I'd never heard Gabrielle desperate before. I stared into her eyes for what felt like minutes. The eyes are where you can see the truth, and I saw honesty in her words.

So, I caved.

I believed then as I do now that sacrifice is a normal part of romantic diplomacy. She bought me a new tie and a nice shirt; my khakis were deemed acceptable. Thinking it might reduce my embarrassment, I bought myself the dress shoes I needed for graduation.

I was feeling pretty good about my sacrifice, but as we exited the Macy's, I saw Gabrielle's real face. It was the look of victory. That's when I realized it wasn't her *honesty* that found those pleading words in the car: it was her *politic*. She was always on, and I was but a line item on the day's to-do list. I'm sure of it; I'm sure she imagined striking a big red "X" through the checkbox labeled "Fix Nicolai" as we strode across the parking lot; my former outfit hiding shamefully in the extra bag I had to request at the register.

8.

When he was ten, Gabrielle's brother, Alejandro, told his father that he wanted to change his name to Adam. His father explained that "Adam" could be a nickname, even if 'Alex' was more appropriate. But the boy didn't like girls, and the name would've confused, so Alejandro insisted the change be legal. Father agreed with little fuss; a reward for the boy's sophistication and manner.

I put little stock in this story—Adam told it to me himself, so most likely it's a lie. Still, I think the story summarizes how Adam Zacapa came to be. His father believed that men should live to their own tune, and that all Zacapa men possessed a pedigree of automatic ascension. This paradigm of parenting created the Adam I met; whether he changed or not, I do not know, for the day ended badly and I never saw him again.

Adam attended a for-profit art school in Northern California until he dropped out halfway through his third year. His only seeming life restriction now was a requirement to live near his parents. At some point, I asked Adam about his occupation. He called himself a wood sculptor, and I suppose that's technically accurate, even if he'd only completed seven jobs in the last five years.

After passing by a landscaper who was pruning thorns from the roses in Adam's garden, Gabrielle and I entered his lake house through an undecorated atrium. We turned a corner and emerged into a grand room with big-window views of the lake and tall pines swaying in a light breeze. You could practically smell the water through the walls. But beyond that and the home's impressive size, the place was a joke; clothes and cans and paper plates and plastic utensils littered the tables and carpet and rugs. In contrast to this, the window sills and countertops shined dust-free; even the portraits of his family hanging over the room's huge sectional couch reflected like mirrors with cleanliness. Adam's lake house had all the signs of weekly maid service. *This must be the sixth day*, I thought, but I couldn't be sure. There was no way to know.

Adam was cooking something on the stovetop in his gray granite-topped kitchen when we entered. He turned briefly and lifted his chin in salutation. Gabrielle directed me to sit at the small marble entry table as she pulled her mobile phone out. She held up one finger as if to say *give me a second*, then she left the room. I just sat alone, not knowing what to say, looking dumb and out of place.

I saw Adam eat soup straight from the pot. (I didn't need eyes; I could hear him slurping.) The place smelled like beer, there was nothing to look at on the white walls, no books or magazines to peruse on the shelves or coffee table. All I could think was, *this is a mistake. I have to get away from here.*

"What's up, bro," Adam said as he approached to shake my hand. I stood up and reached out. He squeezed aggressively with his sweaty hand, but I managed to keep my aggravation hidden. This wasn't difficult; it's not like Adam was introspective.

"You want a beer?" he asked casually.

"Umm…no, I'm good," I said.

"Whatever," he said. "What time's the thing?"

"Gabrielle's thing?" I asked.

"Yeah, Gabby's thing. What else?"

"I think it starts in about—"

"I got it over here somewhere," Adam interrupted, then he returned to his kitchen, scratching his ass as he went.

Gabrielle returned. She told me to stay with Adam while she went home to oversee the place-settings. I had no idea what that meant, but I told her I'd happily tag along. "That's sweet." she said. "I'll be back in no time and I'm sure Adam wants to show you his boat house. Have some fun, k." Before I could orchestrate another excuse, Gabrielle kissed me on the cheek and was gone.

"Heads up!" I heard.

I turned on a dime.

Adam had tossed a beer can at me. It was already in mid-air. I flinched only a little, and although I caught the can with ease, Adam chuckled and said, "Oh yeah. Soccer player. No good with the hands."

I looked at the beer. "I can't," I said. "I'm only eighteen—"

"What're you, a pussy?" he asked, interrupting me.

I wasn't a pussy, and I was in his house, so I popped open the beer and took down half in just a few chugs. He smiled in approval and asked if I wanted to see the lake. I said, "Yes", stopping myself from shouting, *I'm in for any place other than this giant shithole! Let's go for Christ's sake.*

He pulled a six-pack from the cooler beside the back door. We exited, crossing his cherry wood deck. As we made our way down the woodblock steps leading to his private pier and boathouse, he told me the story about his name. We passed a dune buggy and a tool shack, and next thing I knew, we were on the lake.

His pier harbored two jet-skis, a pontoon, wakeboards, a few inflated rafts, and a rowboat. There was a small entertainment room inside the rec house complete with three gaming systems, a full-sized refrigerator filled with beer, a bar replete with liquor, and a microwave-sized dehumidifier protecting two short rows of august looking cigars: a boy's paradise it was, occupied by a grown man living in boyhood. It only occurred to me then that Gabrielle had set this up intentionally. I'm not sure if she thought this was a cool way of showing off her family or if she thought Adam and I would actually get along (I can't imagine it was the latter), but Adam was about the least enjoyable person I'd ever met. He bragged openly about his wealth and women, swore a lot, spit, chewed with his mouth open, and he peer pressured me relentlessly to drink. He'd lived almost a decade longer, so that peer pressure was effective; I downed three cans before a wash of dizziness alerted me to slow down.

After about forty minutes of exploring his toys and gadgets, we returned to the house. As we crossed the deck, he let slip a secret of great importance. "I think it's because of Papa's cancer," he said at the end of some tirade I'd zoned out on.

The comment snapped me back to reality. "Francisco has cancer?" I asked.

"Yeah. Stage 2. Lungs this time. Never smoked a day in his life either, and now he's gotta fight to survive again. Can you believe that? After how hard he's worked?"

I knew from Gabrielle that her dad *did* have a smoking problem: he'd been struggling with it his whole adult life.

"No," I said. "I didn't know. I'm sorry."

"What?" Adam asked, voice raised.

"I'm sorry," I said, confused. "What is it?"

"Gabby didn't tell you? I thought y'all were serious."

"We are—"

"Wait, holy shit," he said. "I bet Gabby doesn't know. Papa hasn't told her. You can't tell her."

Shrugging with nonchalance, I said, "Okay."

I drank another sip of beer, set the can among many others on a side table, and when my eyes returned to Adam his eyebrows were raised and his finger was pointed between my eyes.

"Don't fucking tell Gabby, dude. I'm serious," he said.

"I'm not gonna tell her. Calm down."

"Don't tell me to calm down," he shot back.

"Look, I won't tell her," I said. "And by the way, she doesn't like to be called Gabby."

"Since when, motherfucker?"

"Since—"

"Doesn't matter," he interrupted. "Point is, she isn't supposed to know yet. Got it?"

I put up three fingers: Scouts' honor.

"What the hell is that?" Adam asked.

"You know? Scout's honor? Means I won't tell."

"Like Boy Scouts?"

"Yeah, like Boy Scouts."

"I knew it! Gaaaaay!" he belted, then he settled his feet on the cluttered coffee table, a smirk on his face exhibiting all the signs of a man very pleased with himself.

A few minutes later, by the grace of God, Gabrielle returned.

I stood like a baby-bird upon hearing the door.

"You're not dressed yet?" she half-shouted at Adam.

"I'm dressed." Adam answered.

"Adam," Gabrielle said like a weathered parent. "Change clothes."

"Gabby," Adam said like an untended brat, "you know Papa would kill me if I showed up dressed like this. Keep your socks on."

"That's not, like, a saying or anything. Just…" In frustration, Gabrielle turned away from her brother and looked at me.

"Good time?" she asked.

"Thrilling," I said. "We ready?"

I propped an elbow, Gabrielle palmed my bicep, and I turned so as to escort her out and away from this dreadful place.

"Be there soon, Gabby," Adam said after us.

Gabrielle stopped, released my arm, and looked back at her brother.

"It's Gabrielle," she said. "I've told you this, like, a million times."

"Big brother privileges. And hey, you" he said, moving his eyes to me, "remember what we talked about."

I nodded.

As we left Adam's lake house, Gabrielle asked. "Remember what?"

"Nothing at all," I told her. "Just the time."

9.

Gabrielle and I drove in silence the few minutes from Adam's lake house to her family's mansion. Her mind was on the luncheon. I didn't have to ask to know.

The car slowed, and we parked on the shoulder of a road near virgin woods. I could see a path going into the forest, and by the smell, I could tell we were still near the lake.

"What are we doing?" I asked her. "Where's this palace of yours?"

"It's not a palace, but this is the property," she said. "I thought we'd go the back way.

I tilted my head at her, unsold.

"What?" she asked, grinning at me. "I can be romantic." Then she reached over the center console and kissed me on the lips, saying, "Come."

I tilted my head the other way, very much sold.

Gabrielle led me through a ditch and into the woods. Though I had a strong buzz going from the beers on the lake—I'd never had alcohol in the morning and it was taking its toll—I had all the energy of a kid on Christmas. I enjoyed the lake air wafting through the leaves, and the pull of Gabrielle's hand on mine as we walked a laid path between the road and wherever we were going. My fingers intertwined with hers, my romantic notions satisfied and thankful and working: this was the last time I ever felt warmth for Gabrielle. Just like that, the empress put her clothes back on.

"Now aren't you glad we got you some new clothes," she said to me.

I stopped. Inertia pulled her fingers from mine.

"Nicolai," she huffed, immediately recognizing my shift in mood. "Don't stay upset. Please. Today is important to me."

"Sure."

"Don't do the sure thing."

"Sure, but I'm not upset," I told her. She didn't really see it—my building anger and discontent. She didn't even notice I was drunk. Thinking me sufficiently persuaded, she took my hand and we walked a bit further along the path.

There, in the woods, just as I was considering how I could most quickly and cleanly break us up, Gabby kissed me. She told me how much she appreciated my affection, and she told me it made her happy that I came to her luncheon. It felt like waking up. She said she understood my discomfort. She said she was excited for her parents to meet me. She said, before kissing me once more and for the last time, "I wouldn't want to be here with anyone else."

There, in the woods, I felt my heart turning back. I believed again in our little relationship and in my ability to sustain us; I believed I could keep my promise whole and glittering. I tried to remember how she loved me. I tried convincing myself that I owned some property in her heart.

"You've got a little something there," Gabrielle said, withdrawing a wet wipe from her handbag. "Just right here, right on your chin." She wiped my chin and cheeks the way a mother would a two-year-old.

That was it.

She straightened my tie and firmly slid down the shoulders of the shirt she bought me: it now tucked appropriately around my neck.

Another box checked, and I never believed in us again.

Once Gabrielle completed her inspection of my face, she smiled.

I did not smile back.

"Nicolai," she moaned.

"Yeah?" I asked.

"Today is important," she reminded me.

"You already said that," I reminded her.

"You're taking this the wrong way." She said it with all the sincerity of a gravedigger. "Think of it like this," she said, "if it were a big soccer banquet and I showed up looking completely different than everyone else, like overdressed in a prom gown, and I—"

"Hey, hey, hey," I said. "I get it. I really do. Sure."

"You say sure when you're upset," she replied.

"No, I don't," I answered. "I'm trying to be helpful."

The beer had kindled my anger, yes, but Gabrielle's misdirecting me into a forest so she could clean my face under the guise of a romantic stroll; *that* choice doused my anger in fuel. I had become the puppet; I had traded authentic loneliness for a false touch.

"We're gonna be late," I said. "Let's just go."

"Nicolai," Gabrielle said again. "I'm sorry." It was almost funny to witness an apology spill from Gabby's face, how badly she wished she meant it, but it spilled out empty and fell flat regardless, dying on the floor at her feet.

"Sorry for what?" I asked.

"You're like a parent. Will you just, like, accept it."

Bickering in the woods was pointless; the faster I got out of there the faster I could get back home. The place wasn't right for me.

"Sure," I said again. "Now come on. We're gonna be late."

Time was running low, so Gabrielle accepted my fake apology for punctuality's sake and we continued our loveless stroll, my hands pocketed, her hands texting.

The way I saw it, we had three options for a quick getaway.

1 – Get more drunk: make myself detestable to her family. This seemed dramatic.

2 – Make a scene: instigate a loud, public argument with Gabrielle. This seemed petty.

3 – Punch the brother: deliver social justice to a man-aged boy. This seemed awesome.

Unfortunately, as it often goes for teenage boys, I underestimated the power of tequila.

10.

Her house was a Monet: an 8,000 square-foot villa situated atop a hill overlooking the same reservoir lake from which I picked flowers for Jessica. This shore was for the already rich: not us. The luncheon took place on an outdoor mezzanine facing the water. The air smelled wonderful. The food smelled even better. Jet skis, canoes, and a sailboat were at play on the water, and all of it was framed by a picturesque view of thick Appalachian forest rolling over the horizon. To call it a luncheon was to understate; this was a banquet complete with 115 guests, eight caterers, a string quartet, two photographers, and white-clothed tables covered in fine china, sterling silver utensils, earthy floral centerpieces, and name badges propped up on decorative holders. The day was sunny, the weather was flawless, and for whatever reason, when I saw this version of heaven, all I could think to myself was, *I gotta get outta here!*

Gabrielle began mingling as soon as we arrived. One of her aunts asked her to say hello to a couple of cousins standing on the far end of the lawn, and, without a word, she left me standing alone, and I just stood there like a dope, brooding over our exchange in the woods, holding a cup of punch in one hand and a small plate of fishy hors d'oeuvres in the other.

"Hey rookie," I heard from behind me. I didn't have to turn around to know it was Adam. He had changed clothes but was still wearing those salmon shorts. His brand new white shirt had been unpacked and pressed for him. The shiny gold buttons of his blue blazer twinkled in the sun.

"What?" I said to Adam.

"A surprise, dipshit. Come on."

Adam led me away from the venue and into the smaller of the property's two guest houses. Once inside, he dared me to take a shot of Patron from a flask he'd smuggled into the party. I was drawn to the rebellion, so I downed a flowing shot. I wasn't ready; not even close. The tequila singed my throat. I spewed and coughed instantly.

Adam's shot went down next. He took an enormous swig without even a scrunch of the face.

Ten minutes and three shots of tequila later, I jumped the *buzzed* hurdle and landed squarely into *drunk-as-fuck*. I knew I was drunk too, because my feet were on the ground and I caught myself enjoying Adam's mindless company. He was assessing the event's sexiest non-family attendees—Victoria topped his list.

"Gabby's gonna get pissed if we don't get back," I said.

"Gabby doesn't like to be called Gabby," Adam said, then he checked his watch, and we rushed back to the party.

There were twelve tables at the banquet with ten settings each. Like a tangent, a buffet line of eleven trays and seven dessert spreads were attended by three servers at-the-ready.

"I dare you to talk to Victoria," I said to Adam, referring to the fifty-five-year-old woman who topped his *bang list* (his term, not mine.)

"You're a kid," he said. "I don't take dares from kids."

"You're a kid, you lake bum!" I bantered back.

The banter didn't take. Adam dismissed me with a smirk and a wave of the hand before saying, "Whatever, son." He turned hard left away from me towards a group of four dudes who I assume were relatives or friends of superior class, and once more, I was left to stew alone, a stranger in a strange place, only this time I was blotto.

I spotted Gabrielle standing on the far end of the lawn near a receiving table, a mountain of gifts stacked atop it. To her left stood a stout man in a dark blue three-piece suit; this was Francisco, Patriarch of the Zacapas. To Gabrielle's right stood Francisco's young wife dressed in red; this was Estelle, Adam and Gabrielle's third mother. Gabrielle, her father and her mother were facing a semi-circle of partygoers standing a step or two below them—an admiring court. Every few seconds, the court let out a belly of laughter. Gabrielle looked happy, but then we met eyes, and as I took first steps towards her, she left her parents, stomping in my direction. She wore a smile fake as Fool's Gold as she neared. Unfortunately for her, I was already turned way, way up.

"Where on Earth have you been, Nicolai?" she asked as she reached for my tie to straighten it.

I swatted her hand away, slapping her knuckles.

She looked aghast. "What's the matter with you?" she exclaimed.

"I'm not Adam," I stammered.

"What does that mean?"

"I'm not a baby. I don't need your preppy little fingers mauling my tie. I don't need your apple sauce."

"My applesauce? You're like Adam—that's not a thing! And what's wrong with you? Are you drunk?"

"You wish I was drunk, so you'd have something to blame."

She shook her head and reached for my tie again.

"Stop it!" I screamed, slapping her hand once more.

"Keep your voice down," she whispered through gritted teeth.

"I already said to you that I'm not a fucking baby boy."

She pointed her finger at me just like her brother had. "Don't you *ever* swear at me."

I leaned close to her pointy, entitled finger, teasing it to poke me in the eye. "That's all you do," I said. "You just point and prod and prop me up."

"What?"

"That's all you do," I said lazily. "You take me and try to take something that's already really, really, really, really good, and you try to make it perfect. Like it's your job."

"No. That's not it."

"I'm not good enough this way and it hurts."

"You're being dramatic, Nico," she said.

"Don't call me that. I'm telling you it hurts!"

"This isn't the time," she shouted, "and it is definitely not the place."

"You dressed me like a doll so your friends and your mommy and your daddy would like me. It's sick."

"You're being dramatic, Nico!"

"Don't call me that!" I screamed. "That was Summer's name for me. You damn sure don't have that privilege."

Gabrielle stepped back. "Go wash your face," she said. "Not for me, but for you. The grime on your brow seems to be turning you into an asshole."

Gabrielle marched away and took her rightful place beside her parents. I've found in my many failures that women are quite poetic when angry, and, I must admit, the whole grime-brow-asshole comment ranks right up there with the all-time comebacks. I took her advice, returned to the guest house, and washed my face in the sink of the kitchenette. Even had one of those cinematic stare-at-myself-in-the-mirror moments. I felt out of body with the booze; I had no car, no way to get home, no exit strategy, and thoughts of the circus outside circled in my head like a carousel; Adam's rejection after our fun, Gabrielle's queenly demands on my attire and words, even the unknown specifics of Papa Zacapa's disapproval. I smiled my game-face on, found some Listerine, rinsed my mouth, and gargled away as much tequila as I could. I left the bathroom with a foreboding sense of disaster, and an expectation that I'd be the agent thereof.

11.

When I exited the guesthouse, the party was transitioning from informal chit-chat to formal lunch. Most of the guests were already seated. I saw Gabrielle and motioned for her to meet me away from the tables. I apologized to her for my earlier comment (a half-lie), told her I wasn't drunk (a full lie), that I was grateful to be here (another lie), and that I'd be on my best behavior (a shamefully, unacceptable lie). Her eyes were suspicious, but appeased.

I escorted her to our table, a twelve-seat round stationed on a low stage in the middle of the party. Gabrielle introduced me to seven family members whose names I promptly forgot.

Then, we sat. Three seats remained empty; one across from us and the two to Gabrielle's left.

"Where're your parents?" I asked.

She shrugged. "Probably fighting."

"About what?"

"I don't know, Nicolai. Married people stuff," then she turned to a cousin sitting three seats to her left and for the fourth time I was left alone.

I reached for a piece of bread but stopped when I noticed no one else was eating. That's when Adam sat in the empty chair across from us. He carried with him an overflowing plate of lobster enchiladas, chips, and a smattering of sides. He ate, sounding his satisfaction in obnoxious groans of pleasure while ignoring the sideways glances coming from me and the seven Zacapas. No one else had served themselves yet because the food line wasn't set, and Adam, either deliberately oblivious or wantonly trying to get the table's goat, looked up and said without prompting, "What? Y'all can wait if you want, but I'm not waiting." He gobbled down more rice and said with a full mouth, "I'm starving."

Eyes rolled. Conversations continued. Had I done something so crass at a family event, Mom would've kicked my ass and been handed a medal for the effort. I decided this was the time. I engaged the enemy.

"How's the food?" I asked sarcastically of Adam. (Where he received only rolling eyes for his impatience, my confrontational words brought table conversation to a standstill.)

"It's good," Adam said. "You should get some."

"I'll wait my turn," I answered, holding his gaze.

"Damn right you will."

Gabrielle patted me on the leg.

"Don't do that!" I shouted at her. She was—to my total satisfaction and for the first time ever—speechless.

Adam set down his fork with a clank. "Boy. Don't talk to my sister like that. You're a guest—"

"Shut up! You don't even know her name. You don't know anything. Just eat your food."

He slammed his knife onto the plate. "After all my hospitality," he said.

"You're drunk!" I yelled at him.

"So are you!" he yelled back.

"No, I'm not. I'm overwhelmed."

"Overwhelmed by what? Being a prick?"

"It's Gabrielle's graduation and you've been an asshole all day. What would Papa Zacapa say if he saw you acting like this?"

"You don't get to say his name," Adam said militantly as he stood.

"Nicolai, stop," Gabrielle demanded, placing her palm atop my hand, but I ripped it away before she could nail me.

"Don't talk about Papa," Adam said, as if entranced. "Don't you ever talk about Papa."

"Sit down, Adam," Gabrielle pled.

"Quiet, Gabby. Looks like your little soccer-player boy-toy has something on his mind." He rounded the table—he was really coming at me.

I stood up.

"We gonna fight?" I said.

"No, son." He said back. "I'm gonna kick your ass."

I'd never instigated a fight, but I was fit, fast, strong from training, and ready to party! But Adam was ten years my senior—maybe more—and it all happened way faster than I could see. Before I knew it, Adam was on me, and he landed a sucker punch from Hell right on my jaw. (I'd never been in a fight, period.) I reached for the tablecloth as I fell, pulling it down with me. Water and tea and bread and butter and forks and spoons and plates and flowers and place-holders sprayed and splashed and clanked and flew about the lawn. One of these items— I'm not sure which—struck my face and opened a cut above my left eye. Gabrielle screamed as Adam pounced to hit me again. I rolled, dodging the attack, then I jumped to my feet and tackled him, and we rumbled on the lawn like idiots as Adam rattled off a string of mostly-invented swears. It climaxed fast. Within seconds, friends and family began prying us apart. I calmed quickly, but it required three wise-looking men to restrain Adam. I hadn't even landed a proper strike. As with the rest of his life, Adam survived the consequences of his personality without even a slight bruise to show for it. I had to even the score. It was incumbent on me now.

I wiped flower petals from my tie. My face was spattered in blood from the cut over my eye, but I barely noticed that over the throbbing pain in my jaw. I noticed two developments; one awful, the other opportune. First, Gabrielle was crying. Second, her parents were hustling down the hill towards the luncheon. Already up to my neck in this fiasco, I chose to sate my new lust, and of all the things that happened that afternoon, this next decision is my only deep regret.

"How can you be so disrespectful," I shouted at Adam. "Especially considering you told me your father has…"

And I just let the sentence trail off.

There were at least two dozen family members in earshot of my deliberate slip. Their imaginations went quickly to work. Gabrielle looked at me through tears, then at Adam, then back at me, asking, "Papa has what, Nicolai?"

I shrugged and straightened myself.

Her eyes turned to Adam. All eyes turned to Adam.

"Adam, what is it?"

"Tell us."

"What's going on?"

"Just tell us the truth."

These were pleadings, a begging for disclosure. The swell of pressure broke Adam's silence before his parents could arrive to reel in the madness. He shouted it. "Cancer, okay! Lungs!"

The world stopped—it was like Jesus himself had hit a mute button—and I summoned a conspiring grin for Adam so he'd know *I did this to him.*

"Add that to your story, you asshole."

When Papa Zacapa arrived, the party parted like the Red Sea, and he found himself soaked in a maelstrom of anger, sadness, and confusion.

"Cancer?" Gabrielle asked him.

The patriarch looked at me, harsh eyed, and I looked away.

He approached Adam and raised a hand. Adam turned his cheek to receive a blow that never came; though composed, Papa Zacapa looked so angry I thought his head might catch on fire.

I was quickly (and rightfully) asked to leave. Gabrielle didn't protest my expulsion. I don't blame her for that. I was escorted up the hill by a gang of very large Zacapas before being passed over to a gray-haired butler who behaved with elegance and polish as he drove me home in the Zacapa family Bentley.

I'd come up: it was and is by far the most prestigious vehicle I've ever sat in. The ride home was sublime, just like in all the stories.

12.

During the ride, neither shame nor embarrassment appeared—all I felt was drunk and shell-shocked—but both feelings washed over me in torrents when I entered my home. I'd loved my house once upon a time, but now it seemed peasanty. Mom wasn't there to ask me about the bruise on my jaw or the dried blood over my left eye or the stains on my clothes or how I'd come by this new wardrobe. She wouldn't have liked it. I'd changed. I'd seen. And I was glad she wasn't there to ask me how or what. I, for one, had no clue as to either.

I took off the empress's new clothes, and after that, angry and nude, shoved the shirt and tie and socks into a trash bag, snuck outside, and pressed the trash bag deep into our trash bin before starting the longest, hottest shower of my life. The water scalded, but I bore it.

After this shower, I downshifted to my very lowest, my terminal denominator.

Dad, I thought.

Loneliness took hold of me. All energy, it seemed, had been suddenly siphoned into my heartache, and I lacked even enough strength to dry off. I lay on my bed, wet and hot and in pain, and thought of my dead father; just him—my Dad—and the fact of his passing. I'd failed him again, more miserably than ever. I had no promise or gift to tend to, *which incompleted me.* I felt naked beyond my nudity, and I cried out in pain, and I hid undercover once more, then passed into sleep.

13.

I awoke.

14.

Gabrielle and I didn't talk for a few days; I think we both knew our relationship was headed nowhere. Though we did share a pretense of repair over the following weeks, we behaved more like a football team down by three touchdowns late in the fourth quarter: it's all formality at that point.

As expected, her father killed our final hope. He commandeered the phone during our last argument. "Son," he said, all big and burly, not a hint of Hispanic in his refined tongue. "I want you to listen very closely to me. This is not some game. This is my daughter. My one and only. And I will not—" and I bet his voice kept rising until a dial tone informed him that Nicolai was long gone.

All for the best, I think.

Gabrielle graduated. I graduated. Our lives moved on. Gabrielle refused to compromise her values the way I had. She wouldn't even test it. I think Dad's philosophy appropriately sums up the shortage that broke us: reciprocity is the currency of relationships; the more you have, the richer you are. In this manner, Gabby and Nicky were dirt poor.

Gabrielle landed a big-time internship at Exxon Mobil after her sophomore year at Emory. She's pacing for *Summa Cum Laude* and still looks the part—big toothy smile, cheerleader energy. I was completely surprised when I saw a picture of her boyfriend, a 6'7" semi-professional black hockey player named Conan.

As for me? Following a brief and depressing alienation from life, I fell into my next romantic adventure. She includes, among other fare, a shoulder stabbing, an accidental marriage proposal, bounty hunters, a little toe lost to a bullet, significant property damage, wedded handguns, and lots and lots of hot, hot sex.

Yeah…all for the best.

LIZA WANES

"I think the quality of sexiness comes from within. It is something that is in you or it isn't and it really doesn't have much to do with breasts or thighs or the pout of your lips."
—SOPHIA LOREN

1.

enior year ended. I graduated 22nd.

I had somehow survived Serena's loathing, Becca's soon-to-be-Mayor dad, something akin to attempted manslaughter by Summer's hand, and Gabrielle's lofty appeal. When my failures pressed their way into focus, I blurred them though accusations of misfortune and poor timing. I wrote often about the challenges I'd faced and the rules I'd collected. I didn't feel incapable, not really. I felt unlucky.

I feel that way still.

I earned a partial scholarship for soccer. My remaining expenses were covered by Georgia's HOPE scholarship program. Mom cried when she left campus, lingering a bit about the details of my dorm and expressing pride about all my (non-romantic) accomplishments. I walked Mom out, thanked her for a lifetime of love, and emphasized a hundred times that I'd be alright. With that, she departed, and my college career commenced.

In one word, freshman year was unremarkable.

The first days of orientation thrilled me—beautiful ladies, free-flowing booze, boyish debauchery building in the halls—but I soon found this setting and these women and time itself disrupting my aspiration. On top of twenty hours of soccer practice per week and a full load of classes, I became involved in student government and worked as a research assistant in the business school. And as for women, well, options for them are a smorgasbord. Besides, they're guarded at the start, warned by fathers to protect their treasures and to stay out of trouble. As a result, my quest *to become the very best* idled in life's background. It was an era of failed mini-romances and fanciful start-ups that never found a market.

I met olive-skinned Claire at an off-campus Olive Garden in November. She was a hostess there. A few teammates and I had stopped in after soccer practice for a meal. For thirty minutes, they prodded my pride, saying I didn't have the balls to ask for Claire's number. So, obviously, I approached Claire. Smiling kindly, I introduced myself and asked if I could call her, and she happily obliged, reciting her digits almost impatiently. This troubled me very much: Woody Allen summarizes the sentiment of easy accomplishment best in his opening to *Annie Hall*. From Groucho Marx, it goes, "I don't want to be a part of any club that would have me as a member."

Claire and I talked a few times on the phone before going on our first and only date. When I asked what she was into, her answer came back flat as a pancake. "I like music," she said. "Oh, and I like movies too."

"No way, you like music AND movies," I joked. "Well, well, what a coincidence. Me too." (She didn't pick up on my playful sarcasm, nor did she get specific about her tastes.)

My concern in dating Claire extended beyond her aloofness. Her foremost quality, if I had to choose a word, was disconnectedness, a lack of curiosity that may have been genetic. She shared with me on our drive back from the restaurant a peculiar factoid about her parents; they did puzzles together, like eight per year. She showed me several pictures she kept in her purse. They were huge works, 3,000-5,000 pieces, and her home, as she described it, was covered wall-to-wall with framed projects. That boredom seems to have trickled into Claire's heart, and while I don't have a formal rule for this, I don't date boring people.

Or bankers.

The next summer, Mona and I attended a concert series on newest Chattahoochee Riverwalk. Mona was drinking beer and let me have my fill from her red solo cup. We were sitting on a red blanket with a few of her friends. Mona had evolved away from her Catholicism, but she retained an outspoken spirituality, which I envy to this day. She was far more honest about her feelings than I thought

I could ever be about mine. I was feeling a bit lit, so when Mona and her friends went to the main lawn for some dancing, I lay down on our communal blanket, closed my eyes, and tried to enjoy the echoes of the far-off stage. The cover band was playing, "Heard it Through the Grapevine." I was relaxing there, soaked in the air, when Shelby Marie Prescott made her approach. As the name suggests, she was a country girl.

"Hi there," she said in full southern drawl; the cute sort, high-pitched, enthusiastic, kind. I looked up and saw her standing over me. "I'm Shelby Marie. You look familiar. Did you go to Central?"

She was dressed simply in a white blouse, jean shorts, and scuffed Sketchers. Her legs were fit, her nails were manicured, her smile was natural; it all made for a very good start. (And anyway, I'm not one to turn down an approach. Pickiness is a terribly cumbersome enemy to romance.) "Central? No." I said, covering my eyes against the sun.

"I could've sworn…you must just look like somebody else then."

"I must look like someone, yes," I said as I sat up.

"You don't wanna dance, do you?" she asked. "I'm bored as a pigeon and, well, you look like the dancin' sort."

A brief vertigo swept over me—the drinking and sitting up converging all too quickly—and I fell over onto my elbows. As I recovered and reopened my eyes, I smiled and told Shelby Marie, "I'm not drunk. Honestly. I promise."

"Then that makes one of us!" she half-shouted. "So? dance? Mr. I'm-Not-Drunk-But-I'm-Stumbling-All-About." She giggled, and I figured a little dancing couldn't hurt.

I said, "Yes."

There were hundreds of people on the lawn. The band was playing James Brown. Sunset colors streaked around us, its purples and navies spread across the backdrop of the Thirteenth Street Bridge, and I thought myself lucky for Shelby Marie's company. This sentiment died, however, the moment Shelby Marie began to dance.

This one didn't dance like a country girl: she danced like a rabid hyena who'd just found a fresh carcass. When she wasn't literally jumping up and down like a kangaroo she was so goddamn grabby you might've thought she was a crab. It was altogether a horribly energetic experience. I hoped it would dissipate, but her energy kept climbing. Three songs later, I surrendered. The exertion necessary to keep up with Shelby Marie beyond my resources, and I wasn't about to sacrifice more of a beautiful evening for spontaneous exercise, especially when I had more sensible company nearby.

"I'm gonna go lay back down," I told her after several songs. "The drinking, you know?"

"I thought you said you weren't drunk?"

"Dancing made me drunker," I said.

"Aww," she pouted. "Alright."

Mona and her friends had returned to our blankets and coolers on the lawn. I introduced them to Shelby Marie, then I set about ending this chance meeting of ours.

"Thanks for the dancing," I said. "It was very…aerobic."

"Yeah, me too," she said laughing. "Aerobic."

Then, Ms. Shelby Marie just stood there…waiting.

"Let me get your number," I said, the standard duty of a gentleman.

She wrote it on a piece of paper I tore from a magazine Mona had along, and I told Shelby Marie I'd call. In the days that followed, I considered it—I really did, "strongly" considered, I'd say—but I never followed through. I threw it away. I asked for her number because my only other option was to *not* ask for her number. She might've interpreted this as, "I don't like you enough to talk to you ever again, so scram!" Delivering romantic hurt in the name of a temporary and meaningless truth serves nothing but the truth itself, a poor master if you ask me. It is neither the purpose of romance nor an element of kind courting. I still had thoughts of being *the very best,* and that responsibility extended to Shelby Marie, even if all we ever shared was a semi-exceptional dusk.

2.

Sophomore year began like the freshman one; unremarkably.

Early in the year, our soccer team participated in a two-day tournament. The fields were 140 miles from campus. On the first day we played two short matches, and I needed to impress because the new coach had me on the chopping block for roster cuts. My first and only playing time came at the end of the second game when I was subbed in on defense to hold a tie. Tragically, in the last moments, I turned during a corner kick and the striker I was supposed to be guarding jumped up and I tripped over my own feet and he headed the ball in for the winning goal, and then, trying to stand up, I tumbled again and fell backwards on my ass. There were over two hundred people in the bleachers; their roar of laughter still haunts my dreams. It was unequivocally the most embarrassing sports moment of my life.

Though they were just exhibitions, I couldn't turn off my remorse. I couldn't rationalize my embarrassment away. I sat staring out the window of our fifteen-passenger van all the way to the hotel. I remember wanting to call Mom.

As we neared the hotel, I refused my teammates' requests to join them for dinner. I blamed my courses and they believed me: the business school was notorious for homework. I dropped my bag beside my bed and took a shower. I ruminated on the scratchy couch, flipping through the few available channels before giving up. Again, I considered calling Mom so she could tell me how awesome I was, but I thought better of it. I was, after all, about to turn twenty. It felt childish to lean on anyone, let alone my mother. I thought I didn't need her anymore.

I needed a change of scene, so I went four flights down to the hotel bar. I just wanted a Sprite, a little *SportsCenter*, and to be left alone. It was in this deflated, half-desperate mood that I met Liza Caplan. I doubt asking for a Sprite ever produced a more wonderful side-effect.

Call it coincidence or call it good luck, the time had finally come for my education in sex.

3.

She was sitting impossibly on the middle stool of an empty, twelve-seat bar. A stout, overalls-bearing bartender, the only other human there, had just handed her a book of matches, and had set before her three tealights in metal-wire holders. The place was red walls and forest green lamps on brass stands, dark wood and no music. I saw myself in the wall-mirror behind the dusty liquor bottles. That's where I first met her eyes, green like grass, but it was only a glance. The three unburnt candles didn't match the place. The bronze, silver, and gold hues of their containers didn't match either. Soon enough, I would learn about the impossible woman's four-year old son, her fat dog, an ex-husband, and the exhilarating occupation that brought her to the bar, but all I knew at first was her smoking hot hotness: she was a twenty-year-old spirit trapped in a flawless, forty-year-old body. She wore a sleeveless dress that gave away nothing, and I could see the lines of the muscles of her shoulder as she lifted the matchbook. She possessed a sexuality emboldened by experience: you could see it in her eyes if you knew what you were looking for. (I didn't yet, but that's not the point.) She lit the match, the gaze of the bartender glued to her steady fingers. As she let the tiny flame settle, I noticed a twenty-dollar bill on the bar, between two of the candles. She lit one tealight, then another, but as she reached for the third, I sat in the fifth seat, and the match went out.

Her name was Liza.

The bartender smiled playfully at Liza, who stared at the twenty as he took it away, then he looked at me. "Ay, friend," he said, Australian or British or Welch or something: I honestly had no idea. "What can I do you for?"

"Huh?"

"Whudya like, mate?"

"Sprite. Just Sprite actually. You have Sprite?"

He nodded and grabbed a glass from the overhead shelf, and when I glanced to my right, I caught the black-haired woman staring at me from two stools down. I smiled and looked away, and for the next sixty seconds, I wondered what all men wonder when they catch the eye of such a woman: *is it me, or is she really an angel?*

A minute later, I caught her eyes again. This time, she grinned and looked away.

"How's it going?" I said.

She fingered the stem of her triangular glass. "Good," she said. "Other than the twenty." She sipped her cocktail.

"How's your martini?"

"Delicious," she replied. The drink had a light red hue to it. I know now that it wasn't a martini: it was a cosmopolitan. She must've thought I was the cutest little thing.

The bartender had been fiddling with his beverage gun the whole time. Apparently,

Sprite had run out. From down the bar, he shouted, "Syrup's all cashed mate. We'll go get 'im switched." The little man then disappeared down some stairs hidden behind the liquor display, where he vanished. Liza and I were alone in record time.

"What're you in town for?" I asked.

"Maybe I just live here and I like the drinks they make."

"OK. Do you?"

"No," she said playfully.

"Oh, OK. I live like over a hundred miles away from here. Well, school that is, my home's like, I don't know, a hundred and fifty maybe. But I'm here for soccer. In Europe, they call it football though." I continued rambling. She made me nervous. Her eyes hadn't left mine but mine couldn't hold hers for more than a second at a time and here I was explaining the linguistics of sport. Yeah; she must've thought I was the cutest little thing.

"That's all very interesting," she said after I finished. "Look, honey, I won't scratch you. I'm having a drink, you've got your Sprite. All's well."

Where is the goddamn bartender? I thought. My crotch stiffened. My heart thumped. I felt unprepared and out-of-place and outclassed, so Liza laid an olive branch at my feet.

"What's your name?" she asked. "Mine's Liza."

"Nicolai," I said.

"Do people call you Nicolai or do you have a nickname?"

"I like Nicolai," I answered.

"Then that's something we have in common."

"What's something we have in common?"

"Liking Nicolai," she answered as she returned the cocktail to her mouth.

Oh, how I wanted to be that glass. I gulped an ocean of nerves, then asked, "Is Liza short for Elizabeth?"

"It is." she answered, withdrawing a tube of lipstick from her handbag.

"Well, there you go."

"Well, there I go, what?" she asked, uncapping it.

"People don't think about this, but it's like nickname rules somebody told me. See, you have to shorten four syllable names—" as I talked, she freshened up her little lips with a thrilling shade of red "—because people don't have time enough to say it. Three syllables though, Ni-co-lai, people don't mind that."

"I'd call you Nicky," she said, puckering her lips and checking the result in the mirror across the bar.

"Nicky's not really my thing," I told her.

"Nico, then," she said. "How about Nico?"

I'd known Liza for only a few minutes, and already I was happy, so it was fine that she used Summer's name.

"I don't mind Nico," I said.

"I'm sure you don't," she answered, not missing a beat.

"I'm sure you don't, too," I retorted, missing beats left and right.

"Nicolai," she said, turning her firm body towards me. "How old are you?"

"I'm twenty-one," I said.

"And you're drinking a Sprite?"

"It's the soccer thing. I can't—"

"When's your birthday?" she interrupted.

"Why?"

"Tell me quick, when's your birthday?"

"October twelfth."

"Columbus Day, nice. What year?"

"Nineteen-eighty…" it was the slightest hesitation, but it was hesitation enough. "Eight?"

"Awww, honey," she said, swiveling her stool back again. "So close."

"So close what?" I asked. "It's eight."

"I bet you're a good liar under normal circumstances, aren't you?"

"I'm not a liar. I'm not lying," I said.

"There you go again."

I was scrambling, trying to claw my way back into contention. "Alright," I said, "I don't lie very much. Is that better?"

"Depends on your amends. How old are you?" Liza asked again.

"Nineteen. I'm a sophomore at State."

"I bet October twelfth is your real birthday, isn't it?"

"What makes you think I'd lie about the year but not the day?" I asked.

"Because a great liar can spot a good liar easy."

"And are you a great liar?" I asked.

"Of course I am," she said. Then she took another sip. "I'm a lawyer."

"But I didn't know you were a lawyer," I said.

"That's because I'm not a lawyer," she replied with a smile. "I was just making my point about being a great liar."

That's when she took a cherry from the bar's little produce tray, bit the fruit from its vine, chewed, and swallowed. It was the sexiest thing I'd ever seen. "A good liar," she continued, "is one who keeps as many truths as possible. It makes the length of lies easier to handle. But I'm sure you already know that, Nico."

I did know that, but not with the thoughtfulness of her explanation. Just as I was settling into the conversation's tempo, the bartender returned with my Sprite. He set it on the bar and it clacked against the wood like the cockblock he was.

"Can I put this on the room?" I asked him.

"Sure 'idn't set to pay as so."

I looked at him dumbly.

"You'll need to pay here, mate," he clarified.

"Mine," Liza said. "I got it. A thanks for the conversation."

"But—"

"Don't fret, Nico. I'm on a per diem."

I had no idea what that meant, but I nodded back, pretending that I had. That's when I noticed the purse hanging from the back of her bar stool; a lavender Chanel, a thing of beauty. I, fortunately, understood the significance of such an accessory.

"It's lovely," I said, a new note of confidence intoned.

"What's that, honey?"

"Your Chanel," I said. "The color matches the stripes on your blouse. Do you have others?"

"Other blouses with stripes?" she asked.

"No. More designer purses. Is that a thing for you?"

Her smile verified to me that the play had worked. "I've been obsessed with purses since before ten, but I just have the one," she said. "It was very hard to come by."

"What do you mean?"

She popped open her purse again and withdrew a glossy beige business card. She set it down like an apple from Eden and slid it down the bar halfway between us.

I glanced at the bartender. He raised an eyebrow at me.

"Call me after your birthday," Liza said. "I'd be happy to tell you all about it."

"My birthday?"

"You're a teenager, Nico. You'll be twenty in a month. That'll do much better for me. We all have our rules."

I picked up my soda and took the card she'd set down. I caught her grinning at me in the reflection of the mirror across the bar. "I can stay a while," I said. "You could tell me about the handbag or your work or…Honestly, you could tell me anything. Anything at all."

"No, no," she said. "I'm sure you have to rest up and I'm in a mood to be alone."

I slipped the card into my sweatpants pocket and turned to walk away. "Can I call you sooner than my birthday?" I asked.

"No," she said.

"Are you sure?"

"Not a day sooner. I'll be very put off if you do. Call it Liza's Law."

"Why though?" I whispered. I'm not sure why.

"Because you're a teenager, Nicky. I already told you twice. Three's no good."

"I don't like Nicky."

"That's okay. It makes sense that you don't understand, but that's the whole why. Now go."

"I won't want to tell anyone," I said. "I promise."

"You promise?"

She turned fully on her stool to face me. The bartender was cleaning watermarks from freshly rinsed wine glasses behind her. Strings of light glowed in parallel lines on her perfectly straight black hair, and the moody lamplight muted every color in the room, spare the light purple stripes across her blouse, her matching Chanel, and the powerful green hue of her eyes. "Honey," she said, confident as a cat, "you're going to want to tell everyone."

4.

I hardly slept a wink. Following our game the next morning, my team returned to campus. Staring out the window of our bumpy van, I daydreamed the whole two hours about that woman at the bar, about Liza. I pained myself trying *not* to think about her: my twentieth birthday was still over a month away.

When I got to my dorm, I hid Liza's business card in an old textbook and began pretending like she didn't exist. My strategy was to wait until my birthday and take it from there—I worried I might go crazy if I didn't.

My strategy failed later that afternoon.

"Honey, you're going to want to tell everyone," she'd said.

Over and over I heard it. Every night, just before falling asleep, I'd hold the card under lamplight and examine its details endlessly. I worried it would disappear if I didn't. I tried to memorize its texture with my fingertips.

October finally showed up. By then, Liza Caplan had consumed me.

Ten days before my birthday, I woke from a nightmare just minutes before three. I sat on the bed's edge and rubbed my temples, as if that would squeeze the crazy out. I'd been swimming peacefully in a pond of white wine, and as I waded ashore, a family of ducks carrying umbrellas strolled by. That's the random part of the dream. The read-into-it part was my former love, Summer, standing on the grassy shore in her basketball uniform urging me out. As I rose to my feet, wine dripping from my fingertips and cock, she said, *"Honey, you're going to want to tell everyone."*

I awoke in sweats. My dick was dry.

Sometimes, honestly, I thought I was suffering from a legit mental malfunction, like maybe I made it all up; like maybe my thirteen years of trying to understand women had driven me nuts. Other times, I thought it was sexual karma returning a favor, like maybe I was being rewarded because I never pressured girls for sex. Most often though, I just thought I was a pervert. I fantasized about sex with Liza constantly. I hoped beyond hope that this singular instant—this far-fetched opportunity and precious moment in time—would materialize my daydreams into reality.

"Honey, you're going to want to tell everyone."

What could it mean? Did it mean what I thought it meant? Was she playing me? Was she a composed drunk messing with a frustrated kid who only wanted a Sprite and some time to himself? My God! Had she already forgotten me?

In class, I'd get random hard-ons remembering her stilettos. At soccer practice, I played sloppily thinking of her eyes. Everywhere I walked, I heard it—drive-thru attendants, radio commercials, billboards. *"Honey, you're going to want to tell everyone."* Lust was at play here—at the beginning it was all I felt, or all I thought I felt—but by October the central theme of my longing had changed. Liza brought my loneliness back into focus. She reminded my heart of what it'd been missing; the thrill of companionship, the sharing of time and of feeling and of warmth, the synergies, the unnatural and naturally perfect state of togetherness, and etcetera and etcetera with every girl I passed on campus and every magazine cover I saw and all the kissing couples on benches and at parties and at games. I was increasingly tormented by my failures during these weeks of waiting, and I felt embarrassed at myself. Malaise descended onto my outlook to accompany the unattractive stubble I'd allowed to fester on my cheeks. I had officially lost control, so I did what I always do when romantic stress takes over my rationality.

Retreat.

At the end of a long morning run, I sat on a bench on the border of our campus's botanical garden. Once again, my thoughts settled on Liza. I closed my eyes. My mind cleared. My breathing slowed. *Consider her,* I thought. *Be the very best and consider what you know. What kind of man would she want you to be? Consider her, then act.* Liza would want cool. She'd want mature. A woman like that, comfortable enough to entice a nineteen-year-old boy, would want forward interest and romance.

It was like Revelations. I knew exactly what to do!

The mere thought of my incredible new plan brought me a sudden and complete calm. I stood and sprinted back to my tiny dorm and began laying this plan as best I could. Liza said I couldn't call her until my birthday—Liza's Law, a law I would never break—but Liza hadn't said a single word about sending mail.

5.

Her card read:

> *Elizabeth Caplan / Ferriter, Wallis, & Keen*
> *103-A McGraw St.*
> *Columbus, GA 31314*
> *719-375-3937*

My plan was to purchase her attention.

Mom and Dad started college trusts for Mona and me on our first birthdays. Since most of my tuition was paid for with scholarships, the trust deposited three thousand bucks into my bank account in May of my freshman year, a service the trust would repeat every May until I turned thirty. When the first deposit landed in my account, I celebrated alone in my room and raised a shot of smuggled Jameson to Dad, with a real smile, one bereft of any sadness. I wrote him a letter and put a fake address on the envelope with no return address at its top, then I slipped it into a post office receptacle around the corner. This, I thought, would be my yearly ritual—a shot and a letter—my little own memorialization.

Fall break began, a five-day recess from soccer and school that began on a Wednesday. After breakfast with Mom and her new boyfriend, Tony, I drove ninety miles to the closest Louis Vuitton store. Combining my trust money with restaurant work and odd jobs, my savings totaled about fifty-five hundred dollars. I withdrew three hundred bucks from an ATM, entered the store, examined a few price tags, and promptly drove back to the bank for more money. I searched the store for over an hour. It was like being eight again, seeking the perfect flowers for Jessica. (Romance hadn't changed really; it just grew up.) Ultimately, I chose a beige bag with leather handles, its body completely yet subtly checkered with Louis' famous monogram. It cost me thirteen hundred bucks, by far the most expensive item I'd ever purchased.

I went to a post office, put her address on the box with a fake return address at the top, then I slipped it to the service clerk, paid another few to get it to Liza, and went about my day. The present would arrive at Liza's doorstep in three days, October eleventh, the day before my birthday. It was perfect. I'd done so well!

…or so I felt for a few minutes…

I left the post office and sat in my car. My anxiety kicked into overdrive. I turned up the radio to drown out my worries but it backfired; the song "Drops of Jupiter" alerted me to my insanity: it *did* feel like I'd just stepped back onto the planet Earth. I couldn't believe what I'd done! I'd just dropped four figures on a woman I didn't know, and while I thought it was romantic, Liza might think it desperate, overreaching, poorly-selected, cheap, stupid, comical or all six. She might think Santa sent it. Maybe she'd laugh at it; at me. I didn't know her at all. She might've been a crazy person or a drug addict or a criminal or an alcoholic or a sexaholic (not the worst possibility).

I returned home, deflected Mom's questions about my day, ran a few miles, chatted with Tony, studied OPIM, ate some food, watched some TV, then lay down in my bed and flipped Liza's business card between and through my fingers for half an hour before finally surrendering to the sandman.

6.

It was my twentieth birthday, and in accordance with Liza's Law, I was now officially old enough to court. One minute after midnight, I picked up the landline and dialed Liza's number.

My teammate/roommate, Marco Farias, was snoring like a sailor in his bed, knocked out by an unusually rowdy Thursday night. I was worried Liza might hear his ugly snoring due to the tininess of our dorm, but I had no other choice: I'd lost my cell phone at the post office earlier in the week.

The phone rang five times before Liza picked up. "This is Caplan," she muttered through sleep.

"Hi, hi, hi. Elizabeth?"

"Who is this?" she asked. "Do you know what time it is?"

"I do, in fact. It's Nicolai. You said I could call you on my birthday."

"Nicolai?" She asked liked she'd never heard the name.

Oh no! I thought. *She doesn't remember me!*

"Nicolai," she continued. "Wait…the kid from the bar?"

Oh no! I thought. *She remembers me!*

"The one and only, yup…unless you meet lots of kids at bars."

I laughed at my joke. She didn't. She didn't say anything.

"I just turned twenty," I said. "Like, literally, just right now."

"Does that take time zone into account?" Liza asked.

Does it? I asked myself.

"I think this is sweet," Liza said. "Happy Birthday. I'm going back to bed."

What!?

No mention of the bag. No clarification on, "*Honey, you're going to want to tell everyone.*" I'd suffered for and fantasized about this call all month. I'd shelled out thirteen hundred bucks. I'd called right on time. I remembered something from our talk at the bar, and it spilled out automatically. "You're lying," I said.

"Excuse me," she replied.

"You said that a great liar recognizes a good liar and I can tell you're lying."

"OK," Liza said stoically. "You're right. I was lying. I think this is desperate and immature and crazy. You're waking a grown woman at 12:01 because it's your birthday and your shorts are stiff."

"No. I was—"

"Trying to be romantic," she interrupted. "I get it. B-minus for effort, C-minus for execution. That's my honesty. Would you like more?"

Defeated and speechless, I sank into my desk chair.

"I thought not. Happy Birthday, Nicolai," Liza said.

"Wait," I replied.

"What now?"

I should've just let her go. I had nothing to say. And if I hadn't already ruined my shot, the explosion of noise that came next certainly did.

Without warning, a grubby senior named Pep Munich swung the door to our room open with such force that the knob left a dent in the dry wall. I didn't like Pep; nobody did. He was always drunk, always crude, and always walked around barefooted, even in the bathrooms.

"Get out, Pep!" I shouted, covering the receiver.

Pep ignored me and began shaking my roommate by the shoulders where he lay in bed. "Marco," Pep shouted. "Marco! I need that forty back. Marco!"

Marco didn't stir. While I knew well enough not to engage a drunk man bigger than myself, Marco was my team. I wedged myself between them, then I pushed Pep back and away from the bed.

"Asshole!" I yelled at him. "What?! What do you need? Beer?"

"You idiot, not a forty. Forty!" Pep slurred. "I need two twenties for these two girls. Marco was 'spose to get some, but he passed out, the little bitch. Look at him now—"

"Don't be a prick. Here," I said, reaching for my wallet.

—But then!

As if Satan himself was orchestrating this disaster-fuck, Marco woke up, rolled on his side, faced the little bit of common space between our beds, and vomited onto Pep's bare feet. A string of profanities followed, ending with, "You vomited on my feet you soccer-playing pussy!"

"Goddammit!" I shouted, "Here," and I handed Pep forty dollars; a twenty, a ten, and two fives.

"I need two twenties. You don't get it."

"I'm sure I don't." I ushered him out and locked the door.

Liza! I remembered. *The phone!*

First I had to pass the deluge of Marco's gut; a path of throw-up from his cheek to his pillow to his bed sheet and then onto the floor in a broken line reminiscent of Dali. Toeprints of vomit led from Marco's mess to our door. I'm not squeamish, but it smelled like—well, the inside of a dying man.

"Marco, goddammit, that's disgusting!" I screamed.

He didn't even move, which only served to piss me off more.

—But then!

I saw the phone standing on my desk; its receiver exposed and facing the room, leaning against a book as if someone had placed it there on purpose for perfect reception.

Oh no, I thought. I whispered a short prayer. *"Jesus, please don't let her still be on the phone."* (I knew he owed me no favors, but asking couldn't hurt.)

"Elizabeth?" I asked.

Then I waited.

"Elizabeth?" I asked again, sure my prayer had come true.

"Elizabeth?"

"It's Liza," she said. "It sounds like you have some cleaning up to do."

"Wait, no," I said again.

"Please don't make me turn rude. It isn't a good look."

"OK, but wait. You didn't get it?"

"Get what?!" She screamed.

Like a scolded child, I said in a whisper, "The present?"

"I'm only going to say this once, and if you don't obey, you'll regret it. Fuck off, Nico! And never call me again."

Then, she hung up.

7.

I spent over an hour cleaning Marco's mess. He woke up when I was nearly finished, stammering through an offer of help even though he was barely conscious. I felt bad for the guy—I'd never seen him so drunk—so I encouraged him to go back to sleep. He owed me, and he was the type who'd be good for it.

After cleaning, it took me another two hours to fall asleep. I spent most of that time wallowing in self-pity. I maybe slept three hours total before my alarm sounded at seven. Marco was already gone when I woke up, but the after-odor of vomit still loomed heavy in the air. He'd left a note apologizing. I opened the window, cranked the fan, and left the room as quickly as I could.

After my managerial accounting breakout and a terribly boring two-hour literature elective, I suffered through sixty minutes of weight training with my position coach. I had more soccer practice coming up later and a few errands to run, but I decided to reward myself with some relaxation first. Besides, I didn't want to waste my whole Friday being productive.

I returned to my dorm just before six. Marco was readying his bag for practice. He'd purchased a few candles and an air freshener. I gave him some shit for his vomitus episode but lightened the mood by insulting his feminine sense of smell.

He took his lumps well and left for practice.

The fragrance treatment had worked, so I sat at my desk, turned on my desktop computer, and did what all good college boys do when spared their roommate's company. I masturbated. About halfway through this adventure, my landline rang. I couldn't be interrupted though—masturbation is, after all, the best source of temporary heartbreak relief. It is Advil to romantic pain, Tylenol to regret, effective and safe, regardless of gender.

Two minutes later, the phone rang again.

It can't be, I thought.

I paused my session, rolled my chair over to Marco's desk, and snatched the phone with my business hand. (Gross, I know. I'm not proud of it.)

"Hello?" I said.

"Nicolai?" the voice said, sweet and subdued.

This was my chance to make a sound impression. All I needed to do now was stay calm. I pulled up my jeans.

"This is Nicolai," I said.

"Nico, Nico, Nico. That was quite a call last night," she said.

"What call? Which call?" I asked.

"You have that many eventful calls, do you?"

"Not really. I'm just doing what I can to pretend away the embarrassment, that's all."

"You don't have to pretend with me. Not ever," she laughed.

My heart relaxed.

"Did you call here a few minutes ago?" I asked.

"I did," she answered. "I'm sorry for shouting at you last night. I'm a monster when I'm trying to sleep. I honestly don't remember it too well."

"You told me to fuck off."

"Sounds like me," she said. "I've felt awful all day."

Awful? She felt awful? Though I didn't know her well, I knew the archetype. Something was amiss. "Ohhhh…"

"Ohhhh, what?" asked Liza.

"I get what's going on," said I.

"What's that?"

"You're lying again."

"I'm not lying. What am I lying about?"

I let out the littlest of laughs, a prodding sound really.

"What?" she asked. "What's so funny?"

"You got the bag," I told her.

"What bag?" she said.

Words through a smile vibrate differently than words angry or neutral, and I could tell Ms. Caplan was smiling ear-to-ear. I waited for her confession, which she turned over in just seconds.

"OK, I did. Thank you. It was completely excessive and inappropriate, but thank you."

"Did I nail it?" I asked.

"The bag?" Liza took time to measure her answer. She was a willing and able liar; she could say whatever she wanted.

"Yes, Nicolai," she said. "You nailed it."

"I was happy to buy it for you—" then the question that had haunted me for weeks "—so maybe we could cycle back to the bar. You said something to me."

"I did, did I?"

"Uh huh. You said, of this something, that I would want to tell *everyone*, and I've been wondering—wondering a lot—what that something might be?"

Sexiness is Liza's foremost quality, and her response to my prompt is, to this day, the sexiest thing a woman has ever said to me. "Oh, Nico," she purred. "The answer is your present, and it's still your birthday 'til midnight. I can show you if you'd like."

I gulped and thought she heard it through the Earth.

"Do you have more classes today?" she asked me.

"No."

"Soccer?"

"Yes, but that's inconsequential."

It was Liza—the woman from the bar—and she was the only woman I had in my life, so for me that meant she was the most important thing I had going. Over the next ten minutes, I collected an address, sent an email to my coach explaining that I'd come down with stomach flu (I called Marco to ensure he'd confirm my alibi; debt paid), showered, readied, and packed some clothes and toiletries. I then began my drive to a hotel in Poke, Alabama, one hundred and fifty miles away. It was highway driving mostly. I told Liza I'd be there in two-and-a-half hours.

"Don't be late," she said before hanging up.

A few miles in, I caught my reflection in the rearview mirror. I tried wiping the huge smile from my face, but failed. *"Honey, you're going to want to tell everyone,"* she'd said. *"The answer is your present."* After a terrible wait of weeks, I would finally learn why.

8.

The path to Liza wove through my hometown, and in my hometown, I knew I was exhausted. Fatigue slapped me at some point, half caused by the sleep shortened drama of the night before, half by my midday workout. I pulled off the freeway for a snack. I noticed a change to the coffee shop I'd frequented with Gabrielle; Tod Durch's Coffee & Cookies. It now had a well-designed logo, cookies had become "snacks", and its new sign—with oddly chosen initials reading *ToDuCoS*—sparkled like Las Vegas lights. Tacky as it was, it stood out against a row of neighboring chain restaurants and the shops in the plaza.

The inside had been contemporized; neutral colored walls, alt rock on surround, average-looking baristas making average-looking drinks, average local art with average prices beneath them. The only exceptional feature was the dessert case and the array of goodies—rows of morsels and cookies and brownies and cakes and candies and chocolates that didn't belong in the company of average anything, but in heaven only. The confections were all protected inside by an enormous, curved glass cabinet begging to be shattered and robbed. I selected a few pieces, had them wrapped for Liza leaving two for myself, and stood in a short line ahead of the store's only open register. I felt nervous about the time. Liza was expecting me by 8:30.

My nerves vanished, and were replaced with luminous awe when I saw the cashier. Her nametag said '*Aya.*' She had a beautiful neck that guided my eyes up her chin to her small ears, short hair, and simply, wonderfully, breathtaking eyes. She was wearing purple contacts. I watched her take orders, grin, pick at her nails. She gritted teeth under a smile for the indecisive patron ahead of me, a sixty-year-old bespectacled black man struggling mightily about his choice. The man asked

Aya what they had that was like a Starbucks Frappuccino.

"We don't have a single thing like that," she said to him. "You'll need to go downtown for that."

When it was my turn, without looking up, she asked how many pieces were inside.

"Five total. Three large, two small. They look amazing," I said.

"They taste amazing too." She looked at me, paused her purple eyes, and stammered a repeat response. "They taste amazing. I already said that. I mean I hope you like them," she said. "I mean they're good."

"Did you make them?" I asked.

She pinched back her face, surprised by the question, but happy it was asked.

"Yeah, I did. I mean, I do. I mean, most of them."

"Could I get a short coffee too? Black," I said.

She looked behind her. "We just tossed it—"

"No worries—"

"But we can make another batch. Just—"

"No need. It's good," I said. "I gotta get back on the road."

"It really won't take long," she interjected.

"No, honestly. It's fine. I'll just have this," I said as I grabbed a ginger beer from the ice tub.

She looked troubled; it was the oddest thing. Her reaction had an immediate, sobering effect on my mood. I paid her for the soda and cakes, and then I left, and all along the way to Poke, I had that look of trouble on my mind.

When I arrived to the hotel, concerns about the barista turned to ash. This was the moment I'd been waiting for! The Poke Historic Hotel emerged just as Liza said it would; out of nowhere, a tiny, secluded getaway for fans of nature and unique accommodations. I texted Liza for her room number.

It was 8:25 PM. Things were looking up.

9.

It was 8:40 PM. Things were looking down.

Fifteen crotch-tightening minutes later, she still hadn't texted me back. Maybe her phone had died. Maybe it was a test. Whatever it was, I had to act.

I got out my car, crossed my arms against the cold on my way to the hotel's reception lobby, and entered through a slow-opening automatic door. Old patterned wallpaper, pink and yellow, covered the place floor-to-ceiling, and the stiff-looking furniture struck me as something better suited for a travel museum. An egg-shaped woman in a weathered uniform waited behind the high reception desk across the foyer. She looked up from her work and smiled professionally.

"Welcome to historic Poke," she said. "Checking in?"

"No, ma'am. Well, yes. Sort of. I'm meeting a…a friend, but I can't remember the room number."

"Alright, sir, well, what's his name and I'll call up a con-firm."

"His name? The name on the room is Elizabeth Caplan," I said.

The receptionist took in a disturbed breath, smacked her lips, pressed her glasses close to her face, and began tapping the bulky keys of her tiny computer. I could see its green letters reflecting in the bifocals. A whole minute passed. She peeked at me several times as she searched.

"There it is," she said, sounding both proud of and surprised at her own success. "I'd put an S instead of a Z for Elizabeth. Oopsy me! Just a moment."

The receptionist dialed the room. After a few nods and cordial hotel-talk, she appeared very suddenly turned off. Then, looking me in the eyes, her look worsened to horror. Mine devolved into a stupor. She hung up, retrieved a key from one of three lockboxes behind her, and handed it to me, the number "357" sewn on its leather keychain. She pointed in the direction of the stairs and looked away.

I turned to leave.

"Sir," the receptionist said.

I stopped.

"Mrs. Caplan wanted me to tell you that you're late. And also, that ladies don't like waiting. And that that's rule number one."

"She did, did she?" I said smiling. "Did she say anything else?"

"Yes," the receptionist said with a scowl. "But I'll let her tell you that herself. This is a hotel, sir, and it's a historic hotel too. You be sure to mind yourself."

I couldn't tell if it was pure southern disapproval or something more childish, but I felt the need to apologize. "Sorry, ma'am."

I remember her next line perfectly, like yesterday's sunset. "Don't tell *me* you're sorry, young man. Tell Jesus." (So yes: pure southern disapproval.)

I was up the stairs and to room 357 in a flash.

I knocked twice and waited.

Liza opened the door.

My jaw could've dropped to the center of the Earth. I never felt more inside of a dream.

She wore a red silk robe that came halfway up her silky thighs and halfway down her neck and breastplate, both glistening with lotion. A pencil-thin silk belt held her robe to her waist, fighting the force of her pert B-cups pressing its nipples in the opposite direction. Her hair was up in sticks. She wore makeup subtle and dramatic; full eyelashes, dark mascara, an inviting pink lipstick that shined off the candlelight coming from inside. The wind wafting around her smelled like I think heaven will, like coconuts in Hawaii, like potpourri, and I had to catch my breath twice at the scent before she reanimated me with a name.

"Nico, honey" she said wantonly. "I've been waiting."

My spirit shifted into overdrive. "I texted you," I said.

"I don't text," she whispered.

"But you get texts?"

"Maybe. I'm different than people of your age. Always remember that. Call it rule number two."

"Do you have these rules written down somewhere?"

"Don't be a fool, Nico. You haven't apologized for being late." She put one hand on her hip while sliding the other up the side of the half-opened door.

"I'm sorry for being late. You feel like letting me in?"

"How about we try, *may* you come in?"

"Are we in third grade?" I asked. "Do you want me to come in or not?"

"Maybe," she said firmly. "You may think this is an everyday practice for me.

That's understandable under the circumstances, but you'd be wrong. I'm the rather romantic sort, Nico, and I'm very, very, very, very picky, so please don't speak to me like I'm your friend. I'm not. To answer your first question, this is not third grade, but you're certainly acting like it is, and to answer your second, yes I do want you to come in. Now, can you do this for me or can you not?"

Can I do this? I thought. *I was born to do this!*

"I can, yes. I hope you can forgive my confusion." I took the hand on her hip and kissed it. "I'm very sorry I was late. Honestly. I didn't mean to be, just got caught up with the reception lady. I'll get better."

"Nicolai," Liza said. "Do you have a girlfriend?"

"If you must know, yes. Yes, I do." I straightened up, took her other hand, kissed the top of it and said, "Her name is Liza. I've missed her terribly." Now I had both her hands, to which she radiated a smile. "May I please come in now?" I asked. "It's cold in the hallway, ma'am."

"Of course you may, Nico." She kissed me on the cheek and led me across the threshold. "But never, ever, call me ma'am."

She set the do-not-disturb hanger on the exterior knob and shut the door quietly behind us.

10.

Candles shot hard shadows onto the maroon and white striped walls. Moonlight poured in through the open window, amplifying the room into a moody blue.

"One question," I said.

"What's that, sweetheart?" Liza said stepping nearer. Her forehead was a breath's distance from my mouth, and when she tilted her head up, our lips were but two inches apart.

"What's the last thing you told the receptionist?"

"She didn't tell you?"

"Wouldn't. Just told me about Jesus."

Liza giggled. Lowered her head. Then she moistened her lips with a little lick and said slowly, "I told her, to tell you, to hurry up—" smacking every few syllables "— and that I wanted, to get out, of this tiny little robe, very, very, very, badly."

She took my cheeks in her palms and kissed me. She must've kissed me a whole minute, her hands caressing my back as she sat me on the bed.

"Where would you like me?" I asked.

Liza jerked back. "Nico, listen to me. It is the least sexy thing you can do," she said, "to *ask* if something is alright during intimacy. If something isn't alright, I'll communicate it with my hands and my body, and you'll come to understand what I'm saying. You interrupt conversations with words, but you interrupt intimacy with movement. Does that make sense?"

"All five," I said.

"All five what?"

"Like the five senses, it was—"

"Never, ever tell jokes," Liza said, serious as a heart-attack.

I nodded my agreement and she smiled.

We fell into the sheets. I tried to take some command at first, but Liza wouldn't have it, pivoting her hips to prevent my turning her. I understood immediately what she'd meant about how to communicate. I surrendered to her want. The grin I felt through her kiss expressed approval at my learning curve.

Then, she made love to me.

When Liza pinned my wrists in her hands, they were strong and soft. When she moved her body, it was powerful and elegant. She controlled me and relaxed me simultaneously, and I let go completely all my vulnerabilities. (This is not a compliment to me, but to her.) Everything glowed. Liza was brilliant; her pace, her touch, her energy. The feel of her naked body on mine exceeded every expectation I'd ever had about sex. She led the way from start to end, and she looked me in the eyes as I finished, and she kissed me sweetly then, on the cheeks and ears and lips, until finally I caught my breath.

Afterwards, she opened the window, sipped from a water bottle, slipped back into that little red robe, returned to bed, and situated her head on my chest; all as I just lay there, staring at her, fighting back a dumb grin.

After a few minutes, the silence unnerved me, so I broke it with a question.

"What are you doing here in Poke?" I asked.

"Work."

"What kind of work."

"Collecting records. Finding people. That sort of thing."

"What kind of records?" I asked "What kind of law do you practice exactly?"

"I wasn't lying at the bar. I'm not a lawyer. But I do deal with scumbags all day. And by that I mean lawyers."

"So what then?"

"Nico. Jobs aren't really the sexiest topic. You don't know that yet, but trust me. Let's stay in the now, shall we?"

She kissed me on the neck. I was drifting back into the mood. "Do you like your work?" I whispered.

"I do. I love it. I have my own schedule. The people I work with are amazing. Blah, blah, blah, yes, it's great."

"It's great, well—" Liza had begun kissing my neck "—what's so great about it?"

"Nico," she said, looking up at me now for emphasis, "I told you, it's boring. Stick with sexy."

"I'm interested. Honestly. That's just who I am."

"Baby. Do you want me to teach you about my job?" (No one had ever called me baby before; it sounded wonderful.) "Or do you want me to teach you about this?"

She moved my hand down her stomach and guided my fingers to the best strategic spot between her legs. I realized very quickly that I'd need to shelf my *best at women* crap: Liza needed her reciprocation! (It is the currency of relationships, after all: Dad's words; not mine.) Though I still had much to learn, I did have my Becca days to draw from. Following a few minutes of touchy foreplay, I ventured downtown and for the next fifteen minutes, all Liza said was, "up," "down," "over," (which could mean left or right—women don't really distinguish), "harder," "softer," and "right there." She also said "under" twice and "over" once, and also, the phrases "God" and "goddammit" were used frequently and interchangeably and throughout. She came for me twice, and almost made third, but she instead fell back into pillows, sank into the bed, and said simply, "Wow."

It was the proudest moment of my life. I fell right beside her.

On Sex

"The Law of Diminishing Returns is true of everything in life, except sex, which seems endlessly repeatable with effect."
—ROBERT MCKEE

 hen you're in the arms of a beautiful, sexy woman, what else is there?

Dear Nicolai, on this we are agreed.

Sex just might be the most stimulating word in English. Included among the effects of its being said are panic, remorse, excitement, terror, insecurity, rage, confusion, joy, and, of course, the numerous, various, and uncontrollable physiological phenomena.

Sex. See.

Most people have opinions about the President. Many people have opinions about health. *Everyone* has an opinion about sex.

For teenage boys, sex is a triumph. Years of anticipation build like loose snow on a mountainside. Then, in one moment, with one success, an avalanche of expectation rushes away, leaving in its wake a new take on the truth about sex—the work, the taking off of clothes, the sweat, positioning, the cleanup, the responsibilities, the reactivities, the sensitivities, the cues, the warning signs. Many teens and young adults learn to manage these non-romantic and formal elements of lovemaking early on as they experiment and gather experience, but my practice had been limited. My experience before Liza was simple to a fault. I'd only had sex with Gabrielle, and only a few times, and none of it was memorable, except for the time and the time in the closet in the office her father owned.

In Liza, I'd found an unparalleled mentor to close this shameful gap. More than just thinking about sex, Liza reflected on it. She was brilliant in her comfort with and practice of the art, and never once did she judge my inexperience. On the contrary, Liza was eager to share with me all her meditations, her knowledge, all her theories, all her expertise. We spoke about lovemaking at length—logistics before, feedback after. She was objective and enthusiastic about this education of mine, an enthusiasm likely inspired by my tangential interest in the subject—sex and romance are, after all, inextricably linked—either that or by the sheer pleasure afforded her from my complete acceptance of her instructions and total devotion to her wants. I was feverishly ambitious to please.

Liza and I met two or three times per month, a function of our Georgia rurality. She was always on the road, working the fifteen counties or so surrounding my hometown and school. She even ventured into Alabama. She lived on the other side of this territory in a home two-hundred miles away, and we'd only convene in hotels of the in-between; none as odd or as isolated as the one in Poke, though some came close.

Once, in mid-December, for our seventh rendezvous, I met Liza at a Holiday Inn near Warren Heights. She had an injury across her right shoulder covered by a pad of pinkened gauzes. It looked awful and fresh—I was sure she'd been stabbed—and upon seeing it I asked her several times what had happened. Successfully, she deflected my questions, her response coming in the form of soft kisses and suggestive touch. When I persisted, she grabbed my belt buckle and relieved me of my trousers with the expertise of a jewelry thief.

We made love and watched television and shared our opinions on sex and life and evolution and law (specifically horseshit traffic laws; I'd gotten two speeding tickets during our first five engagements). We made love and talked about anything but us. It was into this mode we settled, and our ritual normalized quickly.

Over breakfast on a Saturday morning—February the twelfth I remember; our four-month anniversary—I asked Liza, "What do you think separates a good lover from a bad one?"

"Trust," she said.

She'd conveyed to me in that one word—TRUST—that we are our most vulnerable selves during sex. For starters, we're naked in front of someone else, but more central is that we become entirely different people. Most of us would reel in horror if anyone other than our lover saw us in either form, nude or impassioned, carnal or lusty, hence the shuttering of blinds, the checking of locks, the deleting of internet archives, and the like. To be that other someone in front of someone else, to do so comfortably and unjudged; this is among the richest treats of romance. For many, it is the richest.

Somewhere between mid-March and late April—I don't remember exactly because it all meshes with our ending—Liza described to me the difference between trust as it applies to gender. "If a woman trusts her man enough," she said, "the woman can maximize her pleasure with grip and touch and expressive sounds. Words of lust. Moans of acceptance. Screams of surprise if all goes well. A good man," she continued, "will smile, reassure his woman, free her to express her pleasure anyway she'd like, answer her sweet nothings and sexual on-comings with his own. He'll hold her when she's finished—" that I always did "—to verify that she means more to him than just her body. These are his acts of trust. Men, though, most of them, express pleasure with strength. Men don't need to moan. They have biceps. If a man trusts his woman enough, he can maximize his pleasure too; his woman will move with his power, allow herself some submission, accept his grasp on her belly, her thighs, her wrists and her hair. Even the neck is in play, but with care." Liza began kissing me on the neck. So pure were those kisses, my listening drifted away. I think she said that a good woman will kiss her man deeply, guide him thoughtfully, and confirm in the afterglow with interlaced hands and authentic connection that an encore is welcome at his convenience. "Where there is enough trust, the degree of exertion finds itself," she told me. "*The more trust, the better the sex.* This is usually the case with men. This is almost always the case for women."

My grades worsened in the Spring, and soccer suffered too—I still wasn't getting much playing time and I wasn't getting better—but I gave not one iota of a shit. As the saying goes, *when you're in the arms to a beautiful, sexy woman, what else is there?* Nothing was more important than Liza; my life revolved around her whims, my schedule on her desires, my thoughts on her and our next encounter. As our compatibility developed, I took more control, took more risks. And I, saying this proudly, closed the enormous gap between her wants and my abilities in impressive time. The details are less important than the substance; in sum, Liza and I became perfect lovers.

Our arrangement ran eight months unperturbed. Sometimes I wanted to be on campus more, sometimes I wanted to go to parties and get extra practice during optionals. Sometimes I honestly just wanted to study. I'd set a bad precedent by always saying yes to Liza regardless of the distance and inconvenience, but hell—what else is there?

Second semester ended on a Thursday. Summer began again.

My soccer team disbanded with a banquet to celebrate our remarkably bad season. The following day, I drove farther than I'd ever driven before to meet Liza. She'd planned for us a three-day getaway at a luxurious hotel and spa near a hot spring on Lake Napalm. Though it wasn't love, I felt connected to Liza in a way I'd never felt with anyone; not even Summer. I was giddy with anticipation, high as a kite. Yet, as it goes with kites and hopes and airplanes and balloons and dreams and summers and orgasms too, what goes up must eventually come down. In one instant, my status quo shattered.

Firearms tend to do that.

Liza Waxes

"I know every time a woman says, 'we need to talk,' we need to talk about some shit that I gotta do. We don't ever have to talk about anything she needs to do."
—DAVE CHAPPELLE

11.

"We need to talk," Liza said to me a few minutes after we finished.

I was resting beside her in the soft blue bed. We were in a cool-colored, wood-paneled hotel suite, and I remember it being the nicest room we ever shared. I forgot everything else though; specifics erased by the trauma of what happened next.

"Sure," I replied, staring pointlessly at the ceiling, my afterglow still burning bright from the sex we'd just finished. "What about?"

Liza leaned away and gently lifted the Louis Vuitton purse. She turned to me.

Laid it delicately on the bed between us, as one would a pet. I got the uncomfortable feeling that something dangerous was inside.

"Thank you for this," she said. "I don't think I ever said a proper thank you. It affected me more than you think." I heard care and concern in Liza's voice. *A trick of the senses*, I thought. It sounded like a pre-planned opening up, and that just couldn't be right. She was at the foot of the bed, naked, her head perched on her palm. Lamplight from the living room shot shadows across her hips and breasts and neck. Her lips glimmered. This image—possibly because it was the last simple moment we shared—is the one my mind recalls most when I remember us together.

"Good. I'm glad," I said, terribly distracted by her beauty.

She shaped her hair into a ponytail, postured to face me, and covered her naked body in the comforter. "I never told you," she said to me, "but three days after we met, I went, myself, to a Louis store in Atlanta and bought a new purse. I was so—" she paused to measure her words "—I don't know, I guess the best word would be fascinated, I think, by how a nineteen-year-old boy could understand the significance of a Chanel."

"I'm flattered," I said.

"Seriously, Nicolai. I'm trying to be honest here."

"I know."

"I don't think you do. I don't think you know. It takes wisdom about women to recognize something like that. Most grown men can't even see it."

I shrugged and asked, "Did you buy a purse?"

"I did."

"I've never seen it," I said. "I won't be offended if you bring yours instead of mine."

Silence and squinting from Liza, so I smiled. Then, her look turned serious.

"You're not hearing me, Nico. That's not why," she said. "I returned it a few days after I got yours."

"Why?" I asked, forgetting the mood. She was covered up, but still she was stunning, and I still felt like the world's luckiest boy.

"You're not going to believe this, but…"

And then she laughed again—yeah, *again!* I became nervous with anticipation. Something pressing was pushing out. In matters of women, that usually means emotions. I was now a submarine radar man and her emotional torpedo was blipping closer and closer to my position.

"Well, you see." She stopped herself and giggled. I braced for impact. "I bought the exact same purse. The one you bought me, I'd already bought it for myself."

"What do you mean you bought the *exact* same purse?" I asked.

"Not exact, exact," she said. "Mine was a little smaller, but same style and design. And it was Louis, of course."

"That's certainly an interesting coincidence," I said.

"That depends. Do you believe in coincidences?"

"I mean, of course I *believe* in coincidences," I answered. "The world's very big and you run into lots of different people and situations so over time it might—"

"No," she interrupted, forcing a grin to mask her very apparent irritation. "I mean do you believe in coincidences when it comes to love and relationships."

There it was: torpedo impact and *Ka-Boooooom!* I knew enough to know that this was not something people came back from. I was fucked, figuratively. I'm not sure if that was the first time Liza used the word *relationship*, but it was definitely the first time *love* ever escaped her mouth. None of this—and I mean none of this—registered with me in real time. To that point, Liza and I had enjoyed a purely physical connection. Sure, I brought her flowers every now and then. Sure, I paid for our meals and massaged her feet and listened intently to her opinions. She'd been comfortable enough to share with me that she'd been previously married, had a kid, all that jazz, but it didn't add up to love.

Did it?

"There's something I need to tell you," Liza said to me. "It's been a long time coming, actually."

As I opened my mouth to interject, her pager buzzed loudly atop the dresser on the other side of the room. She put her finger to my lips and said very seriously, "Hold that thought, baby."

She kissed me, then she stood and turned and walked away from the bed. I watched Liza the way a film critic watches a masterpiece. I was immersed in her wonders; she was nude, flawless, and worth any cost necessary to remain in her good graces. Seeing her there—elbow propped on the dresser, pager in hand, and a troubled look of disbelief on her face—relieved my concern about this emotional development. Liza retreated to the bathroom and came out in her bra and underwear (that's where we'd started.) She picked up the hotel room's cordless phone, punched a few buttons, and waited. Then, in a voice frustrated and professional, I heard these bits of tense conversation: "Hi Shane…No, not now…Look…Listen—do you have an address or don't you…no, I'm not that far…Hell if I'm waiting on Clark!…OK, Patrol get plates?…He have his friends with him, his buddies?…She? Who's she? And what do you mean he's not sure?" All the while, to my dismay, Liza kept putting on clothes. In three minutes she was fully dressed in loose jeans and a plain blue blouse; I'd never seen her in clothes so simple and unflattering, or in a state so frazzled. She'd lost something, and I had no clue what. Obviously, I was concerned. We were just two hours into our three-day pleasure binge.

Liza hung up. Turned to me with a look half-grim, half regretful. "I have to go," she said. "I won't be long."

"What?" I asked.

"I won't be long."

"Not that. Why? What? How long and what's happening?"

"It isn't serious."

"It isn't serious? It's literally the most serious sounding conversation I've ever heard. It sounds like you're about to kill someone."

She huffed. "Definitely not my business. Not quite. It's just work. I'll be only a few hours."

She looked at the dresser. In the mirror above the dresser, I saw her reflection, and there, after I realized she was eyeing the drawers and cabinets beneath, our eyes met. The look was one of distrust and fear, the counter-us.

"What is it?" I asked bravely.

"I…" she said, but her voice broke off.

"I do care about you," I told her. "You do know that, right?"

"Yes, of course," she said.

"Then you've gotta tell me something. You can't just run off and say it's serious and expect me to not worry."

Liza heard sincerity and I could tell it made her happy; I could see it when she tilted her head down, like she was taking in a fact of long-awaited closure. She hesitated for a long moment—nerve-wracking seconds for me, I felt my heart climbing into my throat—then she sighed an exhale of resignation, reached down, opened the dresser's left cabinet, keyed in the four-digit combination to the room's safe, and withdrew two handguns; the first one was tiny, the second one was Arnold Schwarzenegger.

"The fuck!" I screamed. "Why do you have guns?!"

"Quiet down!" she yelled back at me.

I obeyed: she had guns. I'd never been so close before. I wasn't ready. A subconscious bomb exploded in my chest and lunged me back and away and into the headboard as though the weapons might attack me of their own accord. Liza reached into the safe again and withdrew a sleek, single-pocketed, brown leather holster. She expertly strapped it over her shoulder and around her torso, then she slid the larger of her guns, the hand cannon, into its sleeve. She snuck the littler of the guns into her sock—her white cotton sock, I should add, the least sexy thing I'd ever seen on her.

I asked in my loudest whisper-voice, "Have you always had guns in our room?"

"No," she said at first. "Well, yes. But only because I don't like keeping them in the car. You don't have to worry, Nicolai. I have my licenses."

"You have multiple gun licenses?"

"Well, yes actually. I used to teach."

"You worked at a gun range?"

"Present tense sort of. We—I mean I, own a share of a facility in—"

"Is that why you have guns in our room? Did someone get shot at your 'facility'?" I asked flashing air quotes.

"Nico," she said calmly. "You have to calm down. I can't understand you."

She approached me then, and though my heart was thumping like a bellows, the rest of me froze. She stood right beside me at the edge of the bed, her holstered gun an arms-length away.

"I'm a bail recovery agent."

"You're a what?!" I shouted.

"A bail recovery agent," she said again.

"You mean you're a fucking bounty hunter?"

"Call it what you'd like but don't swear at—"

"Bounty hunter then," I snarked. "That's what I want to call it. Bounty hunter. You're a bounty hunter and you never fucking told me—"

"That sounds awful," she snapped. "That's not what it is, Nicolai, and I'm not a fan of the word and it's not necessary for you to keep swearing about it, so stop. Stop being a baby. It's like you've never seen a gun before. Swearing doesn't make them go away. It makes them bigger. You're an adult now. Treat them like their real, because they are. It's time to grow up."

It was the first time our age and experience gaps came to light, and the first time I ever considered her maternal, how she stood over me and spoke down at me with a tone disappointed and superior. "Now calm down. You're acting like a pussycat," she scolded. "Besides, I don't see how my occupation matters all that much."

Meek as a meercat, I made my case, "Well, it does. It matters."

"Why?" she asked.

"Because it does. I assume by the multiple guns we're not talking pick pockets and petty thieves, ay?"

Her stance relaxed, and her expression, which in a matter of minutes had shifted from sexy to romantic to motherly to scornful, now downshifted into concerned, almost holy, another mode of hers I'd never before seen. Her eyes disarmed me. Her complex and lovely look put me at ease.

"Sometimes, yes, pick pockets and thieves," she said, nearing the bed. "But no, not usually. Listen, Nico. I'm really good at what I do. I've been doing it my whole life, like my Dad did. But I'm a woman. The client doesn't see me coming. Not like you did, Nico. You saw me, so you're safe. That's how it works."

"Was there a bounty on me?"

"Not quite."

She backed away from the bed and slid into a thin jacket. "You were always different." She pocketed her car keys. Fully dressed, readied and equipped to leave, she looked at me one last time and asked, "Will you wait?"

"Like the first time? Like on my birthday?"

"Not nearly that long. Just hours, not weeks. It's not much more."

I rubbed my temples. We'd finished making love not fifteen minutes ago. She'd shape-shifted so much, I couldn't form a coherent thought.

She asked again. "Please. Will you be here when I get back?"

"Of course," I answered urgently, remembering that she had guns.

I didn't think Liza could outdo her hidden guns, but I was sorely mistaken. Just before leaving, Liza told me in an unfeeling mode, as if the need for efficiency was more important than the weight of her words, "I love you, Nicolai," she said. The phrase pitched over my awareness like a Mozartian high-note; it sat atop me, a mountain, deafening in the room's silence. Even with all this—even with the fact of the guns and the insanity of her transformations—I managed to keep my body still and my reaction unreadable.

Liza mined for more. "I don't mean to burden you with this," she said. "But I do. I do. I love you. You've been very good to me—" she continued, looking away as if convincing herself "—very, umm, giving. I know you're only twenty, but you've got so much heart and romance in you. It just…I don't have other words. It's love. That's what I feel. I've loved before, so I know what it looks like. I resisted my feelings. I tried to forget them, tried to put off the coincidence about the Louis purses, but I can't now. I'm not sure why, but I just…I just can't. Or maybe I don't want to. Or not anymore. That you're so young makes me feel stupid in all this, but—" Liza huffed a little laugh; an exhaust of energy "—I had to tell you. I thought you should know."

She fiddled with the keys in her pocket and awaited my response. I didn't think about our weekend, didn't think about her words, didn't think about her compliment and its meaning to my life. I thought for a moment about my quest, *to be the very best*, and all at once it occurred to me that in losing it so long I'd failed again. But then, as it usually does in life, fear trumped my wishes and all I could think about were the guns. I considered saying nothing at all, but I didn't have the bravery, especially not after a pop of light glinted off the trigger guard when she adjusted her jacket. "I love you too," I said, fearful in my heart but not in my voice.

"You don't have to say—"

"No. I do," I said. "Not like, I-do-I-have-to, but like, I do. I love you, Liza. I'll be here waiting when you get back. I promise."

As with all my promises, I meant it when I said it.

Liza squinted her eyes disbelievingly. She almost looked angry, so I crossed my heart with my forefinger—a reinforcement of the promise. I thought she might cry or at least pout, or make some gesture about my words-of-love, but she didn't. She nodded a bit and straightened her harness and looked back at me like she was about to say something, but she turned the knob and didn't. She closed the door behind her. Just like that, Liza was gone.

Now look, I understand that reacting to change is challenging in all relationships—I get that; I really do—but I imagine any non-NRA member would react negatively to the sight of hidden guns. My reaction after Liza left me was massive. It was inspired by something wired as deeply into my soul as my love for women. We all have our fears. Some people fear spiders. Others fear heights. Phobias range from tight spaces to death to even something called *globophobia*, a fear of the noise balloons make when they pop. Me, however, I suffer from and struggle with what I believe to be the world's most reasonable fear. It's called *hoplophobia*. I'm uncontrollably terrified of guns.

12.

As with most of life's important whys, this one remains beyond me, this fear of mine, but it is real, as real as my skin and the blood that runs underneath it. I inherited my hoplophobia either genetically or by means of some cruel childhood happenstance, and unlike my love of women—inspired by words I uncovered later that day—the origin story escapes me. When I was a pre-teen, I was forced—socially that is, via the assumed peer pressure of my tiny collective—to pretend like I was enjoying the rock'em, sock'em, shoot'em up movies of the summer. During these big screen adventures, I'd get panicky, sweaty even, closing my eyes in the dark and hating that my ears lacked earlids to shield my senses the same way. (When available, I'd sneak for several minutes into nearby romantic comedies trying to absorb any wisdoms available on screen: there were few.) I tried and tried to overcome it. I played with my friend Stuart's water gun many times and fired an air rifle belonging to Grandpa, Mom's father, but it never took. By the time I was fifteen, I'd totally given up.

I've managed my phobia well since then, and can certainly sit through a movie with guns, but seeing two guns so suddenly and in the hands of my lover triggered within me a truly psychotic reaction. Following Liza's transformation into Rambo, I transformed into story putty: my thoughts and emotions boarded a rollercoaster wild with speed. One minute I'd be meditating calmly; the next I'd be crying—literally, crying. One minute, I'd visualize Liza returning to the room, her guns left behind in the car. She'd apologize and promise to keep them away from me forever and all would return to normal. The next minute, I'd lose myself to fear-induced daydreams; some as elaborate as Liza returning, kidnapping me, and taking me to Mexico where I'd be forced to dig a shallow grave for myself just before she fires a bullet into the back of my head, others as simple as Liza kicking in the door of our suite and shooting me between the eyes. (For some reason, in that version, she casually puts on lipstick in the dresser vanity as my corpse bleeds out in the reflection behind her.) I sat in bed for an hour hardly moving; agonizing; a mental horror house. Finally, I got up, washed my face, and took inventory of my options. I had two choices, really. On the one hand, I could wait; on the other, I could leave. I could write a note and the note could say I needed to visit Mom, or that I'd forgotten to finish something on campus, or even the truth; that I had a deep-seeded fear of guns. I could leave this note on the nightstand or the dresser or even with the receptionist.

But I didn't.

I thought about the guns again, and a third option presented itself: *Get Out!* (This is not the same as leaving.)

I wouldn't *completely* call it cowardice, but nevertheless I packed my duffle bag as quickly as I could and rushed out as though the room was on fire. I felt a panic to escape before Liza returned. Fantasies of violence plagued me all along the way. I heard scratchy violins in my head. I dreaded her rounding the corner of the long hall I had to traverse on my way to the elevator; once in, I dreaded seeing her on the other side of the sliding doors as they opened to the lobby; a gun in each hand, her cold and evil voice cackling and asking, "Why you rushing, Nico? Where you off to," she'd say, and my eye was zooming into the back of the barrell right before the fireball.

Neither happened.

I blasted through the exit, hustled across the expansive parking lot, entered my car, and burned rubber as I sped out of and away from that place. I recognized immediately that there was only one place I could go, one place I could feel safe.

That's right, ladies and gentlemen. I drove straight to Mommy.

ON WHAT MOM FORGOT TO TELL ME

"Your talents are God's gift to you. What you do with them is your gift back."
—LEO BUSCAGLIA

atters worsened quickly. I should've waited. I went home, which was the mistake.

One hour into my trip, about ten miles from the interstate, I noticed a full moon in contrast on the blue sky; it had come out early, a daytime reminder of nights that would never be again. Even if Liza and I mended this somehow, there would exist a sudden vulnerability. The carefree days were over, ended in part by my cowardice but as much by the non-disclosure that brought my cowardice about. She'd lied to me, and though I understand well the logic of lying-is-love, the logic satisfies less on the short-end.

Mom wasn't expecting me—she had no reason to expect me, of course. Not only was this an unplanned escape from Liza, Mom knew nothing of Liza at all. I didn't tell her in part because of Liza's age, but I think few young men share their sexual lives with their mothers, and that's all Liza and I shared; all we had was sex

(at least that's what I thought earlier in the morning.)

What I knew for certain was that Mom would have questions—questions I wouldn't feel like answering. I wanted very much to go to sleep—three hours of driving following that fear-ridden episode in the hotel had exhausted me—so I devised a simple plan. I'd bribe her senses with something delicious. I pulled off the freeway and stopped into Tod Durch's again for a bag of snacks to bring home to Mom. Nine months before, I'd done the same for Liza. (And to answer the burning question: no. I don't consider it weird that I bought the same gift for my mom-aged girlfriend and my mom-aged Mom.)

I parked and entered, and noticed over the door a sign that announced, "Under New Management." The walls were painted with soft pastels, the logo had changed again—abandoning the silly *ToDuCos* sign from before—and Aya, the barista with whom I'd shared the odd encounter on my last visit, was nowhere in sight. For all the lighting and color and fanciness of the shop's new décor, its snack case remained the centerpiece. Just to the right when I entered, it marvelously displayed in a glass case three times bigger than before a delectable assortment of dozens of different treats; desserts, cookies, cakes, snacks, even ingredients like gigantic chocolate chips and candied almonds.

I pulled a number and waited in a group of several patrons. When it was my turn, I chose six cinnamon-spiced macadamia nut cookies, two flavors Mom adored combined in one concoction. I was confident I could resist them.

I knocked on our front door. Mom swung it open. "I bought you three cookies from that Durch's place," I said, holding up the bag.

"Nicolai!" Mom exclaimed. She hugged me, and we did the initial back and forth; *how are you, it's good to see you, why are you home, are you hungry?*

Her boyfriend was sitting in the living room. I didn't care for his ponytail or how he picked his teeth, but really he was just a big friendly guy; not fit-big or fat-big; he was 6'2", 220 pounds, that's all. They were about to watch the next episode of a new show. Mom pitched me to join them.

"What do you mean it happens in real time?" I asked, interrupting her.

"It's called *24*," she said. "It's got Keifer Sutherland in it."

"Doing what?" I asked skeptically. "Playing a vampire?"

"No," Mom said. "He's a take-names-later, kick-ass special agent working for CTU."

"What the hell is CTU?"

"The Counter-Terrorist Unit," she said excitedly.

"Mom. It's fine," I said. "I'll talk to you tomorrow. It's been a long day."

"Son," she said, and she put her hands on my shoulders. "You're not doing me a favor. Trust me."

I did, as I always did, and she was right again. Jack Bauer entered my life that night, and more than sleep ever could, he made the pain of Liza disappear like the terrorists he brought to justice. It was 10:00 P.M. when the show ended: how Jack would survive the next hour, we had no idea! We sat at the dining room table and shared the cookies I'd bought. Mom loved them; said they tasted like an angel made them.

In just minutes, the wear of the day finally broke through my exterior. Mom noticed my troubled thoughts; I'd zoned out on something she said as I crumbled crumbs between my fingers over the small plate of cookies.

"OK," Mom said, "what is it, dear? Why are you home? You can talk to me."

"I already know," Tony said, freeing something from his teeth with a toothpick. "It's a girl."

My quick look away confirmed Tony's theory for Mom.

"Is it Nicolai?" she asked me.

"No, Mom. It's not a girl. It's a woman."

"What happened, sweetheart? Are you alright?"

"I promise you don't want to know," I said somberly. "And I really don't want to talk about it if that's alright."

"Of course it is."

I'd been crumbling the cookies because Liza and I ate sweets often. I'd buy them for her on my way to the hotels; apple pie and Ferrero Rocher were her favorites. I already missed her.

"You didn't tell me you had a girlfriend," Mom said.

"You didn't tell me you had a Tony," I replied.

Tony laughed. "You weren't kidding, dear," he said as he stood from the table. "He is funny."

Tony kissed Mom on the forehead then retrieved a kettle from a pull-out drawer next to our dishwasher. He filled it with water and set it on the stove as Mom continued her investigation.

"Can you at least tell me how serious it was?"

"Mom. Please," I said.

"That's all I need to know. Was it serious? That's a totally reasonable Mom question, right?"

"Was it serious?" I said, restating her question. "I guess so. And I guess not too. It's complicated."

"Well do you love her?" Mom asked. "Or did you love her or whatever?"

"That's a big question," I said, straightening myself in the chair.

"Yeah," Mom replied. "But the answer isn't. It's a yes, or it's a no."

"No wiggle room?"

"No sir, not on that. I think they call it a Boy-lean right?"

"Boolean," Tony echoed. "It's a Boolean. Love."

"You think so too," I asked Tony.

"I agree with your mother. That's my rule."

They smiled at each other. It made me feel sick.

"If you're asking if I was in love with her," I said, "no, not really. But I care about her. She's dear to me. She was all I had going. All that mattered."

"I'm sure that's not true," Mom said, her maternal instinct attacking my self-deprecation. "Don't be so dramatic." Mom took a sip of milk from Tony's cup, and then, very casually, she said, "I bet she's in love with you, isn't she? Is that the problem?"

My eyes almost jumped out of my head. "What?"

"She's in love with you?" Mom said again.

"Who?" I asked, still jolted.

"The woman," Mom said.

"You mean Liza?" I asked in confusion.

"Thanks for the name. Liza? That's nice. A little dated, isn't it?"

"Not sure on the history of her name, Mom."

"Dear, where'd you put the honey?" Tony blurted out as he rummaged through the pantry on the opposite side of the kitchen.

She turned around to answer him.

"Mom," I said, wanting to keep her attention. "Why would you think Liza was in love with me if I wasn't in love with her?"

"It's on the second shelf, by the beans," Mom shouted to Tony.

"Why is the honey by the beans?" Tony asked.

"Why does it matter?" she asked back.

"Mainly," Tony said, "because I'm looking for the honey."

"Mom," I interrupted again, louder this time. "Can you finish what you were saying?"

"Well, Nicolai, it's simple really. I assume it's because she told you that she loved you. That's usually how one can tell, or do Millennials love *that* much differently?" Then, Mom smiled at me that way parents do when they out-wisdom their kids. She stood, patted me on the shoulder, and walked the few steps to the pantry saying, "Tony, come sit back down. I think I might've moved it."

"Oh, now she tells me. After I've looked," Tony said.

On his way back to the table they passed each other and kissed again. I could see why Mom liked him: she was more alive then I'd ever seen. She was, for the first time I could recall, outwardly happy.

"Mom," I called out, "what would make you think she told me she loved me?"

"First, tell me if I'm right."

"OK, Mom. You're right."

"I knew it!" she shouted out, now hidden in the pantry.

"So?" I asked impatiently.

"Nicolai, you are your father's son. Your dad used to tell me his old battle stories," she said. "His old flings and dates, you know? He said he couldn't go more than a month before they said it was love. He was always warm about it though, you know. He wasn't bragging. He just…"

Her voice trailed off, and then she giggled. Maybe it was this new affection from Tony that opened her heart enough to tell me the truth. This was more than a misread or omission from my history; it fundamentally shaped who I was and who I'd become. It was the straw that shattered me. I lost everything.

"It's like what he said to you the night he died," Mom continued. "Those words. He was close to the end, and he was on so much morphine. I thought at first he wanted me to hear it, but over the years I realize it really was just for you. What a lovely piece of advice."

I felt like a camera was zooming in on me.

"Use the force?" I asked her.

"No, no," Mom replied. "Not that. The *last* words. Oh, how'd he put it?" Then Mom was quiet for a moment. I sensed my hands shaking beneath the table. "Oh—you know," Mom said, "it was that thing you presented when you were little, in second grade, at that Aspiration Day nonsense."

I felt a million little animals holding me still. I couldn't breathe. I couldn't move. Neither Mom nor Tony noticed what was happening to me.

"How'd he put it?" Mom asked herself. Then she came out of the pantry, a bear-shaped honey bottle in her hand. "That's right, I remember." Standing now in front of the stove, checking the kettle and acting all nonchalant, Mom didn't know she'd left it out of my life. "If you want to be happy, if you want to live well, be the very best at loving your woman."

"What did you say?" I shouted as I stood.

"Nicky?" Mom said, concerned.

I'd gotten up so quickly that my chair fell over. As it clattered loudly on the floor behind me, I marched the three steps between Mom and me and took her shoulders firmly in my hands and leaned down a few inches so we'd be eye-to-eye.

"Say it again, Mom."

"Hey!" Tony hollered, objection in his voice. I ignored him, desperately wanting an immediate confirmation before Mom forgot again.

"Please! Say it exactly." It was me and Mom and those words and that was all.

"Nick," Mom said. "Son. Are you alright?"

"I'm fine. Just…" I collected my calm, but I was near tears.

"Nico," Mom said again. "What's the matter?"

"Can you repeat *exactly* what Dad said to me the night he died?"

"I just did," she answered.

"Again please."

"It's not like I've never told you before," she exclaimed.

She hadn't. Or I hadn't remembered. It doesn't matter which.

"Again, please," I said. "Exact."

"Alright. OK," she said. "Your Dad opened his eyes to you one last time. It was past visitation hours already and we knew it was probably his last night. You left right after that. He asked you to take his hand, and you did, and you were crying, but then he got you to smile. There was this scratch on the window he was complaining about—"

"Mom!" I begged. "The words!"

"Your dad said, 'Son. My boy,'…or something like that. And oh, then *he* started crying, which he wasn't supposed to be able to do according to the doctors because—"

"Mom!"

"If you want to be happy, if you want to live well, be the very best at loving your woman. That's exactly how he put it. I swear."

"Mom! Are you shitting me?"

"Don't swear at me," Mom shouted back.

"Hey!" Tony hollered again from behind me.

"Leave it, man!" I yelled, half turning to Tony before my gaze returned to Mom. "Don't swear at you? Don't swear at you?! How can I not swear at you? How could you not tell me this?"

—and I was losing it now as a whirlwind swept through my entire identity and I felt out of body because the woman before me wasn't my mother; she was the warden of information kept captive from me for a lifetime—

"How the fuck could you not—"

"Nicolai!" Mom yelled. "Don't you dare—"

"Hey," Tony shouted once more as he stood to quell the storm.

"I've spent my whole life—" I shouted back, but my words hit a wall before leaving my mouth.

I didn't speak for more than a minute. I didn't cry either. I felt a most surreal absence of self as unprecedented and tangled feelings ravaged my thoughts; I was suddenly imprisoned in a womb of emotional gibberish, lost—lost and out of body—as my heart and mind frantically sought balance against the overwhelming chaos besieging them, and now Tony was standing right behind me, so when I turned to run away to somewhere—to anywhere but here—I had to shove by him and I tried to pivot past the table, but my shin slammed into the chair I'd tipped over, and I shouted, and then my hands squeezed into painful fists as I screamed for many seconds, not at the jolt of pain in my shin and not at Mom and not at Tony, but at and against and in defiance of the skies. Just like that, my energy crested and I found a temporary balance. I surrendered my fury to the comfort of sitting once again at the only empty chair at our table, defeated, and anguished. This was Dad's old chair, and I wanted to smash it into fucking bits.

I looked up and caught Mom and Tony passing glances. Mom seemed to understand the extent of her omission and what that could mean to me. Tony seemed to understand that his role in the story of tonight would be audience and audience only. He'd go on to play the role well.

Mom sat beside me, then Tony beside her. In the twenty minutes that followed, Tony witnessed the connection Mom and I shared in real time; this is not something many can say, maybe not even the skies. No doubt her transgression had been mighty—she'd never told me the last words of my dead father, a memory I'd lost to the winds of time and the whims of grief—but this mistake, mighty or not, was but a blade of withered grass under the fine and flowering oak tree of her love. She was Mom, my Mom, the woman who raised me, alone and without complaint, and having grown up fatherless, Mom was, for most of my life, my one and only everything.

We forgave each other and shared apologies; her for the lifelong omission, mine for the swearing and crazed reaction.

Then, for the first time, Mom shared with me the whole truth.

ON THE NIGHT DAD DIED

"A good plan violently executed now is better than a perfect plan executed next week."
—GENERAL GEORGE S. PATTON

never asked about the last day. I guess I never asked when I was little be-cause little kids don't ask things like that, don't quite grasp the weight of it; not like Mona did, and certainly not like Mom. Then time did its work, and I never sought closure, never felt I needed it, which may have been a side-effect of being mothered so well. Maybe it was simple repression.

Who knows?

I already knew the name of the hospital. Mom told me the floor and the room number, the name of Dad's radiologist, surgeon, and his last oncologist; she couldn't remember the first one. She described the color of the room and the size of the TV and the missing tile over the window facing the trees outside. She told me about the too-yellow pudding and the scratchy wool couch she slept on for eight days and the trash cans full of Kleenex. She said Dad didn't want flowers, that he wanted pictures, and that many of the pictures we kept around the house were given to him that week by his many friends who came to pay their many respects. She told me he didn't smile very much at the end, that bitterness ate away at him, but he knew it was important to let his friends say their goodbyes and have their peace. Mom said he was stronger for his friends than he was for her, but that she held his hand and cherished his touch until the fire inside burned out.

He died the day after their tenth anniversary, and not for ten years did she let an ounce of him go, not until I took Serena to homecoming. She said if she had it to do again, she'd change that. His last great fear, Mom said, was that we'd grow up in the shadow of his ghost, but Mom promised that wouldn't happen, and, unlike me, Mom succeeded in her quest. I was two months from my fifth birthday the night Dad died. Mona was eight.

Mom said that Mona cried non-stop that week. She visited twice per day to mourn and to look on her still-living father. She said I spent very little time in the hospital because Dad didn't think it was appropriate for my age. Grandma and Grandpa on Mom's side came to stay and watched over Mona and me while she tended to him all day and all night in the hospice wing he got moved to. "He thought Mona was big enough," Mom said, "but I'm not so sure. He said he wanted her to confront the loss head on. I don't know that we played that one right."

Mom told me I was wearing a *Star Wars* T-shirt. She didn't remember the color or what was on it, but she said she'd kept it and that it was probably in the attic.

I asked if she could find it for me.

"No promises," she said, "but I'll look." Then she went off after it.

Tony told me, "You'll be alright."

I had it together enough to apologize to him, but he just shook his head and drank his tea, not saying another word, and I wondered, '*Did it happen to him too?*' During the minutes when Mom was upstairs searching, my mood sank into the never-knowing of this question.

Mom returned, an unsure emotion on her face and a tiny red t-shirt in her left hand. When she handed me the shirt I looked at the caricaturized images of Han Solo and Chewy and Luke Skywalker, and at the imposing Darth Vader behind them, looking down on them like death itself, and I asked if Dad had bought me the shirt.

Mom said yes, for a Christmas he never saw.

My heart shattered.

I buried my head in the physical memory of the cloth. The combination of Dad's truth and Mom's story mixed like bad drugs in my soul. My body shivered, overdosing on feelings. I'd never wept like this, *or had I?* I knew, as if for the first time, that Dad would never come back, and I wondered, *'Did it happen to me too?'* It felt like Vader staring down. It felt like I was dying again, falling from the balcony, and I was sure, as is for the first time, that I'd forgotten. Finally, forgivingly, after many minutes, merciful recovery breaths relieved my tears of duty. I was hunched over, forearms on thighs, and I exhaled one last aftershock.

Then, I looked to Mom. "He said it exactly like that?" I asked quietly.

"Yes, Nico."

"And then what happened?"

"Then," Mom said. "Then it was my turn."

The image packed in those words—Mom standing over Dad's bed as he died—muted my self-pity. She'd obviously had it worst; a lifelong lover ripped away, only ten years cashed in on a promise of fifty, and I felt ashamed that I'd never asked her:

"What'd he say to you?"

"Not very much more. He was very weak from the medicine by then and he had such a small window of joy after finally letting go." Mom could've cried—certainly she had cause—but it wasn't what she wanted. She wanted to help me. She had *always* wanted to help. "You two talked for about five minutes," Mom continued, "and right at first, you know what he said?"

"Use the force," I answered, my tears threatening an encore. I'm sure I don't remember it in actuality. Mom always told me that's what he said.

I stood and kissed her on the temple. Then she stood and kissed me back. We embraced, and because we'd never shared it before, we cried in each other's arms for a seeming eternity with the pain of *our* loss—we were together in it, but also abandoned, feeling both the warmth of each other and the cold of his absence as tremors of pain flashed through us in waves.

I said good night to Tony, and just before disappearing up the stairs, I looked back into the kitchen for one last peek.

"Mom," I said.

"Yes, son."

"You're sure he said it like that. Love *your* woman."

"Yes, Nicolai."

"But how can you be sure? I mean, he didn't say be the very best at loving *women*, did he?"

"No, Nick. I'm sure."

"Well, how can you be that sure? It was so long ago."

"It's simple, Nico. I chose."

She tried not to chuckle, and she tried not to look sad, and she tried not to think about it. A smirk and a squint of the eyes were all that remained, the look that said, *'I'm always here for you.'*

"Did Dad choose?"

"I don't know. I just don't."

"I see," and I looked at my hands, and they weren't there again. "Good night, Tony."

He waved, and Mom said, "Night, son."

I didn't change. I lay in bed in my clothes and tried to fall asleep. I couldn't. I missed Dad terribly the night Mom shared the story of his last words. I cried like rain, like a thunderstorm until I passed out; a boy alone, a boy missing his long-lost father.

Liza Eclipses

13.

I woke the following morning, sobered but sadder than I'd ever felt before. I cried silently for several minutes, my tears making a bee line for each ear as I stared at the ceiling. I pictured me as Dad, dying there, my four-year-old self standing beside him. It was all too much, so I forced an off switch.

I didn't think of Liza much that day, or the next, but by the end of day three I caught myself daydreaming about our last hotel rendezvous; about that loving look in her eyes just before she transformed from *My Liza* into *Liza the Bounty Hunter.*

On day four, I sent Liza a text. It read, [Hey. Long time no word. I can explain not being in the hotelroomfiasco. You probably upset. But I need to talk and tell you something Will you call? Or I can meet you? I drive any where, Evn 2day if you can be so let me know I miss you]

Two days went by. Liza didn't respond. On day six, I texted her again, this time with more worry but altogether the same messaging; my bad, need to talk, I can do the driving, missing you millions.

Two days went by without a word. On the morning of the eighth day, I called. The call went straight to voicemail. This happened again later that afternoon and in the evening.

For the next two weeks, I called or texted Liza every day. She never responded.

Very soon, her non-contact took full ownership of my thoughts and feelings. It consumed me. I did long for Liza—her touch and charm and wisdom—but more than that, obsessing about our "relationship" provided a perfect excuse to avoid directly dealing with Dad's words. I knowingly resisted the truth like a big dirty corporation knowingly resists environmentalism; self-preservation is a difficult instinct to overcome. Instead of enduring the noise, I donned headphones. The volume was all too much to bear without this insulation, knowing that my life's work—*to be the very best at loving women*—had begun with a childhood misinterpretation. I'd taken the word *women* for *woman*, and worse, I'd accepted it as Gospel. Logically, this probably meant I should relinquish my quest, but the thought itself felt like a threat. *What of greatness? What of journeys? What of adventure? The quest* was my philosophical structure, my mental framework: it had supplied purpose to my life, it defined me. I felt in a way that if I chose to abandon the pursuit, I'd be abandoning myself. As I lost my faith, other bad news piled on.

First, the internship I'd accepted in Atlanta fell through when the company "was forced" to downsize. In need of money for the next school year, I was resigned to serving tables at a steakhouse a few miles from home. Second, I received word from my position coach that our soccer team had successfully recruited a stud midfielder from New Jersey; all indications now pointed to another year of bench warming. Honestly though, neither setback troubled me much. Liza was my preferred antiseptic to this existential crisis; not my career and not athletics. It had been over a month since I fled the hotel, and Liza still hadn't replied to any of my messages.

My second junior year was now three weeks away, and a gloom settled over my life like monsoon clouds. It came on as a perplexing, scatter-brained depression;

not the mopey, cry-all-day type. My mind swung from Liza's guns to Dad's words to falling from the balcony to soft moments with Summer to hard moments with Serena. I'd wonder often, *would I have been happier with Gabrielle?* My depression climaxed on that cloudy afternoon, when I bought a sleeve of colored pencils because I'd forgotten the arrangement of the bouquet I made for Jessica back when I was eight. I scribbled and sketched for hours that evening on sheet after sheet of printer paper trying to remember until, finally, I passed out on the desk. I could remember nothing about the flowers; all I remembered was the rubber band I used to bind them: it was purple. Mom woke me up the next morning and asked what I'd been doing. I lied and said something fanciful, something she'd never believe, like that I was an artist.

It had been a long and boring summer. I worked my last day at the restaurant on a Wednesday.

A few days later, I awoke on a morning like any other, yet with an entirely different thinking. My gloom dissipated, but it was no dream or quote or specific circumstance that inspired me. I was, I think, more than anything else, tired of *not knowing*, annoyed that I'd let so much time pass without resolution. Sure, life does sometimes offer a watershed moment to inspire personal change, but this was not that. This was the more common story of time doing its holy work, always forward, always progressing, no matter how hard we try to go back. My original theme— the one that won Liza's heart—returned like a shooting star.

Action!

I began about *action* with steps one and two; first, I'd buy Liza another incredible gift; second, I'd personally deliver it to her office.

Action! And I was up like a rocket.

Eager to capitalize on my sudden positive energy, I prepared a coffee, filled a thermos, dressed in the nicest casual clothes I owned (I even tucked in my shirt) and left the house at roughly 9:30 A.M; destination: the mall. No matter what, by the end of this day, I intended to make Liza mine. Best-laid plans take a lot of shit—I mean, really, the phrase "best-laid plans" is only ever used to degrade "best-laid plans"—so the way I saw it, I could figure out steps three through '*X*' on the way to Liza's office.

During the thirty-six hours that followed my sudden optimism about Liza and me, I earned many wisdoms first-hand. It was the second time I almost died, *but Liza's not the one who killed me.*

Who said that?

You guessed it.

14.

My enthusiasm drained as I perused the shelves of our mall's three department stores. Sure, their bags and accessories and shoes were nice, but I couldn't demote my gift-giving from excellent to average: if I wanted success, my selection needed to be extravagant and touching and altogether perfect.

I'll feel it in my heart, I thought.

I'd been window-shopping the boutiques between the department stores and was already two hours into my hunt when I noticed an advertisement in the window of a big, yellow-walled corner store called Wei Jewelers: "A Bounty of Savings," it read. Considering Liza's profession, I entered the shop thinking the phrase an omen.

I knew nothing about jewelry—I'd never bought any—but they had salespeople, and I was confident I could navigate the process with some help. Unfortunately, I landed on a douchebag named Skeller. Now, I can forgive Skeller my harshest criticisms; it's a thin line to recognize, that one between salesman and alchemist, but Skeller was only that: a douchebag. He looked it, he smelled it, and like the storytellers before him, he really fucked me good on this one.

"Hi," I said.

Skeller, a little overweight, his tie a little old, his shirt a little tucked out, looked up from his little calculator with a little smile. He reminded me of Adam. He looked about twenty-three.

"Good morning, sir," he said eagerly. "Looking for something specific today?"

"Yes and no," I said. "You see, I have this woman—"

"Aaaaah, a woman," he said as he postured up and hid the calculator in a manila folder. As though reading from a poorly composed script and with hands that moved robotically, Skeller asked, "Is this for a birthday, anniversary, or else a different occasion?"

"It's something else completely," I said.

"OK, OK. Well," Skeller said, straightening his tie and clearing his throat, "we have some fantastic deals today. Please don't mind me asking this, sir, but do you have a price in mind? It would help me help you, if you know what I'm saying." He laughed. It was an unnecessary and ugly noise.

"Not really," I said. "But I need something…exceptional."

"For an exceptional woman?" Skeller replied, lifting his eyebrows.

"Yes, exactly."

We walked through his island of jewelry, him on the inside, me on the outside.

"There's this," Skeller said, retrieving a necklace with a sapphire pendant. I checked the tag: $1,200.

"No," I told him. "It needs to be better. It needs to splash."

"Well," Skeller said, "there's nothing more exquisite than a diamond. Here we have a nice selection of earrings. Some are studs, some hang, and all of our diamonds are certified conflict-free."

"Conflict-free?" I asked. "What does that mean?"

"It means they're not from Africa," he answered. I knew it had to be more complicated than that, but I moved on.

I spotted a few interesting sets. I held them up to the light, but none made the cut. (Get it?) "Thanks for the help," I said in surrender. If I didn't find a gift, I'd have nothing to aid my amends, nothing to prove my regret.

"Well, hang on, sir," Skeller said. "You could buy her a diamond ring."

"It's not that kind of serious, but thanks."

"I don't mean an engagement ring, sir. Those we keep in a special case on the other side of the store where you came in. Trust me, if you were here to buy an engagement ring, you would've said so right away."

"What's the difference?" I asked skeptically. "A diamond ring is automatic, isn't it?"

Skeller smiled politely. It seemed a sincere reaction, and because all his reactions so far had been forced and amateur, I considered his next words more seriously. "No, sir, not at all," he said. "Maybe twenty years ago, but not today. Today, a diamond ring is only a wedding ring if you're on a knee. You even need some chick—pardon me—like a friend nearby to photograph it or whatever."

I looked at Skeller sideways.

"We've got a great selection at twenty percent off," he said. "Come look."

He walked me to the last glass case on the service island. It contained about two dozen rings; most of them solitaire diamonds. Altogether, they reminded me of Liza, and I wished that I was richer; wished I could buy the whole lot of them. I'm not sure if Skeller got lucky, or if he interpreted my suddenly sullen mood, but just then he said, "You fucked up."

"Come again?" I said, eyes thinned.

"You're apologizing for something. I can tell. Takes one to know one, you know?"

I looked at him, eyes widened; a netted fish I wish. With that angle, he'd found his way under my armor. He'd done it. Skeller Thompson had done it.

As I said before, I can pardon Skeller for leading me down this path. He was just doing his job. He'd aligned with me by uncovering a truth I hadn't shared. Naturally, this made me trust him. With the seller's assistance, I chose a 1.5-karat heart-shaped diamond set high atop a white gold band; it looked more fun than the others, and I thought Liza would like the shape.

She'll love it, I remember thinking. *I said I'd feel it in my heart.*

It cost me $4,302; nearly half my savings.

Skeller placed the ring in a blue felt box, but the proposal it implied was too much. I asked him to wrap it differently; something plain, something to juxtapose the diamond. After conferring with a spy-like jewelry cleaner who I hadn't noticed—a little Asian man sitting hunched over small, iron-built pieces of machinery—Skeller put the ring inside of a necklace case, wrapped the necklace case in paper, then put the paper-covered necklace case into a one-square-foot brown box. He taped the little cube quickly, then ferried me out the store. The last thing I saw was him on the calculator, the one he'd covered with the manila folder when I entered. I caught him on it, busy like a bee, tallying the total of his bounty.

I exited the jewelry store, my purchase complete.

Then, I set a course for Liza.

15.

When Liza and I were together, we had sex. That's what we did. That's who we were. Sure, we ate and watched TV and read and worked and chatted, but it was always impersonal, time to kill before or after or between sessions. When the time came, I packed up, kissed her, left, and waited for the next call. She was consistent enough that I never asked to visit; our time apart was never longer than two weeks. We even met twice during Christmas vacation and spent New Year's trying to time our orgasms to the ball drop. We came close. I knew she'd been married long ago. I knew she worked in law. I knew she had a kid. That was it. Whenever I pried, it upset her, and besides, she had a way with her hands and mouth and body that helped me forget. As our sexual comfort matured, I didn't avoid personal topics; they ceased to enter my mind. We made love and we played and I left and that was that. That is to say, I wasn't being *the very best at loving women* during our time together. Instead, I came to be *the very best at enjoying women*. Only the word *grand* can appropriately describe the canyon between those two concepts.

Hindsight, however, is not a friend of the moment, and at this particular moment I was driving with a hero's heart to return my love to Liza.

Elizabeth Caplan / Ferriter, Wallis, & Keen
103-A McGraw St.
Columbus, GA 31314
719-375-3937

I arrived.

Two identical five-story buildings made of black reflective glass occupied two wedges of a five-point intersection. The other three wedges housed a motel, hippie clothing store, Green's smoke shop, and an eclectic mix of retail and small eateries. Five-Points it was called: it was the epicenter of commercial culture in a commercially cultureless town. I parallel parked in a lucky space a few spots from the lobby door and entered with the brown-wrapped box under my arm.

I looked for signs directing me to 103-A. Problem was, there was no 103-A. I spent fifteen minutes searching frantically—climbing stairs, descending stairs, traversing halls. I marched through both unguarded buildings twice before solving the mystery. Turns out *Ferriter, Wallis, and Keen* reads differently in the building than on the card. Here, the business was simply *FWK*, with "FWK Bail Bonds" reading under the artsy tattoo-styled logo. (I hadn't finished my more advanced business classes, but this struck me as a very dramatic change in brand.) Complicating matters, the suite number was incorrect. On Liza's business card it read 103-A, but "FWK" was hanging on the door marked 4123-F. Not only that, in a building with matching wooden doors, they'd replaced the entry here with a metal one. To the right of this metal doorframe, a dim-red light glowed; a doorbell with a sign instructing me to, "Press The Button."

I obeyed, and heard a sharp buzz inside.

I jumped back when a burly voice asked, "Yes?" (The voice came through a camouflaged speaker to the door's left.)

"I'm here to, uh, here to see Liza," I said.

"You're referring to Lizbeth Caplan, I assume?" the voice asked.

"Yes. Yes sir. I've been trying to reach her."

After a few seconds, the voice told me, "Wait." Then, many seconds after that, he said, "You're in the right place. We'll be with you."

I felt suddenly unnerved, unsure, and very much unprepared. I backed away from the door and leaned against the opposing wall. Examining Liza's gift now, in the context of why I'd come, I regretted having it wrapped so poorly. I regretted its style. I regretted having bought the third cheapest diamond available. I exhaled, but it was like being pressed from the outside, air forced out, and I remembered that women love hearts, and I knew Liza would adore her gift. I stopped worrying and relaxed coolly against the wall; back flat, ankles crossed, a thumb in my pocket, a box to deliver. This was romance after all—real and risky, bold and big—my type of doing it, and though I'd failed before, I believed I could succeed this time with the rules I'd crafted from my earlier adventures and the diamond ring gift I carried under my arm. I can't recall if it was Liza's affection or Liza's sex that rendered me so stupid.

You see, I thought Liza hated me because I'd left the hotel. I'd projected a teenage personality onto her adulthood when the *actual* reason for her betrayal was a grotesque, gut-wrenching deception. It turns out that Liza the bounty hunter got herself shot in the leg shortly after leaving the hotel, but that's not very important. Her gunshot wound ceased to matter within a minute of my learning it, because when the *actual* truth about Liza came out, through a door quite literally, time stopped, and I wished very much that I wasn't afraid of guns, so I could shoot her in the leg myself.

16.

What happened next happened very quickly, and it's not worth going through every detail because…well, I sort of blacked out.

The burly voice over the intercom told me to, "Come in, sir," and the door buzzed open and I entered the cheaply furnished lobby on the other side; metal chairs, a flickering fluorescent light bulb, tattered magazines waiting to be read by no one. A six-foot-seven, ripped-to-shreds, mid-twenties black guy with tattoos of roses on the tops of his hands looked me up and down from behind a five-foot wooden blockade. This barricade covered the room's length and terminated at a metal door on the other end. This man was dressed as a guard, but he had the stature and gaze of a fantasy-story sentinel; posted there, I imagined, with high orders to protect the fair Duchess Liza from her many dangerous pursuers.

"Looking for Lizbeth?" he said, voice rumbling like a truck.

"Yes, I—"

"Please sign in."

He pointed to a sheet. I looked at the sheet. I picked up a weathered black Bic pen and began writing my name. I paused after writing only, *N-I-C.* I looked back to the guard and asked, "Is she in today?"

The guard glanced at what I'd written.

"You Nicolas?" he asked.

"Excuse me?" I said.

"Are you Nico?"

The walls around me seemed to be closing in.

"Umm…yes maybe?"

"You the one's been trying to get in touch, right?"

"Maaaayyyybe…"

The guard smiled, interlaced his fingers, cracked them backwards, then turned his attention to the black rotary phone. He gripped it, but didn't lift. "Go ahead and take a seat," he said. "Worth saying is you don't need to be sheepish here. We all know everything. Apologies for any inconvenience to your leads."

"Oh," I said. "Well that's okay."

"Liz said to update you if you did come by. She was injured a while back tracking a suspect."

"What? When?"

"Maybe seven, eight weeks ago." He lifted the phone.

My heart skipped a beat. "What? What happened?"

"She got shot," he answered. "Nine-millimeter."

My heart upshifted from skips to thumps. That's all he said, too! He said it the way someone says "out shopping" or "grabbing lunch." He'd said *Liza got shot* like it was nothing at all!

"Perp's up for arson," he continued, phone now to his ear. He hadn't dialed. Maybe it was an internal call. My whole body was reacting with panic to the news; my stomach tensed, my vision blurred. I thought I might throw-up. "But he ain't no murderer," the guard followed up, covering the receiver. "Asshole as he was, he knew better than to kill an agent, I guess. Good senses. He'd be fucked if he finished her, and I don't mean the chair. Stole her car and her phone. Mrs. Caplan put your name down right when it happened. Yeah, 'bout two months ago."

Two months, I thought.

"Yeah. Two months to the day."

It's been exactly two months since we last saw each other, I thought.

As my brain attempted to process the information and return to equilibrium, the guard flipped down a small pivoting table near his desk (like the kind they use at banks) and said, "Place the package on the counter here."

I did, but like I said before, I sort of just blacked-out. *Shot?* I thought. *What does he mean, shot?*

"What do you mean, shot?" I asked.

"Yeah, I'll keep him here," the guard muttered into the phone.

Then, he looked at me.

"Don't worry—" he said, in a way that implied I was making a big deal out of getting shot "—a flesh wound on the side of her foot, that's all. I think she just took some time to cope about it. It was the same perp who stabbed her in the shoulder." I remembered that; the time I showed up at the hotel and she wore an awful, pinkened gauze. "You been texting and calling? Nicolas, right?"

"Yes sir, I was. Look, please," I said. "It's critical I see her as soon as possible. Is there a way to do that? Can you tell me where she is?"

The guard crossed his arms and straightened up. "That's being taken care of right now, sir. I promise you that."

The metal door at the end of the room creaked open and out stepped a blonde-mulletted, six-foot-three, sleeve-tatted, leather-pants wearing, rock-star-crazy-man. He removed his thick black sunglasses to greet me with his piercing black eyes.

"Hello there, Nicolas," the man said as he stomped nearer in his heavy black boots. I felt like a salmon seeing the bear too late: the rock-star-crazy-man was already reaching out to snatch me.

He just wants to shake hands, I realized. *Stay cool.*

But something about this man had made me instantly uneasy; for whatever reason, he frightened me. I watched him closely as I readied to meet his handshake.

We shook.

He squeezed hard and smiled big.

I smiled back. My knuckles cried with discomfort.

And then he spoke. His first words are the last thing I remember. This time, I didn't just *sort of* blackout. The information delivered by mister rock-star-crazy-man didn't hit me like the first news when I discovered that right after our last sexual excursion my hitherto unknown bounty hunter sex-partner had been shot in the foot chasing a suspected criminal who stabbed her earlier in the year. No; this time, I *actually* fainted. I passed to the other side, if only briefly.

The rock-star-crazy-man smiled and said, "Hi. I'm Shane Caplan, Lizbeth's husband. I run this outfit, with my wife of course. She told me about you, I think. You are *the* Nicolas, right?"

I didn't even feel the thump of my body hitting the floor.

17.

"What's in the box?" I heard a voice ask.

My next awareness was of a soreness in my right arm and right shoulder, and a banging pain on the right side of my head. My second awareness came after I opened my eyes. Rock-star-crazy-man, Shane Caplan, my lover's husband, was standing over me. I was looking up at him from the floor, his lips just inches away from mine.

I heard the voice again. "I don't know what's in the box. No, actually, hold on. It looks like he's coming out of it now." It was the guard. He was talking into a cell phone.

"What, happened?" I asked.

"Looks like you fainted," Mr. Caplan said. "You gave us a hell of a scare."

I grunted and tried to get up, but Mr. Caplan stopped me with a push.

"Hang tight, brother," he said. "You sure you're OK?"

No, I'm not the fuck OK, I thought, but considering the size of the guard, the size of the husband, and the enormous size of the shit I was in, that didn't seem a wise conversation strategy.

"I have a condition," I said. "It happens every now and then. Honestly, I'm good."

"You're good? You sure?" Mr. Caplan asked again as I tilted up from the ground. "You don't look good."

"I am," I said. "Just embarrassed. Nothing to worry about. It's not going to kill me or anything." I laughed at myself unnecessarily. I felt all at once angry and heart-broken, dead and reborn. One hundred different hypotheses about Liza competed for attention in my mind, but all the feelings and competing scenarios slammed to a stop when I saw Mr. Caplan's gun hanging from the shoulder holster under his black vest. I knew nothing about guns, but I knew it was the same as Liza's.

How convenient! I thought. *Matching firearms.*

Another light-headedness threatened to overcome me. Shane Caplan must've seen it in my eyes, because without any warning at all, this rock-star-crazy-man-secret-husband-of-my-lover snatched me into his arms. "Whoa there," he said.

"Nooo!" I screamed, fearing the worst.

"Calm down!" Mr. Caplan fired back. "You looked dizzy. I don't need you falling again. Once is enough, got it?"

"I'm good," I said.

"I'm not so sure," he said.

"Then I'm fine," I said, but I could feel my heart banging against his body like dubstep. It was an aggressive help and completely unnecessary and the surprise of it caught me off-guard. I noted entry-level suspicion in Shane's gaze.

As I straightened my shirt, Mr. Caplan said to me, "Quite an entertaining visit so far. Mister...?"

There was no way I'd give up my name. I remembered advice from far off: *all you have to do is not die.* Giving him my name would have achieved that. I didn't know if this was some bounty-hunter counter-espionage tactic but Mr. Caplan did say Liza mentioned me before. She'd called me Nicolas, which is *not* my name.

Maybe it was for someone else? Who knows?

Already I had forgotten Liza's injury—she'd been shot, for heaven's sake! My concern over her health vanished under the stress of the quandary I was in, replaced by a new and desperate need to get away from these guns and this place and these bounty hunters. Forever.

The guard still had the phone to his ear. Mr. Caplan looked at him and nodded. "I don't think that's gonna be needed," the guard said, his eyes trained on me. "He says he's good. He's at least alright...Yes, ma'am," then he hung up.

"Thought we might have to rush you outta here," Mr. Caplan said. "I never seen a man faint before."

"It's a condition," I said. "Thanks, and sorry and all that. I need to go splash some water on my face and regroup. My head's still spinning."

"Do what you gotta," Mr. Caplan said.

I walked the few steps to the exit but found the door locked when I gripped the knob. I tried many times with a growing fury and strength before looking back at my hosts.

"We've got one inside, of course," and Mr. Caplan motioned to the metal door out of which he'd come. This led to the back office, where, I assume, the actual business of bail bonding took place.

"Alright," I said. I stalled near the exit waiting for another lie to manifest.

"Well, come on," Mr. Caplan said impatiently.

"I should call my doctor," I said. "That's really why I need to get outside. Private stuff, you know…my condition and all."

"Yes," Mr. Caplan replied, "you keep saying that." Then, without hiding his sudden suspicions, he asked with squinting eyes, "How well do you know my wife?"

My fingertips and toes trembled. "Yes," I answered.

"I know yes, but what kind of contracting do you do?"

"What kind? Oh, all kinds," I said. "Every kind. I don't know Ms. Caplan too well—"

"*Misses* Caplan, Nicolas. It's *misses,* Caplan," the rock-star-crazy-man reminded me.

"Of course, of course, I don't know *misses* Caplan very well, but we worked together somewhat a few times—" I needed more lies. I needed them quick. I needed to call on what I knew. In those rare instances when Liza did talk about her work, she always talked about counties. As good liars know, keywords can make all the difference. "—I help her in Hunt and Muscogee counties mostly. I run some errands. Watch. Shed tanks. Provide straps. Build look-aways. That's all I'd like to say if it's alright."

Shane smiled, seemingly appeased. His big teeth were white as piano keys and just as straight. "So why the visit? Lizbeth's been out a minute. I'm sure I can help."

"Oh, umm, yes. I have information, of sorts that is, well, sort of like information, about…Yeah, it's about a perp. A runaway run-offer runner guy. This one hurdle-jumped his arraigning if you know what I'm saying, and—"

In the midst of my rambling, I experienced a great revelation! I possessed evidence to corroborate my lie; fake news about a working relationship Liza and I shared.

"Here you go!" I said enthusiastically as I withdrew my wallet and presented the business card of my now ex-bounty-hunter-girlfriend to her not-so-ex-bounty-hunter-husband.

Shane Caplan took the card reluctantly. He slowly looked it over back and front. He exchanged a look with the guard, and his face soured like a lime. The logo and the room and the nature of their business crashed down on me. This was a huge mistake.

That wasn't Liza's *real* business card.

Mr. Caplan put his hand on his hip, flipping back his vest in the process. I don't know if it was on purpose, but this posture revealed his handgun.

"Who's the perp?" he asked. And while it wasn't overtly threatening, compared to his giddy demeanor at the start, the question trumpeted in my ears like a declaration of war.

"Who's the who?" I asked.

"The perp?" he asked back.

"Who? Oh, the perp."

Mr. Caplan stepped nearer. He leaned down to meet my eyes more directly. "You still seem a bit...shaky." All the while, he flipped and rubbed the business card between the fingers of his left hand. He wasn't like me. He thought it was all an illusion.

"Yup, that's it," I said. "Shaky. I'm just..."

I needed a lie. I needed one quick. I imagined Mr. Caplan grabbing me and turning me around and punching me in my kidneys repeatedly, one of many nightmare fantasies triggered by the gun he carried. Luckily, my kidneys provided an instant solution.

"Dialysis!" I shouted.

"Excuse me?" Mr. Caplan said.

"I need to call so I can adjust my dialysis. It's a kidney condition that makes me, you know?" I hesitated for effect. "My doctor always wants me to call," I said in a hushed tone. "You know what'll happen to me if I don't sort out my dialysis after a faint?"

"More fainting?" Mr. Caplan asked. The topic clearly made him squeamish, so I upped the bet.

"No, sir. Not more fainting, more pee. The Depends I'm wearing right now—"

"Depends?" he asked, scrunching his face.

"Yeah, adult diapers, you know? 'For Old Folks,' as the slogan goes."

"Is that a thing?"

"Of course, but seriously, I'm at risk of a leak right now. I got all filled up when I fell. Then it comes down to the liver. I mean, if you don't want a nasty green stain on the floor—"

"Green?!"

"Yes. Green. I know, right? My condition."

"Hurry," Mr. Caplan said, turning to his guard. The guard hit a button and the door buzzed open.

"Shane," I said, adding a cough to sell the scene, "I'll be back."

"Take your time," he replied.

"Not up to me."

Thus ended the only conversation I ever had with Shane Caplan. I shut the door behind me, pivoted left, and made a run for it. Once I escaped the sight of the sentry camera over the door, I jogged out of the building's lobby, then sprinted to my car. I sped like hell, wheels screeching, nearly crashing into a fire hydrant, desperate to escape these guns and these lies and these heart-breaking bounty hunters.

Forever.

18.

Never again.

She was a bounty hunter. She never loved me at all.

"Never again. Never again," I repeated to myself, pained with combinations of feeling betrayed, lied to, and utterly embarrassed. So I vowed again, as it regarded Liza, "Never again."

Over and over I said it, resolving that, no matter what—no matter the explanations or offers, not even if Liza showed up to woo me in something skimpy and new, no matter what came to pass—I was finished. Disenchantment consumed me; my soul reacted terribly to the facts, a believer in God who'd just had his God proven false. I was finally seeing romance for what it was; an oversold event of ever-competing men and women, a conference where theories of navigation mean more than sailing a ship, where *happily ever after* never truly was. I settled quickly into this disenchantment; the revelations relaxed me as I drove. I caught myself smiling in relief just ten minutes after leaving the bail bond office, convinced my life from here on out would be divine.

She's married, I thought, and I began to laugh.

I thought of all our visits, and of all our non-conversations, and of all her lies; both the direct ones and the lies of non-disclosure. It all came together in an image of the woman, Liza, who, in my mind, now took the form of a terribly designed movie character; flat and cruel, generic and desperate. I leaned my seat back, turned on the radio, and rolled down all my windows so as to feel freedom whooshing around me. My laughing slowed.

"Never again," I reminded myself.

My cell phone's exterior LED flashed. I flipped it open and read the notification: *Text Message from 733-773-7777.* The numbers primed my instincts. It just had to be Liza. The digits didn't make a lot of sense, but this time, *I knew.*

I flicked the phone over my shoulder. It took reality only a few milliseconds to register from there, but these were only milliseconds in theory.

It felt like my life was ending in slow-motion.

Before my airborne phone had even landed following this cocky toss, as it was floating away from me over the center console, where I saw it in the rearview mirror, as if stuck there, a horror worthy of Edgar Allen Poe struck me, an alarm of crisis that sounded with red flashing lights and blow horns and sirens in my mind's emergency sector. Phone still in flight, the crazy noise drowned out all my other thoughts, thoughts which a moment before were flaming my soul. A mental baptism it was; anger at Liza Caplan, fear of Shane Caplan, my life's history, my life's present, worries about Dad's last words: everything, gone. It was abject fear, so I slammed the brakes.

I skidded along the gravel shoulder, where I froze big-eyed like a deer, hands firm and squeezing the wheel. Had I been strong enough, my grip would've torn the thing from its handle. There were peach orchards to my left and peanut trees to my right and short walls protected both. Ahead were endless rows of almond trees, and beyond that, more. I was already fifty miles and forty minutes into this escape. I very badly wanted to leave Mr. and Mrs. Caplan behind.

No way, I thought. *No fucking way.*

Friction stopped the car. Inertia slid the phone off the backseat, and it hit the floorboard with a little thud.

Nevermore.

I laid my head on the steering wheel in regret, feeling dumb as a rock. The enormity and complexity of my new problem wound me so tight and so fast that once relieved, fatigue took hold of me. If it hadn't, I would've ruptured. Fatigue sank me, washing over my senses and almost putting me straight to sleep. I looked drunk there, elbows and forehead on the wheel, and I felt drunk too.

I tried to lift my head. Tried to power myself. Tried to cut myself free of the physiology of it, but I couldn't. I was near tears at the thought.

I'd left something behind at the office. Something important. Something I needed.

The diamond ring! In the brown box! I'd left it with the guard!

Life put me to sleep, and my last thought, swear to God, was:

How did I forget?

19.

I awoke.

I cannot recall how long I'd slept, but I awoke all the same.

20.

Returning to FWK was out of the question, but I needed that ring: I had no interest in memorializing Liza with a gift worth half my life. The ring wasn't the point. I finally understood what she was after: victory.

I just had to get the box back (preferably without her seeing what was in it.) I recovered my energy, unbuckled, reached around to recover my phone from the floor, opened it, and read the message. It sounded like a declaration of war to me. I brought the whole arsenal. It was time for shock and awe.

[you should not have shown him the card], it read. [That's not the real card.]

[Oh now you text me?] I replied.

[can we meet? wear are you?]

[I guess u know I met ur hubby. He sure seems nice.]

[are you gonna meat mi or not?] she asked.

A minute later she followed that up with, [and please don't use that text talk with me. on me. you know how much I hate textung]. The next moment, she corrected herself, [texting. not textounge obviously.]

So, we engaged.

Our inception fight was a back-and-forth text war that lasted an hour. We brought the Army, Navy, Marines, and even The Coast Guard. We left the Air Force out of it. (They never want to fight anyway, and the Navy's got more planes.) Strength, destruction, irrationality, and even passive aggressiveness, in order of the enlisted, rained down on both of us. We were totally disinterested in grammar, spelling, or thought; my main weapon was a passive aggression about the fact that she was married, hers was a maternal pettiness about the fact that I was stupid. I'd never had a text conversation before that; not really. (It was the turn of the century. Everything was starting over and this type of communication was still novel.) Our only texts before today regarded times, addresses, and ETAs, but now, we abandoned our history of logic and manners completely. It wasn't our fault, not really: the fault belonged to texting itself; a language with only thin ties to English and one so destructive that it has—*on its own accord!*—ended countless promising relationships. I considered calling Liza many times throughout, but this text battle just kept getting better. It was all so easy! We poured wasteful reactions and mindless emotions into our phones. The appeal of text-war had even consumed Liza, a grown woman who, by her own admission, hated text.

I received this line from Liza near the end. [it isn't what you think really. It really isn't.]

"Nevermore," I said to myself.

All summer long, I'd considered my affections for Liza. I asked myself often if I loved her, but never committed to an answer. [Good-bye Liza,] I wrote. [You broke my heart. I truly loved you.] I feel ashamed that I couldn't find worthier words.

I set down my phone and thought, looking to the peaches and the peanuts and the almonds. I'd forgotten my strategic purpose for engaging in this skirmish with my lost lover, but presently, I was unconcerned with the diamond ring and wholly concerned with planting my anger as deep in Liza's heart as possible. For the first and only time in my life, I intentionally lied to inflict hurt on someone who cared for me.

Care: that was the word, and that she had; Liza had taken care of me. She'd filled a huge hole in my life. She was an adventure in and of herself, and certainly I would've died for her. What I felt for Liza was kin to love—love's cousin, maybe—but all I felt now was a great passion to preserve my anger.

To my surprise, Liza didn't text back. I thought of the ring as I shifted into drive.

I got home an hour later. Mom and Tony weren't there, so I settled into the living room couch and turned on the T.V. A lady's basketball match was going: Coach Summit's Volunteers. I barely paid attention to it. After about an hour of this, I caught myself stealing glances at the phone; like I was afraid it would catch me wondering about Liza. She still hadn't texted back.

A once-familiar feeling resurfaced: *how can it be that I need her more the more she's running away.* My want for Liza and need for her attention spread like a grassland fire. By early evening, my resolve had eroded. I needed to feel more of her sincerity, needed to feel more deserved.

She only ever said she loved me once, I thought. *Maybe she'll say it again.*

I snatched up the phone and texted quickly so as not to overthink it. I typed the following message: [I think meeting is a bad idea. Let's just call it what it is, actually let's call it what it was. A affair!] But I couldn't hit the send button. I felt unsatisfied with the note's angle and implications. I paced about the living room and considered more measured words, this confounding forum of *the text message* blocking my heart from proper expression. Ultimately, I chose to do what most texters do when they come back to an angry string: I pretended like it hadn't happened.

[Hi.] I sent.

A few minutes went by without response, so I followed that up with, [What you want to talk about? Why you want to meet?]

To this, she replied immediately. [I want to know why you left the hotel and I want to explain what Shane was all about and I'm not what you think and you don't understand.]

Seeing his name typed directly next to hers hit my gut like a heavyweight punch. I muted the television and lay down on the couch. I became very tired very quickly, and hoped sleep would relieve me of this conundrum again.

It didn't. Fatigue isn't a commanded visitor.

A few minutes later, my phone vibrated on the coffee table. [please,] Liza's text said. [we have HISTORY! this isn't RIGHT. You abandoned me at the hotel. REMEMBER 5!] Apparently, she'd just discovered that all caps meant shouting.

[5?] I asked.

[Typo] she excused.

[Sure] I texted.

Abandoned? I thought.

She thinks I abandoned her? That doesn't make any sense. Why wouldn't she have called? She certainly could've recovered the number; she is a bounty hunter after all!

Who knows?

Feeling worn from the day, and knowing I'd eventually come around to seeing her again—for gravity can't be resisted long—I finally, as I always had, surrendered to her wants.

[We can meet,] I texted her. [No guns. No husband.]

[of course], she texted back. [where?]

Considering I'd always driven to meet her during our many months together, I decided I'd earned the right to minimize my inconvenience. [There's a place called Tod Durch's near me,] I texted her.

[What time? I can find it.]

[Youre a bounty hunter I'm sure u can find it. How about on the morrow afternoon. 4? I need time to think.] Remembering my lost property—and slapping myself with a palm to the forehead—I added this request. [One another thing. I brought a gift to you. I left it in a brown box at the bailer office. I'd like to it back. Unopened if you don't mind.]

A minute later, Liza texted back.

[5 is better] she wrote.

[No. 4] I finally knew what I wanted. I'd stand my ground.

[sure thing, Nico. Half it your way. i'll bring it. I can respect 4.] Then, to my surprise, another text arrived. It said, [For what it's worth, I miss you. And I look forward to seeing you, my love.]

I sat up, heart racing. I was fighting back joy at those four letters, l-o-v-e. I reread the text a hundred times in disbelief, and a hundred more times in bed later that night. I couldn't justify sharing the word love again, so I chose instead to relinquish myself of a truth.

[I didn't abandon you at the hotel,] I wrote. [I was scares.]

I read the text again, rolled my eyes, and sent out my final beacon. It felt good.

[scared], I wrote. [not scares, obviously.]

[Nevermore,] she replied.

Then, [not anymore, I mean.]

And I didn't feel so good again.

21.

Thinking myself James Bond, I arrived fifteen minutes early to Tod Durch's. I thought it wise to assess the place first and prepare myself mentally to meet Liza. The shop buzzed with activity; tables in its main seating area all occupied by chatty customers, several people waiting for service at the counters, baristas and cashiers hustling to meet demand.

I pulled a ticket from the orange dispenser by the snack case: "322", fifth in line. A beefy employee shouted my number two minutes later, I ordered two slices of strawberry cheesecake, paid eight dollars and forty-four cents, then sat at an isolated two-top table away from the main floor.

As I sat there, my mind played through several potential scenarios of what might happen when Liza arrived. In most of my fantasizing, Liza and I made happy amends before proceeding to a nearby hotel for a return to our ways-of-old. The worst possibility I foresaw was a bit of bickering in the shop before we amicably agreed to part ways.

The clock struck four. (I mean that literally; there was a chic, purple grandfather clock near the entrance.) Just after the fourth gong, when the fifth would've rung, the small bell over the entry door sounded, announcing a new customer.

I looked up from my table. There she was: Liza.

She removed her bee-eyed, designer sunglasses, and looked across the atrium. I watched her instead of announcing myself. She looked calm—even happy—and when our eyes met, she smiled at me. I knew her well enough to interpret both warmth and love (either that or my daydreaming caused the interpretation.) I smiled back despite my mixed emotions: man, was I glad to see her. She wore a black and white checker dress that hugged her shape precisely, and she was carrying the Louis Vuitton purse I bought for her before our affair commenced.

Ok, now listen:

Before I share what happened next, it's important to note one very interesting fact about my life up to that point. You see, up until that day, I'd never once been struck hard in the balls. My nuts had been uncharacteristically impervious to attack. I played soccer for years, had been pushed over the edge of a balcony, got arrested for going down on a girl, but no damage to my jewel box. Right after four, where five would've sounded, on that incredible day in Tod Durch's, my incredible streak ended at last.

I stood as Liza neared, and she reached out with both hands as if to hug me. Her nails were painted red. They had little white tips—all but the thumbs—and I could tell by the glare that she'd just had them manicured.

They should call manicures sharpening. Sharpened is the better word.

I reached out to accept her embrace, but just then, the loving look in her eyes turned to scorn and her warmth turned to ice and her nails turned to claws and she grabbed me by the shoulders and lunged her knee so hard and fast into my groin I thought my testicles would rocket through the top of my head. I crumbled. I let out a high-pitched whimper as I fell to the floor, cupping my hands around my bits as though they'd provide anesthesia through my jeans: they didn't. My hands are totally non-anesthetic. I assume the nearest customers were aghast, but I couldn't hear anything over the ringing in my ears. I assume that ringing was a collective outcry from the hundreds of millions of tiny Nicolais she had just massacred. They now seemed to be scurrying about my body, freezing me in time and space so as to perform renovations. Eyes shut, head spinning, I moaned on the ground as a horrific pain squeezed my gut; it seemed impossible to me, but somehow the hurt and discomfort was growing. (I had, in my friendship history, made fun of guys who acted melodramatically following a strike to the man-region; I've never done so since.)

The ringing in my ears faded. My hearing returned.

I faded in from black, and Liza was yelling at me—something like, "So I tell you I love you and you walk out on me, you prick! Just like that. You don't leave a note. You don't ask the receptionist to tell me where you are. What kind of man are you!"

I grumbled something back at her like, "What the fuck is wrong with you!"

"Me! What's wrong with *me*!" she screamed.

And then, swear to God, as hard as she could, Liza smashed her Louis purse straight into my head. The bag hit me like a brick. My skull bounced on the floor. I thought a tiny "LV" might imprint itself permanently on my cheek, and I saw birds. I grabbed my jaw with my right hand, leaving the left on my nuts for protection; they remained within Liza's kick radius.

I finally opened my eyes. Liza was standing over me, hands on her hips. All the customers were just watching from a distance, most still sitting in their chairs, some standing now for a better view. Even the baristas had stopped their work. It's wild, but it actually does happen like it happens in the movies: people don't do shit! I needed a hero.

"You didn't go to the hotel," I screamed. "You got shot!"

"What?" Liza asked as she reached down. I protected my head with my forearms as one does during an earthquake. She just said, "I'm keeping this," and she picked up her bag; the one I bought her.

"Your husband," I shouted, "I repeat, *your husband*, told me that you got shot, so how, might I ask, did you get back to the—"

"That happened three days later, you idiot—" (all they'd said at the office was that she'd been shot; I never confirmed the details, I just assumed it was that night) "—I stopped halfway to my target." She continued. "I realized how stupid I was, leaving a boy I loved for a man I hated—" *See there. She loved me!* "—By the way, not a word about that in any of your bullshit texts last night. I guess you just forgot, huh?"

The store was watching. My next argument did not let down.

"So what?" I said. "You still lied to me. You're still *married!*" Three high-school girls who'd been waiting for service gasped with glee at the drama.

Just then, the door to the shop swung open and slammed into the wall behind it, and we all heard a thunderous shout.

"What the hell is going on!" echoed from a once-familiar voice.

I looked up.

Liza looked over.

The audience did too.

It was Aya; the barista who'd served me nine months ago, back in September, when I first met Liza. She entered carrying four brown grocery bags full of food and a fifth seemingly full of fury. It was clear from her gait and posture that she owned the place.

"Get out!" Aya demanded.

"Wait," Liza said.

"No. Get out. Both of you. Before I call the police."

The customers' heads swiveled back to Liza.

"Please," Liza said to Aya. "I promise he deserves this."

Something about Liza's plea struck a chord with Aya. She set the groceries down and crossed her arms.

Liza said to me in a voice both enraged and surrendered, "My husband and I, Shane and I, separated years ago. And anyway, me not telling you this is even less unimportant because you didn't know that when you *abandoned* me at the hotel."

"Funny. Shane sure doesn't seem to know you're separated."

"It's business," she emphasized with an exhausted, parental tone. "Neither of us can afford a divorce, and you didn't know that either when you fucking abandoned—"

"I didn't abandon you!" I shouted. "I left because I'm scared of—" but a choking cough cut off my sentence; probably the side effect of my reproductive system rebooting.

"Oh right," Liza said. "The great excuse. You're scared? Scared of what?" she said. "Love? Did you think I was about to ask you to marry me or something? You ran away like a—well, like a nineteen-year-old. Scared? You think I'm supposed to—"

"I'm scared of guns!" I shouted. The store went embarrassingly silent. I could've heard the proverbial pin drop. "I freaked out, alright. I didn't leave you because I was—"

"Guns?" Liza interrupted.

"Yes," I answered, getting to my feet, hands covering my crotch in an effort to protect Jefferson and his buddies, Hamilton and Lafayette. (Yeah, they *all* have names.) "I'm scared of bullets," I admitted. "I'm scared of guns. I left because I'm scared of guns. I've always thought they'd hurt me. That's the whole why. I tried to call you. I called and texted a million times."

Liza huffed. "Jesus, Nicolai," she said. "Everyone's scared of guns. You're barking up the wrong tree."

"I tried to get in touch with you," I pled.

"Not hard enough. That's the game." She paused and looked whimsically out the window. I thought she'd cry, but she didn't. "I told you I don't do this often," Liza said. "Remember? That first night. In Alabama?"

"Like it was yesterday," I answered.

"I lied," she said to me. "You're the only one. The only man I've had other than Shane. Four years I stayed away. Pointless waiting. And now," she said, looking around, "now I remember why. I'm almost forty—"

"That's plenty," Aya shouted. We'd forgotten her. "It's time for you both to leave."

"I'm going," Liza shouted back.

"Lady," Aya warned.

"Don't lady me, pretty young thing, I said I'm going."

Liza looked down at me, shook her head in disgust, did a one-eighty, and left. As she exited, I couldn't tell if she was talking to me or herself: "Now I've got to explain all this shit at the office. You better hope to God nobody figures it out. You'd better fucking hope…"

I'd better hope, I thought.

Liza trailed off.

Then, she was gone.

22.

The customers resumed eating. Baristas returned to work. Magic had kept them still for our drama, but now they were permitted back to their roles. I wondered how our story would be shared, and I wondered, *who will remember?*

I motioned to sit so I could at least enjoy my cake and recover from the pain and embarrassment, but Aya stopped me. "No way, Jose," she said. "You too. Get out. Now."

I looked at my cheesecake. Desperate for a taste, for some positive takeaway, I sought compromise for the first time. "Can I at least take the—"

"Absolutely not," Aya said, anticipating my strategy. "I *will* call the police. I mean it."

I looked again at the cakes, weighing the option of potential arrest versus instant gratification. My focus on the conundrum was so complete, I didn't see Liza or hear her footfalls when she marched back into Tod Durch's to settle a last piece of unfinished business.

"And another thing," Liza hollered, storming me like a rhinoceros.

Chairs scratched on the concrete floor in a growing rumble as the customers positioned themselves for an encore. Before I knew it, before I even had time to raise my hands in self-defense, Liza took my cheeks in her hands, and kissed me. She kissed me so deeply and so perfectly that my short-term memory vanished along with my self-defense.

I heard, "aww," from our audience.

My pain disappeared.

Everything was right.

I bathed in Liza's touch. I soaked up her lips. The kiss went on for a seeming eternity, and as it did, Liza worked her hands down to my wrists. I thought she wanted to hold hands.

What an apology! I remember thinking.

But then, suddenly and predictably, pulling my arms down at the wrist as her leg lifted, she drove her knee into my nuts once more. Maybe she wanted to kill the second.

I froze, mouth agape, then I stepped back and crashed into four rows of applewood shelving. I destroyed the whole build—steel wires broke loose from the boards, the shelves themselves snapped—and I fell into the mess of deconstruction, banging my head and forearms and elbows as the crash echoed across the restaurant.

I heard, "Ooooooh!" from our audience.

"That's it," Aya said. She marched to and picked up a restaurant phone from its dock atop the cake counter. As Aya dialed 9-1-1, Liza crouched beside me. Her face was so near I could feel her breath. "By the way," she whispered, "my answer is, fuck no and fuck you."

She withdrew and slid onto my pinky finger the heart-shaped diamond ring. I considered explaining myself, but I could find neither a reasonable motive nor sufficient oxygen; I was entirely concerned with protecting Jefferson and his allies from a third attack. All I had to do was not die.

Liza stood. Looked down on me for a final moment. That was the last time I saw her, and this was the last sentiment she shared. "It's the ugliest fucking diamond I've ever seen. Go to hell, Nicolai, or grow up. I don't give a shit which."

Then, like the cougar, Liza left me, leaving only the bones of her prey behind. There, stuck in a mess of wood and metal wire, I smiled to myself, thinking:

At least I have the ring. Alleluia!

23.

Liza admitted to me on our first encounter that she was a terrific liar. Ironically, I didn't believe her. I'm certain she lied at Tod Durch's too, though I can't prove it. I doubt she ever separated from Shane, not ever. I was probably an exploration beyond her years, a need for existentialism beyond my youthful understanding of the word. I think she may have committed the sin of absorbing me into her story.

It was Aya who suggested this theory.

I stood from the debris of wood and wire. The shelves carried baskets for self-serve dried fruits and nuts, and they'd spilled everywhere. (I found an almond in my shirt pocket, actually, and savored it before approaching Aya.) As she instructed two of her baristas to some post-battle duty, she realized I was standing across from her. I kept get distracted by the sweets in the case between us. Without looking, she said, "You need to go."

"Ma'am," I said.

"Don't ever call me ma'am," she snapped. Liza made the same demand during our first meeting in Poke; the coincidence wrung knots in my belly.

"I'm sorry about what happened," I said, "but you don't need to call the police."

"I've already called the police," she replied, resisting my attempt to demilitarize. "I'm just waiting for a new dispatch."

"Hear me out, would you?"

"Do you have any idea how much time and money went into that wall?"

"The wall?"

"The shelves and the wall you ruined."

I looked. She was right. Both were damaged. "No. I don't. But how much?"

"How much what?"

"How much time and money. I mean, to fix the shelves. The wall too."

She pressed the phone between her ear and shoulder and looked on me sideways. Then she looked away, puffed out a big breath, and made like she wouldn't answer me. I didn't move. I stood there for thirty seconds before it paid off. "It was a four-thousand-dollar project," Aya said, still avoiding eye-contact. "But that doesn't include the customers, who've had their experience ruined by a couple of intergenerational assholes."

I laughed. She didn't.

I examined the shelves skeptically. "Four-thousand dollars? Really?" I asked. "What are they made out of?"

"Applewood."

"Applewood? Why?"

"Because it's the best. Would you like to see the receipts? I'm very organized."

"I'm sure."

I considered whether Liza might help cover the costs, and dropped the consideration immediately.

"Tell me her name," Aya said suddenly.

"Who?"

"The woman. Your *lover* I presume." She said "lover" loud enough for the staff to hear. A few grinned.

"Please," I said. "Can I just pay for it?"

"You've got four large sitting around, do you? Nope. Not you. You ain't the type. If you won't give me a name, give me yours and go."

"My name?"

Then—*eureka!*—a solution struck me! I pulled the heart-shaped diamond ring from my pocket and held it up. "Look at this," I said to Aya. "This here, this was a mistake. I bought it as a gift just yesterday to apologize for something, but obviously—"

"Yes," Aya interrupted, "Obviously."

"Obviously," I interrupted back, "that didn't go so well. I bought this at Wei's yesterday. At the mall. I have a receipt in my car if you want to see it. It's worth forty-five hundred."

"You paid forty-five hundred dollars *for that?*" she huffed. "You really *aren't* a liar!"

"Forty-four to be exact, and what do you mean, *for that?*" I asked, confused.

She chuckled at my ignorance and hung up the phone. "They're crooks," she said.

"Who? The police?"

"Them too, but I mean the jewelers. Can you wait at your table while I sort this out?"

"Can I eat my cakes?"

"Depends. You're not going to abandon me too, are you?"

I smirked at that; Aya didn't. She rolled her eyes and walked through the silver swinging door to the back. I sat, and though the cafe had calmed, plenty of eyeballs were still rolling at me. The only evidence of an altercation was the mess of tangled steel and wood and food, much of which had already been swept neatly into a corner. It was like a dream, like it hadn't really happened.

Aya returned carrying a tray of complimentary cakes. She handed out slices to her customers. During her ten minutes of damage control, I slowly ate both slices.

For ten minutes, my worries slept.

As I waited for Aya to finish, I thought of my earlier hopes. I thought it a meeting for reunion and reconciliation. *Me and Liza, Liza and me. Me and Liza, Liza and me,* I thought. *And now it's over.* Pained, exhausted, annoyed, and embarrassed, I crossed my arms onto the table and laid my head atop them.

"Okay, I do," Aya said, the metal legs of her chair screeching across the floor.

"Huh?" I asked, lifting my head with a jolt. Aya was sitting coolly across from me, her chair backwards, her crossed arms imitating mine like a mirror.

"I will," she repeated.

"You do will what?"

"The ring. I accept. I'll take it off your hands and we'll call it square. You walk out of here a free man."

"You want, the ring?"

"Don't move," Aya said as she dusted a crumb from my hair. "That's better. Yeah. Much better. The ring?"

"You want the ring?" I asked again.

"Sure. I'll take it back down to Wei myself. Get full price."

"How about instead *I* do that? I'll bring back the four grand, and keep my change?"

"Because I might never see you again, again."

"Again, again? What do you mean?"

She looked away. "Look, I know the Wei family," she said. "I have for a very long time. I'm sure I can get a better price."

"A better price? They have a money-back guarantee. It's all over the store."

She slapped her hand on the table and laughed. "Good luck," she said. "The second you walk in that impeccable English of theirs will vanish, and he'll mind-fuck you so good you'll never go back. The Wei's are famous for it. Honest people—honestly— but that's just the…Wei it is. Get it?"

I didn't.

"Wait," I said. "The ring was four-thousand four-hundred dollars. That's bad math for me."

"Listen Nicolai," she said, sitting up straight, turning her chair, and moving from friendly to deliberative. "I feel bad for you. Really, I do."

"Don't," I quipped.

She rolled her eyes. "The shelves were about three grand, the work was one, but the customers count too, as does my time. You showed me the ring as comp, now it's up to you. I'm either taking the ring from you right now or I'm calling the police to sort this out. Crooks or not, I refuse to drag—"

"OK," I interrupted. "I get it now."

Though the damage had been swept into a corner, the wall was a mess—snapped wires, sharp-edged wood boards, dry-wall damage. It'd take real work to fix, and for whatever reason, I believed her price point.

"She was lying, you know."

I looked up at Aya. "What?" I asked. "Who?"

"The woman. She was lying. I think you deserve to know that."

"You mean Liza? Lying about what?"

"About being separated. And thank you for telling me her name. That might come in handy."

"Wait," I said, unconcerned with her legality, "what do you mean she was lying?"

"I mean it's clear she's not separated. Probably never was."

"You saw her for a few minutes," I said. "How could you possibly know that?"

Aya shrugged. "A girl knows."

"About women?"

"Among other things."

"You gotta give me more than that," I begged.

"What more is there to know? It's simple. Misses Liza is almost certainly live-in married and almost definitely happy."

I waited in silence for more.

Aya acquiesced.

"Women and men are different," she said. "Big ways, small ways, maybe all ways, I don't know. But one of the big ways is how women and men react to their lies being found out. I mean, think about it. When a lie is found out, she covers it up with anger. She overreacts. This certainly qualifies as an overreaction, wouldn't you say?"

"I suppose."

"Men don't react the same way. At least not in my experience."

"What do men do?"

"They lie more," she answered. "They lie and lie, Nico-lie. You must be great at it."

I'd never heard my name said like that before. It sounded horrible. "Not on purpose," I told her.

Aya made about closing our transaction. "This is simple," she said, "you give me the ring and you can go away like none of this happened. You'll be spared and we'll be squared, get it?"

I did.

"You really think she isn't separated?"

"Focus on the ring."

"How do you know my name anyway? I never told you."

"'Go to hell, Nicolai, or grow up.' I think that was misses Liza's exact quote."

"Then why'd you ask for my name?"

"To catch you in a lie."

"Maybe you're wrong, Aya. Maybe you failed on me."

"I lost to you, Nicolai. Those are very different things. Now do we have a deal or don't we?"

The ring represented half my life. "Not yet," I answered. "You have to tell me one more thing. About Liza, I mean."

"I'm in a rush," Aya said.

"Please," I replied. "It matters. It really does. Anything."

Our eyes were glued to one another's. Aya huffed, considered her options, and because I think the deal was good for her, she observed once more the truth about Liza.

"She's in orbit above you, and you can't even see her. If you need to feel better, just know you never stood a chance *after* she fell in love with you. That's the part you fucked up because you didn't reciprocate. You refused it. A woman like Liza doesn't come back if both parts aren't in place. She kicked the shit out of you for good reason, that's why I let her. You needed it. So you'd stop Nico-lying. That enough truth for a day?"

I considered the details of my relationship with Liza; the way we met, the hotel stops, never texting, never wanting me to call, never wanting to talk about her life. We shared almost nothing but sex, because we had nothing else to share. Until love, of course, but that's when it all went sideways.

"I couldn't tell. It's not so easy as women make it seem."

"We're young, and that's tee-bee-dee," she emphasized. "Time to choose, Nico or Nicolai or whatever it is. Nick. What's it gonna be? Jail or gift-giving. It could go either way."

Aya had been unnecessarily callus, but she was also precise with her descriptions and accusations. I retrieved the receipt from my glove compartment and handed it to her along with the heart-shaped diamond ring.

I said good-bye.

We shook hands.

It was honestly as simple as that.

24.

FWK Bail Bonds rebuilt their website a few months back. The homepage features a portrait of Liza with her husband, Shane, their son, Christoph, and a dog named Banjo. *Bail bonds with a family touch*, their slogan reads.

I never confirmed the truth about Liza—there were no means—but even if I'd had them, I probably would've settled on my chosen truth: regardless of the lies, there was love between us. We had something real, something palpable, and something honest, but it didn't provide sufficient relief in the aftermath. It betrayed me.

As it always happens following my romantic let-downs, I rediscovered all the worst parts of myself. My six relationships had all crashed without triumph. I feared number seven like death. I didn't know Dad. Mom had misled me. I thought myself the butt of a cosmic joke. I began relocating these memories to the attic of my mind, no different than the retired high-schooler boxing up his trophies. I never considered moments again, never considered women. I gave up, and fell in.

The quest itself merged into the folklore of history; the tale of Helen and Hector, the epic of Cleopatra and Antony, the myth of Montague and Capulet, the films of Bogart and Bacall, Hepburn and Tracy. The new adventure captured me like a spider web, consuming and dispelling the romance I'd spent my whole life harvesting.

It began when Aya sat down across from me, and plainly stated, "I do."

On The One

"A great soul serves everyone all the time. A great soul never dies. It brings us together again and again."
—MAYA ANGELOU

The One is an ancient concept, a perfect match crafted by heavenly forces that manifest a first meeting and guide you to lifelong love and happiness or whatever. Grownups who still believe in The One are often ridiculed like grown children who still believe in Santa Claus: like fools.

But who knows.

First, if you have a predestined One, it means you don't need to make choices. It means romance will happen *to* you, not *by* you. Just sit in a chair and wait, and love will, like the chair, unfold as it should. Second, if you think you found The One, and it turns out you're wrong, you just go on looking for a New One. Really though, you shouldn't be looking at all because it's your One, and you can just sit in a chair and wait, leaving love to unfold as it should. Third, The One rejects the notion that effort is at the core of relationships, that enduring hearts win the joy of love. It implies that the choice *of our* partner is more important than the choices we make *for our* partner. One cannot simply sit and wait and *receive* love, but apparently your One can. Fourth, what happens if your One dies? Humanity itself would need to be designed and shaped around the preservation of two Ones meeting and falling in love, so if your One dies before you meet them—via an accident or an overdose or any number of random or self-inflicted methods—you're completely screwed. You'd be sitting in a chair waiting for a ghost (though I believe interdimensional, hetero-spiritual relationships are acceptable under most theories of Oneism.) Fifth, clearly some people never fall in love, never engage in permanent romance and live otherwise non-passionate lives. Where are their Ones? Did they not get Ones? Did something they do negate the One meeting? (Get it?) Did they sit in the wrong chair? And sixth, so good it could be seven—an unflappable fact of reality that overwhelms all rational sense and sensibility—you can never, *ever* know if *your one* was *The One.* Never or not for long; those are the two choices. There are no threes when it comes to Ones. There are no special exemptions from disagreement, no reprieves from calls to battle. The One simply cannot be sated, right?

...Right?

...Wrong.

She was there when I stumbled into Tod Durch's before my first rendezvous with Liza. There she was when I found her, when I fell into the truth.

I remember now that it was her. She is the One.

Even with all this—even with the weight of logic pulling me down like chains at the neck, even with these six reasons and hundreds more bearing down—I believe in The One like I believe two plus two equals four, for two twos add up the way two ones cannot. There is foolishness to it, yes, this star-crossed, destined-to-be-together version of Oneism, but it makes for the better story, right up until the accompanying prison sentence comes to bear. It is thus:

There does, or did exist, somewhere, at some point in time, the greatest potential love you could possibly ever have had.

Remember, there does, or did exist, somewhere, at some point in time, the greatest potential love you could possibly ever have felt, and remember.

This is not an opinion. It is a truism: *it is because it is.* You *will* encounter your greatest potential, but you must encounter, and you must know. And when you meet the One, and she sets death in her sight, and you've burned bridges to the hearts of younger loves who've long since moved on, changed, or forsaken you, the promise of your One—*The One*—rises to incalculable heights. Evidence of the truism abounds: many is the man who cursed marriage as a youth but came to marriage nonetheless. Certainly, that is more common than he who perseveres in the wisdom of singlehood to the end of his days.

Considering the nature of my obsessions, I awoke to the brutal truth of my One very differently. I was standing outside of her bakery in the rain when the revelation hit me like a bag of bricks; but yeah, that's how it happened to me, like lightning.

I'd given her the ring as recompense. She said she'd return it for repairs, but she never did. I left her shop that afternoon with the belief that my rejected, heart-shaped diamond ring would be refunded, that I'd be given another chance. Instead, Aya kept the heart for herself, and I, oblivious as a cloud, did not know.

AYA

"And yet women——good women——frightened me because they eventually wanted your soul, and what was left of mine, I wanted to keep."
—CHARLES BUKOWSKI

1.

n paper, junior year was by far my most successful. The Jersey kid bailed on his scholarship so I got more playing time, and coach said I'd start at left back as a senior. I excelled in my advanced business courses and discovered a knack for operations, and at the end of it, I landed a prestigious internship with a Savannah consultancy.

Off paper, however, junior year was my most miserable, an existential abyss. Every indication suggested my lifelong ambition *to become the very best at loving women* was dead, and that's exactly how it felt every time I spoke with one, every time a conversation began, every time I reflected on my romantic past or those misinterpreted words: dead, like Dad.

I thought often of my father; every day, sometimes every hour of every day. In my effort to stay single, I avoided parties, bars, and all extra-curricular mingles. I made sin an enemy, all but self-loathing. I was so far gone that on my twenty-first birthday, I skipped class and soccer altogether, legally purchased my first flask of Bombay Gin, combined it with a two-liter tonic and some limes, and lay all day in bed watching sports. After sports, around three, I started the Star Wars trilogy. Mom purchased and sent the DVDs to me as a gift, but her attempt to warm my heart through memories of Dad backfired badly. Ten minutes into the first film, treachery brewed and bubbled out of me. I considered my retreat from life a betrayal of Dad. I looked at the half-empty bottle of gin on my night stand, and deciding it didn't look remotely half-full, I casually tipped it over. As it drip-dropped out and onto the carpet, I fell asleep. It wasn't even five. I'd never been so drunk, not since Gabby's party. I woke to an awful smell marinating in the carpet.

This wave returned, and ultimately it consumed all of me. The good did not last; the bad did. My internship sucked, my position as a starter came under threat, and once more I faced the prospect of a year without romance. Mom's relationship with Tony was racing towards marriage and whenever I saw them all happy and together and whatnot, it was like a microscope for my pain. They made love look easy, natural, and perfect. As my final year approached, as the real world neared, I felt my soul on the brink of rupture.

2.

The start of senior year wasn't nearly as bad as the junior one. Sadness has a way of normalizing, I guess, and anyway, during week two, I met a sophomore exchange student named Mae, and we got down a few times. It ended quickly; apparently my cool-quiet dynamic had become melancholy-depressed. And also, I talked about my ex-girlfriends too much.

It was a very cold October that year. My twenty-second birthday fell on the Sunday of Fall Break. Unaware, Tony bought a Caribbean cruise package for him and Mom that same week. Mona had just hit the two-year mark at her job in Charlotte doing something in marketing or publicity, so I was going to be home alone for five days. To make up for their poor scheduling, Mom and Tony visited me the weekend before they left. Mom suggested I stay with my "friends" on campus because she didn't know that I didn't have friends, not even on the soccer team. I passed thousands of people a day, but campus felt like a ghost town, and the thought of even one night in an empty dorm with its odd odor and creaky halls terrified me. I chose to Macaulay Culkin it. Fall break would be but an extension of my tired reality. I'd be home alone, but I'd be home.

Tuesday afternoon, I packed a duffel bag with all the basics and began my drive home. The day's slow transformation into night had begun, and I was drawn to the prospect of watching it. At six, I pulled into a new rest stop that Georgia had built over the summer. I ascended a small hill and found a semi-ellipse of stone cylinders under a white, wood-beamed veranda. The stones had been placed for sitting. They oversaw a postcard-perfect, west-facing vista; rolling hills and colorful deciduous trees just beyond yellow warning signs asking people not to go beyond them. There were protected flowers on the other side of the hill.

I slid into my most comfortable hoodie and watched the whole two hours of it; hints of darker blue on the horizon at early dusk, yellow and gold paint strokes in sheath a little later, highlighter oranges flaring with pinks, sudden pops of brighter pinks like bells, and, finally, moody purples, which swept away every other color in the sky. Night conquered then, like a patient infantry marching east to west, leaving only blackness and pinpointed twinkles in its moonless wake. I watched the stars glitter, and I pined for her though she hid her face. Tonight, the rustling oaks reminded me of Jessica; the green grass reminded me of Serena's favorite color; a cool breeze chilled my bones reminding me of Becca's touch; and when I laid on the Earth and looked at the stars, Summer's love blazed into my heart. The flickering red light of a small airplane buzzing overhead brought Gabrielle to mind as the smells of honey-suckle returned me to the similarly scented hotel beds I'd shared with Liza.

Those words—those stupid words!—played on repeat: *to be the very best at loving women, to be the very best at women. To be the very best.* I was a few days from my twenty-second birthday and I didn't even know how *to just be.* I hadn't felt whole for so long—hadn't been loved, hadn't given love—I wondered if I was giving up, wondered if it was appropriate to, if maybe I'd be better off that way.

I stood. As I walked to my Civic I pressed the soft wrists of my sweatshirt against my damp cheeks. It was a secretive wiping away of the evidence so as to avoid attention from passers-by. I didn't want anyone to see me crying, but there was no one else at the rest stop.

It was clear. I'd been hiding from myself, and I thanked the sunset as I descended.

3.

It's a dark drive, those last seventy miles into my hometown. Then, slowly, the first signs light up with McDonald's arches and exit signs welcoming you to its outskirts.

My belly's grumbling reminded me that I hadn't eaten a proper dinner—just a bag of Doritos and a sandwich before I left campus. My sweet-tooth began to nag me for satisfaction too, but it was already late.

I could think of just one place. Risky? Sure. But there was nothing to match it in town: Tod Durch's it was.

I pulled up, parked, got out of my car, and went in. Odds were that Aya wouldn't be there, but even if she was, nothing in our deal constituted a restraining order. A dozen people or so quietly enjoyed small bites and espresso drinks. Jazz played over the speakers. The applewood shelves I'd destroyed were returned from the dead; the ring had been put to good use. Aya was nowhere in sight.

I perused the cakes and donuts and miscellaneous sweets. I chose a macadamia nut cookie and a beautiful slice of key lime pie. I salivated at the thought of our imminent ménage-a-trois.

"Just this?" The cashier asked as I withdrew my wallet to pay.

I was so distracted by the mini-snacks in front of the register, I didn't look up. "Yes, ma'am," I said, fingering through bags of jelly beans.

"You sure you don't want a knee-to-the-nuts?"

I looked up.

There she was. Right in front of me. *Aya.*

"It's a painfully good drink," she added.

I'd missed noticing her because her hair was much shorter now, revealing a lime-green tattoo of a heart and a flower behind her left ear. She'd flared her bangs down and dyed the tips purple. It was dramatic and beautiful.

She was beautiful.

"Aya, Hi," I said. "You cut your hair."

Aya fought a pleased reaction to my observation—I could see this in the flash of a grin that popped up. "Nothing else?" she asked.

"No. Thanks."

"Eleven dollars, eighty-seven cents."

I withdrew a twenty-dollar bill from my wallet, paid her, and took my change silently. I interpreted two positive signs during our third transaction. First, when Aya handed me my change, she did so in a very specific way. She used a method I mastered as a grocery store clerk in college. It's a reach that requires a touch of your fingertips against the customer's. I'd do it whenever a beautiful lady or pretty teenager paid with cash. You'd have to be a major cynic to notice, and an even worse curmudgeon to make a big deal out of it, and I was neither. Her fingers brushed against mine; and yes, I knew she'd done it on purpose.

Second, as I took my tray of cakes, she said, "See ya, Nick."

"No one's ever called me Nic before," I said. "Well, my Mom, but forever ago."

"Anything's better than Nicolai," she said, "considering that's what your cougar screamed across my store."

"Alright," I said. "Alright."

She ran her fingers through her bangs and shook her head smiling as she rolled her eyes, altogether a bit of body language that implied, *just kidding.* "Have a nice night. Come back, K?"

She didn't *have to* say that. She didn't *have to* smile or look on me so warmly. She didn't *have to* wish me well on my night, and she didn't *have to* ask me back. *This is a reaching out,* I thought.

I left Tod Durch's with an image of Aya's smile plastered against my consciousness. Feelings pumped through my veins for the first time in a long time, and I felt alive with the promise of romance.

4.

I thought about Aya all night at my deserted home; during *SportsCenter*, during dinner, during my very special me time (of course.) I thought of her as I tossed and turned, and again right when I woke up. Only sleep spared me the thinking, although I'm sure I dreamt of her too. This obsession was fueled in part by my unprecedented loneliness, but seeing Aya again had triggered in me a most remarkable shift in mindset. The next morning, over a breakfast of Special K and yogurt, I felt it.

Doubt, gone. Loneliness, gone

My regret over past failures: gone.

My revelations about Dad's words: gone.

I had put away everything else, everything that had troubled me for a year-and-a-half. Everything but her.

Her, I thought.

Then I felt the stir of a most irrational sensation. The sensation consumed me like an earthquake to the land; a heart monster it was, eager and hungry and wolfish.

Nothing else mattered: nothing but her.

Her, I thought again.

Her, I felt.

Just the one word, over and over again: *her.*

Sitting there, alone at the little breakfast table at my house, my chewing slowed to a stop and I froze with a certainty I hadn't felt since high school.

Love.

I was in love again, in a love as doubtless as Summer. Far-fetched but true; and worse, I *knew* it was true: I recognized love's mysterious shape immediately. I wasn't spinning this. I wasn't making something out of nothing. Something new had transpired; new connections had been forged, new destinies written.

Yes! I was in love!

"Finally!" I shouted to no one, excess energy standing me up and moving me about the kitchen aimlessly. I sat on the couch and got up again and lay in my bed and got up again and walked a block or two around my neighborhood before repeating those steps in different orders a thousand times. Nothing worked. I couldn't relax. It was 1:00 P.M, and I'd just spent four hours thinking five words: "I'm in love with Aya."

I knew I needed to temper my feelings. I couldn't just barge into Tod Durch's and tell Aya I loved her. I couldn't even tell her I had feelings; there were no roots, they had no base. So I did what I thought I do best even though doing this had backfired majorly in all six of my prior relationships: I laid a plan.

My birthday fell on Sunday, four days away. I decided I'd go to Aya's coffee shop that morning. Either I'd talk to her directly and try to earn an inroad, or I'd file a complaint and demand her contact information. By *then,* I thought, *a poetry will come to me.* I circled the date on Mom's calendar and readied myself for the gym. In four days, I would go back to Tod Durch's, but for four days, I would wisely wait.

Best laid plans, right?

Well, the gym thing didn't happen. I couldn't tame it, couldn't reel me in. I just had to see her. At three o'clock, emotion carried me to my car and I drove back to Tod Durch's. To my heart's disappointment, Aya wasn't there. I at least had the sensibility not to execute my plan of complaint. (If I knew anything about Aya, it was that she was very serious about work, certainly more than me.)

I went again on Thursday and Friday, transacting with the same cashier on both occasions. His name was Zander, and he made a joke about my suddenly frequent visits. I asked Zander about Aya's schedule, but he said he didn't know when Aya would be in.

"Fine," I said, "I'll take a coffee too," and he added it to the enormous cheesecake I'd just purchased for twenty-three bucks.

The cake was delicious. I drowned my sorrows in it, and added a huge bottle of cheap sangria, an ode to Steinbeck's Flat.

Aya wasn't there on Saturday either. I went twice. I sat in my Civic in the parking lot until the place closed, listening to pop music in the dark, still painfully hopeless and entirely alone.

This morning, my birthday, the truth finally settled in. *I'm being ridiculous.* As I flipped through channels on the new big screen television Tony bought for

Mom, I settled on Cartoon Network. I watched The Jetsons and The Flintstones.
I never considered them family shows, one remanded to the future, the other liberated by the past, a means through which storytellers could teach children about adulthoods they might find and adults about the childhoods they'd certainly lost. This wisdom calmed me, then I ate food, ran some miles, and cleaned up around the house.

Noon came and went. I ate the last slice of cheesecake. That was the end of it.

It happened today. It was very violent and very uneven.

My Aya addiction returns. My heart-monster's hibernation ends. I guess that means it's the Spring. It attacks me with fresh vigor. It screams and scrapes its way out of me, like lava boiling from my pores. I roll off the couch in frightful agony. My skin is alight. I thought my appendix would explode. I clutched my suddenly sick stomach, but realize I am in the wrong. I see me now, and I'm palming my liver.

I rose to a knee, anew, but like I say, it was all very odd.

I see me grab the keys.

I saw me walk out of the house.

I see me speed like a maniac back to Tod Durch's.

And I never saw me again.

5.

It's my birthday today.

Classes start up again tomorrow, which is why I packed my duffel bag and tossed it in the trunk earlier. If Aya isn't at Tod Durch's, I think I'll come back next week. I can afford the hours.

My contingency plan proves unnecessary when I arrive at her shop. It's early evening, and a poorly forecasted thunderstorm is brewing over dusk. I've parked directly in front of the store's big plate glass window, and I catch Aya working a register.

Oh, how I'd missed her.

She looks more beautiful than ever. In my eyes, she glows. I feel flush in my chest as I watch. I can't believe she's real. I know this is my moment, my opportunity, my purpose, but it's like I dreamed it up. I ready to trample my principles, prepare to change myself entirely, whatever it means. I care no longer about *the quest*, which means that in just a few days, Aya, this peculiar passer-by, this afflicter of my heart, has changed me more than any woman before.

If Mom must know, that's how I know—*and yes, goddammit!*—love does that.

6.

There may be a few judges out there who've only seen my immature transgressions and romantic sins. They might be saying to themselves, "I hope he gets it. I don't care if someone kneed his balls. I hope this motherfucker Nicolai really gets what's coming for him. Lord knows he deserves it."

Blessed be the patient. Here it comes.

There'd been a rush of vacation-goers from a tour bus presently idling outside. Why they were touring our little patch of rural Georgia; I could not tell you. They were certainly either lost or in the middle of an evening trek from one meaningful site to another. Regardless of which, Aya's coffee shop was now full of the oldest old people I'd ever seen, the kind with skin spots and walkers, the ones who go one mile-per-hour, wearing big survivor smiles and holding hands with their partners of god knows how many decades. The winners, some say.

I sat in my car and watched Aya like a cop on a stakeout. I investigated her for twenty minutes. At first, it was because I didn't know if she was real, but that's not why I stayed in the car. I'd noticed something else: something terrible and terrifying.

A smile.

Her smile.

Aya was smiling.

She couldn't stop, not for a second. It was a big smile, a fanatic smile, not the reserved grin I'd seen in my dreams. Maybe she wasn't real. The smile was disconcerting, disconnected, and in all ways disproportional to how I'd seen her before. It wasn't the calm-cool demeanor and playful face of the girl I'd just fallen in love with. This was coming from some place I didn't know or hadn't seen or willingly ignored. She was completely, over-enthusiastically, not-at-all-coolly smiling big and toothy at all these annoying, chattering guests.

I did not like it. I did not like it one bit.

I should've fled. I should've recommitted myself to the loneliness I'd chosen—I'd been so safe for so long—but I was in love—*am* in love—so, also because I'm in love, I went in to investigate like a fool in a horror movie. I should've expected death, but I didn't.

There I was, in the back of the line, when I verified her peculiar facial expression. She was giddy-happy, and far too busy to notice me. I was tenth or eleventh in line when I got this awful feeling in my gut—my body preparing for shock, possibly—and I remember distinctly—very, very distinctly—that I was standing seventh in line behind three hand-holding old couples from the tour bus—yes, seventh exactly—when I solved the mystery of Aya's smile. I was standing there, seventh in line, when she broke my heart.

On Aya's left ring-finger was a staggering marquise-cut diamond. It must've been three carats at least. It centered three oval gems; a ruby, a sapphire, and an emerald. The diamond was far superior to what I'd bought Liza; far bigger and much more beautiful. A white diamond over red, blue, and green, the Aya ring: *how had I not thought of it?*

Aya was spoken for. She was engaged. My Aya had chosen someone else.

She didn't have it on before. I would've noticed; you can't miss a ring like that. She was drying her hands last Wednesday, so she must've had it off.

Gut rot punches me. Maybe Aya is wearing the smile of newness, like maybe it just happened. That's what it is—it just happened. That's why she hasn't been in the store. Probably a passionate multiday sex-celebration with her beau!

I feel near throwing up. Luckily, Aya can't see me. I lift my cell phone to my ear, pretending to take a call, pretending like my torso isn't churning. I turn around while mumbling fake salutations, and I exit Aya's store, remembering Liza, but not quite—a tremor of *lostness*, a manipulative *deja vu*.

My Civic is here, but I don't get in. I stare at Aya through a window, through a maze of adorable, elderly couples who somehow—*miraculously*—held onto to theirs. Déjà vu overwhelms me—*I've been here*—but the feeling is new. It feels cosmic, astronomical in scale, and many of the elders are looking at me. Aya isn't. I doubt any of them can see me with the lighting and all.

Still, I can't be sure.

A minute passes before I realize I'm still having a make-believe phone conversation. I lower the phone and see lightning flash terrifically far away. I now see I'm standing in the dark. It was bright a moment ago. I'm still paralyzed with pain and gut rot. Life is still breathless, until fear sweeps me away. It feels like a stroke of professional mercy.

She didn't even notice my coming and going.

I'd felt heartache before, but not emptiness.

Is this what I'd done to them? Is this how Serena felt in freshman year? Had Summer lived with it all those months? Did it burn Liza when she reached the hotel?

God, I hope not.

If that's not enough, it started raining. It starts raining right there and then, right here and now, as I'm looking at the shop-girl I'd accidentally fallen in love with, but she's getting married now, and I wanted time to rewind so I could avoid this whole piece of terribly dramatic bullshit, because I don't deserve it, and I wanted a refund for one hundred hours of wasted daydreams and childish fantasies, and I want a reprieve from a lifetime of hunting, and I wanted to talk to Dad to make sure Mom heard his words correctly because if he got them right and said them to me then shame on him, but most of all I want whatever movie director is out there punching up the drama with the lightning and the thunder and the rain to go fuck himself.

That's right when I say it, of course. Right when I'm at the very bottom. Right when I know. Right to be unafraid, so fear sweeps me away mercilessly.

"I'll forget every woman in the world." I whisper. "I'll love you."

Then it spilled out of me, and I know who picked up the remains.

"Fuck forgiveness," I say.

It was her.

And that's right when she saw me—right when she sees me. She looks up from her register, exhaling exhaustion from the rush. She wipes her brow and slides her red-tipped bangs aside, and she sees me standing there, my powerless phone in my powerless hand, the other hand fingertipping her window. She tilts her head and waves to me, flashing the underside of her beautiful engagement ring. I guess she *does* see me through the window.

I gave you a ring too, I think, *and you sold them for shelves.*

I don't return her smile. I watch the joy drain from her face. I amp the anger in my eyes and watch. I turn around, step into my car, flash the brights, and I'm gone—we're gone, my heart-monster and me. I blow through speed bumps, turn out and away and onto the freeway, then I drive with jaw-clenching fury into the storm. I have plenty to be angry about, but one motive shouts sirens above all the others. A crush on a girl is an utterly terrible thing, but love unrequited; that has the makings of a curse.

7.

It rains in sheets. As my car slides into the concrete median, me inside it sliding hopelessly towards my death, I relive it all in one instant. I rewind once and twice in my head trying to remember. I do this to establish the scar, to make it permanent, to commemorate the pain, losing my grip on reality as my wheels lose grip on the asphalt.

I rewind once and twice and over again in my head and remember the joy as it drained from her face while my car rumbles over the shoulders' rumbling divots. I can hear them one by one. I have more time than I thought…

Had there been anything else? I hear my heart-monster asking.
The way she tilted her head, her casual wave.
Was there more?

I do not seek reconciliation. I want his anger, nothing more. I need the work. I want to remember the flash of her engagement ring and the joy as it drained from her face and the emotional shock so intense it took on a terrifically physical form; my fingers shake, my torso thickens, pellets of sweat condense on my forehead; I feel it all as my arms tense down to my hands, wrapped around a wheel I cannot control. I do not calm—cannot calm! I want—need, must have—this scar, for scars remind. That is their purpose.

There'd been something else, son. There always is.

I hear again.

I hurl my arms instinctively to the right, a last-ditch effort to save my car and the life it carries. I struck something invisibly dark on the road just two seconds ago. It lifted my front left tire. I was doing ninety miles per hour when I hit, and it's raining heavily, and my tires are no good, and I am distracted by the fact-checking, digging up the blurred files of my short-term memory, and the moment not thirty minutes ago when Aya shattered my dream. I was distracted by hope, and that's when I veered off the road and sped towards the concrete median of the freeway, and as I slam the brakes and pray, an ultimate revelation strikes me a mighty blow.

The joy drained from Aya's face.

It didn't take much thinking. It was clear. The joy *did* drain from her face, but I missed the corollary, the point of it all. *The joy drained,* I realize, *because there'd been joy at the start.*

Aya was happy to see me. She'd been expecting it.

But possibly, I realize this too late.

On Forever

I don't die, obviously.

Rain is pouring down as I speed south on the slick freeway back to campus, checking my speed and failing on many occasions to keep it under 100 miles-per-hour. My head feels hot. My chest feels like its squeezing my soul. Just as a boy relinquishes his dream of sports stardom, so too must I.

Ahead of me, I see backlit gray clouds opening to the hidden stars beneath. They twinkle weakly under the gray-white glow of the Moon, but I see them still. They're there.

And steadily I think to myself, *there'd been joy in her eyes at seeing me.*

Right then, my left front tire collides with highway debris—maybe a small log or a rubber flap; it is too dark to see—and my car skids and slides halfway onto the shoulder. My car and I bump and vibrate on the road's margin. I regain control thanks to the asphalt's jagged grading: I've never been so thankful for high quality civil engineering.

I slam the brakes. My car stops. My Civic is safe.

Mostly...

The bitter smell of burnt rubber penetrates and fills the car. A cloud of smoke rolls over the hull lit by my misdirected headlights. I look out the window to my left. My view is entirely obstructed by the concrete divider. The driver-side mirror dangles like a head from a broken neck. I came dangerously close to crashing, to dying; and far worse, to never seeing Aya again.

I can't hear my heart-monster anymore.

Back on the freeway now, I maintain a more reasonable speed. The sheets of rain stutter to a stop, leaving only the pitter-patter of raindrops. I know a truth with certainty now. It is my truth, and quickly it takes a shape comfortable and acceptable and calm.

Love is a rebellion, and a rebel am I.

The clock reads 8:00 PM. Tod Durch's doesn't close until ten.

Plenty of time, I think to myself. *Feels like forever.*

NICO

"Love means never having to say you're sorry."
— FROM THE END OF *LOVE STORY*,
BY ERICH SEGAL

he rain stops.

I pull off the freeway and onto the first exit, State Line Road. My ankles shake with impatience at the red light. My foot presses the pedal and I speed through the stop, turning left. I cross the freeway bridge, turn left again, and fly through a second red-lit intersection. I'm down the on-ramp heading north, and soon pass the spot where I hit the wall or almost hit the wall, then north some more, on my way to Aya.

Romance is a perilous quest—I know that now. There is no point fighting the truth underneath, because I am in that knowing. I know I'm in danger. If my life quest to become the very best was an incidental side-effect of misinterpreted words, so be it. It is but a fact. It changes nothing. "Love is a rebellion," is what Dad meant to say, "and God bless the rebels," maybe.

I speed by lollygaggers on the dark freeway, water shimmering on the surface.

I cannot help but think of Aya's ring. I worry her answers are obvious ones—that she is spoken for, engaged, and that I am but a passer-by, some guy who got his ass kicked in the middle of her store. I may be less than that; I may be forgotten, buried in the cemetery of Aya's reminiscences.

That's fine. I could cope with that. What I couldn't cope with—what I won't bear—is the *not* knowing. I know my fear cannot stay if I face it, no more than a morning dew can against the sunshine: physics won't allow for either.

Love is a rebellion, I think as I turn onto my hometown road, the one leading to Durch's.

I park in the same spot. It's like I never left. The tour bus is gone, along with its elderly caravan. I glance into the shop as I shift into park and turn off my car. I look through the plate-glass window between me and the inside of Aya's shop.

I don't see Aya.

I close my eyes.

I breathe.

I exit my Civic. I enter the bakery. I look at the cakes and cookies in the glass display case to my right, but I've stopped in the entry. I step aside after inconveniencing three high-school couples who enter ahead of me. I enter seventh.

I still don't see Aya.

My eyes are open.

I'm still breathing.

Aya is not at the register. She is not near the desserts. She is not catering to her ten customers, who are smiling without exception. I know she's here. I *feel* it. I cross the threshold between front and back, and nod at four cupcake-decorating prep workers writing "Troop 211" in frosty cursive on dozens of red velvet cakes. They receive my gesture as the nod of someone who belongs. They aren't entirely incorrect.

Fluorescent lights, white walls, shining silver tables, and bustling noise—clanging, shouting, water pouring, four-hundred-pound mixers mixing—all surprise my senses as I come through. Because I've never done the holy work of food prep before, I overestimate my traction. The employees wear shoes that grip (I would later learn), but I'm sporting weathered cross-trainers; three years old, they don't grab shit, let alone the burgundy floor tiles of this easy-to-clean culinary factory. Three steps into my super-climactic romantic moment, my left foot misses the ground or whatever, and I flip up and backwards and onto my ass. I protect my head as I thump to the ground like a bag of sand.

The food prep professionals race to me like angels.

My mood sags.

Does he belong here?

I'm sure that's what they're thinking.

Yes, I belong here.

My eyes open. I scrunch my face. Everything's blurry, and I know this is it. This is the moment.

I moan quietly as the delayed pain of trauma floods my awareness. *It's real*, I think. *I'm going to feel this tomorrow.* I squeeze my eyes shut a few times, and the next thing I know, the faces of the prep workers are looking down at me. They've formed a circle around my body. They're wearing the same white aprons, but they themselves are varied and eclectic. There's a skinny dread-headed white guy. Next to him, there's a short lady with big blonde hair, colorful nails, and enough jewelry for a bank vault; bracelets that dangle and necklaces that shine and a very big, very colorful engagement ring on her left hand: red, blue, green, and white.

Then, in between a bespectacled grandma and a hipster black dude with three studs in a line over his right eyebrow...like a reason to wait...someone new arrives to the circle.

She's smiling. It's her—Aya—and her hand is bare.

"Back to work," Aya says patiently to her workers, her eyes never leaving mine. "Back to work."

As her employees mobilize, she crouches beside me.

"Aya," I say, "Sorry for busting in."

"Nicolai," she says. "Don't be. You're good."

"Really?"

"Sure. Can I help you up this time?"

She reaches for my hand and I accept. Her touch is rough and dirty with work, but tender too.

Then, I'm standing.

Aya shoots a wide-eyed, get-back-to-work glance to those who've continued watching. This time, they truly obey. The kitchen loudens. That's when I see the blonde again; the one with the big hair and the colorful nails. When she reaches up to pull at a roll of parchment paper, her ring shines like a star. I've seen it before. Its diamond is marquise-cut, set atop three small gems; a ruby, a sapphire, and an emerald.

Red, blue, and green? The ring Aya was wearing?

My heart accelerates, but calms when it hears Aya's cool voice.

"Nicolai."

I turn.

"Come over here," she says.

I join her at a prep station countertop and lean slowly against it.

"Are you hurt?" she asks.

I shake my head and say, "No. I'm perfect."

"Is that so?" She smiles, then she runs her hands down her cheeks and clasps them together just under her chin as if to recite rehearsed words. She's wearing no jewelry, spare a braided silver chain with a pendant hidden under her blouse; no earrings, no watches, no bracelets and, most importantly, no engagement ring.

I stare at her bare hands, my hopes expunging the next question automatically, as if wringing water from my soul. I ask before considering its appropriateness or the proper intonation. I just ask it: I'm not afraid. "Do you have a fiancé?"

The clatter of the kitchen provides us privacy. "No," she says, taken aback. "No. Engaged? What? No. Why?"

"You had a ring on when I came in earlier."

"I did see you!" she says, and again she runs her hands down her cheeks and clasps them together. "That was you. You were out in the rain. It was so hard to see with the streetlamp right there and the clouds and everything. But that was you, right?"

"Yeah, I uhmmm… I had to answer a very important call."

"Oh," Aya says. "The ring belongs to Aurora."

We look at Aurora, the blonde with the big hair and the long nails and the glowing ring.

"She just got engaged," Aya continues, "so we're all suffering through her story—she talks about it constantly. She wanted to see it against *my* complexion because she needs to decide how much spray tanning to do come wedding day, like, three years from now—" Aya leans close and whispers "—Then, as we're trying to get that hideous ring off my much fatter finger; literally, we slid it on with butter, I'm not kidding—a tour bus with, like, dozens of people stopped in. And you looked in and thought that—"

"Regarding those old couples—" I interrupt, not needing to dwell on my now-ancient misunderstanding, "—did you ask? Were they between two points or were they trying to get somewhere?"

"Neither. They got hungry. They got lost. Lucky us."

"Luck," I say.

"Can I ask you a question now?" Aya says.

I nod.

"One of my cashiers told me you came in here? Twice, he said. He said you were looking for me. Is that true?"

"No." I say. "I was lost and hungry."

"Oh."

"Twice isn't close. It was way more than twice. I'm very interested in who you are."

Aya looks over my shoulder and flashes her get-back-to-work look again, but this time, the look is sheepish and playful. I turn my head.

It's Aurora. She's looking at. She sends a charming smile our way, then resumes decorating the top of something delicious-looking.

"Don't mind her, Nicolai."

"Nicolai? What happened to Nic?"

"I like Nicolai," she says, and she meant it both ways.

"Me too," I say, and finally, it's true.

She's cupping the pendant under her apron. It looks like she wants to say something.

"What?" I ask, standing straight. I didn't realize I'd moved so close to her. *Or*—I think—*she moved closer to me.*

We're looking at each other now. The pause is hers; the hesitation unbearable. Aya slides her finger under the latch of the necklace behind her short hair, and reveals the secret hanging atop her breastplate.

It's the heart-shaped diamond ring; the one I gave her for the shelves.

She kept it? I think.

No. Better. She's wearing it.

I'm not just a passer-by—I'm a pendant! That means hope, the greatest thing a stranger can be! Every husband and wife in history start as strangers; every mom and dad too. Everyone starts as a stranger, delivered by and into hope. This was perilous romance, and I—for a change—had been its recipient. It felt like a miracle.

(And I think, for once, how lucky the six might have been.)

"Can I see you when you finish tonight?" I ask.

"Well. I do own the place," she says to me.

"Then can I see you?"

"Give me a sec, then how about a quick slice of pie?"

"No problem," I tell her. "I'll wait."

I go, and as I do, it occurs to me in one firework moment that everything I am came from everywhere I'd been; from Dad's words to Mom's sadness to Jessica's flowers; from Serena's heartbreak to Becca's seduction to Summer's temper; from Gabrielle's luncheon to my education with Liza to the heart-monster that brought me into Aya's life.

However it came to be, I am glad for it.

And how it came to be, I know, all began with Dad.

The One Who Killed Me

"I'm not sorry. And I'll not apologize. And I'd as soon go to Hell as to Dublin."
— FROM *BARRY LYNDON*, THE FILM,
WRITTEN & DIRECTED BY STANLEY KUBRICK.

I look across the table at Aya over our two pieces of half-eaten cobbler, mine raspberry, hers appropriately peach. She's flattered every time the taste steals my attention.

I can't believe I'm sitting with who I'm with. She's funny as hell. She kills me with her little quirks and mannerisms. I see her now, through steam rising from our coffee mugs. She pours more from a pot she brewed in anticipation of this conversation.

The steam clears, and now I see she's really there.

One-by-one, the customers leave. Then, more slowly, but still one-by-one, the employees clock out and say good-bye. Aya has to approve things here-and-there, but her absences grow shorter as midnight passes into morning. I don't care: I'd wait forever to feel that way again. I have much to learn, but we know plenty in just hours. Our connection is affirmed: our potential, doubtless.

I wonder who's still watching.

"I like that we're laughing," I say.

It's ten past one when we finish our premiere. We stand and, reluctantly, we leave.

"I think I should tell you something in advance," I say.

"Oh yeah," she says. "What's that?"

"I've never dated a white girl."

"Is that okay?"

"Of course. No. It's nothing. I'm not sure why I needed to tell you that, but I needed to."

"In that case, I have to be honest too."

"That's okay. I'm sure I deserve it."

She giggles, then stares at me stone-cold. "I've never dated an Asian guy before," she says, which is funny because, clearly, I'm not from Asia.

"You're funny. I like that we're laughing."

"You mentioned that already."

"How long have you been wearing the ring? Not all this time, have you?"

I ask her my question after I kiss her on the cheek in the cold outside. "It doesn't matter," she whispers, "but no. Not all the time. I tried."

I realize I'm standing on the spot where I saw the bolt of lightning earlier. I wonder about the lightning, and if it was really there. Aya senses I'm getting lost, so she tugs me back with a warm kiss in return. One, two, three seconds and it's over. She's *bliss*. That's the word.

She's right. She rubs my cheek with her thumb, and I close my eyes to soak in her touch, and she's still right, even after that. It doesn't matter.

"What matters is how you feel when you're with them," I say, looking up at a fingernail moon. I have no idea if its waxing or waning—I never paid attention before—but at least I know the storm is over.

Aya's lips turn down as her eyes look up. By morning, all the clouds will be gone. She looks at me. She's glad to have found someone who understands why love makes her sad. I don't try to change her mind. It is my first surrendering, and it feels sublime.

I step into my Civic. Aya steps into her Accord.

She waves. I wave. It is a lovely and first good-bye; our first of thousands, I'm sure.

I'm five miles into my two-hour ride back to campus when I swear to myself. "I'm going to marry her," I say. I say it again, louder, so as to transform the loose thought of it into a binding contract; the other signatory: myself.

"I'm going to marry her," I say.

I swear on everything I am, and everything I've lived and loved. I swear louder now, this time on Mom, "I swear I'm gonna marry her, just you wait."

My smile is an atomic bomb.

I swear on Dad, and I think he hears me, and I think he's prouder of me now than ever before, *his little rebel*, and I glow and shiver, telling him, "Yes sir. I'll marry that girl. I can and I will. I promise."

As with all my promises, I mean it when I say it.

About the Author

astian R. Carden was born in Bremerhaven, Germany. He moved to rural Georgia as a toddler, immigrating with his twin brother, older sister, German mother, and drill sergeant Dad. He completed his first major work, a short text about Policy Debate, as a senior at Columbus High School.

In 2005, Bastian graduated from the University of Pennsylvania with a B.S. in Economics. A few years later, he and Marta Peters from Saint Peter, Minnesota were wed. They now reside in Arizona with their two preposterously adorable children.

Who Killed Nicolai is his first published work.

For more information and updates on upcoming titles, please visit
www.bastianrcarden.com

You've reached the end, Dear Reader. I'm sorry it's over too. Thanks for reading *Who Killed Nicolai* I hope you loved it.

This is my first novel, but I'm already hard at work on my second. So I'll have more for you to read soon.

As an independent author, I count on readers like you to spread the word and support future work. If you enjoy this book, please join the ranks of my readers who make it all possible. You can:

- Write a review on Amazon <= hyperlinked.
- Subscribe to email updates at www.bastianrcarden.com and be the first to know about future works. You'll get early access to discounted or even free versions of my upcoming books, and the chance to communicate with me via email.

Please connect, I'd love to stay in touch.

Thanks again,
Bastian Carden

Made in the USA
Middletown, DE
24 January 2020